Born in Great Britain, Lewis Orde now makes his home in Chapel Hill, North Carolina. His earlier novels, EAGLES, HERITAGE and THE LION'S WAY, are also available from Corgi Books.

THE LION'S PROGRESS is a continuation of the story of Daniel Kerr which began in THE LION'S WAY. To avoid disappointment, the reader is advised to read THE LION'S WAY before THE LION'S PROGRESS.

Lewis Orde

The Lion's Progress

CORGI BOOKS

THE LION'S PROGRESS
A CORGI BOOK 0 552 13183 0

Originally published in Great Britain (as part of THE LION'S WAY) by Judy Piatkus (Publishers) Limited of London

PRINTING HISTORY
Piatkus edition published 1985
Corgi edition published 1987

This book is set in 10/11pt Baskerville

Corgi Books are published by Transworld Publishers Ltd., 61–63 Uxbridge Road, Ealing, London W5 5SA, in Australia by Transworld Publishers (Aust.) Pty. Ltd., 15–23 Helles Avenue, Moorebank, NSW 2170, and in New Zealand by Transworld Publishers (N.Z.) Ltd., Cnr. Moselle and Waipareira Avenues, Henderson, Auckland.

Printed and bound in Great Britain by
Cox & Wyman Ltd., Reading, Berks.

To Ruth, Lionel and the Ross clan of
Stanmore Hill

Death is afraid of him because he has the heart of a lion.
ANON . . . ARAB PROVERB

BOOK 1

THE BENT NAIL

CHAPTER ONE

The tea had been allowed to grow cold.

Roger Hammersley picked up the dainty Royal Adderley cup and looked suspiciously at its contents. The ring of congealed milk floating on the top deterred him from drinking. With a faint expression of disgust he replaced the cup in the saucer and pushed it away. Then he lifted his eyes to glare across the desk at his visitor.

'Daniel Kerr, exactly one year ago a promising young tenor entered this office because he had suddenly discovered the beauty of opera. So far, The Grand has offered you three roles in this season's productions and you have yet to accept one. Exactly what, in the name of all that is holy, are you interested in doing?'

Daniel mulled over the question while he tried to think of the best reply. He had known immediately why Hammersley had called him to the office — his constant refusal to accept any of the roles that the company had offered him during his first season with the house. 'I'm not interested in minor parts,' he said eventually.

Hammersley blinked at the audacity of the answer. 'Just because a certain role is small in volume does not mean it is minor in impact,' the general manager pointed out. 'The lamplighter in *Manon Lescaut* is hardly minor when one recalls that Jussi Bjoerling used it for his debut in Stockholm in 1930. Unless, of course, you regard Bjoerling as a minor artist.'

Daniel shook his head vehemently. 'No, sir. I do not. He's an exceptional artist.' He had gone to see Bjoerling at the Met following the Swede's return to the United States after the end of the war. What he had listened to on Martinelli's records in England had been nothing short of an insult to the power and clear quality of the barrel-chested Swede.

'What about the other two roles we offered you?' Hammersley asked. 'Parpignol, the toy vendor in *La Bohème*? Or Borsa, the courtier in *Rigoletto*? Are they also too minor for your consideration?'

'Who debuted in them?' Daniel wanted to know.

'I made my Covent Garden debut as Parpignol.' Hammersley's bushy white eyebrows bristled threateningly for an instant. 'Daniel, I am forced to be brutally frank with you. This house's board of management is becoming increasingly impatient with a contracted tenor who simply refuses to perform. You are being paid one hundred and twenty-five dollars a week while you are permitted to continue your career as a cantor. We have bent over backwards to accommodate you. So what is it you want from us?'

'I want a lead role.' Daniel realised he was playing a dangerous game as he pushed brinkmanship to its extreme limit. At the end of the New York season in April the Grand Opera Company might simply choose not to renew his contract. When the others went away on tour, he would be left behind; a cantor in Paterson, still no further along the road to an operatic career than he had been when he'd returned from Europe. If he accepted a smaller role, though, he feared that he would be stuck in a rut. He was in a win or lose situation; for him, place and show did not exist.

Since being accepted by the Grand, Daniel had studied diligently with a voice teacher recommended by Hammersley — Enrico Rosati, who had coached Gigli and Lauri-Volpi. He had learned the lead roles of Chevalier des Grieux in *Manon Lescaut* and Rodolfo in *La Bohème* — two of the current productions — in the hope of being chosen. But despite his constantly improving artistry and his obvious willingness to learn, Daniel had only been offered supporting roles by Hammersley. The major parts had been given to established tenors. Other newcomers to the company had accepted the minor roles eagerly, but Daniel remained a stubborn holdout. It was a calculated gamble on his part; he would settle for nothing less than the best.

'As I have stressed to you countless times there are no lead roles available this season,' Hammersley told Daniel. 'Now that the war is over, we are settling down to something approaching normality and are planning our productions a year in advance. There is nothing for you this season. Look' — he softened his voice as he tried to place himself in Daniel's position — 'I also wanted a lead role when I started. Who doesn't? But the Covent Garden management was not about to push some established tenor out into the cold to make room for me. I had to wait my turn, work for it, just as you will have to.' Against better judgement, Hammersley reached out for the cup and drank the cold tea. He grimaced sourly at the taste.

'Daniel, I thought that by concentrating on Amercian talent — with only the minimum imported — I would be able to avoid the problems that have plagued the Met in recent years. Prima donnas who feel they're too important for such mundane events as rehearsals, a complete breakdown of discipline. You're going all out to prove me wrong.' Hammersley spread his hands on the desk top and smiled sympathetically. 'I hired you because I believed you had the potential to become an outstanding tenor, given hard work and the time to mature. But this cuts both ways. You have to bend a little as well. Leads will come, I promise you.'

'I'm sorry, Mr. Hammersley, but I'll settle for nothing less. Tucker over at the Met got a lead role the first time out, as Enzo Grimaldo in *La Gioconda*. And he was a cantor as well.'

'Then I suggest that when your contract at the Grand expires at the end of this season you approach the Met. I'm sorry too, Daniel,' Hammersley said, closing the discussion, 'but we cannot allow you to run before you've learned how to walk.'

11

After leaving Hammersley's office, Daniel trudged disconsolately down to the auditorium. The same cleaners who had been working when he had taken the audition a year earlier were still pushing their brooms, and he was still unknown to them. Just being among the cast would not have helped either. Who knew anything about a tenor singing Parpignol? Who gave a damn? Only the lead artists were known and admired, talked about and celebrated. Nobody except the immediate family and a couple of close friends cared about who sang the lamplighter.

The knowledge that he would have to write to Enzo Martinelli in Milan increased Daniel's dismay. A reply to the Italian's last letter was almost a month overdue, put off again and again as Daniel waited in vain for a break. What would he tell Martinelli this time? That the Grand's management was still saving him for something special? Or that his career with the company was almost through? Visions of Martinelli stepping off an ocean liner in New York with a shining scalpel in each hand did nothing to ease Daniel's misery. Even his father said nothing now, but Daniel knew that his continuing refusal to accept a minor role aggravated Isaac Kirschbaum as much as it did Hammersley.

He left the opera house and looked along West Thirty-fourth Street for a taxi. Seeing none, he walked towards the subway entrance at Herald Square, momentarily cheered as he recalled a story Hammersley had once told him about the conductor Thomas Beecham trying to find a cab to take him to the Met for a rehearsal during the war. The cab driver had explained that because of gas rationing he was forbidden to take anyone to a place of entertainment, to which Beecham had frostily replied that going to the Met was not entertainment — it was a penance. Obviously Hammersley still regarded it as such, constantly criticising the Grand's competing house for its lack of discipline and control over its artists and technicians.

Daniel changed his mind about the subway and started to walk the ten blocks north to Times Square. He went slightly out of his way to pass the Metropolitan Opera House on Thirty-ninth Street and Seventh Avenue where he stopped to look at the aging yellow brick building. The sidewalk was almost completely blocked with theatrical sets; pedestrians were forced to walk in the gutter as the opera company's technicians prepared for that night's production. Daniel looked at the label stuck on the back of one set — *Il Trovatore*, it read — then he tried to peek inside the building. A burly man in a worn suit barred entrance. Hands jammed deeply into his coat pockets, Daniel walked away, irked by the knowledge that had Hammersley given him one of the leads that season, the man in the worn suit would have been more respectful.

In a few days, he would be thirty-one years old. That was almost ancient for an operatic debut. Bjoerling had been only nineteen. At nineteen, he could afford to accept a minor role like the lamplighter. Even then, that small part had been followed a few weeks later by a starring role as Don Ottavio in *Don Giovanni*. At thirty-one, Daniel could not afford the luxury of starting at the bottom. He had to begin high up the ladder. There was no longer the time to make it step by step.

Entering the lobby of a building on West Forty-fifth Street, between Sixth Avenue and Times Square, Daniel ran up the stairs to the second floor. He still found it amazing how Moishe had managed to get back his original office after closing up the law business for four years. Having enlisted so early, Moishe had been among the first to be discharged, as a major; he had even turned down the opportunity to participate at a junior level in the war crimes tribunal. Back in New York, he had taken a lease on his old office, traced his former secretary and persuaded her to work for him again and gone back to civilian life as if he had never been away.

'What's doing in the world of highbrow wailers?' Moishe greeted him.

'Nothing. And that's the problem.' For the first time, Daniel noticed how sparse Moishe's hair was becoming on top. When he had seen him in England, at the hospital over Thanksgiving, Moishe's hair had been cropped short,

13

disguising the onset of baldness. Now that the hair was growing back to its normal, unfashionably long style, the patch of scalp in the centre was more noticable. The sight of the bald spot confirmed Daniel's earlier feelings. They weren't kids anymore; and he could not settle for a minor role. Time just wasn't on his side.

'Pull up a chair,' Moishe invited. 'This lawyer's time and advice are at your disposal.'

Daniel sat down and let out a long, painful sigh. 'I've been given what amounts to an ultimatum.'

'Take whatever the company offers you or get the hell out?' Moishe guessed.

Daniel nodded. 'I've turned down three roles so far this season. Walk-ons in *Bohème, Rigoletto* and *Manon Lescaut.*' He knew the names meant little to Moishe. 'And I sweated blood to learn the major roles in *Bohème* and *Manon Lescaut.*'

When he paused, Moishe waved a hand at him to continue.

'So I'm being given a last chance. To do the lamplighter in this season's final production of *Manon Lescaut,* or get lost.'

'When's the production?'

'Two weeks' time.'

'So take the lamplighter, then,' Moishe suggested to Daniel's amazement. 'At least it'll get you on stage.'

'For a minute or two, that's all.' Daniel felt as if he was arguing with Hammersley all over again. He had expected support from Moishe. Support for his own point of view, not for the company's. 'I don't want the lamplighter, Moishe. Any cretin can do that. I want des Grieux, the hero of the opera, the main tenor role.'

'Who's singing des . . . des . . . ?'

Daniel helped him out. 'Des Grieux. Cesare Scarlatti, an Italian tenor. Which makes the whole damned business even more ridiculous. Hammersley's always going on about pushing domestic talent, yet he hires Scarlatti as soon as he returns from Europe.'

Moishe knew of the Italian tenor, but not through any operatic fame. Cesare Scarlatti had sung in New York during the thirties before going home to Italy at the start of the war in 1939. In the fall of 1945, he had returned to New York to resume his career, expecting the same adulation he had received before. Instead, his first appearance had caused near riot-level demonstrations outside the opera house and police had been called to escort the terrified tenor into the building. 'Daniel' — Moishe pushed the glasses to the top of his nose — 'tell Hammersley that you're willing to sing the lamplighter or whatever. Make your peace with the man. You need him right now a hell of a lot more than he needs you.'

'Are you serious?' Daniel spluttered. 'Whatever happened to the grandiose schemes that were the hallmark of Moishe Wasserman?'

'I buried them with the name of Moishe Wasserman,' Moishe answered quietly. 'Maurice Waterman thinks with his head, not with his heart. And it wouldn't be a bad idea if Daniel Kerr did the same thing. Just suppose that something comes up? Someone falls ill, maybe, and they need an understudy? How can they call on you if you're not there? Go back and tell your man you'll take whatever he gives you. Go on, beat it. I've got other work to do.'

As Daniel left the office, he heard Moishe tell his secretary to telephone an inspector at the immigration and naturalisation service. Now Daniel understood. Moishe Wasserman — the kid who was going to be a big show business lawyer — had ceased to exist. Maurice Waterman handled immigration cases, something Moishe Wasserman would sooner have starved than do.

Sadly, Daniel decided that he liked the impractical lunatic he'd known before the war a lot more than the pragmatic lawyer who worried more about meeting his overheads than anything else.

Daniel returned to the Grand and informed Hammersley that he would accept the lamplighter role for the season's final *Manon Lescaut*. With his contract for the following season assured — providing he did not fluff the role — he went to the one-bedroom apartment he rented in Greenwich Village, close to where Moishe lived. The last letter from Martinelli beckoned to him and he sat down to answer it.

The first few words made him stumble as he attempted to disguise his disappointment at being forced to accept a minor role. Finally he recognised a way around the predicament. He would cable Martinelli instead of writing. He'd send him a telegram just as he had done when Hammersley had first offered him a contract to sing with the Grand. He'd cable Martinelli the simple message of 'Debut February 26, Grand Opera Company of New York, *Manon Lescaut.*' That way, the Italian would not know that Daniel had been cast in the lowly role of the lamplighter.

Daniel visited a Western Union office to send the cable. When he returned to the apartment he called his father with the news. Isaac Kirschbaum said that he was glad to see his son had finally decided that humility was also an asset.

Standing deep in the wings, arms folded grimly across his chest, Daniel watched the first two acts of the rehearsal for *Manon Lescaut.* His envious eyes followed the short, dumpy figure of Cesare Scarlatti as the middle-aged Italian tenor strutted pompously around the stage, playing the Chevalier des Grieux to Manon, a young attractive soprano called Anna Markova. When he had first seen the soprano, Daniel had thought that Hammersley had thrown away his policy of emphasising domestic talent and gone completely overboard with imported singers; then he had learned that Anna Markova was really Annie Markowitz from Brooklyn. It made Daniel feel happier — but not much — that one native New Yorker had made it to stardom at the Grand.

Hearing his cue, Daniel stepped out onto the stage and sang the few lines allotted to the lamplighter before wandering off down the narrow street built into the set of a square near the French port of Le Havre. Behind, he could hear Scarlatti and Anna continuing their duet. Just great, Daniel reflected gloomily; nobody in the audience will even notice me. If they choose that exact moment to sneeze or

16

blink they'll miss my debut. Walk on. Sing a few words. Walk off. Swallow your pride to ensure next year's contract and pray like hell that there's something better in it than this stinking role.

He returned to the wings and looked out onto the stage. When he could bear to look and listen no longer, he switched his attention to Hammersley in the auditorium, sitting between the Grand's musical director and stage manager. What was Hammersley thinking now? That Daniel's voice merited more than the lamplighter? Or that such a small role was all he was really worth? Daniel chuckled grimly as the most unwelcome thought of all slipped into his mind: maybe Hammersley had chosen that goddamned moment to blink.

As Daniel watched and wondered, Hammersley's secretary made her way along the row of seats, followed closely by two men dressed in almost identical dark grey suits. They spoke a few words with Hammersley, and one of the men showed something that he held cupped in the palm of his hand. Hammersley's smooth face creased up in annoyance as he listened. After a few seconds, he excused himself to his two colleagues and followed the secretary and the two men in dark grey suits out of the auditorium.

Five minutes later, Hammersley returned by himself. He clapped his hands and called for silence. 'Thank you very much, ladies and gentlemen. That will be all the rehearsing for today. Signor Scarlatti' — he beckoned to the Italian tenor — 'would you please be kind enough to come with me?'

Everyone involved with the rehearsal stared in amazement at the retreating figures of Hammersley and Scarlatti. Rehearsals at the Grand were sacred. Maybe at the Met nobody bothered to turn up, but attendance at Grand rehearsals was on a level only slightly below a presidential summons. Nothing short of war or plague could be allowed to interrupt them. An excited buzz began as members of the cast tried to guess what had happened.

Eager to stop any speculation, the musical director yelled out for silence. 'Please clear the stage. Rehearsals are over for today.'

17

'Wonder what the hell that was all about?' Daniel mused, falling into step beside Anna Markova as they returned to the dressing rooms two floors up from stage level.

Anna turned to see who had spoken to her. Recognising Daniel, she smiled warmly, disregarding the unspoken tradition that established singers did not socialise with aspirants. Her own background in Brooklyn's Crown Heights was too close to Daniel's to allow any divisions, and she admired the way he had stood his ground against the Grand's management before finally being blackmailed into accepting a minor role. 'God only knows,' she replied. 'I'm just glad it happened, There's no need to keep rehearsing this production. We've already done it four times this season.'

'You might have done it four times,' Daniel said. 'But it's my first shot at it. Maybe they're rehearsing for my benefit.'

'Keep dreaming, Daniel.' Anna squeezed his arm affectionately in case he took offence. 'The Grand's not that loaded with money to pay technical staff and musicians overtime so a walk-on can rehearse. Anyway, you sounded good enough to me.'

'Thanks,' he said, then quickly added, 'Short but good.'

'They'll get longer. Give yourself time.'

'How much time, for God's sake?' He remembered asking the same question of Martinelli after that first aria had blown a gasket in the hospital recital in England. Anna could talk quite blithely about time. She had been only twenty-two when she had been recommended to the Grand four years earlier. The two years she had spent — first in the chorus and then in supporting roles — before being cast as Gilda in a production of *Rigoletto* had not mattered at that age.

Before Anna could think of an answer, a woman's strident voice called after them. 'Mr. Kerr! Phone call!!'

Daniel turned around to see one of the office staff waving at him. 'Who?'

'A Mr. Waterman. He said it's urgent. You can take it in the dressing room.'

'Excuse me.' Daniel left Anna on the stairs and hurried up

to the crowded communal dressing room that was used by the minor players. A telephone extension was located next to a loudspeaker which piped in sound from the auditorium.

'Moishe? What do you want?'

'Anything happening, Danny boy?'

'What do you mean, anything happening?' Now what was Moishe on about? Did he want a blow-by-blow description of how it felt to rehearse the lamplighter?

'In the opera, *schmuck*!'

'I don't know what you're talking about, for Christ's sake!'

'I can't make it any plainer,' Moishe hissed. 'We're on an open line. Think!'

'You mean about Cesare Scarlatti?' That was all Daniel could think of, but he failed to see how Moishe could know about it, or how it could interest him. 'Those two men who came . . .'

'Jesus Christ! You bigmouthed jerk!' Moishe snapped. Then he slammed down the receiver.

Daniel looked in bewilderment at the dead telephone before replacing it. A hand touched him gently on the shoulder and he wheeled around. Hammersley's secretary was standing behind him.

'Mr. Hammersley would like to see you in his office, Mr. Kerr.'

'Now?' So he'd blown the lamplighter role, and Hammersley was going to throw him out.

'Right away, if you please. It's extremely urgent.'

That's what the woman had said about Moishe's phone call as well, Daniel remembered. And that had not been as urgent as it had been confusing. Why had Moishe snapped at him and suddenly hung up? It didn't make any sense. He just hoped that Hammersley's idea of urgency was better defined.

'Close the door and sit down, please,' Hammersley invited from behind the desk.

Daniel pushed the door closed and sat down, facing the general manager. For once, the office looked reasonably

19

tidy. The only costumes that were visible were piled neatly in a corner, and Hammersley's desk was almost clear.

'Do you know anyone in the Immigration and Naturalisation Service, Daniel?' Hammersley asked conversationally.

'Where?' Hammersley was making about as much sense as Moishe. Moishe? Wait a minute. Forgetting that Hammersley was waiting for a proper reply to his question, Daniel forced his memory to unwind. Moishe handled immigration cases. Moishe had just called him. Now what scheme had that harebrained madman dreamed up?

'Never mind,' Hammersley said. 'More to the point, we have an emergency. An emergency of tremendous consequence.'

'We?'

'The royal "we",' Hammersley explained. 'Like Queen Victoria, I am speaking on behalf of everyone. At this precise moment, Signor Scarlatti, our Chevalier des Grieux, is being escorted to the offices of the Immigration and Naturalisation Service to be interviewed, pending possible deportation proceedings against him.'

'What?' Daniel fervently wished that his conversation could consist of something more substantial than amazed, one-syllable questions; he also wished he could make some sense out of what Hammersley was saying, although a bizarre idea was beginning to take shape in his mind.

'Those two gentlemen who interrupted our rehearsal were immigration investigators. Although Signor Scarlatti was allowed back into the United States after the end of the war, so he could continue his operatic career, it now appears that certain discrepancies have arisen concerning his claim that he disassociated himself from the Fascist party of Mussolini. He contributed — or so the immigration people are saying — more than was necessary to the party's welfare.'

As Hammersley continued to talk in a low, even, accented voice, Daniel at last fully understood the meaning of Moishe's phone call. Moishe had put in the fix. He worked on immigration cases. He knew people in the service. As

20

Daniel had left his office that day, Moishe had told his secretary to call some immigration inspector. It had to be. There was no other possible explanation. Coincidences like this didn't just occur; they were carefully planned. Whether or not there was any truth in the claim against Scarlatti — that he had been a supporter of Mussolini's Fascist party and, therefore, an enemy of the United States — was of little concern. The Italian tenor's appearance as des Grieux in the season's final *Manon Lescaut* would be ruined. Newspapers would get hold of the story. They'd tie it in with the original controversy over his return and have a field day fuelling public indignation and emotion. They would crucify him. Just as they'd crucify the Grand if Hammersley took the foolish step of having him back.

'How can I help?' Daniel asked.

'Need you ask?' the general manager replied cynically. 'Or are you seeing if I'll crawl to you and beg?'

Daniel stared at the man. The reality of the situation had still not fully penetrated his brain; he was too busy thinking about Moishe.

'You've told me countless times you want a lead for your debut,' Hammersley continued. 'You've told me that you've studied for des Grieux. Now you have the opportunity to stand or fall by your claims.'

'What about the lamplighter?' It was the most inane question Daniel could have asked, yet he could think of nothing more constructive.

'Let him light blasted lamps!' Hammersley said irritably. 'If push should come to shove, even I could fill in for those few lines. I need a des Grieux. The Grand Opera Company of New York needs a des Grieux. The role is yours.'

Daniel stretched his hand across the desk. 'Mr. Hammerlsey, you'll never regret this. I promise you.' Words of gratitude bubbled uncontrollably from his mouth. 'It'll be the finest *Manon Lescaut* the Grand has ever put on.'

'I'll make that judgement only after the end of the final act.' Hammersley gazed at the outstretched hand and decided to ignore it. 'To be very honest with you, Daniel, this entire business is extremely repugnant to me, although for you it is a fortuitous coincidence. I asked you before' — despite himself he began to smile — 'if you know anyone working at the Immigration and Naturalisation Service. Do you?'

'No, sir!' Daniel protested vehemently. But he could not stop the blush that spread quickly across his face to damn him as a liar. 'I don't know anyone there at all.'

'It doesn't matter,' Hammersley said, finally taking the hand which Daniel continued to hold out. 'I am a fatalist. To my way of thinking, whatever happens, happens eventually for the best. You were fated to debut in a lead role. Fate has indeed smiled on you, even if it has chosen to scowl most ferociously upon the unfortunate Signor Scarlatti. Do not disappoint fate, or me.'

The performance was due to begin at eight. Daniel left his Greenwich Village apartment just after five and rode the subway up to Herald Square. For fully a minute he stood outside the opera house to admire the poster — Anna Markova as Manon, and introducing Daniel Kerr as des Grieux.

There it was. In black and white. Nothing could change it now. His operatic debut would be in a lead role!

Office workers on their way home walked past Daniel as if his existence were solely in his own mind, just as they had when he had first visited the Grand to audition for Hammersley. Now he felt like grabbing one of them by the arm and pointing to his name. That's me! he wanted to yell. See! I'm going to be on that stage tonight! The applause you'll hear will be for me!

What was the use? he finally decided. These lemmings streaming past him into the subway didn't know who he was. They didn't know who des Grieux was. Nor did they care. But tonight, at eleven o'clock, the people inside the opera house — the only ones who mattered — would know the name of Daniel Kerr. And the following morning, after the reviews had been read and discussed, his name would be on everyone's lips.

He entered the building and walked to the ticket cage. 'Do you have my tickets, please?'

The woman looked at him questioningly. 'What's the name?'

'Kerr,' he said slowly, enjoying the consternation that suddenly flashed across the woman's face. 'Daniel Kerr.'

'Oh' — the woman hesitated, obviously embarrassed — 'you're Daniel Kerr. Here you are, sir.' She handed him an envelope containing three complimentary tickets.

'Thank you.' He returned to the sidewalk and looked around. When he checked Fat Benny's gold watch he saw that it was only five-thirty. Moishe was not due until six; he had half an hour yet to wait.

Standing alone, he could feel the nerves beginning to build up, the same way they'd done at the hospital. Tendrils of fear that started deep in the pit of his stomach and slowly spread out until their icy touch had affected every part of his body. Despite the cold, he started to sweat. He needed company, a warm, friendly atmosphere to see him through the next half hour.

He walked across the street to a bar and sat down with a rye and ginger, trying to nurse the drink to make it last. He shouldn't be drinking now; that would only dull his concentration, not sharpen it. Inwardly he smiled as an odd idea struck him. Everyone else wanted the clock to go back, to turn back the years. He wanted to advance the clock. He wished it were eight already, more than two hours in the future. No. He changed his mind. Not eight. He wished it were eleven o'clock, when the fourth and final act would be over and he would be standing in front of the Grand's gold curtain, side by side with Anna Markova, bowing graciously in acceptance of the applause for which he'd hungered all his life. And for which so many others had worked and made sacrifices — Fat Benny, Kawolsky, Martinelli. Now, even Moishe. Daniel thought back to the conversation he'd had with Moishe following Scarlatti's abrupt disappearance from the opera house and his own instant elevation. Moishe had simply shrugged his shoulders and said that a lot of

23

Germans and Italians tried to hide their wartime records when they came to the States; when he could find the time, he'd look into Scarlatti's case through contacts in the immigration office.

To his surprise, the glass was empty. He ordered a second drink and began to sip it, enjoying the relaxation it brought while he spared a thought for Joe Feltz, Lucy's father. After he had been given the contract at the Grand, he had gone around to Feltz's apartment to thank him. Feltz had opened the door just wide enough to see who it was. He had listened expressionlessly to Daniel's thanks and closed the door again, without inviting him inside. Later, when he had gone to listen to Bjoerling at the Met, Daniel had waited outside after the performance for Lucy's father to leave. Carrying his violin case, Feltz had completely ignored Daniel, walking straight past him as if he were not there. Since then, Daniel had not even bothered trying to make contact.

There had been a good side to that evening, though. After Feltz had left him standing in front of the opera house like a fool, Daniel had gone around to the stage door in time to catch Jussi Bjoerling leaving. Daniel had pushed his way through the crowd of well-wishers until at last he was face-to-face with the Swede. Bjoerling had looked amused as Daniel blurted out that he was a tenor with the Grand. Knowing that Bjoerling had never heard of him, Daniel felt like an idiot. But the Met tenor had eased the situation by clapping him on the arm and inviting a fellow artist for a drink. They'd parted company two hours later, after Bjoerling had regaled Daniel with anecdotes and tales of his career. Daniel had willingly picked up the tab as the Swede only had enough money in his pocket for the cab ride back to his hotel.

Halfway through the second drink, Daniel glanced through the bar window and spotted Moishe on the other side of Thirty-fourth Street, outside the opera house. He gulped down what remained of the rye and ginger and hurried to join his friend.

'Three tickets,' he said, passing the envelope to Moishe. 'Two for my parents, and one for you. Don't lose them.'

'Are your parents that hard up for a good laugh?' Moishe joked.

'Knock it off,' Daniel warned. 'I'm shit scared as it is without any wisecracks from you.'

'You can handle this, kiddo.' Moishe assured him, still grinning. 'Anyone who can take on the Leishman brothers like you did can get away with mumbling a few words in Italian. Just make sure you don't start singing in Hebrew instead, not that half of them would know the difference.'

'Including you?'

'Especially me!' Moishe roared. 'Good luck.'

'Thanks. See you after the show.' Daniel ducked into the building and made his way up to the dressing room. No more shared dressing rooms for him; as the lead he rated his own. He knew he would be among the first to arrive, but he needed time to think, time to prepare himself. There were no worries about the role, but he was more frightened now than he had been eighteen years earlier when he had stood on the *bima* of the *shul* in Claremont Parkway to sing his *bar mitzvah* portion. In the eyes of a thirteen-year-old boy, the *bar mitzvah* had loomed as the most terrifying prospect in the world. In retrospect, it was nothing to fear. What he faced now — four acts to a full opera house with his triumph or failure splashed across the reviews the following morning — was sheer unmitigated terror.

To hell with dreaming about accepting applause gracefully. First he had to earn that applause. Tonight was his real audition for the Grand Opera Company of New York. What he had done for Hammersley the previous year had meant nothing. This performance — the tenor lead in a four-act opera — would make or break him.

His costume and wig were lying on the chair. First he tried on the white, powdered wig and made preposterously serious faces at himself in the mirror, anything to drive away the nagging tension that had him in its unrelenting grip. The two pre-performance drinks hadn't helped. Maybe he had time to slip downstairs for another one? He dismissed the idea as folly.

Taking off the wig, he slipped into the costume. Panic screamed from deep within him as he tried to stand up. He could not. He felt like Quasimodo, the hunchback of Notre Dame. The costume was too short, and billowed out at the sides like a shapeless sack. It made him look deformed. Des Grieux was a handsome, young aristocrat, not a hobbling, amorphous cripple. The panic turned to near hysteria as he imagined himself staggering onto the stage dressed like this. The audience would howl with laughter. They would think Rigoletto had gotten drunk and turned up on the wrong night. Or that the Grand was staging *Die Fledermaus* instead of *Manon Lescaut* and Richard the Third had dropped in as one of the surprise guests.

Daniel bellowed for the wardrobe mistress.

'What is it?' she wanted to know.

'What is it?' he repeated, unable to believe the woman had to ask. 'What the hell do you call this?' He pointed furiously at his deformed shape.

'The costume was altered to fit Signor Scarlatti,' the woman tried to explain.

'That doesn't help me! I'm a mile taller than Scarlatti. I can't go on looking like this.'

The wardrobe mistress refused to be cowed. She had dealt with temperamental tenors before. 'Take it off. I'll see what I can do with it.' She took the costume and walked away, leaving Daniel standing miserably in his underwear.

The make-up man appeared, Unaccustomed to the procedure, Daniel allowed himself to be pushed back into a chair while the man went to work. Watching the reflection in the mirror, Daniel marvelled at the man's skill as he transformed the fleshy face, changing the shape of eyebrows, rouging cheeks, giving the nose an aristocratic, aquiline curve. When the wig was in place, Daniel was certain he could have passed himself on the street without the barest trace of recognition.

The wardrobe mistress returned with the silk and brocade costume. She had pinned in the trousers at the waist, lengthened the legs and let out the jacket seams.

Fearfully Daniel tried on the costume again. It fitted well enough to be passable. The woman stood studying him for several seconds before adding more pins to the trousers, all the while explaining that the costume had been altered to fit Scarlatti. Scarlatti was much fatter around the thighs than Daniel. Scarlatti had shorter legs. Scarlatti had a broader, squatter body. Daniel began to wish that Scarlatti were here, that Moishe had not set the INS on the Italian. The role of the lamplighter was becoming more attractive with each pin the wardrobe mistress inserted.

'What about my shoes?' Daniel asked, pointing to his white-stockinged feet.

'Shoes?'

'I can't go on without them.'

'I'll find some for you.' The woman disappeared again.

Daniel took a break from his own concern to wonder if his parents had arrived yet. Had they found Moishe and gotten the tickets? His father had been ecstatic about Daniel getting the lead, first laughing with the joy of it, then crying because Fat Benny and Tessie — who would have given anything for this day — were no longer here, and then laughing and crying simultaneously. And Harry Feldman from Temple Isaiah in Paterson was supposed to be coming, Daniel remembered. He'd been as happy as Isaac about Daniel's good fortune. Not only did the temple have a tenor from the Grand Opera Company as cantor, but an important tenor! Just don't bring any of your nieces, Daniel prayed. Leave them in Brooklyn.

The wardrobe mistress reappeared, holding a pair of brown shoes with elegant silver buckles. Daniel tried them on. They were at least a size too large and rattled on his feet like empty boxes. 'Who wore these, an elephant?'

'Signor Scarlatti . . .'

'Yes, I know. Signor Scarlatti has bigger feet than I do.' How on earth did a fat midget like Scarlatti manage to have size thirteen feet? 'Can you do anything with them?'

The woman stuffed wads of cloth into the toes. 'Try them now. Just be careful how you walk in them.'

27

Daniel slipped on the shoes and turned to admire himself in the mirror. If nothing else, he looked the part of des Grieux, a young nobleman in eighteenth-century France. Providing none of the wardrobe mistress's hastily inserted pins fell out. Then he'd look like a huge tent flapping in a hurricane.

What time was it? Seven-thirty. Time for his exercises. Vocalise to loosen up the chords. He'd started early that morning, right after breakfast. The voice had sounded bad but he hadn't pushed it. He'd waited until after lunch before trying again, a one-minute workout that was more satisfactory. Before he had left the apartment he had vocalised again. The voice had come easily and he had continued for two minutes. Now he was certain that it would be there, loud, clear and perfect.

From other dressing rooms he could hear his fellow artists going through the ritual. Basses, baritones, tenors, all sounding like a herd of distressed cattle. Above them all, Daniel heard Anna Markova's pure sopranco, and the darker mezzo-soprano of the woman who would play the role of the madrigal singer in the second act. Daniel joined in, no longer self-conscious as he had been when conducting the warm-up session in the English hospital.

After a minute he was satisfied and turned to singing the first lines of 'Donna non vidi mai,' his major aria of the first act. How far could his voice carry? A few blocks north to the Met? Was Bjoerling — his drinking partner of that night, his inspiration — even now shaking as he recognised the voice that would push him off the top of the heap? Was Tucker trembling? Was Gigli?

Watch out! Daniel felt like screaming. Make room for me or get trampled in my passing!

Hammersley entered the dressing room, resplendent in white tie and tails as he made his customary round of the dressing rooms to wish his artists good luck. He stood in front of Daniel and inspected the costume closely. Then he held out his hand. 'Your sudden replacement of Signor Scarlatti has created a tremendous amount of interest,

28

Daniel Kerr. Live up to it.'

'I intend to, Mr. Hammersley.'

The general manager pulled a sheaf of papers from his pocket and passed them to Daniel. 'Read them before you go on.'

Eyes wide in pleasure, Daniel snatched the telegrams from Hammersley's grasp. The first one he tore open was from Harry Feldman. Another was from Jack, his brother in Chicago. From his parents. From Moishe. Even one that read: 'Now I know who you are,' and was signed Jussi Bjoerling. But one was missing.

'Is that all?' Daniel asked, trying hard to keep the biting disappointment out of his voice.

'Five aren't enough for you?' Hammersley asked in amusement.

'There was one I was kind of expecting . . .' Daniel tried to explain and then gave up. Hammersley wouldn't understand, just as Daniel himself could not understand why Enzo Martinelli had neglected to wire him. Maybe there was something wrong with the overseas cable service, he reasoned, trying to ease his disappointment. He couldn't imagine the Italian forgetting an occasion like this.

'Maybe it will come later,' Hammersley said. 'Good luck. I'll be listening carefully.'

'Thank you.'

A uniformed figure appeared in the doorway, blocking out the activity that bustled along the corridor outside the dressing room. Daniel recognised one of the doormen from the front.

'There's some guy outside to see you, Mr. Kerr. Says he's got to talk to you before the performance.'

'Who?' The opera started in fifteen minutes. He didn't have time to talk to anyone now. It would just have to wait.

'He wouldn't give his name, sir. Just told me to pass this on to you' — the doorman held out a thin object wrapped in white tissue paper —'and you'd know who it was.'

Puzzled, Daniel took the package, unwrapped it and began to laugh. In his hand was a gleaming surgical scalpel

29

'Where is he? Quick, take me to him.'

Enzo Martinelli was waiting in the corridor outside the dressing room. His darkly handsome face lit up with a delighted smile when he recognised the bewigged, costumed figure approaching him. He clasped Daniel around the shoulders and hugged him warmly.

'What are you doing here?' Daniel asked, completely forgetting the disappointment over not receiving a good-luck cable from Martinelli.

'Nothing in the world could have kept me away from your debut, Daniel. Not even another Mussolini.'

'When did you get in?'

'Two days ago.'

'Why didn't you call, for God's sake?'

'I did not want to call you. I wanted this to be a surprise. And imagine my surprise, Daniel, when I find that you are cast in the role of des Grieux. I thought Edmondo, perhaps, if you were very lucky. Or even the lamplighter. For any of those roles I would have come, but the lead? *Magnifico!*' He hugged Daniel again.

'We're almost ready to go,' Daniel said, unwilling to break off the conversation but knowing he had to. 'Can we get together afterwards? We've got a celebration planned in Wheeler's, the Grand's restaurant. Say you can join us.'

'I would be delighted. *In bocca el lupo.*' A third time he hugged Daniel and kissed him on both cheeks. 'Do not forget to vocalise. I will be listening.'

'I already did. And watch out for my make-up!' Daniel joked. 'Do you want your scalpel back?'

'It is yours, a souvenir. I am convinced I will never need it.'

Daniel shook the Italian's hand and returned to the dressing room as one of the stage staff walked past calling out that only ten minutes remained. From the auditorium he could hear the orchestra warming up; an even stranger sound than his own vocalising; the musicians didn't want their instruments to be tight either.

He left the dressing room and began the long walk

downstairs, almost unaware of other costumed figures that accompanied him.

'Worried?' a woman's voice asked as he stood in the wings, fidgeting while he waited for the overture to begin and the curtain to rise.

He turned to see Anna Markova standing beside him, dressed in a high wig and an elaborately embroidered dress. 'Out of my goddamned wits,' he answered truthfully.

'It'll pass.'

'That's just what it feels like it's going to do any second now,' he answered flippantly. As he said the words, his stomach began to churn and he wished he'd kept quiet. That was all he needed now, a trip to the washroom. Once he went, he'd never return.

He looked away from Anna to the stage where the scene was set for the first act of the opera — a spacious square near the Paris Gate at Amiens, an inn with a porch under which were tables, and an avenue leading off to the right. Students, soldiers and villagers strolled around the square, or stood together talking. One of the students, Edmondo, was preparing to address his colleagues.

Applause sounded from the auditorium. 'The conductor,' Anna whispered. 'Whatever you feel like doing right now, hold it in for twenty-five minutes.'

The lively overture began. Majestically the heavy gold curtain rose. Edmondo's words — *'Ave, sera gentile, che descendi'* —began the first act.

Daniel clenched his fists and pressed them against his stomach as he listened carefully, waiting for his cue to enter. The rumbling in his stomach refused to diminish. Why the hell hadn't he gone before? He'd had plenty of time. He couldn't go now, that was for damned sure. His cue would come and go and he'd be sitting on the toilet. And down that same toilet would go his entire career. Desperately he sought an object on which to focus his attention. He gazed beyond the footlights, past the orchestra pit and tried to see the audience. It was black out there, like night. Would he be able to see anyone once he stepped onto the stage? He'd even forgotten where Moishe and his own family were sitting. And Martinelli, where was he?

Martinelli! He hadn't even asked the Italian whether he had a ticket for the performance. Daniel forgot all about his troublesome stomach as he cursed himself for his thoughtlessness. Of all people, Martinelli should not have to pay.

'Be ready,' Anna whispered.

Daniel nodded, concentration straining for the cue. He felt Anna's warm, drying hand clasp his own damp one and squeeze gently. Sweat broke out beneath the make-up on his face and over his body. He turned to look into Anna's wide brown eyes and murmured, 'Pray for me.'

'Like I've never prayed before,' she promised.

His cue drew closer and he fretted like a greyhound in the traps when the hare goes streaking by. As he started to move forward, Anna continued to hold onto him. With her free hand she swatted him playfully across the buttocks. 'Give them hell, Daniel,' she told him. Then, in the most atrocious parody of a Brooklyn accent that Daniel had ever heard, she added, 'Show dose bums out dere dat New Yawk can sing like Naples!'

It was all Daniel could do to choke back a laugh.

On cue, he stepped out of the wings and onto the stage. A chorus of *'Ecco des Grieux!'* erupted from the students while a round of applause from the audience greeted his debut appearance.

Daniel glanced down into the prompter's box. The sight of the prompter waving an arm gaily in time with the music while he sang quietly along drove the tension away. This guy had to know every operatic score by heart. And he was probably the only person in the world who could truthfully claim that he had sung every role of every production the Grand had staged during the last ten years.

Daniel's stomach settled down. The perspiration dried. Never had he felt more at ease, more at home. He fitted into the action around him as if he had been born solely for this occasion. The lines flowed surely and musically from him

32

and each time he looked into the wings he saw Anna nodding encouragingly.

The ovation that greeted his bantering serenade, 'Tra voi, belle,' warmed Daniel, lingering in his memory until he head the sound of a horn announcing the arrival of the coach from Arras. Daniel joined the group of students and villagers who clustered around the coach to view the new arrivals. Anna as Manon stepped down, accompanied by her brother, Lescaut, and Geronte, her elderly suitor. As she passed close by Daniel on her way to the inn, she went far outside the score by winking quickly at him.

The act continued smoothly until it reached the point where Manon stood on the balcony of the inn with her brother. Then Daniel turned away and gazed into the blackness of the auditorium. Reality had taken over from enchantment. His moment of truth had arrived. His first major aria that would either stamp him with greatness or expose him as a fraud. He thought of the five telegrams he had received, four that had wished him luck and the one from Bjoerling that said, 'Now I know who you are.' When this aria was over, everyone would know who he was. Daniel opened his mouth and began to sing.

Donna non vidi, mai simile a questa!
A dirle; io t'amo,
a nuova vite l'alma miasi desta . . .

His voice felt wonderfully loose. It seemed to float above his head as if he were singing out of his body, on a plane removed. He stole a quick look at the prompter. The man was still singing along, smiling broadly as he waved his hand up and down. Daniel knew in that single moment that nothing could go wrong, nothing could ruin the moment he had dreamed of since returning from Europe.

'. . . deh! non cessar! deh! non cessar!'

The applause that greeted the end of the aria was both instantaneous and overwhelmingly deafening.

Daniel stood perfectly still, a statue as he revelled in the adulation. This was what it was all about. Applause ringing out from an audience that had hung enraptured on every word, every note. He wished for an instant that he were in Italy, in one of the small provincial opera houses where singers took bows after each aria. Such displays were strictly forbidden by Hammersley, who wanted nothing to interfere with the dramatic continuity of the performance. Bows were fine at curtain calls, the general manager had stressed; but at the Grand they had no place during the actual performance.

At the end of the first act, Daniel stood in front of the gold curtain, first by himself, then with the act's major characters, and finally with just Anna, holding her hand while he let the continuing ovation flood over him.

'They must like you,' Anna whispered out of the side of her mouth. 'They can't all be from Claremont Parkway.'

From one of the boxes a single rose was thrown down. It dropped in front of Anna and she stooped to pick it up, presenting it to Daniel. 'Here, it'll be the first of many.'

Another rose dropped down onto the stage. As Daniel bent to retrieve it, intent on returning the compliment to Anna, he heard the sound of cloth tearing and felt a ripping sensation in his trousers. He heard Anna start to laugh. He stood up quickly, the rose forgotten, and felt pins jabbing him painfully in the back of his right thigh.

'Exit backwards,' Anna advised. 'And make sure you take small steps or we'll be closed down on an obscenity charge.' She pulled him through the gap in the curtains and gave in to helpless laughter as she examined the gaping hole in the back of his trousers. Daniel looked around for the wardrobe mistress. All he could see were technicians changing the scenery for the next act. Finally he spotted the stage manager.

'I'm falling apart, for Christ's sake!' Daniel cried out.

'Don't worry. We'll get you fixed up.' The stage manager sent off his assistant to find a seamstress while Daniel limped carefully up two flights of stairs to the dressing room, clutching the errant folds of fabric in his hand. Anna followed, laughing every step of the way.

By the end of the final act, Daniel's costume was soaked — not with the sweat of fear but with the sweat of exertion. He reckoned he had worked off at least five pounds, an admirable side effect he'd never even considered. Each time he tried to leave the stage, curtain calls encouraged his return. The ovation lasted for fifteen minutes before Hammersley appeared backstage to signal the end.

'Bravo,' he congratulated Daniel. 'A magnificent debut. You were right. Fate was right. And I gratefully acknowledge that I was wrong. You would have been wasted as the lamplighter.'

'Thank you, Mr. Hammersley.'

The general manager followed Daniel up the stairs to the dressing room. 'By the way, I have a snippet of news that might be of interest to you. Before the performance, I spoke with Signor Scarlatti's lawyer. Apparently the investigators at the immigration office have dropped the case. It appears that Signor Scarlatti was the victim of mistaken identity.'

Daniel swung around at the words, towering over Hammersley from the step above. 'So now what happens?' Surely they couldn't relegate him to the bench after he'd turned in such a debut? Hadn't Hammersley taken any notice of the applause? The audience had loved him; they hadn't wanted to let him go.

Hammersley shrugged philosophically. 'Absolutely nothing happens. Signor Scarlatti has refused to ever again set foot on American soil. He's leaving for Europe tomorrow.'

Daniel turned back up the stairs so that Hammersley would be unable to see the gleam of triumph that flashed across his face. There was no longer any competition.

After he had cleaned up and changed, Daniel walked slowly down to the empty auditorium. He knew that his family and friends would be waiting in the restaurant for the post-performance dinner that was a tradition at the Grand. They would have to wait a few moments longer, he decided selfishly. First he needed time alone to come to terms with such sudden success.

Choosing a seat in the front row of the orchestra stalls, he gazed up at the massive gold curtain and tried to imagine how he must have looked on stage. His entrance; had he still been clasping his stomach? That magnificent first aria. And the curtain calls after the first act when his trousers had given way.

Somehow he could not picture any of it. No visions came to mind, nothing but the mute gold curtain and the auditorium empty as he had first seen it, a shell that only hinted at the glory it contained.

'Daniel?'

The spell was broken. He moved in the seat and recognised Moishe walking down the aisle.

'Get the lead out, Danny boy. We're all waiting for you in the restaurant. Your parents. Martinelli. The champagne's going flat.'

Reluctantly Daniel rose and followed his friend into Wheeler's. As he entered the crowded restaurant which adjoined the auditorium, the maître d' grabbed him by the hand and congratulated him on the performance; loudspeakers had carried the opera into the restaurant. Diners set down their cutlery to applaud as Daniel made his way to the table where Martinelli and his parents sat. Even his mother stood up to greet him.

Daniel shook hands, clapped people on the back, kissed. His father was crying again, tears running unashamedly from his eyes as he tried to tell his son how beautifully he had sung. Words collided with each other and Daniel gently pushed him back into the chair. He felt awkward at the praise. From his audience he expected it. It was his due, as Martinelli had once pointed out. But from his own father it embarrassed him.

'Well?' He let his gaze run over the people at the table. 'What's the verdict?'

'Every bit as good as Caruso,' Isaac announced. He held out his glass to the bottle of champagne Moishe was lifting from the ice bucket. 'A toast to the second Caruso!'

Martinelli who had been observing Daniel's reception

36

with a quiet enjoyment, felt it was time to speak. 'No, Mr. Kirschbaum. Not to the second Caruso.' When he saw Isaac's face sag at the contradiction, he raised his own glass. 'The correct toast should be to the first Daniel Kerr.'

Delighted by the toast, Daniel lifted his own glass in response. Then he looked at Moishe. 'And to the immigration office,' he whispered so that only his friend could hear him.

'You might have to sing for their pension fund,' Moishe replied just as quietly.

'And fork over ten percent to you, I suppose, *gonef.*' Daniel looked up as the maître d' hovered over the table, offering another bottle of champagne. Attached to the bottle was a small white envelope. Daniel read the note inside, written in a dainty script: 'See how hard I prayed ... Anna.'

Laughing, Daniel accepted the bottle and looked across the crowded restaurant to where Anna sat with a small group of people. When she saw him looking in her direction, she waved happily. Daniel excused himself to his guests and walked to her table.

'You must have a direct line to God to get prayers answered like that,' he said. 'Thanks. And thanks for the champagne.'

'Enjoy it. You only get one debut.' Anna introduced the people at her table as friends. Daniel nodded to each one, thanking them as they congratulated him. He seemed to be thanking everyone tonight, and he was loving every moment of it. They had thanked him the way they had applauded; now it was his turn.

'Do you want to come over and join us for a while?' Daniel asked Anna. 'If you can bear the din and the tears.'

Anna shook her head. 'Celebrations are private affairs. You don't get too much privacy in this game so enjoy it while you can.'

'Okay, see you later.' He returned to his own table.

'Who was the girl?' Yetta Kirschbaum wanted to know.

'Anna Markova. The soprano who sang Manon.'

'So young,' Yetta mused. 'What kind of a name is this Markova anyway? Russian?'

'It's Markowitz.'

'Jewish girl?'

Daniel looked helplessly around the table until his eyes rested on Martinelli. The Italian was chuckling quietly. 'Yes. A Jewish girl. Happy now?'

'Why did you both have to change your names?'

'Enzo, do me a favour and answer that question.' For once Yetta Kirschbaum had said something funny and Daniel knew he would never be able to reply without laughing.

Martinelli gazed across the table at Yetta. 'Mrs. Kirschbaum, can you even begin to imagine what effect it would have on an opera-loving public if the Grand Opera Company of New York staged a production of Puccini's *Manon Lescaut* and the two leading singers were named Markowitz and Kirschbaum?'

Moishe, busy pouring more champagne, stopped to think about the question. 'Sounds as crazy as a lawyer with a name like Moishe Wasserman,' he grunted to himself. He pushed back his glasses and continued to pour.

As they drank coffee after the meal, the maître d' stopped by the table once more. This time he cleared a space in the centre and set down copies of that morning's early editions. Moishe's hand snaked out and grabbed the *Times,* while Daniel scrambled frantically through the *Herald*.

' "Cesare Scarlatti was not missed," ' Moishe began to read aloud, ' "because in his place as des Grieux was Daniel Kerr, a young American tenor whose voice — if not his tailor — will assure him of popularity." ' He threw down the newspaper and burst out laughing.

'Wait!' Daniel cut in. 'Wait till you hear this gem. "The most exciting noise of all was not Mr. Kerr's high notes — which he reached with impeccable ease — nor the well-deserved if lengthy ovation which followed Act Four. It was,

38

instead, the unusual sound of Mr. Kerr's trousers ripping at the seams." '

Martinelli reached out for the newspapers and smiled broadly as he read the reviews. 'Next time, Daniel, you will be able to ensure that your costume fits properly. That, and that alone, is the mark of a star.'

CHAPTER TWO

Dropping the score of *Tosca* onto the top of the grand piano, Daniel walked thoughtfully across to the living room window and gazed out over Washington Square. Traffic around the square was sparse because of the blanket of snow that covered the streets. The few people braving the early afternoon cold were wrapped up like Arctic explorers, faces invisible behind thick woollen scarves, hats pulled down low, earflaps fastened. All wore trousers bundled tightly into boots; there was no way of identifying men from women.

Daniel was grateful for the eerie silence brought by the snow. He needed the quiet to concentrate. Any other opera, any other score he could have studied despite the noise of traffic which drifted up from the street to his fourth-floor apartment. But *Tosca* held more difficulties for him than memory alone could conquer.

In the four years since he had debuted at the Grand in *Manon Lescaut,* Daniel had twice turned down the tenor lead of Mario Cavaradossi in *Tosca,* a steady favourite which Hammersley insisted on including every season. This time, though, the general manager had demanded that Daniel undertake the role. It was a special performance for which Hammersley had obtained the services of Italian soprano Claudia Rivera and was being billed as the finest *Tosca* ever produced by the Grand. Hammersley had spent countless hours drumming into Daniel that he was perfect for the role, how vital it was for him to sing this one performance with Claudia Rivera. It would establish him internationally.

Realising that Hammersley was right — and that he would be unable to avoid the role forever — Daniel had chosen to study for the part. It would be some consolation — no matter how minor — that when Claudia Rivera sang the fateful words of *'O! Scarpia, avanti a Dio!'* Daniel's Cavaradossi would already be dead. Wrenching memories of that lipstick-scrawled message on the dressing table mirror would not cause him to choke on his words.

A figure in the snow stumbled and fell, sending a brown paper bag of groceries skidding across the sidewalk and road. Daniel watched sympathetically while the unfortunate pedestrian staggered upright and tried to collect the groceries, then he returned to the piano and picked up the score. As always, morbid curiosity forced him to turn to the final page. The closing words of the opera loomed menacingly at him from the page. As he looked, the page became indistinct until he could no longer see words, notes or staff. All he could see was what he prayed each night to forget. Lucy lying on the patio, the baby cold in its crib. God, would he never be allowed to forget that night, to wash it from his memory? Or was it to be forever etched into his mind, an eternal, indelible punishment for going to the club in Harlem and making love to the woman he'd met there, while he left Lucy to nurse her agony by herself?

Throwing down the score again, he went to an old-fashioned mahogany secretary which occupied a small alcove in the living room. From a drawer he pulled out a large book and began to leaf through the pages. Those first reviews from *Manon Lescaut* were frayed at the edges, turning yellow, and Daniel knew he should buy transparent sheets to protect them; but who had time for such everyday tasks in between rehearsals, performances, tours and recordings? He smiled as he remembered his trouser seams splitting and Anna Markova pulling him back through the gap in the curtains at the end of the first act.

Daniel knew he would feel a lot easier about doing *Tosca* if

Anna were playing opposite him. Anna gave him confidence. She could sense when he was nervous before a performance, which occurred more frequently than he liked to admit. Everything was fine once he had taken that first step onto the stage, sung that first note. But until that time . . . the waiting drove him to distraction. Even the two drinks he'd made a custom of having before a performance did not help; they had merely become part of his ritual, a superstition. His stomach still churned before each production, and then the anxieties magically disappeared once he became involved. When he worked with Anna, she knew this. Her bantering and joking helped him through. In this production of *Tosca*, though, he'd be working with Claudia Rivera, an aging, overweight prima donna who specialised in upstaging everyone around her. The woman even employed a claque in case the applause was not quick enough in coming.

Taken with the scrapbook and the wealth of memories it contained, Daniel turned the pages. *Cavalleria Rusticana*, which he had sung in his second year at the Grand — 'A spirited, full-voiced Turiddu,' one critic had written. *Rigoletto*, which he had conquered the following year — 'A suitably lecherous Duke.' Only in Verdi's *Un Ballo in Maschera* — done that same year — had the critics come down on him; not for his singing but for his acting. He had kept the review anyway because he thought it was amusing — 'If everyone died as smilingly as Mr. Kerr's Riccardo did in last night's final act, then heaven must indeed be a wondrous establishment.' The next time he had sung Riccardo, Daniel's acting abilities had been of no concern. It was in a two-part recording broadcast under Toscanini — after Daniel's voice teacher Enrico Rosati had recommended him — in Studio 8-H with the NBC Symphony Orchestra. The soprano who had played Amelia opposite him, under the baton of the white-haired, fiery Toscanini, had been Claudia Rivera.

It was the success of the Toscanini broadcast and recording which had prompted Hammersley to sign up the

Italian soprano for one special performance of *Tosca*. She and Daniel had created magic on record; the sorcery they would produce together on stage would be unmatched.

For Daniel, though, the recording and the live production were two totally different worlds. In the studio he had sung to Toscanini, obeying the instructions of the baton. He had not sung to Claudia Rivera. In comparison, the first rehearsal of *Tosca* at the Grand had been a nightmare. Daniel had sung well enough, but he had found it impossible to think himself into the part. How could he be in love with a woman who weighed almost two hundred pounds and was twenty years older than he was? No matter what miracles the wardrobe staff and make-up artists performed, nothing could change that. He had sung of love in the *Tosca* rehearsal not because of Claudia Rivera, but despite her. On a recording, where he would be judged by voice alone, he would be found faultless. On stage, where he had to react visibly and emotionally with the soprano, was a different matter.

To exacerbate the situation, the soprano had taken it upon herself to give Daniel acting lessons. He was never to stand in front of her, she told him firmly; he was never to shield her from the audience. When she sang, she always stood slightly forward of the man playing opposite her. That was the way she had always performed and she would change for no one; she was the star and deserved the most exposure. Daniel had looked to Hammersley for help. For once, the general manager was anything but master in his own house. To get Claudia Rivera to appear at the Grand, he had been forced to compromise himself by submitting to her contract demands. If he tried to clamp down on her, she would flounce off the stage and probably never return.

Daniel realised he had been spoiled by his many performances with Anna Markova. She was the rarest of all operatic singers — an attractive, slim, untemperamental soprano. Working with her was a joy. There were no tantrums, never a sharp word. She applied herself diligently to the task at hand and encouraged everyone around her. When things started to fall apart she was always the first with a humorous line to dissipate any tension. Claudia Rivera was somewhere beyond the other end of the spectrum, a tempestuous butterball whom Daniel could not stretch his arms around, even if he had wanted to.

The bell on the small alarm clock set on top of the piano began to ring, signalling to Daniel that it was time to go to the opera house for the dress rehearsal. Sticking to his ritual, he poured himself a shot of rye and downed it quickly, shuddering as if it were unpleasant medicine. Before he left the apartment, he lifted the piano lid and played part of his third-act aria, 'E lucevan le stelle,' so reminiscent of Al Jolson's 'Avalon.'

He was honest enough to know that he dreaded only one thing more than today's dress rehearsal.

And that was the performance itself.

Long lines of people shivered in the biting cold outside the Grand Opera House while they waited to enter for the paid dress rehearsal. As the taxi for which Daniel had waited fifteen minutes deposited him on the icy sidewalk, the orderly lines broke and he was besieged by autograph hunters. He stopped long enough to sign a dozen of the pieces of paper that were thrust at him. Then he pushed his way through, smiling at everyone, grateful when he saw the doorman coming to his rescue. He knew he could have entered secretively by the stage door, but he enjoyed the sensation of being besieged by his fans. If such things could happen to a skinny singer with a limited range like Frank Sinatra, why couldn't they happen to him? The smile split into a wide grin as he pictured a group of paid bobby-soxers in the front seats screaming with hysterical delight every time he opened his mouth. That would outdo any claque that Claudia Rivera might organise.

There was little for the make-up man to do. Daniel had grown a full beard for the role of Cavaradossi. After four weeks, he decided that he liked it so much he would keep it after the production. It covered his fleshy skin and lengthened his face. Anything that made him look thinner should be considered in a permanent light, he decided.

Maybe he should pay more attention to his diet instead and lay off the calorie-ridden delicatessen food that was his favourite. During his four years with the company his weight had seesawed between one ninety-five and two thirty-five. But he was tall; he could handle the excess weight with ease.

The telephone rang as the make-up man finished his work. It was Anna, calling from her apartment on Fifth Avenue, overlooking the park.

'There's something for you in the drawer,' she said.

Jamming the receiver to his ear with his shoulder, Daniel rummaged through the dressing table drawer. He found a white envelope with his name on it and shook the contents onto the table. A bent nail soldered to a fine gold chain dropped out. He laughed delightedly.

'It's beautiful!' he exclaimed. 'For good luck?'

'What else? Unless you want to stick it into the *diva* if she gets on your nerves,' Anna suggested. 'Has she turned up yet?'

'I don't think so. She makes a habit of being late.' Although he had come to expect Anna's encouragement, Daniel was especially glad that she had called. Anna fitted comfortably into his life. Her interests and goals were the same and they complemented each other, both onstage and off. Sometimes Daniel wondered if she fitted in just a little too comfortably. Often he had compared her with Lucy but it was a difficult match to make. Lucy had been a child, a girl who had led a totally sheltered life, while Anna was a woman mature enough to handle herself under any conditions. Being exposed to the glare of a constant spotlight did not bother her. And when the time came for her to reestablish her privacy, she retained the attributes Daniel had first admired — her consideration toward others and her supportiveness for any project she deemed worthwhile.

'Being late's a woman's privilege,' Anna remarked lightly.

'Don't you dare turn out like her,' Daniel warned.

'I don't eat that much. You should worry about yourself, though.' She laughed and hung up.

45

Daniel placed the chain around his neck, shivering as the cold metal of the nail touched his skin. He felt immensely cheered by both the call and the thoughtful gift. The woman who had prayed for him on his debut as des Grieux was still standing by him; even if she wasn't appearing in the same production, her presence was felt. He was never certain how he felt about her. He knew he needed her. Sometimes he even thought he loved her, but then the spectre of the tragic relationship with Lucy intervened and he questioned whether he knew what love even was.

He checked his appearance once more in the mirror, then began his vocal exercises, stopping when there was a knock on the door. Roger Hammersley stood outside.

'Has madam arrived yet?' Daniel asked after inviting the general manager into the dressing room.

'She's changing now.' Hammersley pulled out a chair and sat down. 'Daniel,' he said quietly, 'do me a big favour and be nice to the woman. You've only got two performances with her — today's dress rehearsal and Saturday's performance. After that, she'll be out of your hair forever.'

'And yours, too, eh?' Daniel chuckled.

Hammersley nodded in agreement. 'Mine, too.' He knew now that it was a mistake to have hired Claudia Rivera, but he had been so swept away by the success of the *Ballo* recording that he could only see the triumph the Grand would reap with the same pairing; he had been blind to the pitfalls. Now that he had worked with Claudia Rivera, he knew that his heavy reliance on American singers had been the correct path to take. There was no doubt that the pairing would be an artistic success, but he was wondering if the price he would have to pay would be too high.

'I won't stand in front of her,' Daniel promised. 'I'll let her blot me out completely.'

Hammersley just grinned sourly.

Five minutes before the curtain was due to rise, Daniel stood in the wings talking ice hockey with two stagehands. A flurry of activity announced the arrival of Claudia Rivera.

She was preceded by her manager, a voluble rake of a man who had been flown over from Italy at the Grand's expense as part of the soprano's contract, and her favourite New York hair stylist; the one supplied by the opera company was not good enough for Claudia.

Daniel watched the procession with a degree of amusement. When Claudia spotted him, she crooked her finger imperiously.

'You, come here.'

Daniel obediently ambled over to her.

'Remember, in duets I always stand in front of you. You are never to stand in front of me.'

'I'll remember,' Daniel promised and backed away a few steps. If he had his choice, he'd stand as far away from her as he possibly could. Never mind about behind. Viewed from close quarters, the make-up artist's work usually looked grotesque, a clown's face, heavy cosmetics which seemed normal from the other side of the orchestra but not from a yard away. With Claudia Rivera, even the clown's mask was an improvement if it only served to disguise the double chins and puffy eyes.

Claudia paced after him, unwilling to let him escape so easily. 'And do not breathe over me, either. I do not want your germs,' she warned. 'Although I have protected myself by taking garlic.'

From somewhere behind, Daniel could hear the stagehands laughing. As well as being repulsive to look at, the damned woman would be blasting garlic fumes all over him. He fondled the bent nail resting on his chest. If it were really a good luck talisman, Claudia would be struck down with terminal laryngitis before the overture began.

The soprano dismissed Daniel and waddled over to the stage manager. 'Is my mattress ready?'

'Extra soft as you requested.' He led her around the back of the stage to where the sets for later acts were stored. Daniel followed, watching as the stage manager pointed out the mattress that would cushion Claudia's fall after she had jumped off the ramparts of the Castel Sant' Angelo in the final moment of the opera. The drop was only four feet, after which she would crouch below the level of the parapet, out of the audience's sight. When you were as heavy and ungainly as the soprano, though, four feet could be as dangerous as forty. As he watched Claudia examine the mattress, wickedness began to form in Daniel's mind. He drew one of the stagehands off to the side.

'Just the one mattress?' Daniel asked conversationally.

'Sure.'

Daniel looked earnestly at the man and shook his head. 'Look, far be it from me to tell you guys how to do your job, but I think you'd be a lot safer using two, maybe even three.'

'Why?' The man seemed perplexed.

'She's a very heavy lady. She's vain as well, won't admit that she needs more than one mattress. We've got the proper performance coming up on Saturday and I'd hate to see anything happen to Miss Rivera today, like breaking her neck because one mattress wasn't enough.'

The stagehand looked doubtful. During the first rehearsal, Claudia hadn't bothered to jump; they hadn't even had the set completely erected. But surely the woman knew how many mattresses she wanted? 'I don't know, Mr. Kerr. We were told just the one.'

'I'll give you twenty bucks if you use two or three. Make it three, just to be on the safe side.'

The prospect of money for nothing more strenuous than finding two additional mattresses convinced the stagehand that Daniel was right. 'Sure, Mr. Kerr. Miss Rivera will be happy to know that she's got friends like you.'

As the volley of musket shots rang out across the stage, filling the area with acrid smoke, Daniel dropped to the floor, fervently grateful that his active participation in the opera was over. Standing close to Claudia Rivera had been a waking nightmare. Not only did her breath stink of garlic, but he was certain the soprano had not taken a bath for at least two days. Maybe that was her good luck charm, he reasoned; her bent nail. Dirt. A body odour that would have

48

felled Scarpia just as surely and swiftly as the knife she had used at the end of the second act.

He was surprised at how easily he had managed to sing 'E lucevan le stelle.' The memories of Lucy and the child that had plagued him when he was studying the score had disappeared. That was what working with Claudia Rivera was doing for him, he thought; making him forget everything else but her. Didn't Hammersley have any control over the soprano at all? Or was it also written in her contract that she could take as many bows as she thought fit after each aria? Daniel felt especially sorry for the baritone who had sung Scarpia. The man had been left to stand alone, looking like a fool while Claudia took bow after bow following her 'Vissi d'arte.' Sure she could sing, but so could Anna Markova. And with the Brooklyn soprano they would all be spared the histrionics that went with the Italian's performance.

Daniel tried to shut down his senses as he felt Claudia's sagging body hanging over him, crushing his head to her overabundant bosom while she sang in anguish at his death. He didn't know what was worse, the nauseating odour that oozed from her pores or the garlic on her breath. But soon, if the stagehand had earned his twenty bucks, Daniel would have his revenge. And the house would have a grand finale it had not reckoned on.

Daniel only breathed out when his Tosca stood up and ran to the ramparts to escape from the police. Without moving his body, he opened his eyes and watched in fascination. Standing on the parapet, Claudia sang Tosca's final line. Then with what she considered to be a dramatic touch, she threw both arms high above her head and leaped to her death.

A gale of laughter swept through the opera house when Claudia's head and shoulders reappeared as she bounced up from the three mattresses, accompanied by a loud, terrified shriek that Puccini had never intended to be included in the score.

It took every ounce of determination in Daniel's body for

him to lie still and not curl up in a fit of laughter. Maybe he'd give the guy thirty bucks instead of twenty.

Isaac Kirschbaum shook his head slowly in admonition, but he found it difficult to keep a smile off his face. 'A joker, you are. A practical joker. Daniel, how could you? Miss Rivera's an internationally famous opera singer. Before the war, she sang with Gigli.'

'I'm also a famous opera singer, Pa,' Daniel defended himself. 'I'm entitled to some respect as well.'

'Of course you are. And you'll get it without playing silly tricks like that. The poor woman might have been seriously injured.' When he saw Daniel cross his fingers, Isaac shook his head again. 'Aw, what's the use of talking to you anyway? You don't listen. You know best.'

'Pa' — Daniel grabbed his father's hand as he tried to communicate his own high spirits — 'if you'd have heard the audience laughing when she came back up, you wouldn't be complaining.'

'Daniel, an opera like *Tosca* is not a comedy. That final act is very tense drama. That last scene, when Tosca jumps to her death and the orchestra plays the refrain from ''E lucevan le stelle'' is supposed to send shivers down your spine. It's not supposed to make you laugh.'

'Hammersley said the same thing,' Daniel admitted.

'And the stagehand lost his job because of you, huh?'

'No. I took all the blame.' Daniel stood up and looked out of the window. It was snowing and he could barely see Van Cortlandt Park. Without the view, his parents might just as well have stayed in Claremont Parkway. 'You getting out at all?' he asked his father.

Isaac shrugged. 'A little bit. When the weather's not too bad.'

'You should try to get out more.'

'Daniel, I'm not a youngster. When the winter comes, I stay indoors. Your mother has places to go, but I'll wait for the spring.'

It was not Yetta Kirschbaum about whom Daniel
50

worried. Since he had persuaded his parents to leave Claremont Parkway a year earlier and move into a house he had bought for them close to Van Cortlandt Park, his mother had immediately launched herself at the local women's committees, eager to be the centre of attraction as she had been in the old neighbourhood. But his father, retired from work, no longer had a routine to force him out of the house. Daniel feared that without the friends from Claremont Parkway who would drop in on the off-chance, Isaac would simply sit at home and waste away. During the warm weather, the problem had not been so critical. Although he had been deprived of going into the city every day, Isaac had made the trip to Claremont Parkway to keep up his friendships; and he had walked in the park, meeting people there, finding games of chess and cards in which he could join. With the advent of winter, however, he had shut himself away in the house, only venturing out when Daniel took him somewhere.

The move had affected Daniel as well. No longer a visitor to the Claremont Parkway section of the Bronx, he had almost lost all contact with Tommy Mulvaney. The last time he had seen Tommy had been a chance encounter in the Village. He had been on a dinner date with Anna, and Tommy had been with his wife; Daniel was ashamed that he could not even remember the girl's name. Both Tommy and his father had left the police department. The older Mulvaney had retired and gone south and Tommy had switched from one law enforcement agency to another — he had joined the FBI and was working from the bureau's New York office. During a jubilant reunion, Daniel had promised to send Tommy two tickets to one of his performances, a promise that was forgotten as soon as the two couples had parted company. Occasionally Anna would remind him and Daniel would feel guilty at his neglect; and each time he would push it to the furthest recesses of his mind again. After all, what cop was interested in opera? It was best this way. He and Tommy had gone their separate ways. Happened all the time, close childhood friends drifting apart once they grew up and split in different directions. They'd be an encumbrance to each other now.

'Pa, if I leave tickets for you at the box office, will you be able to get down to the opera house by yourself on Saturday night?'

'So we can see you play practical jokes on your soprano?' Isaac queried.

'No tricks, Pa. I promise you. This is the real thing, not some crummy dress rehearsal.'

'We'll take a cab,' Isaac said grandly. 'And arrive in style just like the lead tenor's family should arrive. Where will you be that you can't see us before?'

'I'm having dinner with Anna before the performance.'

Isaac smiled happily at the answer. 'I think, perhaps, that you would rather have Anna as your Tosca instead of this Italian mattress prima donna.'

'You bet.' Daniel took his coat from the closet and put it on, preparing to leave. Isaac called him back.

'Daniel, I'm very proud of you. I hope you know that.'

'Of course I know.' He opened the front door, wanting to leave before his father became sentimental. He knew that Isaac did not want him to go, leaving him alone in the house. His mother had adjusted to the move from Claremont Parkway, but his father — although continually praising Daniel for buying the house — had not. The open spaces of the park frightened him. Walking upstairs to go to bed frightened him. The whole new environment frightened him. Combined with the absence of the routine imposed by going to the garment centre each morning, he was becoming lost.

'Your mother, too.'

Again Daniel said he knew. The funny thing was, he realised that his father was right. Maybe Yetta had mellowed with age; perhaps he had. She still watched every single penny as if it were her last, and she was still prone to the sudden illnesses that would assure her of attention and sympathy. But she was no longer the virago to whom Daniel had promised to deny any pleasure from his achievements. It was his own maturity, he decided. He viewed his mother now in a different perspective, no longer dependent on her for his well-being. And he realised that with Jack and his family firmly entrenched in Chicago, he was the only close relative his parents had. He remembered well the private vow he had taken after deciding to become a cantor. It was a promise that was impossible to keep. To deny his mother any enjoyment, he would have to harm himself; to make her miserable, he would have to forsake his own career. Above all, to do so he would have to hurt his father.

'Sure, Pa.' Christ almighty! he wished his father would stop. But whom else did he have to talk to?

'Daniel, come back here a minute. I want to ask you something.'

Daniel pushed the door shut and moved close to his father. 'What is it, Pa?'

'On Saturday night, make a big show of your mother. Do it for me.'

'I'll be with Anna. I'll have time to say hello and goodbye after the performance.'

'Then make it a fond hello and goodbye. Please?'

'Okay, Pa. We'll grab a bite to eat in Wheeler's afterwards.' He leaned forward to kiss his father on the cheek, then he got out of the house as quickly as he could.

Daniel tried his hardest to picture Claudia Rivera in the full-length mink coat that Anna was wearing. He gave up. Probably there were not enough minks in the entire world to make a coat that would fit that gargantuan body.

Damn! All he could think of was that bitch. It was bad enough that he'd have to sing with her in a couple of hours, with the garlic on the breath and the stink of unwashed flesh, but did he have to ruin his precious time with Anna by thinking about her?

'Penny for them,' Anna said.

Daniel switched his attention from the Fifth Avenue shop windows to look back inside the cab, to Anna sitting beside him. 'Give you one big fat stinking guess.'

'La Rivera?'

'Who else? The b.o. and the whole *schmear.*'

'Try stuffing wads of cotton up your nose,' Anna suggested brightly.

'Interfere with my singing. Pity that something doesn't interfere with hers.'

Anna leaned back and laughed. Then she became serious. 'Daniel, watch out for her,' she warned. 'She'll want to get back at you for the other day. I know that if someone pulled a trick like that on me, I'd want to get my own back on them, sure as hell.'

Daniel dismissed Anna's warning out of hand. 'I know the stagehands better than she does. Rivera couldn't pay them enough to put real powder and shot into the firing squad's muskets.' He smiled suddenly and took Anna's hand. 'Do you mind a snack with my parents after the performance? I promised my father.'

'No problem.'

'I'll make it quick,' Daniel promised. 'Then we can go to a club.'

She squeezed his hand fondly. 'Sounds great.'

Claudia Rivera ignored Daniel completely as they stood together in the wings before the opening curtain. As far as she was concerned, Daniel did not exist; he was on a level with the technicians who rolled the scenery on and off the stage. Claudia Rivera did not stoop to acknowledging the presence of such people.

Hammersley appeared, dressed in his customary white tie and tails. He whispered in Daniel's ear that President Truman and his daughter were in the audience, seated in Hammersley's own grand tier box. Daniel flinched, but before he could make any reply, Hammersley had moved on to Claudia and her manager. Daniel watched while a white envelope was passed across. Payment before performance, another trick of the Italian soprano. Daniel knew what he'd do if he were in Hammersley's shoes. He wouldn't give Claudia a cheque; he'd pay her in dollar bills. See what she'd do with a parcel that size! But you'd think with what she was getting paid she would be able to afford a bar of soap and some deodorant.

'Next time she sings here put something in her contract about taking a bath at least once a year,' Daniel whispered as Hammersley walked by, on his way to his box and the President.

'Try not to breathe too deeply,' was Hammersley's reply.

Daniel thought of Lucy just once during the performance, while he walked along the ramparts and sang 'E lucevan le stelle'. As applause for the aria rang out, he closed his eyes and pictured what Lucy must have seen the moment she jumped from the window. No mattress. Only a cold stone patio. No lifeless Scarpia or Cavaradossi behind her. Just a mercifully dead child and an uncaring husband. He fondled the bent nail hanging under his shirt and thought about Anna instead. Sitting in the audience, waiting for him. And about the President up in Hammersley's box. During the interval before the second act, he'd peeked through the curtain and seen him. Hammersley was probably planning to introduce the cast to Truman after the performance. The unwelcome vision of Lucy passed.

Claudia appeared on stage to tell him how she had deceived Scarpia into signing two safe conduct passes and how she had then killed him. Daniel delicately angled his head away to avoid the smell as he sang 'O dolce mani' — sweet hands that would kill for him. Anna's warning of revenge had been for nought. Notwithstanding the odour, Claudia was behaving perfectly. Never had there been even the slightest hint of her trying to upstage him. She must have learned something from the mattress episode, Daniel decided. That he had more friends at the Grand than she did.

More applause followed 'O dolce mani' and Daniel's confidence reached new heights. The Grand was his opera house. Claudia Rivera was a guest, nothing more. When she and her tantrums and her God-awful smell had gone, he would remain firmly established.

American tenor and Italian soprano played against each other beautifully as they neared the climax of their duet, discussing how wonderful life would be in exile after the mock execution had taken place. Until at last they joined voices for the four words *'armonie di canti diffonderem'*. Daniel closed the final note on cue, ready for the pause that preceded *'Trionfal'* and the last verse. He was startled and then horrified when Claudia held onto the note for a full second after he had finished.

'You fucking Italian bitch!' he hissed at her.

She smirked back at him.

He caught himself quickly and picked up the duet again. Sheer professionalism kept his voice singing while his mind raged at the soprano. She had held onto the note and made him look short of breath! In front of thousands of people! In front of the President of the United States!

The duet ended among cries of *'Brava,* Rivera!' And hisses and catcalls which Daniel knew were directed at him. The audience had turned on him, and Daniel knew that Claudia's paid help — the leader of the claque she had organised — was responsible. If he knew who the guy was, where he was sitting, he'd leap off the stage and plaster him against the nearest wall, President Truman in the audience or not. The slimy little bastard would never lead applause or catcalls again.

Hammersley would realise what had happened. The orchestra would. The cast. So would everyone at the Grand who had worked on the score. But the audience would have only one thought, a single idea that had allowed them to be led into hissing him. That he had been physically unable to hold onto the note for as long as necessary.

They would forget all about his successful arias of the night, where he had held onto more difficult notes for far longer. Only the question mark surrounding that one short note would remain.

Daniel left the curtain calls to Claudia. As soon as the curtain dropped, he stormed off the stage and raced upstairs to his dressing room. Hammersley was there less than a minute later, closing the door, cutting the two of them off from the rest of the opera house.

'Daniel, I know what happened out there. I promise you that she will never work here again.'

'Are you going to tell that to the audience? To the critics?' Daniel snapped. 'To the President and his daughter? They sure as hell don't know. All they know is that I screwed up monumentally.'

Hammersley stood patiently, letting Daniel finish. 'President Truman and his daughter have left. And they know what happened.'

'Fine!' Daniel spat out, not even bothered that now he would not get the chance to meet Truman. 'What about everyone else? That bitch made a fool out of me.'

'She cut you up like a professional, Daniel,' Hammersley replied evenly. 'You should take it the same way. After all' — a slight smile illuminated his smooth face — 'you did manage to make her look like a complete jackass during the rehearsal.'

'Looking like a jackass and looking like a rank amateur are two totally different things,' Daniel retorted. 'What she did to me is unforgiveable.'

'I told you, she'll never work here again while I am general manager,' Hammersley repeated. 'If she were under contract for further performances, I'd tear up the contract and send her packing. Do you think we can leave it at that?'

Daniel did not answer. He looked in the dressing room mirror and started applying cold cream to his face. Some of it stuck in his beard and he rubbed furiously with a towel, transferring his anger from Claudia Rivera to the cold cream. God, what wouldn't he give to get one final crack at that fat bitch! He could have had his revenge when she was sprawled on top of him in grief after the firing squad had done its work. A sharp jab with the point of Anna's bent nail, a pinch, a grab at her tits; something upstage, out of the view of the audience that would have ruined her lines. She'd have

57

croaked instead of singing. Or she'd have hit a note she never dreamed she could reach. But it was too late to think about it now. The performance was finished, and the joke had been played on him.

'Daniel.' Hammersley watched warily as Daniel threw off his costume and began to clean up. 'May I please have your word as a gentleman that you will take this unfortunate incident no further?'

'How the hell can I take it further?' Daniel swung around to face the general manager. 'You said it yourself — we're not appearing together any more.'

Hammersley inclined his head in acceptance of the words. 'Perhaps it's just as well. I'll go to see Rivera now and explain how disappointed I am with her behaviour.'

'Make sure you tell her how pissed off I am as well!' Daniel yelled after him.

'I imagine that your feelings on the matter go without saying, which, from your choice of language, is just as well.' Hammersley closed the door on the way out. Two seconds later there was a knock.

'Come in!'

Anna entered the dressing room with an exaggerated display of caution. 'Are you going to shout at me as well?' she asked meekly.

'Did you hear what happened out there? In front of Truman, everyone, that fat bitch pulls a stroke like that.'

'She did a job on you,' Anna said unnecessarily. 'It was disgusting.'

Hearing Anna agree so readily with his own thoughts had a soothing effect on Daniel; the woman's own steady calmness influenced him. 'What do you think I should do?' he asked.

'Be a pro and forget about it. I'm sure that Mr. Hammersley will talk to the critics about what happened. He wouldn't allow you to get a black mark like that. It would be bad for both you and the company.'

Daniel thought about it before finally conceding that Anna was right. He reached out to embrace her. She recoiled as his cream-clotted beard brushed against her face.

'Hurry up and get ready,' she told him. 'I saw your parents before. They're waiting for you in Wheeler's. Your father's a bit upset by the reception you got.'

'Great!' Daniel said sarcastically. 'Even he thinks I screwed up.' He washed and dressed quickly, then accompanied Anna down to the restaurant. When he entered Wheeler's, the customary polite round of applause was missing. In its place was a subdued buzz, the sound of cutlery on china. Face turning crimson from embarrassment and rage, he looked at the nearest diners. They turned their heads away. Daniel knew why. Rivera and that goddamned note she'd hung on to. They all thought he'd blown it. Choked and missed the note. Timed his breathing so badly that he couldn't hold on. Nothing Hammersley could say or do would be able to change it.

'Don't worry, Daniel,' he heard Anna whisper. 'You'll live through it.'

Daniel nodded grimly as he led Anna between the tables to where his parents sat. Remembering what he had promised, he bent down and kissed his mother. Then he clasped Isaac by the hand.

'What happened?' his father asked. 'In that last duet?'

'That Italian whale held onto the note for longer than she was supposed to.'

'Why would she do a thing like that?' his mother asked.

'Why? To make people think exactly what you're thinking. That I blew it.'

'She got you back for the other day, huh?' Isaac said. 'Picked her moment well, in front of the President and all. That will teach you to play schoolboy tricks.'

'Yeah, sure.' Daniel looked around the restaurant uneasily. Tonight he didn't feel at home. Wheeler's was suddenly enemy territory. 'Can we get out of here? Go somewhere else?'

'Sit down,' Anna told him firmly. 'You belong here. If you don't stick this out, you'll lose in the long run.'

'Okay, I'll stay.' At least Anna was standing by him. He

started to sit, then stood up again. 'I've got to go somewhere first.' He walked quickly to the washroom and locked himself in a cubicle, certain that everyone in the restaurant was talking about him now that he had gone. He needed time to think, time to cool off. The way he was feeling right now he would antagonise everyone. His parents. Even Anna. That would be all he needed to cap a disastrous night.

Five minutes later he emerged from the cubicle, his mind set to accept the embarrassment. Anna was right. His next performance would knock this evening to the back of his history books; the short note would never be remembered.

The washroom attendant brushed his jacket. Daniel tipped the man and prepared to rejoin his party in the restaurant. As he opened the door, he had an idea. He spoke a few words to the attendant, who took something from the storage cupboard and passed it to Daniel. Daniel slipped it into his pocket and reentered Wheeler's.

'Did you wash your hands?' Anna asked lightly as he sat down.

'Before and after,' he replied. 'See?' He showed her his hands, back and front.

'Feel better now?'

'Yes.' He picked up a menu. 'Let's order.'

As the waiter appeared, a single cry of *'Brava,* Rivera!' rang out through the restaurant, magnified as other diners took it up. Daniel swivelled on the chair and looked towards the restaurant entrance to see the Italian soprano entering like a triumphant Caesar returning to Rome with the spoils of victory, beaming in pleasure at the reception, waving a fat, beringed hand in recognition of the praise. Daniel knew whose voice had started the cries. The same worm who had instigated the applause during the performance and who — he was certain — was responsibile for the hissing and catcalls that had followed the short note. Now he could see who it was. He got up from the chair and took one step away from the table. Anna pulled him back.

'Daniel, leave it alone,' Anna whispered. 'Rivera will be gone by tomorrow. You'll still be here.'

'It's not her I want. It's that little *vuntz* over there.' He pointed to the claque leader, a tall, skinny, middle-aged man dressed in a tuxedo. As Daniel watched angrily, the man stood up and clapped his hands enthusiastically, leading the restaurant customers into a louder, more sustained ovation. He stopped clapping long enough to pull out a chair at the table he was occupying, holding it for Claudia.

'Leave it alone,' Anna repeated.

Daniel chose not to hear the warning. He shook himself free and marched across the restaurant. About to sit down in the chair being held for her, Claudia stopped halfway when she saw Daniel.

'A word of advice!' Daniel called loudly to the claque leader over the suddenly silent restaurant. 'Use two chairs. One for each buttock!'

Chairs scraped as people moved to better witness the eruption of the volcano. Claudia straightened up, the pudgy face drawn tightly. 'A pity you do not sing as well as you shout, Mr. Kerr. Perhaps you would then draw the applause a true artist deserves.'

Daniel kept his eyes on the claque leader. 'I don't like paid applause. Especially when it's led by a creep like the one you hired.'

The man took his hand off Claudia's chair and squared his shoulders. Daniel moved swiftly and grabbed the man by the lapels of his tuxedo jacket, lifted him clear off the ground and deposited him firmly in the centre of the table, sitting him in a bowl of iced water which held two bottles of champagne. The claque leader's screams drowned out the anguished cries of the maître d' who was trying to stop his restaurant from being turned into a battlefield.

Turning from the stricken claque leader, Daniel reached into his jacket pocket and presented to Claudia the wrapped bar of soap he had been given by the washroom attendant.

'Madam,' he said loudly enough for everyone in the restaurant to hear. 'In the United States we call this soap. I would suggest that you try using it. It will stop your body from singing as powerfully as your voice.'

61

Then he turned to address the entire restaurant. 'I, too, can hold a note for an unnecessarily long time. *Armonie di canti diffonderem!*'

He held the last note for seven seconds. Then, with a wide grin of satisfaction that mirrored his pleasure at the ovation he received, he walked triumphantly back to his own table. He covered three steps when something smashed into the back of his head and he fell to the ground, unconscious.

A face topped by a shock of white hair swam drunkenly into his vision, alternately sharp and fuzzy as Daniel tried to bring it into focus. Daniel blinked three times in rapid succession, and Hammersley's face stabilised.

'What the hell happened?'

'Rivera crowned you with a bottle of Dom Pérignon, which you wholeheartedly deserved from what the maître d' told me.'

Daniel sat up, surprised to find himself in Hammersley's office. Anna was sitting in a chair, her concerned face beginning to relax as she saw that Daniel was all right. 'Where are my parents?' he asked. 'How did I get up here?'

'I sent them home in a taxi,' Anna replied. 'Your mother was hysterical.' She would be, Daniel thought. 'Fortunately there was a doctor in Wheeler's. He took care of her.'

'Then we brought you up here,' Hammersley continued. 'So Wheeler's could return to normal. Fat chance of that,' he added quietly.

Daniel struggled to his feet, feeling his head to be sure it was still there. A lump the size of a golf ball greeted his questing fingers. 'Jesus,' he muttered, half in shock, half in admiration. 'Rivera did that? Where is she?'

'Forget about Rivera,' Hammersley answered. 'She left.'

'Can I press charges?' Daniel asked hopefully. 'Assault?'

'For the good of the company I would prefer it if you did not. Besides, her friend could do the same to you, remember?'

'But I only dumped him in a bowl of ice water!' Daniel protested. 'She creamed me with a full bottle.'

Hammersley waved away the justification as having no significance. 'Stealing five cents and stealing five dollars is still theft. So you can forget all about pressing assault charges. There is, however, one matter I would like to discuss with you if you feel well enough.'

'What?'

'My artists do not make a habit of insulting each other in private or in public. An apology is in order.'

'To Rivera?' Daniel asked incredulously. 'You're kidding!' He looked to Anna for support, but he could find no expression in her face to give him comfort.

'No,' Hammersley said. 'Not to Rivera. To me. To Anna. To everyone who witnessed that disgraceful exhibition in Wheeler's. And to all of our patrons. I would suggest a public apology in the columns of the New York *Times*.'

'That's crazy!' Daniel burst out. 'Rivera's the one who should apologise.'

'If she were under further contract to the Grand, she would. Otherwise, she would no longer work for me,' Hammersley explained. 'You, however, are still under contract.'

'If I apologise, I'll admit I was wrong.'

'You were. You made a fellow professional — no matter how obnoxious a person she might be — look a complete and utter ass in front of a restaurant full of patrons. And you physically assaulted one of her party.'

'He deserved it,' Daniel muttered.

Hammersley ignored the comment. 'I leave the choice to you,' he said with an air of finality. 'A public apology to our patrons against the continuation of your contract. Think about it over the weekend. I'll expect your decision first thing on Monday morning.'

Daniel watched sourly as Hammersley held open the office door. Then he took Anna's hand and left.

'I'll see you home,' Anna offered as they stood outside the empty opera house and looked along West Thirty-fourth Street for a taxi.

'You don't have to,' Daniel said half-heartedly. 'I'm not an invalid.'

'I never said you were. But I think you need company more than you're willing to let on.' She flagged down a passing cab and helped Daniel inside. His head ached abominably and he felt nauseated. Far above the physical discomfort, though, rose a sensation of horror that he would have to apologise in public for the mayhem in Wheeler's.

The cab turned south towards the Village and Daniel slumped back in the seat, angry at Hammersley for demanding an apology as a condition for continuing with the Grand, and even angrier with himself for disregarding the advice of both Hammersley and Anna that he should conduct himself like a professional and not be provoked by Claudia's antics. But didn't they understand that she had made him look like a rank beginner? That she'd harmed the reputation he had worked so hard to establish? Even his father — and what stronger supporter did he have? — had thought he'd fluffed the note. It was ingenious, though. He had to admit that. Claudia Rivera — that fat stinking bitch — had chosen her moment of revenge well. Insults, abuse he could have taken and still laughed. But to be left stranded, apparently short of breath while she continued the note, had been like a dagger thrust between his shoulder blades. Grudgingly he forced himself to admit that the Italian soprano's revenge bore the trademark of a real professional at the game. She'd picked her audience well — everyone from Harry S. Truman on down — and she'd picked her method well. Daniel was still learning the business.

The cab stopped outside his apartment house. Anna paid the driver and helped Daniel out. 'Keep the cab,' he told her. 'I'll be all right from here.'

She shook her head firmly, brooking no argument. 'Nothing doing, pal. I'm tucking you in tonight.'

He managed to grin. 'Are you going to undress me as well?'

'I've seen you in your underwear before.' She put an arm around him for support. 'Come on, you wounded soldier. The war's over for today.'

Unprotesting, Daniel allowed himself to be helped up to the apartment. In the living room, he dropped heavily onto the divan, not even bothering to remove his topcoat.

'Where do you keep the aspirin?' Anna asked.

'Bathroom. Medicine cabinet.'

Anna disappeared, returning seconds later with a bottle which she held upside down. 'Empty,' she said needlessly. 'Why do you bother keeping empty aspirin bottles?' She threw the bottle into the trashcan in the kitchen, put on her coat and opened the door. Daniel asked where she was going.

'There's an all-night drug store over on Sixth Avenue. I'll be back in a few minutes.' Before Daniel could stop her, she left the apartment. He stood up and put away his coat, then he went into the kitchen to make some coffee. By the time it was perking, Anna was back with a large bottle of Bayer aspirin.

'How's the head?' she asked, measuring out three tablets into the palm of her hand. She gave them to Daniel, who swilled them down with a glass of water.

'Still there. Aren't you going home? It's past one.'

'Before I leave tonight we're going to write that apology for Mr Hammersley,' Anna said evenly.

'I'll do it in the morning.'

'Like hell you will. You'll sit up all night long and work yourself into a frenzy, find a thousand and one reasons why you shouldn't have to apologise. And you know damned well you should.' She watched him pour the coffee and take two cups into the living room. 'Where's the notepaper?'

Daniel pointed to the mahogany secretary. Anna pulled open the doors, took out a pad of notepaper and began to write.

'What are you putting down there?' Daniel asked, alarmed by the speed with which the words flowed from her pen. 'He wants an apology, not a book.'

Anna held up her hand for him to be quiet. A minute passed while she continued writing, crossing out words, substituting new ones. Finally she held the pad away to read off the message. 'To Mr. Roger Hammersley, the members and patrons of the Grand Opera House of New York: Following the disturbance in Wheeler's Restaurant on Saturday night I wish to apologise for my unprofessional behaviour. Although I was provoked, I now realise that my unfortunate response was ill-conceived and I regret any embarrassment or discomfort I may have caused.' She paused and then added, 'Sign it, Daniel.'

Daniel exploded. 'I can't sign that!' he yelled, instantly regretting the force of his words as the anvil chorus in his head picked up pace. 'Rivera will bust a gut laughing. So will everyone.'

'Daniel, Rivera's career is almost over; she's got another five, maybe ten years tops. Yours is just starting. She'll have damned good reason to laugh if your career ends right here. Then she would have won.'

Anna's logic cut through his pride and anger. She was right. She had been around far longer than he had, knew the ropes more. Despite his successes in *Manon Lescaut, Cavalleria Rusticana, Rigoletto* and *Ballo,* he was still a virtual newcomer. If he refused to apologise, Hammersley would terminate his contract at the Grand and let him go. He knew the general manager well enough by now to realise that he would stick to his word, even if it meant losing one of his top tenors. Hammersley was a man of unyielding principle who demanded complete loyalty and obedience from his artists.

'Give it here,' Daniel said quietly. 'I'll keep you happy and sign the damned thing.'

Anna rewrote the apology neatly, then passed it across for Daniel to sign. When he had finished, she took back the sheet of paper, folded it carefully and deposited it in her purse. 'Just in case you change your mind by Monday morning.'

Daniel grinned and was pleasantly surprised to find that his headache had subsided slightly. He held out his hands to Anna. 'You're a doll.'

She shook her head but took his hands nonetheless. 'I'll be an Aida, a Mimi or a Gioconda. But I refuse adamantly to be a doll. Another apology, please.'

'Uh-uh. That's one I'm not apologising for.' He pulled her onto the divan beside him and kissed her lightly on the lips. 'That's how my speechwriter gets paid.'

'Speechwriter, hell!' she shot back. 'I'm your career-saver.' She ran her hand across the back of his head and tenderly felt the bump. 'That Rivera should have been a boxer,' she murmured. 'A heavy-weight contender. She punches her weight and then some.'

'Smells it as well.'

'You'd better go to bed, Daniel. Make yourself a cold compress and get some sleep.'

'You mean you're going to leave me?' Daniel asked plaintively. 'Leave an invalid, a dying cripple all alone? How can you? Where's your sympathy?'

'In my purse with your apology. Daniel' — she leaned forward to kiss him — 'if I don't leave now, it's going to be very tough for me to leave at all. Some other night.' She stood up and walked to the closet for her coat.

'Where did your family come from?' Daniel asked out of the blue.

'My family? Why do you want to know about that?'

'I'm curious about the name Markowitz, that's all.'

'Poland,' she said. 'Two generations ago.'

'Good.'

She looked at him strangely, but he made no attempt to clarify the comment. She let him help her into the mink coat, then he walked her down to the street to find a cab. When he returned to the apartment, he waited for half an hour — enough time for her to have gotten home through the snow — and dialled her number.

'How do I make a cold compress?' he asked.

CHAPTER THREE

The telephone rang shortly after eight o'clock in the morning, disturbing the Sunday tranquillity.

Daniel reached out to lift the receiver from the bedside extension, grateful for the diversion. He had hardly slept at all, kept awake by the dull throbbing pain in his head and the even sharper pain that a public apology about his behaviour would surely bring.

He hoped it was Anna calling to find out how he was feeling. After last night's débâcle, the soprano was about the only bright star on his horizon; he was convinced he was in love with her.

Instead, it was his mother.

Yetta did not ask Daniel how he was feeling. She did not ask what happened after she and Isaac had been sent home in a taxi by Anna. All she said was, 'Your father's been taken to the hospital.'

Daniel sat up in bed, suddenly alert, the ache in his head forgotten. 'What's the matter with him?'

'He was up all night, complaining about chest pains . . .'

'What's the matter with him?'

Yetta carried right on, dramatising the situation until Daniel felt like screaming at her. 'He thought it was indigestion. He took some seltzer for it, but the pain wouldn't go away.'

'For Christ's sake! What's the matter with him?'

'He's had a heart attack.'

Holding the receiver to his ear, Daniel jumped out of bed and began looking around the room for his clothes. 'Where did they take him? Which hospital?'

'Montefiore. On Gun Hill road and Bainbridge — '

'I know where Montefiore is. Are you there now?'

'Of course.'

'I'll be there in half an hour.'

Without bothering to wash or clean his teeth, Daniel dived into the clothes he'd worn the night before and rushed downstairs to the garage where he kept his car. Because of the snow and cold, he had not used the car for two weeks, but he knew he had little chance of finding a cab to take him to the Bronx at eight on a snowy Sunday morning. When he turned the ignition key, his efforts were rewarded with nothing more encouraging than a dull click. The battery was dead.

He jumped out of the car and, in blind frustration, lashed out savagely at the fender with his foot, leaving a deep dent. The icy wind that whistled around his unprotected head and throat held no discomfort for him. All he could think of was the damned car, and his father lying in a hospital with a heart attack. How ill was he? Critical? Dying? Daniel prayed that his mother had transferred some of her own hypochondria to Isaac. Maybe it was just indigestion and his mother had done what she used to do to him — call in every doctor and ambulance within a ten-mile radius.

Of course it wasn't indigestion. His father had suffered a heart attack and the car was useless! Now, how was he going to get to the Bronx? Subway? Daniel started running towards Sixth Avenue and the closest station. He slipped on the ice and fell, skinning his hands and knees, tearing his trousers. Tears of anger almost froze as they sprang to his eyes and started to roll down his cheeks.

Moishe! That *meshuggeneh* would drive in this kind of weather. He wouldn't even see it had been snowing. He'd get Moishe to run him up to the Bronx. Mind made up, Daniel walked quickly but cautiously over the icy sidewalk to

Moishe's building and ran up the stairs. Moishe opened the door in pyjamas and dressing gown, sleep-filled eyes widening in shock as he surveyed the tattered figure of Daniel.

'What happened?'

'Get dressed!' Daniel snapped. 'I need you to run me to the Bronx. My father's in the hospital with a heart attack.'

'Where's your car?'

'Dead battery. Jesus, are you going to take me or not?' Daniel demanded.

'Okay, okay. Give me five minutes to throw some clothes on, will you?'

Daniel paced the living room while Moishe dressed. What was taking him so long? Was he taking a shower? Cleaning his teeth? Shaving? Daniel wanted a driver, not a tailor's dummy! When Moishe came back, fully dressed, less than two minutes had elapsed. To Daniel, it seemed like two hours.

'Where is he?'

'Montefiore. Gun Hill Road and Bainbridge Avenue.'

'You'd better direct me.' Moishe led the way downstairs and started the car. The rear wheels spun on the icy road surface and then gripped. Daniel held on tightly, hoping there would be no traffic. Moishe was dangerous on dry roads; on ice it would be like flying co-pilot with a Kamikaze.

'What happened to your father?' Moishe asked, gripping the wheel as tightly as he could. Thirty yards ahead, a traffic light changed against him. Moishe debated about whether he should brake and decided not to. He gave the engine gas, sending the car speeding through the intersection moments after the lights had turned to red. A chorus of angry honking applauded his efforts as cars coming across braked wildly to avoid an accident. Daniel screwed his eyes shut and prayed.

'I asked you what happened,' Moishe repeated, oblivious to the multiple accident he had nearly caused.

Daniel forced himself to open his eyes again, amazed to find that the windshield was still intact. 'Last night I had a run-in with Claudia Rivera in Wheeler's after the

70

performance. Didn't you read anything about it in the newspapers? I imagine it was in them.'

'I haven't seen a paper. I was in bed when you tried knocking the door down.' Moishe pressed harder on the gas pedal as he sensed the next light about to change. The car's speed rose to forty-five miles an hour in his quest to catch all the lights along East Houston Street to the East River. The car swayed drunkenly as it hit potholes left by the winter, and Daniel felt that he was going to be sick at any minute.

'I got hit over the head with a bottle,' Daniel explained. 'It must have upset my father. Now he's in the hospital suffering from a heart attack.'

'Quit worrying. It's probably minor,' Moishe said hopefully.

'How can a heart attack be minor?'

From a hundred yards behind, a siren began to wail. Daniel swivelled in the seat and saw a patrol car gaining on them. 'Pull over,' he told Moishe.

Moishe ignored Daniel's instruction. 'This is an emergency,' he pointed out.

'Pull over, you idiot, or we'll wind up in a hospital, too.' Daniel reached across and turned off the ignition, pulling out the key. The engine died and Moishe guided the car to an abrupt halt. The police cruiser pulled to an angled stop in front of them, and the driver climbed out. He pulled his coat collar up around his ears and went to Moishe's window.

'You in a hurry to get to church or something?' His breath left clouds of vapour hanging in the freezing air.

Daniel leaned across Moishe to answer. 'My father's just been taken to the hospital with a heart attack. We're trying to get to the Bronx to see him.'

'What hospital?' the police officer asked dubiously; he hadn't heard this excuse for almost two days.

'Montefiore.'

'What's his name?'

'Kirschbaum. Isaac Kirschbaum.'

'Wait a minute.' The officer returned to his car. Three minutes dragged by while he spoke on the car's radio. Then he rolled down his window and signalled Moishe to follow him. Lights flashing, siren blasting, he led the way uptown, over the Harlem River and into the Bronx. When the police car pulled up in front of Montefiore, the driver waved to Moishe and Daniel, executed a wide u-turn and headed back to Manhattan. Daniel left Moishe to lock the car while he hurried into the building. A woman at the reception desk told him what ward his father was in. Unwilling to wait for the elevator, Daniel ran up the stairs to the third floor.

Yetta Kirschbaum was sitting in the corridor outside the ward. She stood up when she recognised Daniel running heavily from the stairway.

'How is he?' Daniel asked.

'The doctor's in with him now.'

Daniel peeked into the ward. He could see three patients, but the far corner bed which his father occupied was surrounded by a screen. As he watched, the screen was pulled back and wheeled away. Daniel could see his father lying on his back, chest rising evenly as he breathed. His face held a ghostly pallor, and the bones seemed to stick through the skin.

'I'm Mr. Kirschbaum's son,' Daniel said, grabbing the arm of the doctor as he left the ward. 'What's his condition?'

'Resting comfortably.'

'Will he be all right?'

'Of course. He's suffered a very mild heart attack. He'll just have to take things easier in the future, that's all.'

How much easier could his father take life? Daniel wondered. Isaac never went out of the house as it was. What was he supposed to do now? Stay in bed for the entire day and never move a muscle?

'Is it all right if I go in and speak to him?'

The doctor nodded. 'Try to keep it quiet and short. He needs rest right now.'

Forgetting about his mother who continued to sit in the corridor, or Moishe who would be trying to find out where he was, Daniel entered the ward and quietly pulled up a chair beside his father.

'How are you feeling?'

Isaac made a disgusted face. 'All this fuss over a little bit of indigestion.'

'You haven't got any indigestion. You didn't get to eat anything in Wheeler's last night.'

'Okay, a chest cold then, not indigestion. But never mind about me.' Isaac tried to sit up in bed. Daniel pushed him back gently. 'How about you? How's that lump on the back of your head?'

'Don't worry about it. It's going down,' Daniel replied. 'I think that cow hurt you more than she hurt me. Why did you have to get so worked up about it?'

'What did you expect me to do?' Isaac countered. 'Clap with the rest of those turncoats?'

'I'd have disowned you if you had.' Daniel smiled at his father's question. Isaac could not be feeling that bad if he could manage to make jokes. 'Why didn't you let Ma call the doctor when you first felt ill last night?'

'Ah, you know what your mother's like. First sneeze and we get ten specialists lining up outside the door, all counting on us to build their new swimming pools in time for the summer.' He struggled to rise again; a second time Daniel pushed him back. 'What's going to happen to you about last night?'

'I'm publishing an apology in the *Times*. To everyone, Hammersley, company members, patrons.'

'Good,' Isaac said in approval of the decision. 'That's the right thing to do. I'm proud you thought of it.'

Daniel laughed drily. 'I didn't have much choice in the matter. Hammersley decided it for me. It was either that or kiss goodbye my career at the Grand.'

Isaac chuckled. 'The man's got you under his thumb. And I think he knows what's best.'

'Maybe.'

'Anna got us a cab home last night, you know. Don't forget to pay her back. She's a nice girl, Daniel.'

'I know. She even wrote the apology for me.'

'Because you would never have done it yourself?' Isaac guessed.

Daniel nodded. 'Apologies still come hard, Pa.' He leaned over the bed and kissed his father on the forehead. 'Get some rest. I'll take Ma home and we'll look in again later in the day.'

Daniel left the ward and went outside to his mother. Moishe had arrived and was sitting alongside Yetta, reading a newspaper he had bought in the kiosk downstairs.

'I'll wait a few hours and then call Jack,' Daniel told Yetta. 'There's no sense in him flying in, but he should be told what's happening with Pa.'

Moishe suddenly held the newspaper aloft, startling Daniel. 'Here you are, Danny boy. Fame at last. Real fame!'

'What?'

Moishe showed him the review of the previous night's performance. The story centred around the fracas in Wheeler's with a quote from Hammersley explaining that the episode had been provoked by Claudia Rivera holding onto a note for an unnecessarily long time to make Daniel look bad. Daniel grinned as he read the article. Hammersley had been true to his word. He had spoken to the critics. The article finished by commenting that Daniel Kerr was establishing himself as a wit as well as a singer. He might even find new challenges in *opera buffa* — comic opera — once he had recovered from Claudia Rivera's knock-out-punch.

'Very funny,' Daniel said. He passed the newspaper to his mother who wanted to read the article.

'Do you want me to stick around?' Moishe asked.

Daniel thought about it before shaking his head. 'Just drop us off at the house. I'll be able to cab it around for the rest of the day.'

'Your father's going to be all right?'

'Sure. Nothing a bit of rest and proper attention won't cure. Thanks for all your help.'

Moishe drove Daniel and Yetta to Van Cortlandt Park before going home to the Village. Taking into account the one-hour time difference between New York and Chicago,

Daniel waited until almost midday before calling his brother. It was like speaking to a stranger. Jack had made a life for himself in Chicago and came east only once a year, during the fall. It was a duplication of his relationship with Tommy Mulvaney, Daniel decided. Grow up and you split. Sometimes he wondered how he still managed to remain friends with Moishe.

After assuring Jack that their father was all right, Daniel exchanged news politely and hung up. Then he called Anna. She promised that she would come over right away.

That evening Isaac was looking better and feeling brighter. Colour had returned to his face. The bones no longer seemed so prominent. He sat up in bed, eyes alive with pleasure as he surveyed his visitors.

'They know who you are,' he whispered to Daniel, pointing to the other three beds in the ward. 'I told them who my son was. Now I can tell them who you are as well,' he added to Anna.

Daniel glanced around the ward. The other patients were surrounded by visitors. He was grateful. As much as he liked the adulation that went with his career, he did not want to see a hospital ward transformed into a celebrity parade. 'The doctor says you should be able to come home within a week. Do you want to go down south, to Miami, for a month?'

'No. I'll be fine in the Bronx. I'll get my strength back, and when spring comes I'll be able to get out some more.'

Daniel turned to his mother. 'Do you want to go to Miami? Until the weather breaks?'

'I think it would be an excellent idea, Mrs. Kirschbaum,' Anna cut in. 'This cold won't do your husband any good once he gets out.'

'He doesn't want to go,' Yetta replied stoically. 'How can I go if he doesn't want to?'

'If you say you'll go, he'll go as well,' Daniel pressed. Why did everything still have to be decided by a big conference, another Yalta? 'I'll get the train tickets for you, make the hotel reservations, everything. All you'll have to do is go. Okay?'

'Why not?' Yetta shrugged. 'Who needs the Bronx in the winter?'

'Pa, you're going to Miami to convalesce. No arguments.'

Isaac reached out and grasped his son's arm. 'No arguments.'

Daniel stayed in the house long enough to be certain his mother was all right, then he took Anna home in a taxi. Only after she had invited him in for a drink did she notice his dishevelled state, the torn trousers, the skinned hands.

'What did you do?' she asked.

'I took a dive on the ice this morning. Almost broke my neck.'

'Did you forget to take a shower as well? You're reeking enough to be Rivera's twin.'

Daniel wrinkled his nose in self-disgust. He was still wearing yesterday's clothes, and he hadn't even cleaned his teeth in the panic of the morning.

'You'll find a spare dressing gown hanging up in the bathroom. Give me your apartment key. While you're taking a shower, I'll get a cab over there and pick up some fresh clothes for you. You stink like last week's garbage.'

Unprotestingly, Daniel handed over his apartment key. When she left, he drew himself a scalding hot bath and sat luxuriating in it for almost half an hour. It would take Anna the better part of an hour to get to the Village and back, and sort out clothes for him. Why was she bothering anyway? She could just as easily let him go home by himself, to clean up there.

He thought about his father in Montefiore Hospital. No matter how he tried to look at the situation, he felt guilty, responsible for his father's heart attack. If that scene in the restaurant had never taken place, his father would have been all right. At least he approved of the apology that would appear in Tuesday's *Times*. Funny how Isaac had been right, that apologies were still hard to force out. Not as difficult as

76

they had once been, perhaps, but tough all the same.

He dried himself off briskly, cleaned his teeth with a new brush he found in the medicine cabinet and looked on the back of the door for the spare dressing gown. It was made of heavy wool, but to Daniel's horror it was bright pink and far too small. Probably it looked fantastic on Anna, but Daniel was not certain that tightly fitted pink was really his style. Still, if he was to avoid walking around the apartment in the nude, it would have to do.

Anna returned fifteen minutes later, a small leather suitcase in her hand. 'Pink's your colour, Daniel. Suits you like a dream. But I think you'd be better off wearing these.' She set the suitcase on the table and opened it, pulling out a pair of grey trousers, a sports coat, a roll-neck sweater, underwear and socks. 'Where's the stuff you took off?'

Daniel pointed to a chair. 'Don't worry about it. I'll pack it all away.'

'Like hell you will. It's going down the incinerator.'

'The suit as well?' he asked in disbelief.

'Why not? Unless you think torn trousers are going to be the fashion rage one day.' Without another word, she started sorting through the clothes, removing money and keys, wallet and comb. With the exception of the topcoat, gloves and shoes, she threw everything down the incinerator in the hallway.

'Now, what would you like to drink?' she asked brightly on her return to the apartment.

'Got any pink champagne?' Daniel gestured at the dressing gown. 'To go with this creation.'

'Funny man.' She went to a cabinet and took out a bottle of cognac. 'For medicinal value.' She poured some in a snifter for Daniel, but only took tomato juice for herself. 'You still feeling guilty about your father?'

'How do you know?'

'It's pretty obvious, Daniel. Every thought you ever have runs right across your face like a newspaper headline. You'd be a lousy poker player.'

Daniel stared moodily into the snifter of cognac before

77

replying. 'I can't seem to get rid of the feeling that I'm the one who put him in Montefiore.'

If he expected any sympathy from Anna, he was disappointed. 'Daniel, you can't say that you weren't warned about starting anything with that fat cow. Sometimes you've got to think of people other than yourself. For one thing, I'm not sure I like the idea of seeing my favourite tenor get smacked across the head with a bottle. And I'm damned sure that Mr. Hammersley wouldn't approve of any of his artists going out in sub-zero temperatures without a scarf or a hat. Unless you're planning to sing an off-key bass the next time out.'

'I never thought about it because I was in such a hurry to get out this morning,' Daniel admitted lamely. He drank some of the cognac. It burned a pleasant fire throughout his body. Coupled with the hot bath, it was the first time he had felt warm all day. Anna was right. He was probably going to get a cold; he'd done everything possible to deserve one. Not that it really mattered at the moment. He had no performances for almost three weeks. He could afford a cold. He moved on the chair and felt the dressing gown begin to open. Quickly he pulled it closed.

'Would you feel more confortable if you changed?' Anna asked. 'I promise I'll turn my back. Won't even peek.'

'I'll use the bathroom.' Daniel picked up the fresh clothes and went off to change. Anna called after him that she would make something to eat. When Daniel emerged five minutes later in the trousers and roll-neck sweater, Anna was in the kitchen, carefully watching over two steaks under the broiler.

'Can you make salad?' she asked.

'Does anyone make salad?'

'Where do you think it comes from then?'

'A deli?' he guessed. 'That's where I always get my food from.'

'It shows, Daniel. It shows. If you've split the seams on my dressing gown, you can buy me another one.' She turned the steaks over and concentrated on the salad. 'Do you ever cook for yourself?'

'Coffee,' he replied.

'Marvellous diet. Grow strong on that,' she said sarcastically. 'Here, make yourself useful and take this inside.' She handed him the bowl of salad. 'How do you like your steak?'

'Large.' He returned to the kitchen, found knives and forks and set the table.

'Why did you ask where my family came from last night?' Anna queried while they ate.

He looked up in surprise from his plate. 'I told you. I was just curious about the name Markowitz, that's all.'

Anna didn't say anything for a while. She toyed with her food, and then staggered Daniel by asking, 'Were you checking to see if I came from a Russian background? Because of Lucy?'

Daniel slowly set down his fork and stared open-mouthed across the table. 'Who told you anything about that?' he gasped. 'Hammersley?' No, it couldn't be. The general manager knew that Lucy had killed herself, but he was not aware of the details. He didn't know anything about the child. Martinelli? No again. He and Anna had only crossed paths once, on Daniel's debut in *Manon Lescaut* four years earlier. They hadn't even spoken to each other.

'Your father,' Anna said. 'He told me about three months ago.'

'Why? What business was it of his?' Daniel exploded, forgetting that his father was lying in a hospital bed.

'It came out in a conversation, that's all,' Anna explained. 'We were talking about the production of *Tosca* that the Grand had scheduled, with you and Rivera. Your father was worried about whether you'd be able to handle Cavaradossi. I asked him why, and he told me.'

Daniel's flare-up of anger at his father subsided. 'Why did you wait this long to bring it up?' he asked Anna.

'I didn't bring it up at all,' Anna replied quietly. 'You're the one who did.'

Daniel switched subjects so swiftly that he left Anna foundering. 'I just had a bath. If I go out there now, I'll catch pneumonia.'

79

'What?'

'You've got a guest for the night. See?' he added proudly. 'I'm thinking about other people by taking care of my health.' Anna smiled as she understood. 'Good. It's about time.'

At nine the following morning, Daniel took a taxi with Anna to the Grand Opera House. While Anna waited in the reception area, Daniel kept his appointment with Hammersley. The general manager read the letter of apology which Anna had prepared on Daniel's behalf and nodded approvingly.

'Excellent,' he declared. 'I'll get our publicity department to push this out to the *Times*. Let me assure you, Daniel, that I'm greatly relieved you've decided to follow my advice.' Hammersley called in his secretary and gave her the letter, instructing her as to its disposition. When she had left he continued talking to Daniel. 'As you may have noticed, I managed to speak to the critics about Saturday's unhappy episode. The emphasis of all the stories was on the fight, not on your short note. Perhaps it's just as well that you did bait Rivera. It took everyone's attention off the obvious.'

'Except that it put my father in the hospital with a heart attack.'

'Oh?' Hammersley's eyebrows rose a fraction. 'I'm terribly sorry to hear that. How is he?'

'Not too bad, considering. A few weeks' rest and he'll be all right again. I'm sending him down to Florida when he gets out of the hospital.'

'Good idea,' Hammersley concurred. 'But to happier events. Now that you've decided to stay with the Grand, perhaps we can talk about next season.'

'Could we leave it for another time? Anna's waiting outside.'

'Bring her in,' Hammersley invited. 'It concerns her as well.'

Daniel called Anna into the office. They sat down facing Hammersley. 'We've been doing the current production of *Bohème* for so many seasons that I think it's becoming a little jaded,' Hammersley said. 'It's time for a new one.'

Listening to Hammersley, Daniel felt the excitement building up within him. He perched on the edge of the chair, hands clasped tightly together. Hammersley noticed the effect his words were having and smiled.

'We're planning an entirely new *Bohème* for next season's opening night. New production, new sets, everything. Do you want Rodolfo?'

'Do I?' Daniel was out of the chair in his eagerness to snatch up the role. Of all the romantic tenor parts, Rodolfo was the choicest. He had never sung the role; suddenly he wanted it more than anything else in the world. 'You bet I want Rodolfo!'

'And we can write you in for Mimi?' Hammersley asked Anna.

She nodded.

'Good.' Hammersley clapped his hands in satisfaction. 'We want this to be a *Bohème* that will be remembered by everyone. Although not, I hope, for the same reasons our *Tosca* will be.'

'Tell me something,' Daniel asked. 'Did anyone ever write an opera where the tenor and soprano lived happily ever after?'

Hammersley scratched his head. 'Daniel, it's Monday morning. Very early on a Monday morning, in fact. Why are you asking me such a question?'

'Because the situation's just arisen. As soon as this season is over, Anna and I are getting married.'

Hammersley leaned back in the chair, his face blank, then smiling as he accepted the news. 'That's marvellous. Absolutely wonderful. My congratulations to the pair of you.' He picked up his telephone and called for the secretary; he had something else he wanted the Grand's publicity department to work on.

After leaving the opera house, Anna took a cab to her voice teacher for her regular instruction period while Daniel returned to the Village to get his car fixed. Once the battery was charged, he went to a travel agency to confirm tickets and hotel reservations for his parents in Miami. Then he picked up Anna. Together they drove to the Bronx.

'Shouldn't we call on your mother first?' Anna suggested as they stopped outside Montefiore Hospital.

'Later. I want to tell my father first. We'll go to the house afterwards.' He led the way into the hospital, happily surprised to find his father sitting up in a chair, talking animatedly to the man in the next bed. Daniel was certain he knew what Isaac was talking about.

'Feeling better?' he asked Isaac.

'When can I get out of this place?' Isaac protested. 'I don't need to be here any longer with all these sick people.'

'Think I might join you if there's a spare bed anyplace around.' Daniel felt awful. His head seemed to have swollen to twice its normal size and he had difficulty in breathing through his nose. Yesterday's folly in the snow and ice was beginning to exact its toll. 'I've booked your tickets to Miami so you can't back out.'

'Fine. Let me go now. I'm ready.'

'Only after your doctor says so.' The words came from Anna. 'You've got a couple of big dates coming up this year, so you've got to be healthy.'

'What big dates?'

'An opening night *Bohème* with Daniel in November,' Anna replied. 'An entirely new production.'

'What else?'

'And a standing-room-only date under the *chuppah* in April,' Daniel finished off. 'Get better because there'll be no room for wheelchairs.'

'A *chuppah*?' Isaac pointed at his two visitors. 'You two?'

'Us two. Now are you going to get some rest?'

'Does your mother know yet?'

'We're on the way there now.'

'Good. Tell her soon, otherwise she'll feel left out. Go on, go!' He shooed them away. As they passed through the ward door, Isaac called back his son. 'Daniel, this might sound funny, but believe me it's no business to make fun of.'

'What do you want, Pa?' Daniel asked uncertainly.

'Do everyone a big favour this time. Make sure you tread on the glass.'

Tuesday's New York *Times* carried the public apology from Daniel, alongside a story concerning the impending marriage of two of the Grand's brightest stars.

He considered it fortuitous that he had a cold. It allowed him to stay in the apartment for the entire day, reading telegrams and answering calls about the apology and the story. Of the two dozen cables he received concerning the apology, not one criticised his action. He had, the common message read, proved himself to be a gentleman, rising above the antics of an unpopular Italian prima donna. Daniel decided to include the cables in his scrapbook.

Midway through the afternoon, Martinelli telephoned from Milan. The story of the apology had been sent over the wire and eagerly picked up by the Italian press. Daniel had taken the only proper course, the doctor stressed. His action had been honourable. When Daniel told him excitedly of his plans to marry, Martinelli promised that he would create time off from his practice to attend.

By evening, Daniel's eyes were streaming and his nose was raw from wiping. Anna had called twice. The first time she had offered to come round and nurse him. Daniel had put her off, fearful that her own performance in *Norma* that week would be imperilled by exposure to his cold. She had told him to drink plenty of hot liquids. The second time she had called was to find out if he was following her instructions.

Late that evening, when Daniel was preparing to go to bed, Moishe turned up. The probability of catching Daniel's cold didn't bother him. All he could think of was that Daniel had risen above the boring role of opera singer. He was now a national celebrity, a man who had his name plastered all over the New York *Times*. When Daniel inadvertently mentioned that the story had been sent over the wire and picked up in Italy, probably elsewhere, Moishe's delight was unbridled. He would have braved flu and pneumonia for this.

At last, he had in Daniel what he had always dreamed of: a marketable product.

CHAPTER FOUR

'Hey, Danny boy! Happy new house!' Moishe lifted his glass high in the air to make the toast.

Daniel looked up from the drink he was holding and gazed absent-mindedly at his friend. As much as he tried to avoid it, he could not help being fascinated by Moishe's head. It was almost as shiny as the lenses in his glasses. The baldness Daniel had first noticed four years earlier had spread like an epidemic. All that was left of Moishe's hair was a ring round the crown, a monk's tonsure. No small wonder that Moishe was still unmarried, Daniel decided uncharitably; what girl would want a thirty-seven-year-old lawyer with a head like a cue ball?

'Thanks,' he finally replied to Moishe's salute.

Moishe came closer and sat down next to Daniel. 'Didn't no one ever tell you that comparisons are odious?' he asked.

'Who says I'm comparing anything?' Daniel challenged.

'Be goddamned hard for you not to be.'

Daniel knew Moishe was right. He found it impossible to stop making comparisons between Lucy and Anna. He supposed it was the natural thing to do. If you didn't compare, how did you know where you stood? Whether you were better off than before or not? There was no doubt about that. Every comparison he had made had been favourable. This time he had broken the glass on the first attempt, shattered it to dust with the heel of his shoe. The four-day

84

honeymoon he'd stolen in Niagara Falls with Lucy looked shabby when compared with the two-week luxury cruise he had taken with Anna in the Caribbean before picking up the Grand's annual tour in Denver. He and Anna had been celebrities on the cruise ship, just as they had been fêted on their return to the Grand's tour. The company's publicity department had worked overtime on the pair, two star-struck lovers whose romantic duets on stage contained more than just mere acting.

It wasn't only that Anna was a different person from Lucy. Daniel knew his own character had a lot to do with it. He'd also changed. He'd grown up at the Grand. The opera company had been like a finishing school for him. He had learned how to cope with others, learned how to care for others. He often wondered how successful his first marriage might have been had he entered into it with the perspective he now possessed.

He looked away from Moishe to see Anna walking across the living room towards him. The long pale green dress she wore shimmered with every movement of her body.

'What mischief are you two hatching up?' she asked suspiciously.

'Nothing. Nothing at all.' Daniel smiled up at her. 'Just doing a bit of reminiscing, that's all. Deeds done and best forgotten.'

'Oh? Anything I should have known about before I said yes to you under the *chuppah*?'

'We were trying to put together a list of the places that never asked us back for a return engagement,' Moishe joked. 'We had to stop when we ran out of fingers and toes.'

Anna laughed at Moishe's answer. She'd heard countless stories of their club dates, and each tale was more embroidered than the last, the drunks more obnoxious, the premises more seedy. The only club date Daniel had never mentioned was the Deuces Wild, the night Lucy had died; that he would continue to keep as his own secret.

'They never realised the treasures they were passing up,' she said. She took Daniel's arm and pulled him up from the chair. 'You're going to have to reminisce by yourself for a while, Moishe. Daniel can't ignore his other guests and sit here to shoot the breeze with you all day long.'

'Sure.' Moishe nodded. 'Catch you later.'

Daniel allowed himself to be led through the French windows into the back garden. A huge, multi-coloured marquee was set up in the centre of the lawn. Inside, a red-jacketed barman dispensed drinks to the seventy guests who had been invited to the housewarming party. Primly attired waitresses in black dresses and white starched aprons carried trays of appetisers to the groups of people who stood talking on the lawn and patio. A chef — complete with a tall white hat — basted steaks over a sizzling barbecue.

The housewarming had not been Daniel's idea. If anything, he had been firmly set against having any kind of celebration to mark the possession of the new house in the northern New Jersey town of Teaneck. He'd been through the performance before and held no desire to take the same route again. It had been at the housewarming in Paterson that they had first noticed Rachel was unwell. Again those damned comparisons! he thought. No matter how hard he tried to avoid them, they kept on cropping up. Anna had wanted a party, though, to show her friends and colleagues how well she had settled down to suburban life, so Daniel had given her one.

The early evening August sun sent long shadows spilling across the carefully manicured lawn, and the temperature was steadily dropping from its high of seventy-nine degrees reached during the afternoon. Through a crowd of people, Daniel spotted his father sitting on a lawn chair with a plate balanced on his knees. The summer months had done him good, following the six weeks he'd spent in Florida after he had been discharged from Montefiore Hospital. Isaac had more colour in his cheeks than Daniel could remember seeing for a long time, and there was a spring to his step that belied his recent heart attack. But what would happen in another couple of months when fall began, with winter not far away? Would his father lock himself away in the house again and pray that he survived until spring? Daniel looked around the garden for his mother but was unable to see her. Probably stuck in the middle of a group of people, he decided, playing to the gallery until she bored them. Maybe it would be better all around if he moved his parents out of New York altogether. Where would he put them? In New Jersey, somewhere close enough to keep an eye on his father? Or should he send them down to Florida permanently?

'Daniel, don't you think you should be spending some time with Mr. Hammersley and Robin Duguid?' Anna whispered. 'Politics.'

Daniel glanced to where the Grand's white-haired general manager stood. He was talking quietly with a tall, dignified-looking man in his late thirties, clean shaven, with a high brow that made his light brown hair appear to be receding. Daniel, Anna and the new house might have been the day's main objects of attention, but Hammersley had managed to dim some of their lustre by springing the party's major surprise. During the summer months, rumours had permeated the structure of the Grand — and found their way into the press — that Hammersley wanted to retire and return to his native England. Everyone associated with the company had treated the rumours as just that. Hammersley had neither said nor done anything to confirm or refute the gossip, as if — like the performer he had once been — he was enjoying the Machiavellian atmosphere the stories were creating.

Until today, when he had arrived at the house by taxi with a guest of his own — Robin Duguid. Hammersley had introduced Duguid as the man who would take over the reins as general manager of the Grand Opera Company of New York at the beginning of the new season in November. Duguid's credentials, as vouched for by Hammerlsey, were impeccable. For the past four years he had been with the San Francisco Opera Company, working as an assistant to the company's founder and director, Gaetano Merola; before San Francisco he had managed small companies in Seattle and Vancouver, from where he originally came. Duguid was both experienced, Hammersley said, and young enough to push through his own innovative ideas.

Both Daniel and Anna had been shocked by Hammersley's announcement, as had other members of the company who were present at the party. Where did that leave the season's opening night *Bohème*? Daniel had asked. The new production that Hammersley had proudly planned? Eager to dispel any uncertainty, Duguid had assured everyone that the season would run as it had been planned. Any changes he instigated would come at a later date. Even with his assurances, however, the party had taken on a more sombre note.

'Having a good time?' Daniel asked conversationally as he joined Hammersley and Duguid.

'Splendid,' Hammersley replied. 'A thoroughly enjoyable party. Much health and happiness in your new home.'

'Thanks a lot. You?' he asked Duguid.

'It seems to be a very pleasant area. Perhaps not as pretty as San Francisco, but nice all the same.'

Daniel stole a look at Anna out of the corner of his eye, trying to gauge her reaction to the remark. He was uncertain whether Duguid had just offered him genuine praise or a left-handed compliment.

'How did it ever get a name like Teaneck?' Duguid asked. 'Is that an Indian name?'

'I don't know,' Daniel admitted. He had asked the same question of the real estate agent through whom he had bought the house shortly before he and Anna were married at the end of the New York season. The agent hadn't known either. Not that the agent's ignorance had deterred Daniel from buying the five-bedroom brick house. As well as being a desirable area, Teaneck was equally convenient to either New York or Paterson, where Daniel continued to conduct the Jewish High Holy Day services. He had once punned to Anna that singing at Temple Isaiah was his *'Shabbatical.'* It was true. Despite the work involved, he continued to find the peace he had first discovered that day he had left Lucy alone in the house and sat by himself in the temple until the janitor had wanted to lock up. The money the temple gave him for his *Rosh Hashanah* and *Yom Kippur* appearances did not mean a thing to him. Each year he wrote down the full amount on a cheque and sent it off to the United Way.

The immensity of the house had been dictated by his and Anna's needs. They both required privacy for practising. With five bedrooms there was no way they could continually be under each other's feet. And when they decided to have children — Anna had said that as she was starting late, she wanted the first child in one hell of a hurry — all those rooms would not go to waste.

'What kind of name is Duguid?' Daniel asked in response to the question about Teaneck. 'Sounds like the kind of name a philanthropist should have.'

Duguid smiled thinly at the comment. 'My father was a Scot. Do you still think it's a philanthropist's name?'

Daniel didn't know what to say.

'Mr. Hammersley tells me that you'll be doing some work in Europe next year,' Duguid continued.

'I'm considering an offer to sing Turiddu next spring at the Royal Opera House in Covent Garden,' Daniel replied. 'That would be after the Grand's New York season is over, of course.'

'Just as long as it doesn't interfere with the tour,' Duguid pointed out. 'You're quite an attraction.'

'Rest assured, Mr. Duguid. I wouldn't let that happen.'

Daniel's contract specified that he could take engagements with other houses as long as they did not conflict with the Grand's schedule, but he was always to be available for the tour that followed the close of the New York season. His private thoughts, however, were the opposite to the words he spoke to Duguid. He hated the tours. Weeks spent crammed together in a train while the sets rolled along behind on flatbeds, like the circus come to town. Fêted like conquering heroes by local committees in towns you would never dream of visiting. Dragged to parties in this house and that by wealthy community leaders who had guaranteed money for the tour and wanted their pound of flesh in return.

No matter how hard he tried, Daniel could never bring himself to understand what prestige there was in playing host to a company of opera singers, most of whom could think of nothing other than their next meal or their last performance, providing it had been a memorable one. But the tours helped to keep the Grand solvent and to pay his own salary, so he knew he should not complain too loudly. And he realised that the minor players — on small salaries and even thinner expense accounts — looked to those free meals as their main sustenance.

The last tour had not been so bad. He and Anna had a sleeper reserved for themselves. Daniel had bribed an amazed waiter — amazed because touring opera companies were notoriously cheap when it came to tipping — to serve them their meals in the compartment. Whatever laughter had been generated by their spending most of their travelling time in their own compartment had been small payment for being spared the tedium of the never-ending card games and gossip sessions that passed the journeys.

'I'm relieved to hear you say that,' Duguid observed. 'Now that Bing's knocking the Met into shape, we must stand doubly alert to prevent the Grand from slipping.'

When Daniel went the rounds of his other guests, his mind was preoccupied with Robin Duguid. Liking or disliking the man didn't enter into it, although Daniel wondered how he would respond to a general manager who was only a couple of years older than himself. Would he command the same respect that Hammersley had?

Daniel supposed he resented the manner in which Duguid had turned the housewarming party into his own launching party. To a degree it was Hammersley's fault for bringing him along. Hammersley should have known better. But what was he to do? In all decency, he could not have left Duguid out in the cold when the appointment had just been announced by the Grand's board of management, and the man was in town.

'A bit overbearing, isn't he?' Anna murmured, reading Daniel's thoughts. 'He didn't seem very happy about you doing *Cavalleria Rusticana* at Covent Garden.'

'There isn't much he can do about it,' Daniel answered. 'I'm entitled to take other engagements as long as they don't interfere with my work at the Grand.'

Anna gazed at him with increased interest. 'Has something else cropped up that you haven't told me about?'

'Well ... ' He hesitated, debating whether to tell her. 'Moishe mentioned an idea before, when we were sitting talking in the living room.'

'Ah, so that's what the pair of you were plotting. What scheme is brewing under that gleaming dome?' Sometimes Anna felt that Moishe had been included as part of the *ketubah,* the Jewish marriage contract. She knew that Daniel regarded him as a talisman as well as a friend, but that did not stop her from viewing Moishe's ideas with a healthy dose of scepticism. 'Let's hear the latest.'

Daniel took a deep breath. 'Moishe knows someone ... '

'Who knows someone else,' Anna continued as she guessed the next line. 'Go on.'

'That's about it. There's a movie producer called Joel Pomerantz who's trying to get together the money for a musical based on the life of Al Capone.'

'Capone?' Anna almost shrieked. She backed away from Daniel and burst out laughing. 'Did you say Al Capone?'

'Quiet!' Daniel hissed as heads turned in their direction. He was frightened of being overheard. He was still concerned about Robin Duguid and the impending change in the Grand's management. As he had told Anna, there was nothing the general manager elect could do if he took operatic engagements elsewhere. But Duguid might decide to put his foot down and establish his authority immediately if he learned that Daniel was thinking about accepting a role in a musical movie.

Anna was already in bed when Daniel came upstairs. She watched him undress before going into the bathroom to clean his teeth and gargle. The house was full of cigar and cigarette smoke, a memento of the guests who had stayed long into the night. Despite the open windows, the smell refused to disappear, clinging to the drapes and upholstery. Neither Anna nor Daniel smoked, and she knew the exposure had irritated his throat.

'Tell me more about this Al Capone scheme,' she said when Daniel returned from the bathroom.

'It's a musical based on a very simple formula. English-language light opera for want of a better description. A musical centred on the life of Capone, or a part of it, is a two-edged sword. Capone's still a folk hero to a lot of people, mostly Italians. You link that with the Italians' love of music by throwing in some strong numbers and you've got a ready-made audience. Anyone else who pays to see the movie will be gravy.'

Anna could not help laughing at the idea. The whole scheme was preposterous. Only Moishe could have thought it up. And only Daniel would have listened. 'There's a third edge to this sword you're talking about, Daniel,' she finally managed to say. 'And I think you've forgotten what it is.'

'Oh? What's that?'

'The very sharp edge that will come slashing down across the back of your neck if you even think about appearing in something like this. I'm damned sure that even Mr. Hammersley wouldn't let you get involved in a madcap scheme like this, and you're one of his favourites. God only knows what Robin Duguid would think. Anyway, what part in the award-winning movie would you play?'

'Nothing's been decided yet,' Daniel answered, ignoring Anna's disapproval. 'The whole idea's up in the air while the producer tries to bankroll it. All I'm asking right now is that you don't laugh.'

'Why not?' She began to giggle, unable to control herself. A vision of Daniel wearing a chalkstripe suit, two-tone shoes and a grey homburg while he carried a tommy gun under his arm and sang something rousing and ferocious like 'Di quella pira' from *Il Trovatore* was too much to bear straight-faced.

Daniel slid into bed beside her and turned off the lamp on the night table. 'Do you know what the biggest box office hit is going to be next year?' he asked.

'The *Capone Chorale*?' she baited him. *'Dillinger's duet?'*

Daniel enjoyed the banter. Anna had a knack for the absurd, a way of removing the tension from any situation so that it could be discussed on a rational basis. With Anna around, Daniel knew there was little chance of his becoming pompous or taking himself too seriously like some of the other tenors he knew. Basses and baritones hardly ever seemed to be afflicted by the problems from which most tenors suffered as a matter of course. Tenors were an operatic breed apart — insecure, perpetually worried about their voices, their looks, their weight, as demanding as any neurotic prima donna whose pet dog or cat was not allowed onstage during rehearsals. It wouldn't happen to him, though. He had Anna always ready with a sharp pin to prick any promising bubbles.

'It's a movie with Mario Lanza called *The Great Caruso*. You've heard Lanza sing, right?'

'Sure.' Anna raked her memory for a moment before coming up with the names of movies. *'That Midnight Kiss* and *The Toast of New Orleans.'*

'That's it. This guy has a natural, God-given voice. But he's never seriously sung opera in a big house. Never will, either.'

'How do you know?'

'Because he refuses to take any direction. Says he hasn't got the time to mess around with learning from the bottom while he can be making money in the movies.'

'That sounds like someone I used to know, someone who didn't have the time to take any minor roles.' She sat up in bed as she became more interested. 'Who told you all this about Lanza anyway?'

'I bumped into Bob Merrill from the Met in the Russian Tea Room the other day. He mentioned that he'd once recommended Lanza to his own teacher, but he didn't want to know anything about studying. Yet this guy with an uneducated voice is going to be busting box offices wide open for the next few years.'

Anna listened patiently, waiting for Daniel's enthusiasm to wane. When he had finished, she spoke quietly. 'Daniel, you said it yourself. Lanza's going to be in *The Great Caruso*. The story of an operatic tenor. Lanza's a matinee idol with a voice who can make a movie like this; he'll be upgrading himself. You're thinking about going in the opposite direction, an operatic tenor going into a dubious musical movie. The Grand will never buy it. They'll argue that you're bringing down the tone of the house by appearing in such a thing, and they'll be right.'

'I'll make a fortune if the movie's a hit.'

'Great! You'll be the richest out-of-work lyric tenor in the country. Singers of your reputation don't make musical comedies.'

'It's not a musical comedy,' Daniel argued. 'It's just a musical.'

'Daniel!' She reached out in the darkness and hugged him tightly, rejoicing in the warmth of his body. 'Al Capone's life set to music has to be a comedy. Very black comedy maybe, but comedy nevertheless.'

Daniel lay still for a moment, breathing evenly, his arms around Anna. Then he said, 'Should I tell Moishe not to bother?'

'Tell him whatever you like. Just keep a watchful eye out for Duguid.'

He snuggled in closer, pressing his knee in between Anna's thighs. 'I've just had an idea that's even funnier. Nothing to do with Moishe.'

'What?' She wrapped her legs around him, imprisoning him, arching her back in anticipation as he pressed against her.

'We're opening *Bohème* in twelve weeks, right?'

'So?' She could feel his teeth nibbling gently on her ear lobe. The teasing sensation sent shivers streaking down the length of her spine.

'You know that scene in the first act, where Rodolfo's

94

sitting alone in the garret after Marcello, Schaunard and Colline have split for the Café Momus?'

'Yes.' His mouth left her ear and began working its way down to her neck. 'What about it?'

'There's a knock on the door. Rodolfo opens it and sees Mimi. First time they've ever laid eyes on each other,' Daniel said.

'That's right.' She closed her eyes and trembled in delight as his tongue traced delicate patterns on her breasts.

'Think what a scream it would be if Mimi was pregnant. Say three months gone. And no one in the audience had the faintest idea that Rodolfo was the louse responsible.'

'I might be sick,' she said. 'How would you like me to throw up all over you while you're singing "Che gelida manina"?' Her stomach muscles tensed as Daniel continued his downward journey.

'I thought morning sickness only happened in the morning,' he murmured.

'What will Mr. Duguid say when I cry off after *Bohème* because I'm pregnant?' Anna asked. 'He'll have to recast for the remainder of the season.'

Daniel chuckled at the question. 'He'll look at me with jealousy in his unphilanthropic Scottish eyes. And I'll have to start making love to sopranos who outweigh me by fifty pounds.'

'You think such a sacrifice would be worth it?'

Daniel didn't answer. He simply took her hand and guided it down, breathing raggedly as her long fingernails trailed tantalizingly across him.

Moishe telephoned two weeks later to arrange a lunch date between himself, Daniel and the movie producer. When Anna answered the call, there was no need for her to tell Daniel who it was. The expression on her face — and the way she pointed her index finger at her temple — made it clear the caller was Moishe.

'What do you want?'

'I've lined up Joel Pomerantz for a lunch meeting.'

'Who's Pomerantz?' Daniel asked; he'd already forgotton the man's name.

'Joel. The producer I told you about from Carmel Studios. He wants to get together with you, to talk about the project.'

Daniel turned to look at Anna standing beside him. She was making faces, mouthing the words 'Say no.' Daniel grinned at her. 'Where do we meet?'

'Katz's on East Houston Street. About twelve-thirty tomorrow.'

'Where did you say?' Daniel demanded, unable to believe what he had heard.

'Katz's. You know, on the corner of Ludlow.'

'I know where Katz's is. You're buying lunch I take it.'

'Yeah.' Moishe sounded baffled. 'How did you know?'

How did I know? Daniel repeated to himself. Because only a cheap sonofabitching lawyer like Moishe would pick a place like Katz's for a business lunch. Rub shoulders at the same time with diamond peddlers and the bums from the Bowery; share a pickle with them. 'Haven't you got any class?'

'The guy wanted a good deli, for crying out loud.'

'There's a million classier ones in the city, you cheap *mamzer*.'

'Are you coming or not?' Moishe wanted to know.

'Yeah, I'll be there.' He hung up and turned to Anna. 'Katz's, would you believe?' He still could not believe it himself. Movie careers did not start in Katz's. Jewellery deals, yes. Indigestion, yes, when you gave in and ate too much. Maybe even the occasional bank robbery. But never a movie deal. Unless the guy who was handling your end of the deal was a pennypincher like Moishe.

Anna let a triumphant smile cross her face. 'Does that tell you something about the idea then?' she asked quietly.

'It tells me Moishe's cheap. But I knew that already. Look, what harm can it do if I go along and say nice to meet you to this guy?'

Anna knew there was no way of dissuading Daniel so she

96

gave in. 'I suppose not. But one sandwich only, and no knishes,' she warned. 'I'm the one that's supposed to get fat, not you.' Since the housewarming party, she had come down on Daniel like an avenging angel, cutting down his calorie intake until he feared he would waste away. In two weeks his weight had dropped eight pounds to two-sixteen. Anna wanted it down to two hundred at least, maybe even one ninety-five. If he were to be the father of the child she was certain she was carrying, she wanted to make damned sure he would be a healthy one.

Daniel gazed at her through reproachful eyes. What was the fun in going to a deli if you weren't allowed to eat? All tenors were large; that power had to come from somewhere.

'Daniel, please think carefully before you let yourself get talked into signing anything. Don't pay too much attention to what Moishe says. Think of your career first. If you're doubtful, talk it over with Mr. Hammersley and Robin Duguid before you make any decisions.'

'I promise.' He held up his right hand like a man taking the Oath of Allegiance. 'Only one sandwich, and no commitment without clearing it first.'

The promise to Anna about only one sandwich was forgotten as soon as Daniel sat down. The corned beef had melted in his mouth like butter; the pastrami would be insulted if he didn't try that as well. What the hell! he decided. Anna would never know; he'd make up for his indiscretion some other time.

He bit into the second sandwich with all the relish of a gourmet savouring the most exquisite delicacy. Satisfied, he looked across the table at Joel Pomerantz.

The movie producer reminded Daniel of a German shepherd dog. Pomerantz had a sharp pointed face, large, oddly shaped ears that seemed to stand away from his head and watchful brown eyes. He had a habit of punctuating every few words with a grin, drawing his lips back from teeth that were so white and perfect they had to be false. 'We're calling the movie *South Side Serenade*,' he said. The grin flashed on and off his face like a light switch being flicked. 'Obviously we've got to catch the feeling of the Capone era in Chicago and at the same time put across the message that it's a musical.'

'Great title, eh?' Moishe commented. 'What do you say, Danny boy?'

'Not bad,' Daniel acknowledged. He took another bite of the sandwich while he waited for Pomerantz to continue.

'We've already got Diane Orsini to play the part of Capone's mistress.'

'I never knew she could sing,' Daniel said. A spray of crumbs erupted from his mouth, scattering across the table. He hadn't thought that Diane Orsini could act either, the two times he had seen her on the screen. She was always being touted as the hottest sex symbol since Mae West, bleached hair, icy blue eyes and a bust that would have made three-dimensional movies a public outrage. In both movies Daniel had seen, she had played a gangster's moll, wiggling across the screen in obscenely tight dresses, flaunting her proudest possession at the camera. No wonder Pomerantz had cast her in the role.

'We'll be dubbing her in,' Moishe interrupted.

'We?' Whose side was Moishe on? Had he decided already that Daniel would take the part?

'The studio, I mean,' Moishe said quickly. 'The studio will be dubbing her in. Joel needs a name to set the ball rolling. But you'll be doing most of the singing; all the big numbers.'

'Yeah, that's right,' Pomerantz agreed eagerly. Again the smile flickered on and off. 'The entire movie will be a vehicle for your voice, for Daniel Kerr. Opera singers in movies are big business right now. Look at Mario Lanza.'

'Mario Lanza's not an opera singer,' Daniel pointed out as he remembered his discussion with Anna. 'He's a matinee idol who happens to possess a good, natural voice.'

'Same difference,' Pomerantz said, not wanting to be drawn into a battle of semantics in a field about which he knew next to nothing. 'Are you interested or not?'

'There are a few other points I'd like to discuss first,' Daniel said. 'I'd like the opportunity to read the script.'

'Of course. Goes without saying.'

'And I'd like to check out the music, make sure it's suitable for me. Who's writing the songs for you, anyway? Berlin? Porter?'

Pomerantz flashed the grin yet again and waved a hand in the air. 'What do you take me for, a goddamned novice? You're an opera singer so I'm going to get you opera-type music. Do you think I'm going to pay good money to get a score written when there's ten tons of uncopyrighted junk floating around? Beautiful music! The kind of stuff you know already. I've got good writers putting in English words. I'm modernising those opera songs.'

'Arias,' Daniel corrected him. Then he leaned back in the chair and began to laugh. 'You're a character, you know that? You want me to play a musical Al Capone, which is preposterous to begin with, and sing English transpositions of famous operatic arias? You're crazy.' As usual, Anna had been right. Another one of Moishe's scatterbrained schemes. Why had he even considered meeting Pomerantz? He should have known better. If Moishe was involved, it had to be on a lunatic level. And for his troubles he'd have a guilt complex about eating that second sandwich.

Moishe watched his friend cautiously. He felt embarrassed, having dragged both parties together only to see Daniel laughing at Pomerantz's proposal. But he thought he recognised a way to wipe the grin off Daniel's face. 'Danny boy, don't laugh too hard. If you accept, and we agree on any musical changes you want, it's six weeks' work for forty grand.'

The laughter vanished. 'How much did you say?' Daniel gasped.

Pomerantz repeated the figure. 'For six weeks' shooting, that's all. Plus a percentage of the profits. I'll leave you a copy of the script so you can make up your own mind.' He pulled open the heavy briefcase on the floor next to his legs and tossed a bulky brown envelope onto the table. 'The songs are in there, everything you'll need to decide.'

Daniel decided not to open the envelope until he arrived home. He would read through the script with Anna and get her opinion before forming his own. 'There's no way I can put six weeks together until next summer,' he said. 'When the New York season ends, I'm doing a *Cavalleria Rusticana* at Covent Garden, followed by the Grand's spring tour. Maybe June or July.' He said nothing about hoping to be a father around that time; that would remain his and Anna's secret until they were ready to tell everyone.

Pomerantz nodded. 'Maurice here already told me that. We've got a lot of details to iron out first, but I'd like a decision from you by the beginning of November. You should know by then whether you're interested or not.'

'Fine.' Daniel set the envelope down on the empty seat next to him and concentrated on eating again. He didn't feel like laughing anymore. Forty thousand dollars was a sum of money he could not afford to pass up. On top of that he would have the final word on the music. He could write his own ticket.

Anna's face reflected a mixture of amusement and interest as she put down the final page of the script for *South Side Serenade*. 'I know I should be laughing at this entire thing,' she said, 'but it contains some very good ideas. What they've done with the music is clever.'

'I know.' Daniel had been happily surprised when he had read the script. The plot was simple, a period in Capone's life when he had wrested control of Chicago from the other mobs until he had made himself king of the heap. The strength of the movie was contained in the music, twelve numbers for Daniel to sing including the complete 'M'appari' from Flotow's *Martha* — turned into a love song entitled 'Those Smiling Eyes' — and portions of some Donizetti and Verdi arias. Daniel wondered what Martinelli would think of him putting commercial English lyrics to the words of the composers he idolized.

'What you have to ask yourself now, Daniel, is whether

this is going to be beneficial to your career,' Anna said.

Daniel nodded. 'I've got to look at it as being part of my career,' he said. 'Everything I do or sing is part of my career. That one song ''Those Smiling Eyes'' will leap into the hit parade. You accompany me on the piano and see how it sounds.'

'I know how it will sound,' Anna said. 'And I'm with you. But you have other considerations. When are you going to speak to Mr. Duguid about this? To Hammersley as well? It's common courtesy to tell them both that you're thinking about this.'

Daniel told her that he did not have to tell anyone yet. He had until the beginning of November to make up his mind. He would know one way or the other before the opening night *Bohème* which would mark Robin Duguid's first official function with the company. Daniel was certain that there would be no problems should he decide to take work outside of opera.

'You've made up your mind already, haven't you?' Anna said.

'It shows?'

'Does it ever!'

Daniel tried to compose his face, to leave it so blank that no one would know what he was thinking. It was an impossible task. The screen was beckoning to him with promises of fame outside the world of opera. He knew it was a summons he would never be able to ignore.

CHAPTER FIVE

Opening night required tuxedos for men and long dresses for women employed by the Grand Opera Company, from the most anonymous ticket taker to the highest-paid, most celebrated singer. Roger Hammersley had always insisted on the tradition as a gesture of respect for the patrons who would dress up in their finest for this annual social occasion. Robin Duguid, in his first act as general manager, had decreed that the practice would be continued.

Standing in front of the full-length mirror in the bedroom, Daniel studied his reflection carefully. He decided his father would approve of the new tuxedo. It had been brought home from the tailor only two days earlier, after Anna decided that Daniel's old suit could no longer be altered enough to fit him. Since the summer, he had lost twenty pounds and he looked and felt better than he had in ages. Despite the occasional lapses when he cheated on his diet, there was no need tonight to cinch in his middle with a cummerbund as there had been last year. The middle had almost disappeared. Just as long as the loss of weight had not affected his voice. If it had, no one had noticed anything at rehearsals.

Anna stuck her head around the bedroom door and watched him quietly for several seconds while he continued his self-admiration. 'Have you quite finished?' she asked eventually. 'Or should I call the Grand and tell them to hold the curtain for you?'

'Athletic-looking, that's the way I'd describe myself,' Daniel said, patting his stomach. 'I look like a model for a clothing company.'

'Sure you do,' Anna agreed. 'Outsized clothing. Come on or we'll be late.'

The housekeeper Daniel had hired a month earlier was waiting by the front door with their coats. Daniel took his own while the woman helped Anna into hers. Outside, he gave his new Cadillac a minute to warm up, then he headed on Route 4 for the George Washington Bridge and New York.

'When are you going to tell Duguid?' Anna asked.

'Tonight. After the performance.'

'You're pushing your luck,' she warned.

Daniel disagreed. 'The man's had plenty of other things to occupy his mind without me wasting his time.' He had purposely refrained from telling the new general manager that he had agreed to take the role in Joel Pomerantz's production of *South Side Serenade*. He was waiting for the most favourable moment, and what moment could be more favourable than tonight? Robin Duguid would be walking on clouds tonight. The season's opening. The smash hit of a new *Bohème*. And his own beginning as the man in charge of the Grand. Psychologically it would be the best time to strike. Duguid would be so buoyed up that he would find it impossible to say no. As the final applause died away, and Duguid was besieged by well-wishers, Daniel would tell him.

A week earlier Daniel had undertaken a screen test that Pomerantz had arranged in New York. He had sung 'Those Smiling Eyes' to Diane Orsini who had been flown in from the West Coast. The test had been successful even if his first encounter with Diane Orsini had not. She immediately made it known that she was put out by having to fly across the country to test with Daniel, whom she kept referring to as 'Mario Lanza's understudy.' She had done her best to put him off while he was singing; yawning, poking a finger into her ear and even turning her back on him. Her antics had no effect on Daniel. As Moishe had once so rightly pointed out, if he could take on the Leishman brothers, he could take on the devil himself.

After the screen test, Daniel had taken Moishe, Pomerantz and Diane Orsini to Sherry's, the Metropolitan Opera House's restaurant for dinner. The Met had opened its season earlier than the Grand, and Daniel's appearance in Sherry's brought him a lot of attention from Met patrons who wondered if he was planning to join the company — and from at least one aging, concerned tenor who was wondering the same thing. Daniel had enjoyed the attention. Here, even in a competing house, he was known and respected while Diane Orsini was nothing more than his guest. She sat sullenly throughout the entire meal. Daniel had also enjoyed signing the contract which Pomerantz had brought with him, and accepting a cheque for twenty thousand dollars; the remaining twenty thousand would be paid on completion of shooting.

'And when are you going to tell anyone about us?' Anna asked. 'Duguid knows and that's about all.' She had already told the new general manager that she was pregnant and would be unavailable for the remainder of the season.

'Tonight,' Daniel replied. He pulled up to the bridge toll booth and handed across a dollar bill, waiting for change. 'I'm going to tell everyone tonight. I'm going to tell them everything. By tomorrow morning we'll be the most talked about couple in the whole wide world.' He reached out and squeezed Anna's arm fondly.

'For all the right reasons, I hope,' was her response.

Once all the pre-performance anxieties had been eased — finding his parents to give them tickets, making certain that Rodolfo's costume had been altered to fit his new slim figure — Daniel forced himself to relax. He'd taken two quick shots from the half bottle of rye he brought from home, and now he sat back in the chair, eyes closed while the make-up artist went to work on his face. At Duguid's insistence the beard had come off. Rodolfo, the new general manager maintained, was always clean-shaven. He might be a starving, idealistic artist but he was not a scruffy existentialist. Daniel had considered arguing the point purely on principle, but he had given in. He wanted Duguid on his side when it came time to broach the subject of *South Side Serenade*. Anyway, he knew the beard would have no place in the movie so he might as well get rid of it now and score points with Duguid at the same time.

As the make-up artist finished his work, Duguid entered the dressing room. Like everyone else he was wearing a tuxedo with the added touch of a white carnation on the left lapel. To Daniel, though, the tuxedo seemed out of place on the general manager. Only when he remembered that Hammersley had always worn white tie and tails for every production — not just opening nights — did Daniel realise why. Duguid had toned down the general manager's image.

'Come to wish me good luck?' Daniel asked. 'No need to. I carry my own.' He pulled out the gold chain from beneath his shirt and displayed the bent nail to Duguid. 'Anna gave it to me years ago.' Without waiting for an answer, he stood up, walked to the wall and rested his elbow against it while he cupped his hand to his ear. This was the only way he could hear how his voice sounded. Satisfied with a few scales, he switched to the first lines of the fourth-act aria which he would share with the baritone playing Marcello, 'O Mimi, tu piu non torni.' From his position by the dressing room door, Duguid watched impassively.

'I understand you had dinner in Sherry's last week,' Duguid said when Daniel finished vocalising.

'That's right,' Daniel answered cheerfully. Enough people had recognised him there; word had to get back to the Grand. 'That's not against the rules is it?'

'No.' Duguid shook his head in firm denial. 'I'm just a bit curious about the contract you signed while you were there, that's all.'

'It wasn't for the Met, so don't worry.' Despite his easy answers, Daniel began to feel uneasy. Duguid had something — or he thought he did — so why the hell didn't he come right out and say what he wanted? The few dealings Daniel had shared so far with the new general manager had all been straight forward. Why was he beating about the bush now?

'Let me assure you that your deciding to sing with the Metropolitan Opera Company would not perturb me in the least,' Duguid said. 'Although I think you'd be a fool to give up your career with the Grand.'

'So what's the problem then?' Come on, man, Daniel thought irritably. I've got to go out there in a few minutes. Quit making me tense.

'I also think you'd be a fool to appear in garbage like *South Side Serenade*.'

Daniel flinched as the name of the movie was tossed at him. 'Who told you anything about that?'

'You have an excellent press agent.'

For the first time Daniel noticed that Duguid was carrying a rolled-up newspaper. The general manager held it out. A story on the show business gossip page was outlined in red ink.

Stunned, Daniel read the article. Carmel Studios had acquired the services of Grand Opera Company tenor Daniel Kerr to sing the lead in their forthcoming production, *South Side Serenade*. The story even mentioned where the contract had been signed — at Sherry's — and quoted Joel Pomerantz as saying that Carmel Studios was gearing up for a no-holds-barred, head-on clash with MGM and Mario Lanza; and with Daniel Kerr, Carmel would come out on top.

'I think you could have had the decency to mention this to me,' Duguid said quietly.

Daniel took a few seconds to recover from the shock of seeing the news in the paper. 'I was going to,' he said shakily. 'Tonight, after the performance, when you'd officially taken over as general manager.'

'Were you really?' Duguid asked, his voice icy. 'Or were you going to wait until the end of the season? Or even later, until after this, this' — he seemed stuck for the right word —

'piece of garbage had been shot. And then presented it as a *fait accompli?*'

'Hey!' Daniel protested. 'Hold on just a minute! Aren't you running a bit fast? There's nothing in my contract that says I can't make a movie.'

'True,' Duguid agreed. 'But there is one little clause that stipulates if you accept any undertakings the management deems to be detrimental to the reputation and welfare of the Grand Opera Company of New York, we will have grounds to consider discontinuing your contract.'

Daniel heard a man's voice yelling that only five minutes remained until curtain. He didn't have the time to stand around and argue the finer points of his contract now. He had to get downstairs. 'Why don't you wait till the movie's finished, Mr. Duguid. Then decide what to do.'

'I would rather avoid an embarrassing catastrophe than have to apportion the blame afterwards,' Duguid said.

'I've got to go,' Daniel snapped. 'If that curtain goes up and there's no Rodolfo, you'll have an embarrassing catastrophe all right. Your first night as general manager will be your last.' Ignoring Duguid's presence, Daniel pulled the half bottle of rye from the dressing table drawer and swigged quickly. He hoped it would relax him before the curtain went up. Then he brushed past the surprised general manager and ran down the two flights of stairs to stage level. Anna was waiting in the wings, looking anxiously for him. When she saw him, she smiled in relief.

'Why are you so late?' she asked.

'I just had a massive fight with Duguid. Something slipped out to the press about *South Side Serenade*. It's in tonight's paper. Our new general manager' — he said the title caustically — 'is not a happy man right now.' Daniel looked out onto the stage where the singers playing Marcello, Schuanard and Colline were clustered around the pot-bellied stove in the middle of the garret set. From the way they were laughing quietly, Daniel guessed that someone had just told a joke; he wished he'd been out there to share it.

From the auditorium came the sound of applause as the conductor appeared and took his place on the rostrum.

'Tell me all about it later,' Anna whispered. She pushed him out onto the stage. As he turned back to say something, the overture began. There was no time. He walked quickly to the centre of the stage and took his position as the curtain began to rise.

He knew he had never sung better in his entire life than he had in that first act.

The knowledge made Daniel proud. And to a certain degree it made him sorry. In a way, tonight was his swan song because it would be at least one full season before he sang again with Anna. It was as if knowing that she was pregnant had changed his voice, increased its power and its sensuality, made it more caring.

Anna's response to his 'Che gelida manina' had been breathtakingly voluptuous, from the simple beginning where she told him her name to the final lines of their love duet which carried high up to the ceiling of the auditorium, reaching into every corner to fill its space with sweetness.

The effect was not lost on the opening night audience. From the way they applauded — calling the two main characters back in front of the gold curtains again and again — the audience realised that it had been allowed to share in a magical moment, an instant in musical history that went far beyond the realms dictated by composer and conductor. The audience had witnessed an event, a *Bohème* first act that would never be surpassed.

When the applause finally died, Daniel slipped through the curtain and rushed up the stairs. He slammed the dressing room door and picked up the phone.

'Moishe! It's Daniel. Did you see what Pomerantz has done?'

'The story?' Moishe asked.

'What else? I'm getting shit from the new guy here.'

'Why?' Moishe sounded puzzled.

'Because I hadn't damned well mentioned it yet.'

'Jesus Christ,' Moishe muttered. 'Why the hell not?'

'I was saving it for after tonight's performance. Why did Pomerantz rush to get it into the papers?'

'Because he wanted it to coincide with your opening night,' Moishe tried to explain. 'He thought it was timely.'

'Why didn't anyone bother telling me?' Daniel wanted to know. 'Give me Pomerantz's number.'

'He's on the Coast.'

'Just give me the number.' Moishe did. Daniel broke the connection and called the operator, asking her to put him through to Los Angeles. When Pomerantz's phone rang unanswered for fully a minute, Daniel slammed down the receiver in disgust.

A woman's voice called his name. He spun around to find Anna waiting behind him. She asked what had happened with Duguid.

'I don't know yet,' Daniel answered, his mind still full of Pomerantz and what he would like to do with the man. 'He wants to see me after the performance.'

'I thought we were seeing your parents then, to tell them about our news.'

Daniel laughed bitterly. 'I might have some other news for them instead.'

'Daniel, take it easy. Don't slam any doors behind yourself. You might want to go back through them.'

After the performance, Anna sat in Wheeler's with the Kirschbaums. She had not told them anything, preferring to wait until Daniel arrived. The meeting with Duguid had been going on for fifteen minutes. Anna was uncertain whether that was a good sign or not. Looking at it optimistically, she decided the new general manager was at least listening to Daniel's side of the story.

People stopped by the table to offer congratulations on Anna's performance as Mimi. They did not know yet that it would be her one and only role of the season. The Grand would publicise that information the following morning. Anna smiled graciously at each compliment but her

109

expression was automatic, an extension of the acting she had performed on stage. She was too preoccupied with Daniel to put her heart into accepting praise. She had told him all along that his timing was wrong, but he had insisted that tonight would be the best time to publicise the start of his movie career. He should have informed Duguid immediately about his plans to make the movie, not have the man read of it, secondhand, in a newspaper. As general manager, Duguid was entitled to know what his artists were planning. Letting it come on him as a surprise was like a slap in the face, as if Daniel wanted to show that he did not care about the man's feelings.

'Where is he?' Isaac asked. He was becoming anxious. Daniel never took this long after a performance to come down; he was always early, wanting to hear the applause that would ring out when he entered Wheeler's. Especially tonight, when he had opened the season in a new production.

'He's in an urgent meeting with Robin Duguid, the new g.m.,' Anna replied, trying to make her voice dismiss the concern she felt. 'There's a contract problem that Daniel wants to get sorted out.'

'Money?' Yetta asked hopefully.

'No, not money.' Anna did not try to explain further.

'What then?' Yetta pressed.

'It's a personal problem, something in the contract he doesn't like. If Daniel wants you to know about it, he'll explain it when he comes down.'

'Oh, I see.' Yetta became subdued and Anna wondered if she had offended the older woman. Had the short replies seemed rude?

'He's not in any kind of trouble, is he?' Isaac asked gently.

'Not that I know of,' Anna replied. Either Daniel's father was more intuitive than she had given him credit for, or else she was doing what she always claimed Daniel did — wearing her feelings in plain view.

When Daniel finally entered the restaurant five minutes later, his face was devoid of expression, like a man sleepwalking. The broad smile of pleasure he usually wore after an outstanding performance was missing. Anna feared the worst. He pulled out a chair and sat down. Before he could say anything about the meeting, Anna cut in.

'Can we book you as babysitters for next June onwards?' she asked her in-laws.

Isaac forgot that he had been worrying about his son. His face exploded into a beaming smile and he leaned across the table to grasp Daniel's hands. 'Is that what your big important meeting was all about? It took you so long to tell your new boss that Anna was going to be a mother?'

Daniel looked blankly at his father, apparently mystified. Anna replied for him. 'Tonight was my only performance of the season, but no one else knows that yet. I'm taking off the rest of it. Daniel was telling that to Mr. Duguid.'

'That's what you call a personal problem?' Isaac exclaimed. 'A contract problem, something Daniel doesn't like? That's not a problem. That's magnificent news!'

Daniel looked at Anna. She nudged his thigh under the table. He got the message and remained silent, content to let Anna do the talking. Following the lengthy meeting with Duguid, Daniel had more than enough to fill his mind.

For the second time in less than a year, his career at the Grand was on the line. It was as simple as that. Unlike the last time, though, when a public apology had served to soothe everyone's ruffled feelings, there was no easy avenue of escape. He was involved in a clash of wills. Duguid wanted him to back out of his contract for *South Side Serenade* and forget about the movie. Against Daniel's arguments that his appearing in the movie would have no adverse effects for the Grand, Duguid had bent as far as to say that the company would not object if Daniel's voice was used on the sound track; they would have serious reservations, however, if he appeared in the movie as he would be doing both himself and the company a disservice. Daniel had resisted stubbornly. He needed the movie to establish himself in another entertainment field. Opera was a love. He enjoyed it, just as he took pleasure in his cantorial singing. Never

111

could it pay the kind of money that a popular movie could. Never could it give him the kind of thrilling reward that a hit song might.

To close the meeting, Duguid had told Daniel that the company's board of management did not expect him to reach a decision immediately. The general manager suggested that Daniel think very carefully about the matter and be prepared to make his choice by the end of the New York season. Only Daniel's mind was already made up. He would continue with his plans for the movie. If he continued to turn in the kind of performance he had in tonight's *Bohème*, the Grand would never let him go. They would not be able to afford the luxury of principle.

'What about next season?' Yetta asked Anna. 'The child will be a few months old by then. Will you be coming back?'

'I'll probably take that season off as well,' Anna admitted. 'We haven't decided yet.'

'You can always hire a nurse to look after the baby,' Yetta suggested. 'Are you sure you can afford to be away for two seasons?'

Anna stopped to think about the question, uncertain how her mother-in-law meant it. That long without singing, or that long without making money from singing? She decided to be charitable. 'I'll be able to make my comeback whenever I decide to. I've waited a long time for my first child and I want to nurse it myself.'

'If I had a career like yours, I would never let anything stand in my way,' Yetta said.

Anna smiled as she recognised the sniping tone in Yetta's questions. 'My career only came first until something better came along.' She knew of the friction that had existed between Daniel and his mother, until he had decided the best course was to simply pretend to tolerate her for his father's sake. She could understand why.

'Daniel, are you all right?' Isaac asked suddenly, switching his attention from his wife's conversation with Anna to his son.

Anna turned to look at Daniel. He was staring down at the

tablecloth, apparently unaware of what was taking place around him. She knew that she would not have to ask him how his meeting with Duguid had gone; the result was imprinted on his face. 'Daniel, your father's talking to you.'

He lifted his head abruptly, blinking in surprise like a man rudely awakened from a deep sleep. 'Sorry, I was thinking about something else. What did you want?'

Isaac regarded him oddly. 'I was wondering if you were all right, that was all. You look tired.'

'I am,' Daniel confessed. 'I'm shattered. Would you be very upset if we called off dinner? I'll run you back to the Bronx, then I want to get home and sleep.'

Isaac agreed readily, eager to believe that only fatigue was affecting his son. Yetta, though, did not seem pleased by the prospect of having her evening cut short. She had dressed up to the teeth for tonight's opening. She had been spinning tales of it for weeks to her friends. Who would be there. Whom she would meet. To be shunted off home early was not an agreeable prospect. 'Haven't we even got time for a cup of coffee and a pastry?' she protested; that could always be expanded among her friends to a banquet, a feast where she was surrounded by opera lovers who all wanted to meet Daniel Kerr's mother.

'Daniel's feeling exhausted,' Anna said quickly. 'So am I. It's been a very hectic, very exciting day for the pair of us.' She wanted Daniel out of the restaurant as quickly as possible, before he could say or do anything that would publicise the argument she knew had taken place with Duguid. 'Would you mind very much if we left now?'

Isaac stood up immediately and pushed back his chair. 'Of course not. Come on, Yetta. We're leaving.'

Yetta surveyed the still empty table unhappily. 'First we get invited to dinner and then we don't get any dinner,' she muttered. 'What kind of invitation is that to give a person?'

'Just be glad you're getting a lift home,' Daniel shot back as he transferred his smouldering anger at Duguid to a more readily accessible target. 'I don't feel like eating anything

113

tonight, okay? If you want to stay, suit yourself. But you'll have to get a cab home.'

'Don't you want to be seen with us?' Yetta asked. 'Are you such a bigshot now that you're ashamed to be seen with your parents?'

'Of course he's not,' Anna said. 'He's just tired, that's all. You try standing up in front of the lights for two hours, wearing all that make-up and costumes. See how you feel.' She pushed Daniel towards the restaurant exit as she tried to get the ball rolling. A man reached out to stop him, to ask him about the story that had appeared in the newspaper. Daniel pushed straight past as if he were not there. Anna followed, smiling apologetically, whispering that Daniel did not feel well.

Outside the opera house on West Thirty-fourth Street, Daniel breathed in deeply, letting the cool fresh air slowly work its miracles. His head cleared and he thought back to the meeting with Duguid. What would he have done had the roles been reversed? He tried to put himself in Duguid's position, imagining one of the company's singers approaching him with a similar problem. He'd understand, he decided. He would know how important an opportunity like this was to an artist. That was the whole goddamned trouble. Duguid had never been a performer. Hammersley would have understood better, but Duguid would never know the feeling if he lived to be a hundred and fifty. He'd always been an administrative man, unable to relate to the pressures and problems of artists.

No matter how Daniel tried to view the situation, he failed to see any conflict between his work at the Grand and appearing in *South Side Serenade*. The two worlds would complement each other, not conflict. And he'd have the best of both worlds — he'd be a popular singer while enjoying a career as a lyric tenor. What was so wrong with that?

'Daniel, are you going to get the car or should I call a cab for all of us?' Anna asked as she watched him anxiously. She'd never seen him like this before, withdrawn, moody.

Daniel snapped out of his reverie. 'Would you drive? I don't feel up to it.'

She gave him a long, searching gaze and said, 'I think I'd better.' Taking the keys, she went to the parking lot while Daniel remained outside the opera house with his parents.

'Are you sure everything's all right?' Isaac queried. 'This isn't the way you normally celebrate wonderful news like you gave us before. What's the matter?'

'I'm tired, Pa. That's all. Dead beat.' He was relieved when he saw the Cadillac's headlights coming out of the parking lot. More than anything else, he just wanted to go home and go to bed.

'Okay, buster, what the hell happened back there?' Anna switched to a B-movie aggressive tone as she tried to shake Daniel out of his depression. She looked at the Kirschbaums' house, saw the front room light come on and steered the Cadillac away from the kerb. 'What did Duguid say that's got you so down in the mouth?'

'He's given me until the end of the New York season to make up my mind about what I want to do. Opera or movies.'

'In other words, if you take the movie role you're finished at the Grand. Is that it?'

'That's what he thinks. But he's wrong.'

'Daniel.' Anna dropped the gravelly aggressive tone and became serious. 'I know what you're thinking and it's you who's wrong, not Duguid. You are not bigger than the company. They can always replace you. Look how easily they replaced a tenor called Cesare Scarlatti in *Manon Lescaut*.'

'You're a fat lot of help.'

'Do you want me to tell you that you're right when you're wrong?' she asked. 'I won't.'

'You wouldn't stand by me on this?'

'I'll stand by you on everything. But my loyalty doesn't stop me telling you what I think.'

Daniel stared gloomily through the windshield. Some opening night, he thought; some new production. Blackmailed by Duguid on his first full day on the job. Was it blackmail? he wondered. Of course it was. And on top of everything else, it had blunted what should have been the joyous occasion of telling his father about Anna and the child. He should have sent Isaac home overjoyed. Instead, he had sent him home hungry and bewildered.

'What do you think I should do?' he asked Anna,

'You've made up your mind to ignore Duguid, haven't you?'

'He's giving me until the end of the season to reach a decision. Or, as he so succinctly put it, the moment I set foot on the set of *South Side Serenade* my future at the Grand ends.'

'Daniel, call Moishe first thing in the morning. He got you into this mess, with quite a bit of assistance from you. Now he can help get you out of it. Otherwise there'll be no Markova and no Kerr in next season's productions.'

Daniel supposed he could blame the entire mess on Moishe but that would not be at all fair. Anna had hit the bull's eye when she'd said that he'd assisted Moishe. Sure Moishe had waved the magical lure of Hollywood in front of his ambitious eyes like a wand, but he'd been the one who had grabbed at it. He'd wanted a crack at the movies, the opportunity to show himself and everyone else that whatever Lanza could do, he could do a damned sight better. He'd wanted the chance so much that he hadn't even stopped to consider how it would affect his standing with the Grand. Now he'd found out. 'If worst comes to worst, I could always go back to being a cantor, I suppose. Full time,' he remarked drily.

Anna spared a moment's concentration from the road to glance sideways at him. 'If that's what you really wanted to do, I'd say go do it.' Then she asked, 'You know something, Daniel? I think you'd really like to be a cantor again.'

'Sure I would. When I'm old and grey and too fat and lazy to do anything else.' He closed his eyes wearily and tried to sleep for the remaining few minutes of the journey. He'd call Moishe first thing in the morning and let him straighten everything out. Anna, as usual, was the voice of reason, the moderating force in his life that kept him firmly on the

116

narrow path. *South Side Serenade* would be a risky gamble, at best a dubious long shot. And the stakes might turn out to be considerably higher than he could afford.

Moishe shook his head emphatically as he faced Daniel across the desk in his office on West Forty-fifth Street. 'You signed a contract, Danny boy. It's been witnessed, it's binding. There's no way out of it for you. You're committed to making *South Side Serenade,* like it or not.'

'What do you mean I'm committed?' Daniel asked belligerently. 'You're acting as my agent on this deal with Pomerantz. I'll give you the four grand you'll be out of my pocket. Just get me out of it!'

'I can't, for Christ's sake! Will you get that through your thick skull? And that's a lawyer speaking, as well as an agent and a friend. I must have spoken to Pomerantz five times since you told me you wanted out of the deal. He won't let you out of it. He got his bankroll by showing your name on the contracts. He's got too much invested to let you back out on him now.' Moishe had been aghast when Daniel had called him that morning after *La Bohème* and insisted he get the contract invalidated. On Daniel's urging, he had telephoned Joel Pomerantz at Carmel Studios and explained Daniel's position, that he might lose his Grand Opera Company contract if he went through with *South Side Serenade.* Pomerantz had been adamant. Daniel had signed the contract, accepted and banked the cheque. He was legally bound to appear in *South Side Serenade.* If he backed out now, Carmel Studios would have no alternative but to sue for damages to cover the prospective losses of cancellation or recasting. The amount Pomerantz had mentioned to Moishe had been a staggering half million dollars.

'What made you all of a sudden decide that you wanted to stick with opera and not try a musical?' Moishe demanded as he tried to understand what had brought about Daniel's abrupt reversal.

'I was never forced to make a choice before. Only when I

had to pick one over the other did I realise what I wanted to do!' Daniel shot back.

'So now I suppose you're going to blame me for getting you involved with Pomerantz. Is that it?' Moishe asked acidly.

Daniel opened his mouth to say something, then thought better of it. Moishe was giving him a lesson in truth. Or maybe they'd just known each other for too long. Moishe realised how Daniel's mind worked, how he would throw any blame right onto Moishe's head.

'No, I'm not blaming you,' Daniel said at last. 'I'm blaming myself and no one else. I should have done a bit of thinking before I signed Pomerantz's bit of paper. I should have asked a couple of people what they thought.'

Moishe listened to what constituted an apology. He felt he had to offer something himself. 'Maybe your new general manager will thaw out by the time spring comes around,' he said hopefully. 'Right now he's chafing at the bit. He's just been made number one and everything that goes with it, so he wants to show the entire world right off that he runs the Grand. You were the first target to pop into his sights so he picked you off. Come the time they start shooting *South Side Serenade* he might have changed his mind about you. So wait as long as possible before you tell him that you're not going to back out. He might surprise you.'

'Sure he'll surprise me,' Daniel muttered without any real conviction. 'Sure he'll change his mind.'

South Side Serenade had better be the biggest blockbuster since *Gone With The Wind*. Otherwise he'd be out in the cold with nowhere for shelter.

CHAPTER SIX

London in April was damp and chilly. A cold, grey, persistent drizzle formed a semi-opaque curtain across the city, dulling the edges of buildings, transforming the roads and sidewalks into greasy pools.

Coat collar pulled up and a heavy woollen scarf drawn tightly around his neck, Daniel left the Park Lane Hotel and walked slowly along Piccadilly towards Piccadilly Circus. More than ninety minutes remained before he was due at Covent Garden for the final rehearsal of *Cavalleria Rusticana*. He would use the time to window shop, to reacquaint himself with the city he had not visited for more than six years.

He had arrived in London the previous day, flying in from Idlewild after appearing in the Grand's last *La Bohème* of the season. Reporters had met him at London Airport and he had happily answered the inevitable questions. Yes, he was thrilled to be appearing at Covent Garden for the first time. That's right, it was in England that he had been given his first real break and he was delighted to be back. Yes, his wife, the Grand Opera soprano Anna Markova, was expecting a baby in a couple of months. The reporters had been kind to him. They had mentioned his commitment to *South Side Serenade*, but no questions had been asked about his problems with Robin Duguid and the Grand. Not that Daniel had really expected any. The rift between himself and the management had been kept quiet. So far, anyway. Duguid was content to sit back and wait for Daniel to make his move, one way or the other. If Daniel chose to put the company first, Duguid would be delighted; if he decided to forgo his contract at the Grand, Duguid was certain he could find other tenors to fill in. But Daniel knew he could go only one way. His sole course of action was to present himself in July for the start of shooting *South Side Serenade*. And then Robin Duguid would undoubtedly throw the book at him; in his very gentlemanly way, of course.

As soon as he had arrived at the Park Lane Hotel from the airport, Daniel had put through a call to Anna. Although the housekeeper was there to help her, Daniel was anxious about leaving Anna alone in New Jersey. Even in her advanced state of pregnancy he had wanted to bring her with him, for herself and for his own sake. She would be his companion, his encouragement when he trod for the first time on a strange stage. Anna had declined. She was perfectly capable of coping at home for the few days he would be away. Besides, she told him, she was so far gone that she was convinced she looked awful and did not want to be seen in public.

Daniel had also called Martinelli in Milan. After explaining that he had to rush back to the States the morning after the Covent Garden performance, he had extracted a promise from the Italian doctor to visit London. When he had ended the conversation, he felt elation about seeing Martinelli and relief that he would have someone he knew in the audience. And with the way Martinelli felt about him, Daniel knew he would have to be disastrous to draw anything but praise.

He crossed the busy Piccadilly Circus junction, stopping long enough to look up at the statue of Eros, then began to walk slowly along Shaftesbury Avenue. A record store attracted his attention. His *Un Ballo in Maschera* — recorded under Toscanini with Claudia Rivera — was displayed prominently in the window. So was the *La Bohème* he had made with Anna following the Grand's opening night. Thrilled to see it already on display, Daniel entered the store. A sales clerk asked if he could help. Daniel pointed to the display of *Bohème* records, wanting to know how they were selling. When he explained who he was, the sales clerk called over the manager. Daniel left the store ten minutes later after making a promise that he would return on Friday afternoon and autograph the covers.

There was an added spring to his step as he crossed over the Charing Cross Road and entered Long Acre. He was surprised to see how much the city had changed since he had been stationed there during the war. Bomb damage still showed, but most of it had been cleared and built over. He knew that if he went down to the dock area, though, he would find plenty of reminders of the bombing raids.

Fruit and vegetable warehouses were still open as he entered the Covent Garden area. Daniel could not resist a broad smile as he approached the opera house. The Grand was on West Thirty-fourth Street, the Met was on Thirty-ninth and Seventh, and the Royal Opera Company performed in the middle of Covent Garden fruit market. When you left the house after a performance, he had been told, you had to pick your way through trucks unloading produce as the market went through its busy period. At least, you never lacked for fresh fruit on the way home.

Because of the tightness of his schedule, Daniel had missed the first two rehearsals of *Cavalleria Rusticana,* which would share the bill with *Pagliacci.* The end of the New York season coincided almost exactly with the beginning of the Covent Garden season. There had been some reservations that one rehearsal would not be enough for Daniel to pick up any traits peculiar to the London production. Daniel replied that he had played Turiddu enough times to be at home anywhere. He hadn't missed much by being absent from the first two rehearsals, he decided. Neither had been with the orchestra. The first hadn't even been in the opera house. It had taken place in a room across the street from the opera house; only the principal singers had been present — an understudy had stood in for him — and chairs had been used for scenery. The second rehearsal, at least, had been

121

held on the Covent Garden stage, and the chorus had been involved.

He stopped outside the opera house to look at the calendar of events, curious to see who else was appearing during the season. His eyes drifted down to his own name and then he did a double take. Thank God he was doing *Cavalleria Rusticana* and not *Pagliacci,* he thought when he saw the cast in the accompanying opera. The role of Nedda in *Pagliacci* was being sung by Claudia Rivera.

When he entered the opera house, he was greeted by the company's musical director, who showed him around. Daniel was duly impressed. Covent Garden was older than the Grand, more ornate. The acoustics were marvellous, the sounds bouncing back at him from the furthest points. He decided that he would enjoy singing at Covent Garden, especially when he knew that Claudia Rivera would be watching him.

After three hours of rehearsing, Daniel's anticipated enjoyment was wearing dangerously thin. His throat felt like a sheet of sandpaper and he was starting to cough. He was sure that the overlong rehearsal and the dampness of the city were combining to affect his voice. How much longer was that damned musical director going to keep everyone rehearsing?

'That last scene one more time,' the musical director called out. 'After the *intermezzo*. It's still not right.'

Daniel grimaced at the mezzo-soprano playing Lola, making certain that his feelings were well known. He had two major arias in that last scene — 'Viva il vino spumeggiante' and 'Mamma, quel vino é generoso.' If he carried on singing like this, he'd have no voice at all for the performance in two days' time. 'Do they always drag these rehearsals out?' he whispered to the woman.

'Until it's right.'

'It is right, for crying out loud.' His voice sounded abnormally loud and he realised he had dropped his tactful whisper in favour of his normal tone. The acoustics were too good, and his petulant statement reverberated around the auditorium.

The musical director clapped his hands. 'Is something the matter, Mr. Kerr?'

Daniel turned to face the man in the darkness of the auditorium. 'How many more times are we going to go over this piece? It sounds fine to me.'

'Perhaps it does,' the musical director replied. 'To you. But not to my ear. One more time, please.'

The scene began again and Daniel willed himself to be patient. He felt out of place as it was, being the only American on stage. And no one had warned him that the English company dressed for rehearsals far more casually than did the Grand. In New York, you felt you had to wear a suit and tie for each rehearsal. In London, the style of clothing was dictated by comfort. The suit Daniel was wearing clashed with the sloppy, shapeless sweaters and baggy trousers of the English cast. But what the Royal Opera Company lacked in sartorial style it certainly made up for in lengthy rehearsals.

By the time Daniel went offstage with the baritone playing Alfio for the duel, he had made up his mind. He was adamant; this was the last rehearsal he would do. If the rest of the company didn't have it right by now, he couldn't give a damn. That was their problem, not his. Even with the two extra rehearsals they'd had, they couldn't put it together.

'Was that to your satisfaction?' he asked pointedly into the blackness where the musical director was sitting.

'From your attitude, Mr. Kerr, I would assume it has to be,' the man remarked sardonically. 'You may step down. We'll have one more go with your understudy filling in.'

Exasperated, Daniel took off his jacket, rolled it up into a ball and threw it into the wings where it was caught by the stage manager. 'Okay, one more time.' His voice was sounding hoarser with each minute and he was sweating uncomfortably. Please God, get these frogs out of my throat by Friday night, he prayed silently. As much as he wanted to call it quits, there was no way he could walk out of the rehearsal now. Opera gossip was like an underground newspaper. Word of his refusal to continue with the rehearsal would reach everywhere. His difficulties at the Grand were already troublesome enough without having the reputation of temperamental tenor added to them.

When the rehearsal finally ended, Daniel nodded a curt farewell to his fellow artists and quickly left the opera house. He had to walk back to Charing Cross Road before he could find a taxi. After giving the driver an address, he slumped back in the seat and closed his eyes. God, his throat felt raw, like he'd swallowed a gallon of sulphuric acid. He'd better take something quickly, otherwise he'd sound like a cement mixer on Friday night.

The journey slipped past in a dream, until the taxi stopped outside a newly built row of anonymous, red brick houses. 'Here you are, guv,' the driver said. 'This is the address you gave me.' He managed to make the statement sound defiant, as if expecting his passenger to claim he'd been taken to the wrong place. After all, what wealthy-looking American would want to come to a street like this?

Daniel shook himself awake. 'Thanks. Will you wait a few minutes for me?'

'Sure. Don't bother me none. Meter's still running.'

Daniel stepped out of the taxi and looked around. The buildings were unfamiliar to him, modern two-storey council homes where once had stood old-fashioned, tall private houses. He wondered if the taxi driver could be mistaken until he looked along the street and recognised the public house on the corner. No, the driver had made no error. This was where he had been that Sunday morning with Harvey Berman, the chaplain from Chicago, and the family he was convinced he'd found in London. The old houses were gone, replaced with council homes, subsidised housing. Daniel stepped closer and tried to see through the communal hallway into the back garden where he had played ball with the boy that morning. There was no garden. Tarmac greeted his eyes. Children's swings and roundabouts. Slides and see-saws. It was a playground for the neighbourhood kids.

'You looking for somebody, mister?'

Daniel turned around to see a woman standing behind him. Her hair was in curlers and she wore an apron over a faded blue dress. Suspicious of a stranger loitering on the premises, she had left her home to investigate.

'I'm trying to find an old friend. Phil Berman. Do you know him? He used to live here during the war.'

The woman gazed at him, uncertain about the American accent, about his cashmere coat. 'Don't nobody live around here from that time,' she finally said. 'These places are all new. Buzz bomb landed in the street and destroyed everything that was here before.'

'I know. Thank you very much.' He walked past her back to the waiting taxi, asking himself why he had bothered coming to this street. Had he really expected to find Phil Berman still living there? Or was it because he was so alone in the city that he needed someone he knew — no matter how vaguely or from how long ago? And if he had found Phil, what would he have said? That he'd seen his wife and child die?

'Where to now, guv?' the driver asked.

'Park Lane Hotel.' He'd have a drink and try to get some sleep. Sleep would be the best cure of all. It wasn't only the sore throat that was bothering him, it was the huge time difference as well. That's what had made him irritable at the rehearsal. He had been so tired that he'd almost fallen asleep on his feet. No wonder his voice had sounded hoarse. Pleased to identify the source of his trouble, Daniel resolved to apologise to the musical director when he saw him next.

Back in the hotel room, he ordered a bottle of scotch and some ice. When it arrived, he poured a generous measure into the glass and sat back in an easy chair to relax.

When the telephone rang ninety minutes later, the bottle was almost half empty and Daniel was fast asleep in the chair. He woke sluggishly at the insistent double ring of the bell and looked around the room in bewilderment while he struggled to remember where he was.

'Yes?'

125

'Daniel Kerr?' a clipped voice asked.

'Who is this?' He sounded terrible. His words were slurred, hard to form. His throat ached. The whisky had not done any good at all.

'Roger Hammersley. I had hoped that you might contact me when you knew you were coming to Covent Garden.'

'I was going to,' Daniel lied. He'd forgotten all about Hammersley. The man had left the Grand less than six months earlier to return to England and Daniel had already pushed him out of his memory. 'Any chance of getting together for dinner sometime?' he asked, trying to make up for his lapse. 'Say Friday. Spend the afternoon together and have a bite before the performance? I'm flying back on Saturday, otherwise I'd suggest then.'

'That sounds excellent,' Hammersley concurred. 'I'll meet you at the Park Lane.'

'Do you remember Enzo Martinelli from Milan?' Daniel asked, eager to prolong the conversation as he sought to hold onto a familiar voice.

'Your mentor with the scalpel?'

Daniel grinned at Hammersley's choice of words. 'That's him. He's coming over for the performance. The three of us can have dinner together.'

'That would be nice. I'm sure you'd like to tell us all about the trials and tribulations of an opera singer trying to break into grade-B films.'

'How do you know about that?'

'I still have contacts at the Grand, Daniel. Friends who keep me informed of what's going on, even if you don't. By the way, your voice sounds terrible.'

'I've just woken up and I've got a lousy cold.'

'Look after it. See you Friday.'

Daniel replaced the receiver and picked up the bottle again. He poured himself another large drink, undressed and crawled into bed, certain that he would feel better in the morning when his body had been given the rest it needed to adjust to the time change.

Martinelli arrived the following evening to take up the reservation Daniel had made for him at the Park Lane Hotel.

To Daniel, the Italian never seemed to age. The hair was still as black as he first remembered it, the body still as spare. Only the eyes and mouth had changed. Tiny crow's feet had crept in, almost indiscernible until Martinelli smiled.

Daniel was unable to hide his joy at seeing Martinelli. He had not left the hotel all day, eating his meals in the room, trying to find something in the newspapers he had ordered to interest him. With the exception of Hammersley, whom he would not see until the following day, he knew no one in the city and had never felt so lonely, so cut off. He missed Anna especially and kept wishing that she had accompanied him. After a few hours' separation during the course of a normal day, he was always glad to get home, to be with Anna again. The knowledge that he would not see her for a few days was almost unbearable. To make matters worse, the cold had intensified. He had wondered constantly whether he should call Covent Garden, beg off the commitment and book himself on the first plane back to Idlewild. The musical director had said that there was an understudy available. Good, let him play Turiddu. As he was about to lift the receiver and place the call, he had realised it would be a long time before the Royal Opera Company asked him back again.

'You look awful,' was Martinelli's greeting when he visited Daniel in his room. 'What's the matter with you?'

'A cold.'

'Let me see your tongue.'

Daniel obeyed. Martinelli saw the covering of white fur and told Daniel to close his mouth. 'What kind of medication have you been prescribing for yourself? It smells like whisky.'

Daniel admitted that it was. He had finished off the bottle he had started the previous night and opened another.

'You are a fool,' Martinelli said. 'Alcohol is for sore muscles, not a sore voice.' He left the room and was gone for twenty minutes. When he returned, he was carrying a thermometer which he stuck in Daniel's mouth.

'How is Anna?' he asked conversationally. 'Getting big?'

Daniel nodded. 'Fine,' he mumbled through the thermometer. He had spoken to her in the early afternoon. The sound of her voice, so clear despite the thousands of miles separating them, had served to make him feel even more lonely and depressed. He'd never been away from her this long before. Wherever he had performed, she had always been nearby, ready with encouragement. Without her for the first time, he realised how desperately he relied on that support. Now she couldn't travel and he was on his own, like a small child left at school by himself for the first day. It was frightening. And the knowledge that he'd be on his own in Hollywood as well, when the time came to film *South Side Serenade,* only served to deepen his misery.

Martinelli removed the thermometer and checked the reading. 'A hundred and one. You will live.' He called room service and ordered a bowl of boiling water. From his pocket he pulled out a brown paper bag which bore the name of Boots, the drugstore chain. When the bowl of water was delivered by a curious maid, Martinelli tipped the contents of the brown paper bag into it. Immediately the strong smell of eucalyptus smothered the room. Martinelli forced Daniel's head over the bowl and covered it with a towel.

'Breathe deeply through your nose. You can stay like that for five minutes.' He watched Daniel for a few seconds, then he began to scout around the room. When he found the opened bottle of scotch, he poured it down the basin.

'What are you doing?' Daniel called out from beneath the towel. He tried to look around, but his eyes were streaming.

'Saving your performance for tomorrow night. Saving your career.' Martinelli pulled away the towel and helped Daniel to stand upright. 'Since when did you start drinking like this?'

Daniel wiped his eyes with the wet towel. 'Since I came down with this cold yesterday,' he answered. 'What the hell do you think I am, an alcoholic?' His voice felt better. His

128

nose was clear and his throat seemed more comfortable. The eucalyptus and the steam had done their work. He felt fit enough to go on stage right now and sing Turiddu.

'What was wrong with trying cough syrup?' Martinelli asked.

'I never thought about it.' Daniel sat down heavily on the edge of the bed and breathed deeply through his nose. The entire room was full of steam. The mirror was misted over and condensation clung in tiny drops to the windows. 'Did you come to London to hear me sing or to give me a lecture?'

Martinelli's face tightened into a stern frown. 'Both, if necessary. The scalpel I gave you on your debut at the Grand was not the only one I possess.'

'Why did you pour away the scotch?'

'Because you are not to drink anymore. At least, not before tomorrow night. After that, you may do whatever you like. But I will not allow you to disgrace yourself at Covent Garden while I am in the audience.'

Daniel pushed himself up from the bed and glared angrily at Martinelli. He'd been prepared to sit and listen to the Italian until now, but he'd overstepped the bounds of friendship. He owed the man, sure; but he wasn't certain he owed him this much. 'When did I ever disgrace myself before? Tell me that?'

Martinelli's face relaxed and the smile that Daniel remembered took the place of the frown. The sharp, aquiline features softened and warmth returned to the brown eyes. 'I never said you did. I am just ensuring that tomorrow night will not be the first time. Too many other artists have ruined their careers by relying on drink to solve their problems. I would not like my own personal discovery to be among that number.' Martinelli poured away the inhalation and threw the sopping wet towel into the bath. 'Do you feel up to eating anything?'

'Feed a cold, starve a fever?' Daniel queried, the spark of anger forgotten.

'A fallacy,' Martinelli replied. 'If you feed a cold, you will

129

have to starve a fever later on. Settle for something light. A salad or an omelette.'

'Sounds great.' Daniel went into the bathroom to clean up, ready to go downstairs with Martinelli for dinner.

While they ate, Daniel told Martinelli all that had happened since he had signed the contract to appear in *South Side Serenade*. Martinelli said nothing, listening intently until Daniel had finished. Then he laid down his fork and slowly shook his head.

'Do you dream, perhaps, that you are another Mario Lanza?' he asked gently. 'Gigli, Bjoerling never did these things. No serious opera singer would even consider starring in a musical movie of this nature while he is at the peak of his career. Movies, yes; by all means. But not something like this. You would make a mockery of your entire art.' He stared across the table at Daniel, trying to understand what had made him take such a step.

'Quit looking at me like that,' Daniel said defensively. 'You're making me feel like I've got the plague.'

Martinelli took no notice. He continued staring as he asked, 'Are you quite prepared to abandon your operatic career for this film?'

'Why the hell should I abandon anything?'

'Because if you do not abandon it, it will surely abandon you. I hope, for your sake, that the film is an enormous success. That you make a vast sum of money from it. That you become famous in Hollywood. Because you will not be able to go back.'

'I couldn't get out of it even if I wanted to,' Daniel tried to explain. 'The studio says they'll sue me. We start shooting in a little under three months, and if I'm not there, I'll have their lawyers chasing me.'

'So let their lawyers chase.' Martinelli made it sound ludicrously simple.

'And just where am I supposed to come up with the kind of money they're threatening to sue me for?' Daniel asked. 'Have you got a spare half million dollars you can lend me till it's over?'

Martinelli pondered the question for a long moment.

'Congratulations,' he said at last, with just the finest trace of sarcasm in his voice. 'You seem to have succeeded in digging a splendid hole for yourself.' He thought about adding that success had gone too quickly to Daniel's head; that he thought he was above sensible behaviour. He refrained only when he realised how low Daniel already felt about the situation. 'I think you should pray for this studio to go bankrupt, or that they should decide not to shoot this film at all. Not only would that get you out of an awkward position, but it would also put you in the novel situation of being able to sue the studio for breach of contract.'

Daniel recognised the humour in Martinelli's statement and began to laugh. Thank God he had company tonight. He was frightened to even think what might have happened had he been alone again. Martinelli would see him through. And with Hammersley also there tomorrow night, he'd have no trouble in knocking them dead at Covent Garden.

Martinelli went to his room shortly before eleven, claiming fatigue from the full day of travel. Daniel sat in his own room for almost half an hour, fully dressed, knowing he would never sleep. The performance was still twenty hours away, but the familiar tension was creeping in. He clasped his hands together, closed his eyes and tried to pretend Anna was with him. Anna with her special way of making his nervousness disappear, just as she always did before a performance. The jokes, the soothing conversation, the way of making him laugh at himself, at his worries.

Anna! That was it! He'd call her. He had already spoken to her once today so she would not be expecting a second call. He'd surprise her and help himself at the same time.

He dialled the operator and told him to place the call. Then he sat back and waited, his anticipation heightening. Ten minutes passed and the anticipation turned to anxiety. Why hadn't the operator called back yet? Impatiently he dialled again. The operator explained that he was trying to find a clear circuit. It might take up to an hour to complete the call. Did Daniel wish to cancel it? No, he answered. He did not. Keep trying. He had placed the call and keyed himself up to speak to Anna. Nothing was going to stop him now.

As the wait lengthened, he called room service. A night porter knocked on the door. Daniel ordered another bottle of whisky to replace the one Martinelli had poured away. When the man told him that the bar was closed, Daniel offered him five pounds. The porter looked first at the large white note then at Daniel's face before saying he would see what he could do.

At half past one, when the operator finally called back, Daniel had drunk his way through a third of the bottle of Johnnie Walker the night porter had brought him. The bowl of ice had turned to water without a cube being taken from it. Daniel was drinking the whisky straight.

'Hello?' Daniel answered the phone on the second ring, speaking uncertainly, his mind dulled. Who was calling him at this time of night? Who even knew he was staying at this hotel?

'Your call to the United States,' the operator said. Suddenly Daniel remembered. A confused jumble of whirs and clicks attacked his ear, then he heard Anna's voice.

'Anna, it's Daniel. I'm in London.'

'What?' She struggled to hear him. 'What did you say?'

'I said I'm in London. How are you? I miss you.'

'Daniel, are you all right?'

'I'm fine. I just wish you were here. I need you with me.'

There was a long pause before Anna asked suspiciously, 'Daniel, have you been drinking?'

'Me?' he asked in surprise. He looked in amazement at the glass in his hand and placed it on the dressing table. 'No, I'm just lonely, that's all. And I've got a rotten cold, that's why I sound so bad. I'm frightened it's going to affect my singing tomorrow night.'

'For God's sake, Daniel. Go to bed. You'll be out on your feet tomorrow if you carry on like this.'

'I'm sorry.' He was confounded to feel the warm trickle of tears that dribbled down his cheeks. He was crying. For himself. Crying because he was alone and no one wanted to keep him company through the long night. Not even Anna.

She didn't want to talk to him. she wanted him to go to bed.

'Why don't you want to talk to me?' he asked plaintively. His head felt swollen again. The inhalation had worn off. Or maybe the whisky had overwhelmed it. He hadn't drunk that much, or had he? He picked up the bottle and stared hard at it, trying to see exactly how much had gone. It could not have been full when the night porter brought it up, he finally decided. The man must have raided the bar for an open bottle.

'Daniel, listen carefully to me. I want you to go to bed right now and get some sleep. I'll see you at the weekend when you get home. Good night.'

He heard the connection being broken, and the tears of self-pity increased to a deluge. Now he had no one to talk to at all. Wait a minute. He'd try Moishe. Moishe would be glad to hear from him. He'd be thrilled to get a call from England. So would Isaac! Daniel decided to call up everyone whose number he could remember. He'd show them that he hadn't forgotten them.

Mind made up, he got back to the operator and gave him the numbers of Maurice Waterman and Isaac Kirschbaum, instructing the man that if he could not get through to one, he should try the other.

When the operator called back an hour later with Moishe's connection, only two inches remained in the bottle of Johnnie Walker. Daniel was lying across the bed in a drunken stupor, breathing heavily, too far gone for the bell to ever reach him.

He moaned in his sleep, struggling to free himself from the two steely claws that grasped his shoulders. His legs were moving slowly, dragging him across the floor. His arms were hanging limply by his sides.

Daniel wished the dream would go away. He didn't want to dream. He wanted to sleep, to experience a long dreamless slumber that would leave him refreshed before the big performance at Covent Garden. Turiddu needed to rest before he sang.

He wasn't moving anymore. He was lying still again.

Better. Much better, But he wasn't in bed. He was lying on something cold and smooth. Like a slab? Mortuaries had slabs. He was lying on a mortician's slab. He must be dead. But how? Turiddu was killed in the opera, but it was all in play. It was an act. So if it were all an act, what was he doing lying on a cold slab?

A stream of freezing water cannoned into his face, down his chest and legs. The dream vanished abruptly. In its place was Martinelli's voice, shouting, cursing, cajoling as he held Daniel under the cold shower.

'*Vergogna!* Are you mad, an *imbecille?* What happened to you?'

Daniel tried to force open his eyes. The stream of icy water slammed them shut again. He struggled and fought blindly against Martinelli's unrelenting grip, desperate to get out of the bombardment of water. But he was no match for the combined offensive of both Martinelli and his own aching head.

After a minute, Martinelli turned off the water and helped Daniel to his feet. The clothes in which he had fallen asleep were soaked through, ruined beyond redemption. Martinelli's shirt and trousers were also saturated. The Italian doctor did not seem to care. All his attention was focused on Daniel. He sat him down gently on the bathroom stool, watched him warily for a moment to be sure he would not fall off, then walked quickly to the telephone. Five minutes later, a maid appeared in the room, holding a tray with orange juice and coffee. She looked at the table, at the glass lying on the floor. When she peeked into the bathroom and saw Martinelli briskly slapping Daniel's face back and forth, she put down the tray and ran from the room. Martinelli hardly even noticed her.

'Drink this.' He dropped two large white tablets into a glass of water. They fizzed angrily as Martinelli held the glass to Daniel's mouth.

'What is it?' Daniel asked. The bubbles tickling his nose made him feel nauseated.

'Something to make you feel better.' Martinelli grabbed

134

Daniel's nose and squeezed it shut. As Daniel gasped, the Italian poured the effervescent liquid down his throat. Daniel gagged against it. Martinelli refused to take away the glass. It was choke or swallow. Daniel yielded, then gulped frantically as the bubbles sent his already tortured stomach into instant rebellion. He lunged past Martinelli to the commode and retched painfully until nothing more would come. Martinelli watched impassively.

'Now drink the orange juice,' Martinelli said. 'Slowly.'

Daniel climbed unsteadily to his feet and took the tall glass of freshly squeezed orange juice that Martinelli was holding out. The taste cleared his mouth, but his head continued to ache abominably.

'Do you feel better?' Martinelli asked, satisfied that the orange juice would not follow the Alka-Seltzer down the toilet.

'I feel terrible. What time is it?'

'Ten. You are due to sing in another ten hours.'

Daniel shook his head to refute the statement. The pain inside his skull increased to battering ram proportions. 'I'll never be able to. I'd better call them and cancel, give them time to warn the understudy.'

'You will do no such thing,' Martinelli said. 'You will sing tonight. But first you will put on some dry clothes and we will go for a walk in the fresh air. Before you sing, you have to clear your head.'

Daniel took one look at the stern expression on Martinelli's face and decided not to argue. It would be easier in the long run to do as the Italian said.

The black taxi stopped outside the Park Lane Hotel and a man wearing a bowler hat and a beige Great British Warm topcoat stepped out. He began to walk towards the hotel lobby when he noticed the two men pacing up and down the sidewalk, strolling in the brisk April afternoon air. He stood for a moment, watching, then he went over to join them.

'Expanding your lungs for tonight's performance?'

When Daniel looked round, Roger Hammersley stepped

back in shock. Daniel's eyes were red-rimmed. His face was white and puffy and his breathing was laboured. Hammersley knew that he would never be able to sing that night.

'Good Lord! What happened?'

Martinelli answered. 'He was looking for courage for tonight's performance in a bottle of whisky. Instead, he found a hangover.'

Without another word, Hammersley grasped Daniel's free arm and began to walk with him, talking over his head to Martinelli. 'When did you find him like this?'

As if Daniel was not there, Martinelli explained how he had waited for Daniel to meet him at breakfast. When he had not shown up, he went to the room, where he found him stretched out across the bed, fully clothed and out to the world.

'Has Covent Garden been notified yet?' Hammersley asked.

Martinelli shook his head. 'He will sing tonight. He will not let us down.'

'Impossible,' Hammersley asserted. 'He can't even talk, let alone sing. I'll call in for him. They know me there. I'll make up a story that he's ill. They'll believe me.'

Again Martinelli shook his head. 'You will be doing Daniel a disservice, Mr. Hammersley. If he does not sing tonight, he might never sing again.'

'What?' asked Hammersley in disbelief. 'You'd better explain that.'

'You should know already. Whenever Daniel sang before, Anna was always with him, either in the cast or watching. Tonight will be the first time he has sung without her presence.'

'That's the reason for the whisky?' Hammersley asked dubiously.

'Yes. To give him the courage to sing without her. And if he fails this time, this first time by himself, he might never be able to find the courage to try again.'

Hammersley still had difficulty believing what the Italian

was saying. During the five years he had worked with Daniel at the Grand, he had never lacked confidence. Usually, the opposite was true. Daniel had suffered from overconfidence, the certainty that he would never put a foot wrong, never miss a note, never forget a line or bungle a cue.

'I think, perhaps, that he fooled you as well, Mr. Hammersley,' Martinelli continued. 'Daniel needs perpetual encouragement, someone ready to pat him on the back the entire time.' Martinelli had seen it at the hospital in Hitchin when he had been forced into tricking Daniel into participating in the concert by putting him in a position where he could not back out. And when he had rushed from the hall at the end of the scheduled recital and had to be bullied into returning for an encore. 'In New York he always had Anna to push him. Here, he has nobody and he fell apart,' Martinelli turned around and started to walk Daniel back towards the hotel. 'Do you know what I learned he was doing at one o'clock this morning?'

'What?'

'Placing telephone calls to the United States. He was that desperate to speak with someone he knew. Anyone, it did not matter who, just as long as they would tell him how marvellous he was and what a success he would be at Covent Garden.'

'I see,' Hammersley murmured. 'I guess we'd better start telling him that ourselves. Maybe we can salvage this evening's performance for him.'

The telephone rang at four o'clock just as Martinelli and Hammersley had managed to get Daniel to start vocalising. The first minute sounded terrible. Hammersley wanted to drown out the noise, clasp his hands over his ears until Daniel ceased the travesty of the sweet voice he had heard on stage at the Grand.

'Keep going,' Martinelli urged. 'It can only get better.'

'What about the phone?' Daniel asked. 'Maybe it's something important.' Anything to stop vocalising. He knew how terrible his voice sounded; the more he pushed it, the worse it would become.

Hammersley answered the telephone, watching while Martinelli continued to make Daniel vocalise. God, Hammersley thought; if he sings like this tonight, he'll empty the house quicker than a fire alarm.

'Were you supposed to be at a record shop in Shaftesbury Avenue this afternoon?' Hammersley asked. 'The manager's on the line, saying you had agreed to autograph some copies of the *Bohème* you and Anna recorded.'

Mention of Anna immediately brightened Daniel's frame of mind. Until he remembered the promise he'd made to the record store manager. 'I forgot all about it.'

'Get dressed,' Hammersley said. 'We're going down there now.'

'All of us?'

'All of us,' Martinelli confirmed.

When Daniel marched into the record store fifteen minutes later, accompanied by Hammersley and Martinelli, a small crowd of customers was waiting. In one corner of the store a table had been erected; on it were neatly piled stacks of *Bohème* and *Ballo*. The manager, white-faced and clasping his hands in nervous despair, only relaxed when he saw Daniel.

'Thank heavens you're here, Mr. Kerr. That sign in the window' — he indicated a white cardboard placard that announced Daniel Kerr, of the Grand Opera Company of New York, would be in the store from four until five to autograph records —'aroused a lot of interest. We'd have been faced with a mutiny if you hadn't turned up.'

'I'm sorry I'm late. I wasn't feeling very well.' Daniel waited for either Hammersley or Martinelli to show him up as a liar. They did not.

'If you'll sit over there' — the manager guided Daniel to the table in the corner — 'we can get going.'

'Thirty minutes and no more,' Martinelli told the manager. 'Mr. Kerr has a performance at Covent Garden tonight.'

'Who are you?'

'His voice teacher,' Martinelli lied. 'Mr. Kerr is just recovering from a bad cold and we do not wish to take any chances.'

'Of course,' the manager nodded.

Daniel made himself comfortable behind the table. The first thought to cross his mind when he picked up a pen was to draw glasses, a beard and moustache on Claudia Rivera's Amelia on the sleeve of *Un Ballo in Maschera*.

'Don't you dare,' Hammersley whispered as soon as he recognised Daniel's intention. The Grand's former general manager decided it was a good sign. If Daniel had the alertness to remember his feud with the Italian soprano, he was feeling better.

'Just a thought,' Daniel murmured. He did not know whether it was the brisk walk from the hotel or the work that Martinelli and Hammersley had forced him through in his room, but he was feeling better. Much better. All he needed now was something to eat and he'd be as fit as he had ever been.

He signed record covers and thanked the customers automatically while he let his mind drift back to the previous night. He must have been mad, drinking like that, feeling sorry for himself. Why had he ever allowed himself to feel so miserable when all these people were waiting to boast that Daniel Kerr had personally autographed their records?

They got him back to the Park Lane Hotel just after five. Martinelli immediately sent down for sandwiches and a pot of tea heavily laced with honey. Then they began to work in earnest. Daniel vocalised in one-minute spurts, stopping for five minutes to drink the tea, starting over again. Three times hotel staff knocked on the door to check that everything was all right, their polite method of letting the room's occupants know they had received complaints from other guests about the noise. The manager showed up the next time to say he would throw out the three of them if the noise did not cease.

As sympathetic as the hotel was to Mr. Kerr's need to rehearse, the other guests could not be disturbed.

The prospect of being evicted from the hotel and thrown out into the street made Hammersley decide it was time to leave for Covent Garden. They could finish their work in the dressing room.

'I have to call Anna first,' Daniel said as they were about to leave.

Martinelli sensed that the fear had returned. 'You will never get through in time. We dare not be late.'

'I don't care. I've got to speak to her. I haven't called her yet today. She'll worry.'

Hammersley saw a way out of the predicament. He gave instructions to the hotel switchboard. They were to call Mrs. Kerr in New Jersey and give her the number at Covent Garden where Daniel could be reached. She was to call him before the performance started. The arrangement seemed to satisfy Daniel.

CHAPTER SEVEN

Daniel sat perfectly still in the chair while the make-up man put the finishing touches to his face. Off to one side sat Hammersley and Martinelli, silent as they watched.

Hammersley was now certain that Daniel's voice would not let him down, and he was amazed how his opinion had changed. Daniel was still young and possessed an incredibly strong constitution that had enabled him to shrug off the effect of the previous night's bender. Six hours earlier, when he had arrived at the Park Lane Hotel to find Daniel being forcibly walked by Martinelli, Hammersley would have wagered everything he owned that Daniel would be unable to sing that night. Now it was thirty minutes to curtain time and the voice was as strong and as clear as he had ever heard it.

What did concern Hammersley was the way Daniel would react to singing with Claudia Rivera. Hammersley understood with painful clarity what Daniel must be thinking. That Claudia had only offered to sing Santuzza for the opportunity to cut him up again. This time in front of the sophisticated Covent Garden audience where she had sung many times before. All Daniel would remember as he stood onstage with Claudia would be how the soprano had held onto her note during the Grand's production of *Tosca* and thrown him to the hisses and catcalls of the audience. And, of course, there was the additional matter of a bottle of champagne across the back of the head, Hammersley ruefully recalled.

The telephone in the dressing room rang. Hammersley reached out a hand to answer it. He listened to the switchboard operator and then his face broke into a happy smile as he recognised Anna's voice asking for Daniel.

'Anna, my dear. This is Roger Hammersley. How are you?' He turned away from Daniel and lowered his voice. Perhaps Daniel's insistence on speaking to Anna before the performance would reap benefits Hammersley had not imagined. If anyone could influence Daniel's behaviour, it would be Anna.

'We have a little problem here, Anna,' Hammersley said quietly. He looked sideways and saw Martinelli staring curiously at him. When he glanced towards the dressing table he saw that Daniel's eyes were closed, relaxing under the make-up artist's steady touch. Quickly Hammersley related how Martinelli had first found Daniel at the hotel, the second drinking bout, the tension, the gnawing anxiety that he was alone — all followed by the unexpected pressure of singing again opposite Claudia Rivera.

Anna listened, her mind in a confused whirl. Even the baby's insistent kicking inside her went unnoticed. She could hardly believe what Hammersley was saying. It didn't seem to make any sense. She had suspected that Daniel had been drinking when he'd called her the previous night. One drink, maybe two. That was nothing new. He had a couple of quick drinks before every performance. But an entire bottle? What Hammersley was saying was an unwelcome revelation. This surely couldn't be Daniel — to empty a bottle by himself and not give a damn about his performance. The tension she could understand; he was like that leading up to every performance. So were thousands of others. Drinking this heavily was something new.

'Let me speak to him,' she said finally.

'We were hoping you would,' Hammersley whispered. Then he added in his normal voice. 'Glad to hear you're

142

feeling so well. Don't forget that I expect an invitation to the christening.'

'There won't be a christening.'

'Of course, I forgot.' Hammersley laughed heartily. 'For you,' he said to Daniel. 'Anna to wish you good luck.'

Daniel took the call. 'Anna?'

'Hi. You feeling better?'

'Fine!' he exclaimed. 'Why shouldn't I be?'

'You didn't sound too bright when you called last night.'

'Last night?' Daniel asked, momentarily confused. 'Did I speak to you last night? When?'

'About midway through the bottle, I'd guess, from the way you sounded.'

He fell silent at her reply.

'You worried the life out of Moishe as well. He called me this morning. Said the operator called him with a transatlantic phone call and nobody was there when he got connected.'

'What about my father?' Slowly Daniel began to remember the calls he had ordered.

'Did you call him as well? Were you that down on yourself?'

'Guess I must have been.'

'Your entire fee for singing at Covent Garden's going to be wasted on phone calls,' Anna chided him gently. 'Listen, I understand you're singing opposite Claudia Rivera. She's filling in as Santuzza.'

'Yes.' The single word came out hesitantly, almost grudgingly.

'Are you worried about it?'

'Why should I be?'

'In case she tries to upstage you again?' Anna did not wait for an answer; she carried right on talking. 'Have you seen her yet?'

'No. I don't want to, either.'

'Don't be stupid, Daniel. She offered to sing the part for one reason, and one reason only. Because she's a professional and did not want to see a production ruined

143

because another singer couldn't keep a date. You should be grateful that she stepped in and made the offer, otherwise you'd be playing opposite an understudy who'd make you look awful. So don't go out there and make a fool of yourself by trying to put one over on her.'

'What if she tries something on me?'

'She won't.' Anna wished she felt as confident as she sounded. 'She evened the score last time. Just go out there and sing like you've never sung before.' She blew him a kiss and hung up.

'Ready?' Hammersley asked cheerfully.

Busy thinking over what Anna had said, Daniel did not hear the question. Was Anna right?

'Daniel, are you ready?' This time it was Martinelli who spoke. 'You have just got time to finish your exercises before you are due on stage.'

Daniel snapped out of it, his mind firmly made up. He knew how to conduct himself. He would give Claudia Rivera, Covent Garden, everyone who was out there a performance they'd never forget. He'd do it for Martinelli and Hammersley. For Anna as well. Without their care, their worry, their help, he would never have made it out of the hotel room. He would have lain on the bed, drowning in self-pity until someone came to tell him that his reservation at the hotel had expired and would he please leave so that the chambermaid could prepare the room for the next guest.

'Good evening, Mr. Kerr. I hope your manners have improved since the last time we met.'

'Hi, Claudia. How are you doing, old girl?' Daniel walked right up to the soprano as they waited in the wings, grabbed hold of her and gave her a loud, resounding kiss on the cheek. 'Been looking forward to working with you again,' he lied.

Somehow the smell didn't bother him anymore. To some degree, the tail end of the cold protected him. Mostly, though, the reason was the role Claudia was playing, a nineteenth-century Sicilian peasant girl. If nineteenth-

144

century Sicilian peasant girls didn't stink of sweat and garlic, Daniel reasoned, who did? Claudia was playing the role perfectly; even to the smell.

The soprano was taken aback by Daniel's friendly greeting. Tenors had never kissed her before. Especially one she had embarrassed and then levelled with a champagne bottle.

Still holding the woman, Daniel looked around at other members of the cast and winked; he was in charge and he wanted everyone to know it. 'You know what people have been telling me?' he whispered in Claudia's ear. 'That you only offered to sing Santuzza so you could make a fool of me again. That's not true, is it?'

'I do not know what you are talking about!'

'Good. Unless you want to sing Nedda in *Pagliacci* on crutches, you'd better watch the conductor. One long note and I'll throw you right across the goddamned stage. You hear me?' He moved to kiss her again. Instead, he bit the lobe of her ear. She shrieked loudly enough to be heard out in the auditorium and struggled to break free. Daniel maintained his grip; he hadn't finished yet. 'And none of this standing in front of me crap, either. You take one step in front of me and I'll kick you so hard you'll wind up in the front seats.'

Claudia paled at the threats. No one had ever spoken to her like this. First he had kissed her, then he had threatened her. She had expected gratitude for filling in. Instead, she was being promised harm. He was mad.

'You got a claque out there tonight?' Daniel asked. 'You'd better pray they don't upset me.' The claque was the only thing Daniel feared. No matter how well Claudia behaved herself on stage, he would be unable to control her paid supporters. If she had already instructed them to jeer him, there was little he could do about it. Unless he could persuade Claudia to change her orders before the opera began. 'I get booed just once out there tonight and you're going to wind up on some violinist's lap with his bow shoved right up your ass.'

145

He let go of her finally. She stepped back immediately, face white with fear, breathing unsteady. She turned and waddled away, avoiding the eyes of those who had witnessed the scene. Daniel guessed that she was going out to the auditorium to find her claque leader and change her instructions. When she returned five minutes later, just as applause sounded for the conductor's arrival, she marched straight up to Daniel.

'You need have no fears, Mr. Kerr. My claque will be silent tonight.'

Daniel smiled at her. 'I'm sure the violinists and the people in the front seats will be glad to hear that. *In bocca el lupo.*'

The last of the crowd had gone when Daniel, Martinelli and Hammersley left by the stage door on Floral Street. The sound of trucks and the shouts of men greeted them as the Covent Garden fruit market went through its nightly business.

Martinelli slapped Daniel joyfully on the back as they walked among crates of fruit being unloaded. 'You have never sung better!' he shouted above the market's din. 'Congratulations!'

An orange rolled loose along the sidewalk. Daniel kicked happily at it, a small boy again playing in the streets. The orange skidded along the concrete and thudded into a wall, splitting skin, spraying juice. He knew he'd sung well. He didn't need Martinelli to tell him that. After the final scene, the audience had refused to let him go. They had called him back time and again for more bows until he thought his back would remain bent.

Above his performance, though, he was proud of how he had pushed aside his problems, the loneliness, the drinking. He'd forced himself to fight back with the strongest weapon at his disposal, his own voice. There had been no defence against it, from the audience or from Claudia Rivera. She had known it, too. After the performance — during the interval between *Cavalleria Rusticana* and *Pagliacci* — she had

146

knocked on the door of his dressing room while he was changing. His earlier threats were forgotten as she complimented him on the performance. Daniel had responded in an equally gracious manner, praising her for standing in for the indisposed Santuzza; he had even stayed to watch the production of *Pagliacci,* applauding Claudia as loudly as her own claque.

The evening did not serve to make him like Claudia Rivera; her egotism and her personal hygiene still left much to be desired. It did make him aware, though, of what a consummate professional she was. It was a trait to be admired, to be learned.

'Do you realise now what a fool you've been?' Hammersley asked. He managed to make the question sound like a fond remark, a father trying to guide a wayward son.

'Sure.' Daniel felt so exuberant about his performance that he would agree to anything.

'And what an even bigger fool you'll be if you go through with this stupidity in Hollywood,' Hammersley continued. 'Get a doctor to sign you off ill. Do anything, but get out of it. I know Robin Duguid. I recommended him for the Grand appointment because I thought he was the best man for the job. Don't cross him, Daniel. Because if you ever want his help, you'll have to crawl back on your hands and knees.'

Daniel said nothing. To argue now would destroy the euphoria he was feeling. And he would depress himself again; he could not afford that.

'Are you listening to a single word I'm saying?'

'Of course.' Daniel stopped to kick another orange lying on the sidewalk. This one burst against his shoe. splattering his trousers. He pulled out a handkerchief to wipe the juice before it could dry on the fabric.

They reached Shaftesbury Avenue and Martinelli waved down a passing cab. Back at the Park Lane Hotel, Daniel waved aside suggestions of a late night snack and went straight up to his room, ordering a call to Anna in New

Jersey. He wanted to tell her of his success, how he had come through it, turned disaster into triumph.

The connection was made almost immediately, as if to make a mockery of his previous night's efforts. As the words flowed from him — describing the performance to Anna, the way he'd cowed Claudia Rivera and her compliments afterwards — he did not give a moment's thought to Martinelli or Hammersley. His earlier gratitude to those who had helped him went unrecalled.

When Daniel's flight from London touched down at Idlewild the following evening, Moishe was waiting at the airport. First Daniel called Anna to tell her he was home, then he got into the car.

'Next time you call make sure you stay on the goddamned line,' Moishe grumbled as they drove away from the airport. 'You've got no idea how big an idiot you feel when you're waiting for a phone that's not answered and it's not even you who made the call.'

'I forgot about it, it took so long to get through.'

'What the hell did you want anyway?'

Daniel searched quickly for a reply; obviously Anna had not told Moishe what had happened in London. 'I just got to thinking about Joel Pomerantz and *South Side Serenade,* that's all. Have you heard anything from Carmel Studios?'

Moishe nodded. 'He's been on to me. Checking that you'll be out West once the Grand's tour is over and Anna's had the baby.'

He would be checking, Daniel thought sourly. Pomerantz won't let go of me now that he's got his claws in. Goddamn! I was a stupid son of a bitch to sign that contract. Duguid will let me go, though. He won't be like Pomerantz.

Daniel did not look forward to seeing the Grand's general manager when the tour started in four days' time. They would be in each other's pocket for three weeks — in Cincinnati, Denver, Dallas, New Orleans, Miami and Atlanta — but Daniel knew that Duguid would never mention *South Side Serenade.* The general manager's mind

148

was made up already on how he would handle the situation. He would wait for Daniel to set foot on Carmel's lot and for the cameras to begin rolling. Then, like a patient cat sitting by a hole in the wall waiting for the mouse to be brave enough to stick its head out, he would pounce.

Daniel asked Moishe to make a detour to his parents' home in Van Cortlandt Park. He stopped in long enough to tell Isaac of his success in London and show him the review from that morning's London *Times*. At his father's suggestion, he left the review in the house for Isaac to show Yetta when she returned from visiting friends whom she was regaling with tales of the three months they had just spent in Florida. At Daniel's insistence, his parents had gone south again for the winter. Daniel did not think his father could have stood another New York winter, although the periodic heart check-ups were encouraging. Still, what strain could there be on his heart when he did next to nothing all day long?

Anna was waiting when Daniel arrived home, a bright maternity smock, if not actively hiding her condition, at least pleasantly disguising it. The housekeeper had prepared dinner, but Daniel felt too tired to eat. His body was still on Greenwich Mean Time. The day contained five hours too many for him and he felt as if it were three or four in the morning. He had been up early to see Martinelli off at Victoria Station for the long trip back to Milan, had a late breakfast with Hammersley and then gone to London Airport to catch his own flight. He had stayed awake during the entire flight; the abuse to which he had subjected his body and the lack of sleep were now combining to take their toll.

Realising how exhausted Daniel was, Moishe refused the offer of dinner, claiming he had eaten at the airport while waiting for Daniel's flight to arrive. He was also tired, he said; if they'd excuse him, he'd like to go home.

After Moishe had left the house to drive back to New York, Daniel sat in the living room with Anna. He put fresh logs on the fire and watched the flames dance merrily before

149

he sank down in an armchair. The warmth of the fire settled him. It was time to talk, time to unwind after the exertions of the trip.

'Daniel, do you ever stop to think that you've got other people to consider? Not just yourself?'

The question startled him. It was not what he had been expecting. He had been looking to Anna for support, not an attack. 'What do you mean?'

'You're living your life for your own enjoyment. No' — she shook her head while she tried to think of the words she wanted — 'I don't mean that.'

'What do you mean, then?'

'Whenever the slightest thing goes wrong, you immediately start looking around for a crutch, someone to lean on. You don't know what to do. You're hopeless at handling awkward situations.'

He knew what she was driving at. 'I had nothing to do,' he broke in. 'I was bored out of my mind. That's why I had a couple of drinks.'

'It's not the drinking. It's the way you' — she paused again — 'use people.' Daniel opened his mouth to argue, but she held up her hand. 'Please let me finish what I'm saying, Daniel. You do use people. Whether you realise it or not, you've been using them all your life. After you'd wiped yourself out in London, Mr. Hammersley and your friend Enzo went through hell and high water to get you straight in time for your performance. But you never mentioned them once to me on the phone after you'd got back to the hotel from Covent Garden. It was all you. You'd conquered the world all by yourself.'

Daniel sat quietly, listening to Anna's criticism, thinking of what he could say in his own defence.

'They were both worried out of their minds about you. Mr. Hammersley told me everything that had happened to you in London. The drinking. The loneliness. They weren't helping you for their own benefit. They were doing it for you, so you wouldn't show yourself up in front of the Covent Garden audience. I think they'd both be very hurt if they

150

knew you thought so little of their efforts, I know damned well I would.'

'I appreciated what they did!' Daniel burst out. 'I know how hard they worked to get me fit. It's just that in the excitement I forgot. You can't imagine how high I was, Anna! Even Rivera came into the dressing room to congratulate me!'

Anna raised her hands to her ears to block out his words. 'There you go again! That's exactly what I'm talking about! You're only thinking of yourself, about what you did, how you did it all on your own without any help from anyone else. Everyone has helped you in this business. Me. Mr. Hammersley. Your friend Enzo. Even Moishe. And you're convinced that you've done everything by yourself.'

'Well, I have!' Daniel protested. 'I'm the one who stands up on the stage and sings. I'm the one the people come to see and hear. I'm the one who gives the performance.'

Anna stared at him in desperation. She knew she could never hope to make him understand. She'd learned that a long time ago and still she tried to change him, to make him accept the fact that others were also responsible for his success. How could she hope to change him when he'd been this way all his life having others to help him. There had always been others, she understood that. Daniel had told her about Fat Benny, how his uncle had opened all the doors for him, leaned on someone here, called in a favour there to make the way to the top easier for Daniel. And she had continued the tradition, although the paths she had cleared had been for Daniel's confidence; a timely word of encouragement, a promise to stand by him. How far would he have gotten had it not been for other people? she wondered. He seemed to accept their help as if it were his due. He took it for granted, certain that it would always be there and he would never need to acknowledge it.

She stood up and walked to the window. Bathed in the light spilling out of the living room, she could see daffodils in the front garden, trees beginning to blossom. She felt at one

151

with them. When they bloomed, so would she. Another few weeks and she would be a mother.

Forgetting that Daniel was in the room with her, she let her hand stray down to her swollen stomach, caressing the child that slumbered within. She would need Daniel's help when the child was born. She'd need his support. But what help would he be able to offer? He would need her more than ever once he began shooting *South Side Serenade*. If ever his world was to cave in around him, it would be then, when what he had tried to ignore for five months finally happened. He would be home for the first three weeks after the child was born — enough time to be present at the *bris* if it were a boy — then he would be off to Hollywood. He would need encouragement there as he had never needed it before.

Anna wished fervently that he had sought the advice of others before he had signed the movie contract, that he had been straightforward with Robin Duguid. If he had been honest with the general manager, all this trouble could have been avoided. She was certain that Duguid did not want to lose Daniel any more than Daniel wanted to leave the Grand. They were like two immovable objects, two implacable armies pushing each other to see which would yield. And neither would. What worried Anna most was how the clash would leave Daniel. If his confidence could be destroyed simply by the knowledge that he was performing in a strange city for the first time, what would happen to him once he realised that the carpet had been pulled from underneath him at the Grand Opera Company, from where his strength came?

Mistaking Anna's silence for anger, Daniel stood up and joined her at the window. 'Whom do I apologise to first? You? Moishe? Hammersley? Enzo?'

He was like a child, as naive as the baby inside her. She turned around and smiled warmly at him, unable to resist his innocence. 'No one, Daniel. You are the way you are and nothing in the world can change it. But try to remember sometimes that other people help you as well. Let them know

152

you appreciate their efforts. Show them. Let them share in your happiness.'

He put his hands on her shoulders and kissed her forehead. 'Okay, I promise.'

And she knew he would forget the promise as soon as his next triumph occurred.

Other than greeting Daniel when he joined the tour party at Pennsylvania Station, Robin Duguid did not say a word. The matter of *South Side Serenade,* by tacit agreement, was left unmentioned. Duguid had too many other things on his mind.

He had just completed his debut New York season with the Grand and was embarking on his first tour. A string of successes, starting with the new production of *La Bohème,* lay behind him. Not that Duguid had been totally responsible; much of the work for the season had been accomplished by Hammersley before he had passed over the reins. The tour cities were eagerly awaiting the new Grand. Opera committees in the scheduled cities had raised more money than ever before to ensure the Grand's performances. Special functions for cast members had been planned. Most of the company were dreading it.

Daniel walked along the coach, past the card games that were already in progress and found his seat. Junior members of the company respectfully mentioned his success at Covent Garden and Daniel received their praise graciously. He didn't expect any compliments from his equals — they were incredibly objective when it came to someone else's work — but it was nice to hear the junior singers, who, no doubt, one day hoped to take his place, praise him. Not that he tried to be friendly with any members of the cast. He made a point to keep his relationships within the company on a strictly professional basis. The card games, the riotous behaviour and partying were not for him. He had an image to protect both within the company and outside. The problems he knew would arise when he started on *South Side Serenade* need not be

153

fuelled with scandalous memories of his previous behaviour with the company.

As the train pulled out, Daniel took a sheet of paper from his pocket and began to read. On it was printed a list of boys' names. He hadn't yet chosen one for the child Anna was carrying, the baby he was certain would be a boy. He'd told Anna it would be a boy. He'd told his father. They had both said the same thing in reply; just pray that it's healthy and never mind what sex it is. Deep down, though, he prayed for a boy. He deserved a boy this time. Last time he had fathered a girl, and the memory still burned within him. With a boy, nothing could go wrong.

His eyes flicked over the list, reached the end and started again from the top. Dissatisfaction surged through him that no name had arrested his attention. God, there were enough from which to choose. He moved down the list of A's. Past Barry and Basil. Basil? What the hell kind of name was that for a kid? What kid wanted to be tagged with a moniker like Basil? He'd have every right to kill his parents for calling him that, and no judge in the country would convict him.

He moved further down the list. At Benjamin he stopped. Benjamin. Ben. Benny. Did he want a son called Benny? Maybe not Benny, although other kids — even grown-ups — would probably shorten Benjamin to Benny.

He'd call the kid Benjamin.

He'd show Anna that he cared about the contributions made to his life by other people.

CHAPTER EIGHT

Daniel was right, just as he had known he would be. The child carried by Anna was a boy, a chubby healthy son who would be named Benjamin after Fat Benny, whose gold watch Daniel still wore. There would be another Benny in the family. Not a Fat Benny Kirschbaum, but a Benny Kerr.

Memories of the Grand's successful tour slipped from Daniel's mind as he hurried around to inform everyone of the birth of his son. He was a father again! He'd waited so long — too long — and now it had happened. He busied himself making arrangements, happy to lose himself in an ecstasy he could share with everyone. He took Moishe out to a celebration dinner and told him he was the child's godfather. He made arrangements for the circumcision that would take place in the hospital. Work, his career, the problems he'd faced because of *South Side Serenade* were all pushed aside. They could take a back seat for a while. Anna and his son came first.

Between visiting Anna in the hospital, Daniel supervised the decorators while they finished the nursery that awaited Benjamin — Little Benny as Daniel constantly thought of him. The nursery was on the second floor of the house, in the furthest corner where the sounds of voice and piano would never be able to penetrate. His son would be able to sleep undisturbed through the most rigorous practising; even Daniel's most piercing top-C would never unsettle him

155

there. Daniel had checked on that already, stationing a bemused painter in the nursery with the door shut while he sang part of 'Di quella pira' at the top of his voice, aiming for sheer, shattering power instead of musical quality, blasting the two high notes in the aria. The painter had come down shaking his head, saying that Daniel's voice was barely audible. At other times, under other circumstances, Daniel would have felt insulted. This time he was happy.

On the eighth day, the hospital room was crowded. Daniel watched in fond amusement as Isaac revelled in the role of grandfather. Clustered around the bed, watching, were Yetta, Moishe, Harry Feldman and people from Temple Isaiah in Paterson. Despite his father's urging to watch as the *mohel* performed the ritual operation, Daniel screwed his eyes tightly shut. He heard a short, sharp cry, followed immediately by a happy chuckling noise as Isaac dipped a finger in a glass of wine and brushed it lightly across the baby's lips.

When Daniel forced himself to open his eyes, it was as if nothing had happened. The baby was cooing contentedly; everyone standing around the small, linen-covered table where the *mohel* had operated, was smiling. Daniel felt ashamed that he had closed his eyes until he saw Moishe turn away, eyes blinking rapidly behind his glasses, face changing colour. Some godfather you are, Daniel thought, forgetting about his own qualms; too queasy to even hold your own godson for his *bris*.

A nurse came to take away the baby and suddenly the room seemed to empty. Daniel arranged for his parents to be driven back to the Bronx, then he sat down on the edge of the bed, hardly noticing that Moishe still remained in the room, sitting quietly on a chair in the corner.

Anna reached out and took Daniel's hands, holding them gently between her own. 'Is that how a Manrico or a Radames would behave?' she chided him smilingly. 'Closing his eyes just because he was afraid to look?'

'I'm only Manrico on stage,' he reminded her. 'Watching a *bris*, I'm just like anyone else. Ready to chuck up.'

156

'And your big brave friend over there's even worse.' She nodded to the corner of the room where Moishe sat, his face still devoid of colour. 'He watches and almost passes out.'

Daniel swung around to look, surprised to see that Moishe was still in the room. 'You feel all right?' he asked.

'Someday someone's going to report every *mohel* to the cops for child abuse and molestation,' Moishe murmured weakly. He continued to feel nauseated, although he was certain that any pain the child had felt could have been only momentary. 'Anyway' — he brightened up considerably — 'that kid's going to be proud that his old man's a big movie star.'

Moishe's words, aimed at cheering himself, had the opposite effect on Daniel. The excitement of the *bris* was over and Daniel's defences were down. Mention of *South Side Serenade* darkened his joy, forced him to think of Duguid and the Grand, the threat to terminate his contract once shooting began. He had to go through with the movie; there was no way out of it for him. But was there a way out for Duguid? Daniel had never wondered that before. Had the general manager found an avenue of escape for the threat he had made? Had he found a way to save face? Or was he still as intent as ever about letting Daniel go?

'Moishe.' Anna spoke quietly. The smile had left her face. 'If you're feeling better, why don't you go home?' She looked at Daniel sitting silently on the edge of the bed, knowing what had dampened his mood. She could not blame Moishe; he had only said something he thought was innocuous. He was not to know how deeply Daniel was worried by the prospect of making the movie.

'Another couple of minutes,' Moishe said. 'I'll be all right by then.'

'Go now. The fresh air will do you good.' Her voice was sharper. 'Please. I want to be alone with Daniel.'

Puzzled, Moishe looked at Daniel sitting on the bed. Daniel made no move, staring morosely at the blanket covering Anna. Moishe shrugged his shoulders, got up from the chair and patted Daniel on the shoulder. 'Be in touch,

157

Danny boy.' He kissed Anna on the cheek and left the room.

'Will you stop worrying?' Anna pressed. 'The worst hasn't happened yet and for all you know it might never.'

'I know.' He managed to raise a semblance of a smile. 'I just feel kind of flat, that's all. One round's over — the baby, the *bris,* the tour, everything. Now I've got to lift myself for the next round.'

'You will,' she assured him. 'Now, hadn't you better get home to see that the decorators have done all you wanted? I'm out of here in a couple of days, and I don't want to see paint brushes lying around the house. Unless you want Benjamin to be a housepainter.'

'Got to be a damned sight easier than trying to make his living as a lyric tenor!' Daniel joked.

Anna felt better, happy to see that the mood had passed. She would feel happier still once the movie was out of the way and the dust had settled. Seeing Daniel kept on tenterhooks while he worried was worse than anything that could befall him once Duguid had made his decision.

The first day Anna was home, Daniel spent hours on end in the nursery, sitting by the sleeping child, watching intently. Every cough, every movement startled him; every time his son would change his breathing pattern, he was ready to rush out of the room screaming for Anna. He tried to convince himself that he was worrying needlessly. It couldn't possibly happen a second time. Anna didn't come from a Russian family. There was no chance. And still he maintained an anxious vigil on the child.

That evening the housekeeper peeped into the nursery and saw Daniel fast asleep in the armchair by the crib. Quietly she tiptoed downstairs to call Anna. For fully a minute Anna stood in the nursery doorway, watching. Then she prodded Daniel awake.

'Okay, buster. Your time's up. If we need a watchdog, we can hire a nurse.'

'For what?' he asked groggily. 'A nurse for what?'

'To keep an eye on the baby. Fathers play with their sons;

158

they don't spend the entire time in the nursery watching over them.' She led him outside, guiding him to their bedroom. 'If you constantly worry about that child, you're going to make yourself ill,' she told him sternly. 'Benjamin is a perfectly healthy baby, so will you please stop standing guard over his crib like a vulture on a death watch? You're making a nervous wreck out of me.'

'Does it show?'

'Does it show?' She laughed at the question. 'I've told you before that every thought you have stands out on your face like an illuminated sign. Stop it now.'

'Okay.' A gleam came into his eyes as he pulled her down onto the bed beside him. 'I read somewhere that there's a great cure for being a nervous wreck.'

'How would you know?' She snuggled close to him. 'If it's so good, why haven't you tried it on yourself?'

'Can't do it by yourself. You need a partner, and there's been no one available for the past few months.'

'I'm glad to hear that. Anyway, I've been busy, or hadn't you noticed?'

Daniel grinned, the worry about his son eased. Anna had saved him again, dissipated his tensions and anxieties by understanding them. 'I saw you'd put on a few pounds, but I figured that was because you'd stopped singing. The easy life was making you fat and lazy.'

'The nerve of the man!' Anna exploded. 'Just make sure I don't put on a few pounds again right now. Benjamin and you are the only kids I can handle at the moment.'

The heat smashed into Daniel like a solid fiery wall as he walked the short distance from the airport terminal in Los Angeles to the waiting Cadillac limousine sent by Carmel Studios. Behind him trailed Moishe and a redcap carrying the suitcases of both men. When Daniel had asked Moishe in New York why he was coming with him, Moishe had replied that he was protecting his interests by ensuring that Daniel arrived on time at Carmel Studios; ten per cent of Daniel's forty thousand dollar fee was more than enough of an

159

incentive for Moishe to leave his law business for a few days and pay his own fare out West.

'Pomerantz has set up a press conference tomorrow morning,' Moishe said as the Cadillac left the parking lot. 'Wants to introduce you to everyone.'

'If I'm awake.' The flight in the TWA Constellation had taken twelve hours and Daniel felt numb, even worse than he had felt after the two transatlantic flights he'd taken. He wanted to sleep around the clock.

'You'll be awake,' Moishe told him. 'After the press conference, you can take the weekend to relax, then shooting starts on Monday.'

Daniel nodded automatically, his mind half on what Moishe was saying — although he'd heard it a dozen times before — half on Anna whom he would not see for six weeks, until *South Side Serenade* was finished and in the can. Anna had driven him to the airport that morning to meet Moishe, and he had felt like crying as he watched her drive away, back to Teaneck and Little Benny. He could swear the kid was growing already. Three weeks old and as alert as a sentry, wide blue eyes that followed you everywhere you went. Was going to be a big kid as well. A real bruiser. Just as long as he didn't turn out to be another Benny in size as well as in name.

'Are you listening to a word I'm saying?' Moishe demanded. He jabbed Daniel in the side with his elbow.

'Sure,' Daniel lied. 'Every single word.'

Convinced that Daniel had not heard a thing, Moishe started to repeat what he had said. Daniel cut him off. 'Where are we staying anyway?' he asked. He hadn't even thought about it. Moishe was supposed to have taken care of all those arrangements.

'The Chase. You've got a five-room suite there.'

The trip began to look better to Daniel. A five-room suite in a luxury apartment hotel was more like it. Maybe there was something in this movie business after all; accommodation like that sure as hell beat where you stayed on the Grand's tours. 'Generous of Carmel to foot the bill for a place like that.'

160

'They're not,' Moishe said, dispelling any misapprehensions. 'You are. One thousand a month.'

'Moishe, for Christ's sake!' Daniel yelled. The chauffeur glanced in the rearview mirror to learn the reason for the explosion from the back seat. 'Whose idea was that? I don't have to live in a place like The Chase. If I'm paying, I can live in a small place.'

'Hollywood rule number one,' Moishe said evenly. 'If you live small, you are small.'

'Thanks. With my money, you're a bigshot!' Daniel stared out of the window as the Cadillac passed along a street of white Spanish-style ranches. He supposed Moishe was right and he had to make some kind of impression on these people; show them he was their equal and not some country bumpkin singer just up from the farm or wherever they thought opera singers came from. But one day his friend would surprise him by telling him beforehand of something he planned to do. Surprise him? He'd kill him with the shock!

He began to think about Anna again. What was she doing now? On the East Coast, it would be ten in the evening. The baby would be asleep. Anna would be listening to the radio or reading; maybe she'd be playing the piano. Since she'd stopped singing at the Grand, she had taken more interest in the piano, using it to relax. Daniel grinned as he remembered the difficulty she'd encountered in getting close to the keyboard during the final months of her pregnancy. He'd told her to try growing her fingernails longer so she could reach the keys.

Once they arrived at the hotel, Daniel went straight up to the suite, leaving the baggaage and checking-in formalities to Moishe while he ordered a call to New Jersey. Waiting for the operator to ring back, he looked around the suite, surprised when he found a mixed case of bourbon, scotch, gin and brandy in the small kitchen. 'Where does this stuff come from?' he asked Moishe the moment his friend appeared.

'Don't worry about that. I ordered it ahead of time for when you entertain.'

'You paid?' Amazement tinted Daniel's question.

'It goes on your tab.'

'Get rid of it,' Daniel said. He remembered the fiasco in London, the night porter who had raided the bar so he could get stinking drunk. He didn't want any repetitions; he didn't want to drink again as long as he lived.

'You have to entertain,' Moishe protested. 'Everyone does it.'

'I'll do my entertaining by singing. Now, get it out of here and off my tab.'

Moishe shrugged helplessly and looked for a bellboy to remove the case of liquor. The telephone rang and Daniel answered it.

'Everything all right?' he asked Anna.

'Why shouldn't it be?' Her voice was like music to his ears. In the madness he could already sense was Hollywood, the sound of Anna's voice was like a lifeline thrown to a shipwreck victim. 'Or are you having premonitions now?' she asked.

'Of course not.' He told her about the press conference set for the following morning and promised to call her once it was over. 'Love you,' he whispered, waiting for her to respond before he broke the connection. Then he turned to Moishe. 'What about some food? I'm starving.'

'No sweat,' Moishe answered grandly. 'I'll get some sent up for us. What do you want?'

And Daniel saw more additions going onto his tab.

Daniel and Moishe were finishing a breakfast of lox and scrambled eggs the following morning when there was a double rap on the door of the suite. As if expecting a caller, Moishe leaped to answer and came back with Joel Pomerantz. Daniel finished off the remaining forkful of food and got to his feet.

Pomerantz was wearing the grin that Daniel remembered from their first meeting in Katz's on Houston Street. 'Glad to see you've arrived,' the producer said, shaking hands too heartily for Daniel's liking. 'Thought we were going to lose

162

you for a while back there. Happy that Mr. Waterman finally got everything straightened out.'

Daniel assumed that Pomerantz was referring to the threat that Carmel Studios would sue if he backed out of the deal.

'Hope you're fighting fit and raring to go,' Pomerantz continued enthusiastically, 'because this morning we're going to introduce Carmel Studios' newest star — Daniel Kerr — to the press. By the time our publicity people have finished with you, no one's going to be talking about Mario Lanza anymore. Your name will be on everyone's lips instead. What do you say to that?'

Daniel decided he had nothing to say to that. You don't carry on a jovial conversation with the guy who had threatened to sue you into the poorhouse, he decided; you just kept your distance and hoped that you could get through whatever ordeal he'd planned in as professional a manner as possible. Finally faced with the prospect of beginning his movie career, Daniel found himself wishing for the comparative sanity of the world of opera.

'See? He's speechless,' Moishe said, covering quickly for Daniel who stood mutely in the centre of the room. He could guess what was running through Daniel's mind. In all the years he had known him, Daniel had never been one to forgive easily; to forgive at all, for that matter. Moishe knew that the threatened lawsuit was still burning ulcers in Daniel's gut. He also knew that he would have to stick around longer than he had originally intended to make certain Daniel did not run out of the production.

'I'm not speechless,' said Daniel eventually. 'I just want to get on with this thing. In case anyone's forgotten, I've got a wife and tiny baby waiting for me back home. I'd like to get back to them as quickly as possible.'

'You will, you will,' Pomerantz assured him. 'Six weeks and it'll be all over. If it runs longer, you get overtime. And think about this — by the time *South Side Serenade*'s been shown all over the civilised world and you've had a couple of big hits out of it, you'll have made more money than you could ever have hoped for by singing opera. You won't have to worry about sending your kid to college. You'll be able to *buy* him a goddamned college.'

'Sure,' Daniel said, unconvinced.

'Get your jacket on and let's get out of here,' Pomerantz said. While Daniel put on a pale blue seersucker jacket, part of a complete wardrobe he'd bought for the trip west, Pomerantz crossed to the suite's entrance and rapped unobtrusively on the door before returning to the living room. Less than a minute later, a loud, prolonged knocking came from the door.

'Must be for you,' Pomerantz said to Daniel.

Puzzled, Daniel straightened his jacket and went to answer the door. As he opened it, a woman's high-pitched voice screamed. 'Daaahling! Welcome to Hollywood!' A pair of arms were thrown around his neck and lips pressed against his own; a smothering perfume threatened to suffocate him. He was barely aware of the camera flashbulbs that popped off blindingly in his eyes as he fought to free himself.

When he managed to step back, he recognised Diane Orsini, platinum blonde hair falling down to her shoulders, dressed in skin-tight pink trousers and a blouse that pushed her capacious bosom almost up to her neck. Behind her stood three photographers and a group of men and women whom Daniel assumed were reporters. Moishe had warned him that there would be a press conference, but he hadn't said anything about Pomerantz arranging it to take place in the suite.

'Here he is, folks!' Pomerantz boomed. Daniel was surprised that the producer had such a strong voice when he wanted to use it. A pip-squeak like that should have a soprano, not tones that belonged to a Chaliapin, a giant. 'Straight from the Grand Opera Company of New York City, Daniel Kerr!'

'What the hell is this?' Daniel whispered angrily to Moishe. 'That picture comes out with that broad kissing me and Anna's going to fly straight through the roof!'

164

'Relax, will you?' Moishe said. 'This is for publicity, something to get your face and name in the papers. Without it you're dead before you even start.'

'You going to quit that longhair stuff if you click in *South Side Serenade*?' one man yelled. He pushed himself to the front of the crowd and repeated the question, his face only inches from Daniel's while he waited aggressively for the answer.

The reply came not from Daniel but from Pomerantz. 'What are you talking about, if?' Pomerantz yelled back at the reporter. 'Daniel Kerr's going to be the biggest name in musical pictures after *South Side Serenade*. And you can use that for collateral!' While he let the reporters digest his claim, he hissed at Daniel. 'MGM's already shitting in their pants and we haven't even shot an inch of film yet.'

'Why don't you let them quote you on that if you're so sure?' Daniel shot back.

'Hey, come on! We've all got to get a living out of this world. Be serious, will you?' Pomerantz turned back to the waiting reporters and photographers. 'Why don't you get a couple more shots of Daniel and Di together, the most important pairing this town's ever going to see. Go on, Di,' he urged the girl. 'Get friendly.'

Diane sidled closer to Daniel and draped an arm around his neck, brushing his face with her lips. 'I never knew an opera singer before,' she murmured huskily in his ear. 'And I mean knew in the old-fashioned biblical way, you get what I mean?' The animosity she'd felt towards him in New York had gone. If what Pomerantz was claiming was true, this guy wasn't going to be Mario Lanza's understudy for long. He'd be a name to reckon with, a star in his own right. Besides, he wasn't that bad-looking. Tall. A bit tubby, but so were many of the men she'd been with. A bit of fat never hurt, just as long as there was enough muscle underneath to swing a hefty hammer.

'Blondes don't do nothing for me,' Daniel hissed back, smiling all the time at the cameras that continued to record every detail. If Anna ever got to see any of these pictures, she'd laugh, he was certain of that. But his father would not.

Nor would his mother; she'd be convinced he was having an affair with this celluloid sex symbol, always eager to think the worst about anything or anyone. Most of all, it was Robin Duguid's reaction about which he worried. If Duguid ever saw these pictures, it would be the final nail in Daniel's coffin.

'I'm not a natural blonde,' Diane Orsini giggled. 'But only my best friends know that.' She stared at him inquisitively. 'You want to be one of my best friends?'

'Sorry, I don't like sloppy seconds.' He shrugged her off and gave his full attention to the reporters. So far only Pomerantz had answered all the questions. Maybe Daniel could salvage something for himself out of this three-ring circus of a press conference if he was given the opportunity to make the right replies.

'Mr. Kerr, what made you take a role like this?' a woman asked. 'A lyric tenor of your stature taking a chance on a movie like this is unusual, to say the least.'

Daniel felt like reaching out and kissing the woman. She knew what a lyric tenor was; most of these other creeps wouldn't be able to tell the difference between a soprano and a bass. Maybe he could score a few points here. 'Because I firmly believe that beautiful music has a place on the screen as well as on the stage. Perhaps the words will be different, but the music will be the same.'

'He's being modest!' Pomerantz called out and Daniel resisted the impulse to punch the producer in the mouth. 'He's too shy to say that his voice is too good for opera. That it belongs on the screen where millions can appreciate it instead of a couple of thousand stuff-shirted creeps who probably need hearing aids.'

'Shut up, you imbecile!' Daniel muttered with as much vehemence as he could muster. 'You can't speak for me.'

'Can't I?' Pomerantz replied threateningly. 'You read your goddamned contract better. Carmel Studios can publicise you any way they see fit.'

'Shy men are always queers,' a woman's voice whispered from the other side of Daniel. 'Maybe that's why you can sing so high . . . because you've got no balls.'

Daniel swung around from Pomerantz to see Diane Orsini standing on the other side, finger resting against her lips as she gazed at him mischievously.

'Can get you fixed up with a nice fellow,' she offered. 'Anything to make your stay here more pleasant.'

Daniel let a broad grin creep across his face, Making certain that no one else could see, he mouthed, 'Screw you, baby.' He was beginning to recognise Diane Orsini as a Claudia Rivera, but without even the faintest vestige of class or sophistication. Maybe Carmel Studios was not the Grand, his home turf, but he was damned certain he could take care of Diane Orsini.

'If I let you try it once, you'd never go back to men.' She put her arms around him again and kissed him firmly on the lips. Although the gesture of affection was done for the photographers' benefit, Daniel could feel the tip of her tongue trying to force open his lips. He yielded. As her tongue snaked triumphantly between his teeth, he clamped down hard enough to pinch but not to draw blood. Diane jumped back, hand to her mouth in shock and pain, eyes blazing.

'You sonofabitch!' she cursed.

With ease, Daniel ducked the blow that whistled towards his face and laughed loudly as Diane's open hand cracked into the doorjamb. The woman's anguished scream filled the hall. While the photographers made the most of their unexpected good fortune, Moishe grabbed the opportunity to pull Daniel off to the side.

'Are you mad? That's your co-star, for God's sake!'

'Tough shit. Maybe Pomerantz'll fire me.'

'With a million-dollar lawsuit he'll fire you.' Moishe broke off as the producer came over to them, leaving the press to surround an indignant Diane Orsini, who was giving vent to her fury at Daniel.

'I'm warning you, Kerr.' It was as if he had read Moishe's thoughts. 'You screw up this movie with behaviour like that and I'll sue you for everything you've got!'

Daniel drew himself up to his full height, dwarfing the

producer. 'My behaviour is that of a professional. You'd just better keep a chain on that bitch.'

Pomerantz swung around angrily to the reporters surrounding Diane Orsini. 'Okay, folks,' he shouted, pushing his way through. 'Question time's over. We've got to get down to some work around here.' He reached Diane and said something quietly to his blonde star. No one overheard the words, but they seemed to have the desired effect. Diane simmered down and allowed herself to be led away. Daniel turned around and returned to the suite. Behind him he could hear Moishe close the door, cutting out the din from the hallway.

'Jesus, Danny, what are you trying to pull? Do you want to get us sued for every penny? You can't get away with shit like that.'

'What did I do?' Daniel wanted to know. 'Tell me what I did that was so terrible? Tell me as a friend, an agent and a lawyer.'

'You've got to bow to these people if you want to get on here. When you're a big name, you can get away with whatever you like, but right now you've got to knuckle down and do whatever Pomerantz says.'

Daniel picked up the telephone to place a call to Anna. More than ever, he needed her sanity before he lost his own. As he waited for the switchboard to make the connection, Pomerantz entered the suite. He stood in front of Daniel, oblivious to the fact that he was on the phone.

'Shooting starts Monday morning at six sharp. A car will be coming to pick you up. Make damned sure you're ready.' Then he stormed out of the suite to tend to his wounded star.

The first week's shooting was murder on Daniel. Because of the five o'clock call each morning in order to reach the lot by six, he could not shrug off the feeling of sluggishness. Lines were continually fluffed; simple scenes had to be shot over and over again.

Before coming west, Daniel had never realised how little he knew about acting. He'd never given it any thought. On stage, his singing alone carried him to success. The acting involved was basic with little room for delicacy. Fights and action scenes were carefully choreographed so as not to interfere with complicated musical cues. On camera, though, the style of acting he used at the Grand brought forth hysterical screams and a perpetual torrent of abuse from the director.

'Subtlety!' the man kept shrieking. 'Be subtle, for Christ's sake! Do you know the meaning of the word? This is a movie, not a goddamned pantomime!' And Daniel continued to use the exaggerated style of acting he employed on stage.

Each mistake on Daniel's part gave Diane Orsini an opportunity to laugh maliciously at him. When they broke up for lunch on the fifth day, she passed by him and said, 'Maybe they can find you a role as a homo next time out. You should be able to play that without any need for acting.' Daniel simply glared at her, too tired to even think of fighting back.

Moishe kept him company in the studio commissary during the lunch break. Daniel pecked unhappily at his food, appetite dulled, while Moishe watched pensively. He'd got him this far and he'd be damned if he was going to let Daniel quit now. Moishe was booked on a flight back to New York that night as he could no longer afford to neglect his law business. It was now or never with Daniel as far as he was concerned. 'Keep at it,' he encouraged. 'Once you get to the singing bits, you'll knock them all on their asses.'

'If I ever get that far.' The songs came right at the end when the studio would fill in all of the musical scenes in one long burst. In truth, it was only the thought of recording the songs that kept Daniel at all interested in *South Side Serenade*. It was the one point on which he agreed with Joel Pomerantz, that 'Those Smiling Eyes' would leap straight into the hit parade. It had to; nothing could stop it. And more than anything else, Daniel wanted a hit record to add to his trophy list, the opportunity to show the entire country that he was just as good as Lanza.

169

A middle-aged man stopped by the table. Daniel recognised him as one of the extras. 'Mr. Kerr, I'd like to say something to you.'

'What is it?' Daniel wondered what other insults were about to be heaped on his head. Maybe he'd think twice about hauling off and and slugging Diane Orsini or Pomerantz, but he would have no hesitation in sticking this little squirt on his back. Almost unconsciously he clenched his fists underneath the table, ready to lash out.

'We don't get paid too much, Mr. Kerr, so . . .'

'What?' Daniel asked, his fists relaxing. 'What are you talking about?'

'Us extras. All these scenes we have to replay get us overtime. We want to thank you for lousing them up.'

Suddenly Daniel began to laugh. He threw back his head, filling the entire commissary with the sound of his laughter. Heads turned in his direction, but all he could think of was the man standing in front of him. His wooden, heavy-handed acting was having an effect he had never even considered. No wonder everyone was getting upset with him. He was costing the studio a fortune with each scene he screwed up.

'Knock it off,' Moishe warned, embarrassed by the stares that were sent his way.

Daniel gained control of himself and looked at the man who continued to stand meekly by the table. 'How about if I turned up late a few mornings as well? Would that help you?' he asked.

'Great, Mr. Kerr. Fantastic.'

'You've got my word on it. You're going to get the biggest paycheque you've ever seen.' Daniel burst out laughing again as the man walked away to join his friends at a nearby table; heads went down as he quietly imparted the good news.

'Pomerantz will kill you if you pull shit like that,' Moishe muttered darkly.

'There's nothing in my contract about causing delays through ineptitude,' Daniel retorted. 'Or not turning up because I'm sick. I've read that damned contract so many times since the press conference that I can recite it off by heart. This whole goddamned bunch thinks I can't act. Well, they're right. And it's going to cost them money to find out just how right they are.'

As they walked back to the set after lunch, a uniformed guard approached Daniel. 'Telegram for you, Mr. Kerr.' He handed Daniel a Western Union envelope.

'Thanks.' Still chuckling over the extra's request, Daniel slit open the envelope. He read the words quickly and his face turned white. When he looked at the message again, his mouth slowly formed the words as if he were unable to to read without moving his lips.

'What is it?' Moishe asked.

'Here!' Daniel snapped savagely. 'You read the goddamned thing. It's all your fucking fault anyway!' He threw the telegram at Moishe and strode off angrily towards the set.

Moishe picked up the piece of paper. His eyes first hit the signature block of Robin Duguid, then they took in the complete message area:

DANIEL KERR CARMEL STUDIOS HOLLYWOOD CALIFORNIA

WAS WILLING TO OVERLOOK YOUR FORAY IN- TO MOVIES IN HOPE YOU WOULD RETURN TO YOUR SENSES STOP NEWSPAPER PICTURES OF YOUR RELATIONSHIP WITH MISS DIANE ORSINI MAKE THAT IMPOSSIBLE STOP BECAUSE YOUR BEHAVIOUR NOT IN BEST INTERESTS OF GRAND OPERA COMPANY WE ARE HEREBY TER- MINATING YOUR CONTRACT STOP REGRET THIS EXTREME STEP BUT YOU LEAVE US NO ALTERNATIVE STOP GOOD LUCK IN THE MOVIES STOP ROBIN DUGUID.

CHAPTER NINE

The first phone call Daniel made from his dressing room was to Anna. For once he did not pester her about the baby. Instead, he read out the contents of Duguid's cable. Anna waited until he had finished before informing him that an identical cable had been delivered to the house. Duguid was taking no chances on Daniel not knowing of his decision.

Next, Daniel called Duguid at the Grand. The general manager was icily polite.

'Mr. Duguid, it's Daniel Kerr.'

'Good afternoon, Daniel. How are you?'

'I'm upset, how the hell do you think I am?' Daniel burst out. He closed his eyes and took a deep breath, willing himself to calm down; he could not afford to antagonise Duguid now. 'I just received your cable.'

'Where?'

'At Carmel Studios. It's a bit of a blow,' Daniel added unnecessarily.

'Self-inflicted, I might point out,' Duguid said. 'As I mentioned in the cable, I was willing to live and let live as long as you maintained a certain discretion while you followed this path. Unfortunately, those newspaper pictures of you cavorting with that woman have forced my hand.'

Daniel gripped the receiver harder as he forced himself to remain cool. 'It was a set-up, Mr. Duguid, believe me. A stupid publicity stunt, that was all. She was waiting for me outside my suite with all the photographers. The studio arranged it. I never had a chance.'

'I'm very sorry, Daniel; but there's little I can do about it now. You've chosen the path you wish to follow, and I hope you have success. Goodbye.'

There was a soft click in Daniel's ear and the line went dead. Angry and frustrated, he called the Grand again. When he identified himself, Duguid's secretary said that the general manager had just been called away to an urgent meeting and would not be available for the remainder of the day. Perhaps Daniel would like to try again on Monday morning?

Daniel slammed down the receiver and stormed out of his dressing room. When he saw the other members of the cast happily talking away the remainder of the lunch break, he spun around and headed towards the parking lot. The Studebaker Carmel had loaned him for his stay in Hollywood — Moishe had demanded a Cadillac but had settled willingly for less — was parked close to the exit. Daniel revved the engine savagely. Wheels spinning, the Studebaker tore out of the parking lot, past the guard on the gate and headed towards Los Angeles. The bizarre thought that the extras would have a field day flashed across Daniel's mind. Good! He was glad that someone could make capital out of his misery.

He drove blindly, his mind only seeing the cable that Duguid had sent. He couldn't believe it. He'd kidded himself all along that it would never happen, that Duguid was only bluffing, that he'd find a way at the last moment to avoid the inevitable. The Grand couldn't do without him, he'd told himself repeatedly. Now Duguid had proved that they damned well could.

He saw a bar and slammed the Studebaker to a juddering halt. Inside the bar, he forgot about the way he'd told Moishe to get rid of the liquor. He needed a drink now more than ever. He called loudly for a bourbon. Almost before the bartender had set down the glass, Daniel had emptied it, calling impatiently for a refill. The bartender eyed him

173

curiously before pouring another measure. Then he moved away to the other end of the bar, leaving Daniel alone.

Daniel drank the second bourbon more slowly, letting his mind wander over the ramifications of Duguid's act. Duguid was bent on proving that the opera house could exist without him, but could he exist without opera? It was the Grand that had made him. Without it, he would never have been approached for this part in *South Side Serenade*. Christ, why had he ever been fool enough to accept it? Everyone had warned him against doing it, but he'd gone blithely on, disregarding the advice of people who knew a damned sight more than he did. He looked bleakly into the glass as he remembered throwing the cable at Moishe and shouting that it was all his fault. He knew damned well it wasn't. He had nobody to blame but himself. His own ego had pushed him into it, and now he was out of work; or out of the work he loved more than anything else. He didn't want movies. He didn't want a hit record. He couldn't care less about proving he was better than Lanza. All he wanted was the chance to walk once more on the stage of the Grand and thrill people with his voice.

'Another one?' the bartender asked.

Daniel glanced at his glass, surprised to find it empty. 'Sure. Keep them coming.'

'Whatever you say, mac.'

As the afternoon wore on, more people entered the bar. Daniel took no notice of them, too intent on pondering his own problems, a nightmare that had suddenly become reality. At one point he made up his mind to try calling Duguid again. The general manager would be home by now. Daniel knew the phone number of his apartment in Manhattan. Duguid would answer the phone himself; there would be no way of his avoiding speaking to Daniel. When he stood up to use the pay phone someone was already there. By the time the call was finished, Daniel's determination had waned.

'You all right, mac?' the bartender asked as he passed Daniel's seat.

''Course I'm all right.' Daniel did not realise how distorted his words were. 'Gimme another one.'

'You sure you want another one. Or would you rather I called you a cab to take you home?'

'Gimme another drink!' Daniel declared fiercely. 'I've got the money to pay!' He pulled a roll of bills out of his pocket and slammed it onto the bar; money fluttered onto the floor. 'Fill me up till that runs out.'

'Put your money away,' the bartender said quietly. He bent down to pick up the bills that had fallen on his side of the bar. 'I'll get you a cab.'

'I don't want a goddamned cab!' Daniel yelled. Customers turned at the noise. 'I want another drink!'

'Not here, pal. Not today.'

Daniel's rage at himself found an easier target. He leaned across the bar and grabbed the man by the shoulder. 'Gimme another drink, you stinking sonofabitch! Do you know who I am?'

The bartender turned around slowly, his gaze disdainful as he looked at Daniel's hand on his shoulder. 'I don't give a shit who you are, mister. Get your hand off me and get your ass out of this bar before I call the cops.'

'You can't talk to me like that! I'm Daniel Kerr!' The fury reached boiling point and spilled over. Daniel swung an ill-aimed punch at the bartender. The man stepped back and Daniel flopped across the bar, gasping for breath as his chest slammed into the fixture. The bartender raised his own hand to strike back before deciding it was unnecessary. He left Daniel straddled across the bar while he telephoned for the police.

A minute passed while Daniel lay across the bar, His chest hurt like hell; he was sure he'd busted a couple of ribs. Above the pain, though, he knew he had to get out of the bar. The cops were coming. That was all he needed. He pushed himself to his feet, standing unsteadily.

'Hold him!' the bartender yelled.

Daniel felt hands restraining him as other customers tried to keep him from leaving. Fear of staying and being arrested

175

gave him strength. He lashed out with his hands and feet, hearing yells of pain and surprise. Suddenly there was a clear space between himself and the door. And freedom. He dove towards the door as the bartender vaulted over the bar, a sawed-off baseball bat in his hand. Daniel saw the club swing towards his head, ducked, and then slammed a short right at the bartender. This punch hit home. Coupled with the bartender's forward impetus, the blow was devastating. Daniel's fist smashed into the man's solar plexus. The club went flying through the air to shatter the bar's front window, spilling glass over the sidewalk. Daniel's shoes crunched broken glass as he ran from the bar, swung open the Studebaker's door and started the engine. Figures erupted from the bar. He heard the sound of sirens and floored the gas pedal.

The Studebaker screeched away from the kerb. Ahead Daniel saw a black and white patrol car tearing towards him. He swung the car in a wide, fast u-turn, without realising that he'd just made the chase easier for the policemen. Horns blasted as traffic in both directions took evasive action. Daniel held his hand down on the horn to clear a path. He had to get back to the lot, had to get back to the movie. They'd protect him there. He was a star. Without him the movie could not continue.

There was another patrol car coming from the opposite direction. Its siren drowned out the sound of the Studebaker's horn. Too late Daniel recognised the police driver's intention as the approaching patrol car cut across traffic and positioned itself in Daniel's path. Daniel went rigid in the seat, foot jammed down on the brake. At the last moment, he yanked the steering wheel sideways and cannoned broadside into the police car.

'We were worried sick about you!'

Moishe's voice battered through the waves of pain and dizziness that surged unmercifully through Daniel's head. 'What the hell happened to you? You're lucky you weren't killed, you damned lunatic, driving like that!'

176

Daniel looked around the white-painted walls of the police station. Uniformed figures moved around as if unaware of his presence. He looked at Moishe and Pomerantz standing in front of him. Moishe seemed anxious, Pomerantz furious. 'How did I get here?' Daniel mumbled. He felt terrible. He didn't even know what time it was or how long had passed since he'd been in the crash.

'The cops called us,' Pomerantz answered sharply. 'And they called the papers at the same time. I've got a good mind to throw you out and sue you for what you've cost us in shooting time and bad publicity. You're going to be in all the papers tomorrow. Carmel star in drunken brawl, car chase, smash-up. You name it, you did it. Very nice!'

'I did all that?' For the life of him Daniel could not remember exactly what had happened. All he could recall was the moment of impact, when he'd slammed sideways into the police cruiser. 'Was anyone hurt?' He was amazed to find himself in one piece.

'No, and you're goddamned lucky,' Pomerantz answered. 'Because you didn't kill anyone, I'll be able to square it away. But you're paying for the damage you caused, make no mistake about that.'

Damage? Daniel shuddered as he thought about it. The Studebaker, the cop car; and whatever he'd done during the fight he was supposed to have had. A picture of a window shattering as a club went through it filtered into his memory and he shuddered again. 'What time is it?' he finally asked.

'Just after six,' Moishe muttered. 'I've missed my flight as well, thanks to you. Now I've got to wait till tomorrow. Asshole!'

Daniel got to his feet. 'Can we go?' he asked. 'Or do the police still want me?'

'We can go. Right back to your suite where you can sleep it off until tomorrow morning. And if you're not on the set by six a.m. tomorrow, you're going to be sued for every penny you ever make. And this time I mean it! Understand?'

Daniel looked at Moishe, who nodded grimly. Pomerantz watched while Moishe held Daniel's arm, guiding him outside. Then he followed, shaking his head

Daniel telephoned Anna from his suite early the following morning before he left for the lot. News of the drunken fight and police chase had made the late editions of the New York papers. In one, there was even a quote from Robin Duguid saying he was sad to witness a singer of such undisputed brilliance following such a path, but as Daniel was no longer with the Grand, there was nothing he could do about it.

'What about my father?' Daniel asked. 'Have you spoken to him?'

'He called a little while back,' Anna replied. 'He was very upset. He says you should never have gone to Hollywood in the first place.'

'Great,' Daniel muttered. With the exception of Anna, he didn't have a single supporter left in the entire world. And she probably, rightfully, thought him a fool anyway. He supposed he could always try for the Met when he returned to New York. No; it wouldn't work. No doubt there was a loyalty between the two houses, and Bing would look the same way upon his antics as Duguid did.

He'd have to make his peace with Duguid. But how, for Christ's sake? How?

Maybe he'd make a million from *South Side Serenade* and be able to retire, be able to tell them all to go to hell in a handcart. Some hopes, he reflected bitterly. If he managed to get off the Carmel lot without owing money, he'd be more than satisfied.

CHAPTER TEN

When he returned to New Jersey after completion of *South Side Serenade*, Daniel could not believe how much Little Benny had grown. He was certain he was not looking at the same child he had left just seven weeks earlier, and he was annoyed with himself that he could have allowed so long a period of his son's life to pass without being there to share it. Thick brown hair covered the baby's head, and his cheeks were so chubby that even the most confirmed baby-hater would find it hard to resist pinching them. Daniel picked up the child and lifted him high into the air, laughing as Benjamin spread his arms like a bird in flight.

'Put him down,' Anna said. 'You're scaring the living daylights out of the poor kid. That's why he's waving his arms around like that.'

'Of course it's not. He's enjoying it.'

'Like hell he is,' Anna contradicted. Gently but firmly she took the baby from Daniel's hands and set him back in the crib. Then she went downstairs, leaving Daniel alone in the nursery with his son.

Daniel pulled a chair up to the crib and sat staring in fascination. Occasionally he would tickle Benjamin's hand, amazed at the strength contained in the minute fingers as they clutched at his own and refused to let go. How could he have let himself stay away for seven weeks? Forty-nine days, each second of them absolutely irreplaceable. Even the photographs Anna had taken at every opportunity and the stories with which she had regaled him during their twice-daily telephone conversation could never remotely compensate him for his absence. But now he was back and nothing would ever drag him away again. Not that Joel Pomerantz of Carmel Studios would ever want him back. No matter how much money *South Side Serenade* made — if it made anything at all — Pomerantz would never call him again. In addition to the three thousand dollars he had paid for damages to the two cars and the bar, Daniel had cost the studio a small fortune in overtime. He had made no friends there, unless he counted the extras who had reaped a golden harvest in salary because of his clumsiness.

Benjamin fell asleep and Daniel tiptoed out of the nursery. When he went downstairs, Anna asked about his plans. The Grand was already rehearsing for the next season, and Duguid had been quoted liberally in the press about his efforts to replace Daniel in the production for which he had contracted. In some instances, European tenors were being brought in for single appearances; otherwise, young, upcoming singers would substitute. The cost of the changes was astronomical, Duguid had said, but expense was of secondary importance where such a matter of principle was involved. He had the unequivocal support of his board of management and major patrons. The Grand Opera Company of New York would continue without the services of Daniel Kerr.

'I've got to see Duguid, I suppose,' Daniel told Anna. 'Maybe a face-to-face confrontation will do the trick.'

'Call him soon and set up an appointment,' Anna suggested. 'He probably knows you're back from California, and he'll be waiting to hear from you. The longer you leave it, the tougher it's going to be to patch it up.'

Although Anna continued to offer her wholehearted support to Daniel, she was far from confident that he would have any success with Duguid. Intentionally or otherwise, Daniel had made the general manager look small. Duguid had retaliated by proving beyond any doubt that he was the master of the company and nothing or no one would be allowed to dispute his authority. He had stuck to his threat of firing Daniel. Now that he had gone so far as to publicise how he planned to replace Daniel, Anna could not see any real hope of him changing his mind. He was determined to teach Daniel a lesson and to let others benefit from the example — even if it meant hurting both himself and the company.

Early the following morning, Daniel dialled the Grand. Duguid's secretary placed him on hold for several minutes, then she said yes, the general manager would be able to see him that afternoon. Her tone was frosty and distant, and Daniel held out no great optimism for the meeting.

At three o'clock that afternoon he entered the opera house, forcing himself to walk quickly and confidently up to the offices, determined to show everyone that he had not come to beg. He noticed the difference immediately. Office staff who had always fussed over him now looked in another direction, embarrassed by his presence. When he tried to strike up a conversation as he waited for Duguid to see him, his attempts met with no success. It was as if he were suffering from leprosy; no one wanted to take a chance on catching it.

'Mr. Duguid will see you now.'

Daniel entered the familiar office. Duguid was sitting behind his desk, head bent low as he scribbled in pencil on a sheet of lined yellow paper. He made Daniel wait for almost half a minute before he finished writing and looked up. 'How's Anna and the baby?' he asked conversationally.

'They're fine, thank you,' Daniel answered automatically. He had expected that to be the opening question. Duguid was a gentleman to the last.

'You look well, too,' Duguid said evenly, referring to the deep, even suntan Daniel had achieved. 'The West Coast must agree with you.'

'Not really, Mr. Duguid.' It was time to get down to the reason for the meeting. 'I've learned that I'm much happier on the East Coast.'

'I see.' Duguid looked down at the piece of yellow paper

181

on the desk. 'What do you plan to do now? Have you decided yet?'

'I was hoping we could talk about that today.'

'Oh?' Duguid looked up again, his face devoid of expression, giving Daniel no clue to his feelings. 'I'm afraid that the Grand no longer has a place for you, Daniel. However, I'd be more than happy to furnish references if you decide to work somewhere else. With your talent, though, I would imagine that any references I could offer would be merely redundant.'

Daniel clenched and unclenched his fists while he willed himself to remain calm, to maintain the confident manner he had promised he would show. Duguid was goading him. He was in a position of power and he was rubbing Daniel's face in it. 'Mr. Duguid, I do not wish to work with another company. My entire professional life centres around the Grand.'

Duguid sighed sadly. 'Daniel, I thought I had made the company's position perfectly clear in both the telegram I sent to you and during the phone conversation that followed. Your antics in Hollywood — whether they were of your own making or a publicity stunt over which you had no control — forced my hand irrevocably. And there was that unfortunate business with the police. The Grand does not have a position for an artist, no matter how good, who puts his personal aggrandisement above the overall welfare of the company. I'm tremendously sad that it has come to this pass, but we have no other option open to us.'

Daniel could feel the tears starting to burn behind his eyes. Not tears of pain and sorrow. Or regret because he had done wrong. They were tears of rage and frustration. Duguid was cutting his throat for him and there wasn't a single thing he could do but sit and watch it happen.

'Try putting yourself in my position, Daniel.' Duguid dug through a drawer and pulled out a large brown envelope from which he shook a batch of newspaper clippings. 'If you were general manager of a prestigious opera house, would you continue to employ a singer who behaved as you did?'

He pushed the clippings across the desk to Daniel.

This was the first time Daniel had seen the stories in the New York newspapers. Anna had made certain there were none about the house when he returned from Hollywood. He picked them up, curiosity overcoming anger. There were several pictures of Diane Orsini throwing her arms around him, and there were garish, exaggerated stories of the fight in the bar and the ensuing collision with the police car, turned into a hundred-mile-an-hour drunken chase. Numbly he read each story, looked at each picture before letting them slip from his fingers.

Duguid watched him carefully. 'Daniel, even if I wanted to take you back I couldn't. My hands are tied. The Grand's board of management has professed disgust with your behaviour. On top of that, the productions for the coming season are all settled. Every role is filled. There's nothing I could offer you at this late stage.'

Daniel picked his head up and gazed stonily across the desk at Duguid. 'I guess I wasted my time in coming to see you.'

Duguid pursed his lips in thought. 'Perhaps. And perhaps not. At least you've realised where your priorities should have been.'

'But that doesn't buy the groceries, does it?' Daniel said.

'I'm afraid not. Are you in financial difficulties?'

'Money's no problem, Mr. Duguid.'

'Good. What will you do now?'

Go home and cry, Daniel thought. But he'd be damned if he'd let Duguid know he felt that way. He had entered the building with his head held high, and he was going to leave it the same way. His grief was private. 'I don't think I'll have any trouble in finding other engagements, Mr. Duguid. My agent's already got a number of offers. Concerts. Clubs. I can sing anything. Anywhere.'

'I'm delighted to hear that.' Duguid sounded as if he were genuinely pleased. 'No doubt we'll be running across each other again in the future. Good luck.' He held out his hand. Daniel looked at it for a long moment, debating whether to accept it. Finally he did.

'I enjoyed the season I spent with you, Mr. Duguid. I think it was my best season. Good day.' He turned around and walked quickly from the office. Duguid watched the door swing slowly closed before he returned his attention to the piece of lined yellow paper on top of his desk. He read it through several times, the letter he was thinking of sending to Daniel. It was not a letter of forgiveness; it was a letter setting out the terms under which forgiveness could be made and Daniel reinstated with the company.

Like Daniel, Duguid had refused to let his true feelings show during the meeting. The pronouncements he had made to the press had been for public consumption only. He wanted Daniel back as badly as Daniel wanted to be back. There were no upcoming singers even near Daniel's class, and the European tenors Duguid had booked at short notice were of limited ability. Daniel had a place in the hearts of the Grand's followers. He was local talent, a direct link to the New York audiences.

Uncertain how to deal with the problem, Duguid had spoken with Hammersley in England. Flattered at having been brought into the dispute, Hammersley had recalled the uproar in Wheeler's following the production of *Tosca*. He had suggested to Duguid that a public apology might be in order again. Duguid had accepted the advice, but he had decided to hold off setting out the terms of forgiveness until he could gauge Daniel's attitude. What he had just witnessed during the meeting made him decide not to send the letter. Apart from what could be construed as a token attempt at regret — saying that his professional life centred around the Grand — Daniel had not seemed in the least contrite. If anything, he had been cocky. Overconfident that he would be taken back.

Duguid rolled up the piece of yellow paper and tossed it into the trashcan. He had made up his mind that Daniel could stew in his own juices for a while. It might do his oversized ego a world of good.

Daniel waited until he reached the comparative privacy of

his car, then he hammered futilely at the steering wheel with his fists. All that crap about his agent getting him work, concerts, club dates. Duguid had seen right through it. He must be sitting up there laughing now over Daniel's obvious lies.

He didn't want concerts or club dates. He didn't want any other kind of work. All he wanted was the chance to go back on stage in the roles he loved best, and Duguid was not going to offer him that chance. He banged on the steering wheel again while he wondered what an opera singer did when there was no opera company that wanted him.

When his temper had subsided, he started the car's engine, shifted into gear and headed north. Who said that no other company wanted him? What the hell! He'd try the Met! He'd walk in there and take them by storm. He'd make Duguid squirm by throwing in his lot with the opposition.

Parking the car on West Thirty-ninth Street, he recalled that other time of desperation when he had stopped by the yellow brick building to look at the *Il Trovatore* sets and the man in the frayed suit had denied him entrance to the opera house. This time he was going in by the front door and no one would stop him until he'd got right through to see Rudolf Bing. And he'd walk out of there with the promise of a contract. See what Duguid and his goddamned board of management did about that!

Reaching the offices, he stated that he wanted to see Rudolf Bing. Asked the reason by a surprised middle-aged woman, Daniel could think of nothing to say other than he wanted a job, to which the woman replied that the Met did not give 'auditions just like that.' When Daniel finally identified himself, the woman said that Mr. Bing was away for a week; perhaps Daniel would like to make an appointment for when the general manager returned. Daniel mustered enough courtesy to thank her and left the building.

Back in the car, he wondered what to do next. Go home? And tell Anna what had happened? That he was out of work? He decided instead to drive up to the Bronx and visit his parents. He had not seen them since he had returned from California; now seemed as good a time as any to let his father in on the grim news as well.

It was a mistake. Whereas Anna had made certain that no trace of the newspaper stories remained in the house, Yetta Kirschbaum had clung onto them as if they were made of solid gold. 'A nice time you had in Hollywood,' she greeted Daniel when she opened the door. 'I'm glad you changed your name to Kerr and didn't leave it as Kirschbaum.' She carried on talking without giving Daniel the chance to say anything. 'How am I supposed to feel when I see pictures like this? Read stories like this?' She led him into the living room, where the same newspaper clippings Duguid had showed him were proudly displayed on a table, alongside family wedding pictures.

Daniel ignored the display. 'Where's Pa?' he asked.

Yetta paused only long enough to tell Daniel that Isaac had gone out for a walk. Then she started all over again. 'You're lucky you have a girl like Anna. Me? I would have left home when I heard about the things you were doing.'

'I wasn't doing anything. What time will Pa be back?'

'How should I know? Sometimes he meets his friends in the park. A nice day like this he plays some cards. Why did you have to get involved with this woman?' She pointed at a picture of Diane Orsini. 'All my friends who know you're my son think you're messing around with a *shiksa*, and you're in trouble with the police because you're a *shikker*.'

Before Yetta's horrified gaze, Daniel picked up the pile of clippings and tore them into shreds, dumping them into the trash bag in the kitchen. 'Why did you do that?' Yetta yelled after him.

'I thought you were ashamed of them!' he shouted back even more loudly. 'Don't keep anything you're ashamed of!' He slammed the front door and walked towards the park.

When he found his father, Isaac was playing chess with another elderly man, sitting under the shade of a maple tree so intent on the game that he did not even notice Daniel standing behind him. Daniel watched his father make a

186

move, then he clucked his tongue in disapproval. 'Two question marks for that one.'

Isaac's eyes lit up when he recognised the voice. He turned around on the seat, looked at Daniel for an instant and then stood up to clasp him around the shoulders and kiss him on the cheek.

'When did you get back?'

'Yesterday.'

'Your movie's all finished?'

Daniel nodded. 'Thank God.'

Isaac introduced him to the other man playing chess, then excused both himself and Daniel. 'I give you the game!' he called in farewell. 'What's the news with the opera company and your Mr. Duguid?' he asked anxiously as he walked with Daniel from the park, back towards the house.

Daniel debated whether or not to lie. Anna had told him how upset Isaac had been about Duguid's statement to the press. It might be kindness to hide the truth from his father. Later he could pretend to come down with some illness that would keep him from singing and then his father might never know. Wild fantasies prevailed in his mind as he sought to disguise the truth from Isaac.

'Well?' Isaac pressed. 'Have you been to see your Mr. Duguid? Did you make it up with him?'

'No, Pa. I saw him but I didn't make it up. I'm not with the Grand anymore.'

Isaac fell silent and walked with his head bowed. As much as he rued his folly for himself, Daniel regretted it twice as badly for his father. What did the old man have now? One son was a thousand miles away. And the son who had remained close — who had brought him pride and joy through singing — had deeply disappointed him. Isaac had nothing.

'So what do you plan to do?' Isaac asked. 'Are you and Anna all right for money?'

'Of course we're all right for money.' Why did everyone have to keep asking if he was solvent? Just because he'd lost the job didn't mean he was broke. And if he'd said he

187

desperately needed money, what would Isaac have done? Sold the house that Daniel had bought for him and moved back to an apartment?

'But you've got to do something with your life,' Isaac said. 'You can't just sit back and be idle. What will you do?'

'I wish I knew, Pa. I thought about trying the Met but that wouldn't work. I even went in there before, but the general manager, Mr. Bing, was unavailable.'

'Try again,' Isaac suggested.

Daniel shook his head. 'After the way I've fallen out with Duguid, the Met wouldn't touch me. Guess I'll have to go back to being a full-time cantor again.' He said the last sentence lightly, trying to coax a smile onto his father's troubled face.

'You know something, Daniel?' They reached the edge of the park and looked up and down the road before crossing. 'Ever since you got involved in this opera business, I've had a dream.'

'What about?'

'It was *La Juive* that killed Caruso. The strain of performing it. It's a very difficult role. I always wanted more than anything else to see you in the role of Eleazar, because I know in my heart that you would have done it better than Caruso. I've pictured it a million different times. And maybe, when the baby's bigger, Anna as Rachel.' He reached out and grasped Daniel's hand. 'Looks like it was just an old man's foolish dream, eh?'

Daniel felt a lump grow in his throat. He gulped a couple of times, forced it back so he could speak. 'The only reason you have dreams is so you can sit back and watch them come true,' he finally replied. 'Stick around so you can see this one come true as well.' Empty words to speak, he realised. Easy promises to make. Daniel knew it, and he was certain Isaac knew it, too.

'Then you'd better start doing something about it soon, Daniel,' his father said. He led the way into the house, holding open the door for his son. 'Were you serious about what you said before, going back to being a *chazan*?'

188

'Who knows? I've got to do something.' He spotted his mother in the kitchen. The garbage can was on the sink counter and Yetta was sorting through the torn-up scraps of paper, trying to piece them together.

'Will you look at her, Pa?' Daniel said. 'I tore up all that newspaper junk about Hollywood and she's busy trying to stick it all back together again.'

'Sure I am!' Yetta shot back, surprised at the sound of Daniel's voice because she had not heard the front door open. 'I want you to remember all those terrible things that happened to you there.'

'Yetta, Daniel doesn't need anything to remind him,' Isaac said quietly. 'He's paying enough for it.'

'How's he paying?' Yetta wanted to know. 'I'm the one who's paying. People look at me with pity in their eyes because they know I'm Daniel Kerr's mother. Better I should have died giving him birth than have to suffer this.'

Very deliberately Daniel turned away from his mother and patted Isaac gently on the shoulder. 'I'm going home. If I stick around here I'll say something we'll all be sorry for. I don't need it; neither do you.'

Understanding, Isaac followed him to the front door. 'Don't forget what I told you about *La Juive*, Daniel. I don't have that much longer for you to sort yourself out. I don't care whether you sing it with the Grand, with the Met or with some tiny company that doesn't even pay you. But please God, I get to hear you sing it just once.'

Daniel bent low and kissed his father. 'You will. Don't worry about it.'

While he drove back to Teaneck, Daniel tried to place his thoughts into some semblance of order. Top priority was finding something to do until he could get back into opera. Sure, there would be overseas offers, recording contracts should he want them. And *South Side Serenade* would be out the beginning of the year. But none of those could fill the loss left by Duguid's decision.

He needed something to fill his time completely.

As usual, he would be conducting the High Holy Day services at Temple Isaiah in Paterson. That was something to anticipate, but it would only last for a few days. Even if he did decide to return to being a full-time cantor — and he knew there would be no shortage of offers — the work would not have the same appeal, the same fulfilment that he gained from singing at the Grand.

Then he realised there was one occupation that would pass the time as sweetly as singing. He would be a full-time father to Little Benny. He would spend more time with his son than any father ever spent with any kid before.

CHAPTER ELEVEN

The Grand Opera Company opened the following season with Giacomo Puccini's *Turandot*, the first production attempted by Robin Duguid that was totally free of any influence from Roger Hammersley's tenure as general manager.

When the production had been planned originally, the tenor lead role of Calaf had been given to Daniel. It was a natural role for him, giving full rein to his strong, vibrant voice. At the time he had been offered Calaf, he had admitted that he was overjoyed; it was a role he wanted to sing above most others. But on opening night, instead of commanding the audience's attention from the centre of the stage, he was merely a member of that audience, sitting in the orchestra stalls with Anna, who continually pressed his hand in sympathy with his biting disappointment.

While he listened, he tried to pick holes in the performance of the tenor who had been given his part. He knew it was his frustration and self-directed anger that prodded him to seek flaws in the substitute singer. Some of the mistakes he was convinced he spotted were nonexistent. Only by continually telling himself that the tenor was not as good as himself however, was Daniel able to sit through the first two acts. In the third act, when Calaf began to sing 'Nessun Dorma,' Daniel could take no more. He stood up and apologised his way along the row until he reached the aisle. Then he walked quickly out of the auditorium and stood in the lobby until the performance was over and the crowd began to spill out. Stares of recognition were cast in his direction; greetings hailed his presence. He ignored them all while he waited for Anna, vaguely annoyed that she had not followed his example by walking out in the middle of the act.

'You should feel ashamed of yourself,' she laced into him when she joined him in the lobby. She kept her voice low so that no one would be able to overhear, but her anger was evident. 'If you didn't want to listen, you should have damned well stayed at home!'

'I couldn't take it anymore,' Daniel protested. 'That should have been me up there. I'd have done a better job.' She was right; he shouldn't have come, he reflected. He'd have done himself a favour by staying home and looking after Little Benny. He certainly would have gained more pleasure out of it. Attending the opening night had been Anna's idea. It was the best place to meet Robin Duguid, she'd said. To catch the general manager off guard. To get even the faintest hint that soon Daniel would be forgiven for his sins and welcomed back into the fold. If the opening night performance was a good one, Duguid would be in an expansive mood. Then would be the best time to face him.

'Do you want me to cancel our reservation in Wheeler's?' Anna asked.

'No.' If he had managed to sit through almost the entire opera, he could find the strength to eat in Wheeler's. The best chance he had of arranging an accidental meeting with Duguid was in the restaurant. Taking Anna's hand, he led her into Wheeler's. The maître d' greeted them effusively and showed them to their table by the window overlooking West Thirty-fourth Street; he treated them like valuable customers rather than former artists with the Grand.

Daniel sat down heavily in the chair that was held out for him and gazed through the window onto the street. Cars were being driven up to the Grand's entrance to pick up passengers. Tonight those people in the cars would be talking about another tenor, Daniel thought. And later on, when the maître d' brought around the reviews contained in the early editions of tomorrow's papers, he'd be dropping them off on someone else's table, making some other singer feel that his own personal oyster had just been popped open to reveal the biggest, brightest pearl in history. Daniel envied that man for his youth and enthusiasm. And he pitied him for his innocence, his inability to recognise the pitfalls that might beckon to him in the future.

Daniel turned from the window as the ovation he had once received rang out for the tenor who had substituted for him. Trying to demonstrate how magnanimous he was, he joined in. The simple action of applauding another singer brought an approving glance from Anna. She stretched a hand across the table and gripped his wrist lightly. 'They'll soon be doing it for you again,' she whispered confidently. Her eyes sparkled with the reflection of the restaurant's ornate chandeliers, and for a moment Daniel allowed himself to believe her words; it was easier that way.

'Keep telling me,' he said. 'Say it often enough and maybe it'll come true.' He returned to staring out the window, using the pane of glass as a mirror to see who else entered the restaurant. When he recognised Robin Duguid among a group of people, he did not turn around. The last thing he wanted was for Duguid to think he was waylaying him.

The general manager looked around Wheeler's, nodded politely to several diners, then spotted Anna and Daniel. Excusing himself from his own party, he made his way quickly over to the table for two by the window.

'I'm delighted you could make the opening night,' he said. 'What did you think of it?'

Daniel was uncertain how Duguid meant the question. Before he could decide to be charitable and tell Duguid it was one of the finest productions of *Turandot* he'd ever heard — even if he had walked out in the middle of the final act — Anna answered.

'Very enjoyable, Mr. Duguid. You've every reason to feel

proud. It was the most enjoyable opening night I can recall. Probably because I was watching it in comfort and not working,' she added brightly, which drew an approving chuckle from the general manager.

'Thank you. How's the baby?'

'Growing at an alarming rate,' Anna replied. 'We'll soon be bringing him along for an audition. He's got a pair of lungs you wouldn't believe, holds a note for an hour or more.'

Duguid smiled. 'Perhaps we'll be able to find him a slot as Cio-Cio-San's son in *Butterfly*.' He looked around for an empty chair. While his back was turned, Anna gestured at Daniel, urging him to become involved in the conversation. If he was serious about working his way back into Duguid's plans for the Grand, sullen silence was not the way to go about it.

'I was meaning to telephone you during the week,' Duguid said, pulling a chair up to the table and sitting down. Daniel's heart quickened until he realised the general manager was addressing his words solely to Anna. 'With the baby getting bigger, you must be thinking about resuming your career by now. Obviously I'd prefer that you resume it with the Grand.'

'Daniel and I have been discussing it,' Anna answered, determined to drag her still-silent husband into the conversation. How did he hope to show his repentance to Duguid if he didn't open his mouth? 'Definitely for next season.'

'I'm glad to hear that.' There was no mistaking the genuine sentiment in Duguid's voice. 'Just tell me when you're ready and I'll start arranging for your return.' He switched his attention to Daniel. 'How about your movie? That's coming out soon, isn't it?'

Daniel blinked in surprise at the question, amazed that Duguid would even mention *South Side Serenade*. 'Six weeks,' he murmured. 'There's a simultaneous opening in New York and Los Angeles.'

'Which one will you be attending?'

'New York. I've had more than my fill of Los Angeles.'

Duguid nodded as if he understood Daniel's meaning. 'And the songs?' he queried gently.

'The sound track's due out about one month later. After they see how the movie goes.'

'I must admit I'm quite looking forward to hearing the music. Should be really exceptional.' He nodded again, and Daniel did not know whether he was being sarcastic or just complimentary. In the end, he decided that Duguid was simply being his gentlemanly self. 'You'll have to excuse me now, but I have some people waiting.' He stood up and replaced the chair at the table from which he had taken it. 'Don't forget, Anna. The moment you decide you're ready to come back, let me know. Nice to see you as well, Daniel. Enjoy your meal.'

Daniel seethed while he watched Duguid walk away. The guy hadn't given him any kind of opening to use; not even the slimmest hint that he wanted Daniel back at the Grand with Anna.

'Why not send him a couple of tickets for the opening?' Anna suggested. 'He might appreciate the thought.'

Daniel continued to gaze after Duguid, willing the general manager to turn around and recognise the beseeching expression in his eyes. Duguid did not. He rejoined his party and sat down, involved in their company. 'Yeah, he'd appreciate the thought all right,' he eventually muttered. 'He'd think I was stringing him along, poking fun at him. He's no more interested in the movie or the sound track than I am in doing missionary work in Africa.'

'Then I'll send them to him.'

Daniel allowed a long weary sigh to escape. 'You do whatever you like.' He looked around for the waiter. What he wanted more than anything was a drink, a real drink that would make the throbbing in his stomach go away. Anna would never allow him to have one, though; he'd have to make do with a bottle of wine instead.

Anna sent two tickets to Robin Duguid which he

gracefully declined, stating prior commitments as his reason for refusal. If Anna was disappointed by the rejection, Daniel was not. He had expected no different response. Duguid would not be caught within five miles of the opening of *South Side Serenade*, a musical that featured a man who had been one of his leading tenors. Perhaps he'd sneak in when the movie was on general release, at a small theatre where no one would recognise him; but he would never dare go where the spotlight was certain to fall on him.

South Side Serenade never went on general release.

A preview for critics scheduled a week before the movie's double opening had been panned mercilessly, including one review that claimed it was the biggest mistake Carmel Studios had ever made. Daniel was particularly chagrined when Carmel subsequently slashed the promotional budget that had been allocated to the movie.

When Daniel went to the New York opening — accompanied by Anna, his parents, who had put off their annual Florida trip until February to attend the opening, and Moishe — he fidgeted uneasily in the seat for the entire two hours of the performance. His voice sounded fine and there was a sustained round of applause after 'Those Smiling Eyes' to the tune of 'M'appari,' but he could sense the first-night audience moving just as restlessly as he was. Even from his own subjective viewpoint, wanting to believe it was good, the movie was a disaster, nothing short of an amateurish parody of the type of film that had pushed Mario Lanza to instant fame. Daniel closed his eyes in relief as the credits came up at the end. He could almost hear the MGM top brass laughing themselves sick at Carmel Studios' puny challenge. The same top brass who had been intimidated to the point of panic, as Pomerantz had said.

The applause that greeted the end of the film was nothing more than polite. Daniel remained rooted in the seat, too embarrassed to stand up and take any credit. He wondered what Diane Orsini was doing over in Los Angeles. She'd stand up, that was for certain. She'd jump to her feet and wave around that oversized bosom, convinced that she'd just seen herself in the finest movie ever made. Regretfully Daniel conceded that every warning given to him had been well-founded. He had no place in this business.

'Sorry, Danny boy,' Moishe whispered as they left the cinema in an ominously silent group.

Daniel clapped him sympathetically on the shoulder. 'No fault of yours. Just bad judgement on my part.'

'But that one song sounded great,' Moishe carried on. 'Even if the movie's shit, that number'll make the top twenty.'

Daniel grinned, his mood momentarily lightened by Moishe's enthusiasm. 'I guess I should feel like a pitcher who got one strike-out while giving up ten grand slams. I'll have something to remember when I'm back on the farm team again.' He turned to his father. 'Let's have your two cents' worth.'

Isaac made a disparaging face. 'You want the truth or do you want to hear something nice? Daniel, it will take you twenty lifetimes to live this down. You've made yourself look like a fool.'

'Anyone else got anything to add?' Daniel asked. He could not understand why he was sounding so cheerful about the whole thing. It was nothing short of a tragedy and he was beginning to feel good about it. It was relief, that was it. He was grateful that the damned thing was over and done with. Now he could get on with living again.

'I think what your father said sums it up pretty well,' Anna replied. 'You swam a mile out of your depth and you almost drowned. Now you need artificial respiration.'

'You offering to give it to me?'

Anna shook her head. 'It's a job you've got to do on your own. Come on, let's get something to eat and go home.'

They selected a restaurant far away from the cinema. Even if Daniel had managed to come to terms with his own private catastrophe, he did not want to be recognised by anyone who might have seen the movie. That embarrassment would no doubt come later. Right now he wanted to fend it off for as long as possible.

Within four days, *South Side Serenade* was playing to half-empty movie houses on both coasts. After ten, it was brutally shoved aside and forgotten.

The recording company which was to have released the sound track debated the situation before deciding not to throw good money after bad. The sound track was abandoned.

Moishe visited Daniel in Teaneck to relay the latest bad news. Daniel accepted it stoically. There was no point in displaying animosity. He had resigned himself to *South Side Serenade* being one of the biggest bombs of all time, along with everything associated with it. He wondered how Duguid would react to the news. Would he laugh? Or would he just shake his head and congratulate himself because he had been right?

When Moishe left, Daniel went upstairs to the nursery and played with his son for half an hour. He took pleasure in changing the baby, proud that unlike many fathers, he was not above this necessary chore. Next season Anna would be singing again, and he'd be running the house. It would be his job to look after the child. Little Benny couldn't be left to the care of the housekeeper.

'Your old man's out of work, and he hasn't got a prospect in the world,' he said quietly to the uncomprehending baby he held on his lap. 'Are you ashamed of him? Do you want to change him in for a later model?'

The baby gurgled happily and Daniel smiled.

'Listen to your old man, kid. Don't grow up to be a movie star. Unless you've got a wife who can work to support you.' He laughed loudly, startling the child. 'Don't be a singer, either. Be something smart and sensible like a lawyer.' He thought about Moishe and shook his head. 'Don't be a lawyer either. Just marry a rich girl, then you won't have to worry.' With the utmost care, he placed the child in the crib, straightened the covers and went downstairs to find Anna in the kitchen.

'I've decided what I'm going to do,' he announced grandly.

198

She looked up from the pie crust she was rolling. 'About time. What is it?'

'It's a secret. I'll let you know when it happens.'

'Have you been smuggling a bottle up to the nursery?'

He forced his breath on her. 'Nothing, see?'

'So what are you going to do?' She finished off the piece of dough and placed it carefully on top of the apple pie.

'Take this season off to begin with.'

'Very good.' She carried on with preparing dinner, convinced that Daniel was not going to make any sense. The act he kept putting on to show how little he cared was becoming more extravagant with each airing; half the time he seemed to be rambling. It was a problem he would have to solve for himself, though. Following the conversation in Wheeler's with Duguid, Anna had been to see the general manager to discuss her return to the company for the next season. During their meeting, Duguid had made no mention of Daniel other than to say he was sorry the movie had failed. At no time had he asked Anna what Daniel planned to do; it was as if he had washed his hands completely of his wayward tenor.

'Aren't you even going to try and guess?' Daniel asked wanting to keep the conversation alive.

'I'm too busy,' Anna replied. 'When you decide, you'll let me know.' She looked up sharply as Daniel took his coat from the closet. 'Where are you going?'

'Over to the Bronx. To see my father.'

'Daniel, dinner will be ready in an hour. There's a roast in the oven. You can't go out now.'

He didn't take any notice of her protest. 'You eat. Leave mine in the oven. I won't be home late.'

She watched in despair as he left the house, then she popped the apple pie into the oven. She would wait for him to come back and hope he didn't return so late that the meal would be ruined. Would he even bother going to the Bronx to see his father? Or would he abandon the idea the moment he passed the nearest bar? She supposed she could leave Benjamin in the housekeeper's care while she toured around, seeing if she could spot Daniel's Cadillac in front of any bars. That was no use, though, she finally decided. Even if she found him, what could she do? Make a fool of herself by going into the bar and trying to persuade him to leave?

After half an hour she telephoned the house in Van Cortlandt Park. Yetta Kirschbaum answered. Yes, she said, Daniel was there. He was eating dinner while he and his father talked and listened to records. Anna put down the phone, went to the oven and took out the apple pie and the roast. Without a second thought, she threw the whole lot into the garbage. Then she went into the living room and turned on the television set. She'd kill him when he got home, she silently promised herself. She'd strangle him with her bare hands, smash in his skull with the rolling pin she'd been using on the apple pie crust.

Gradually her anger subsided. It was probably the best thing he could do, talk with his father. Maybe Isaac could make more sense out of what Daniel needed, be better able to give him the right advice, if Daniel would listen to advice from any quarter. At one time Anna thought she knew how Daniel's mind worked. Now she was no longer so certain. Despite the nonchalance he worked so hard to affect, this latest upset had taken away his drive, cut his legs out from underneath him. He had cushioned himself against losing his position with the Grand by being so certain that *South Side Serenade* would be a smash hit, open the doors for a new career. His optimism had been shattered, and Daniel was left to face the irrefutable truth that singing with the Grand was the only work he really wanted.

What disturbed Anna most was that Daniel had stopped practising. While he had continued, his vocalising had been a positive force. The sound of his voice ringing through the house had assured her that he was keeping trim like an athlete, always ready for that moment when Duguid picked him again for the team. His decision to stop seemed to Anna like he had given up the battle, resigned himself to believing that he would never return.

She telephoned the Kirschbaums again and asked to speak to Daniel. In the background she could hear a man's voice singing 'Celeste Aida.' She thought she recognised Richard Tucker. They must both be sitting there, Daniel and his father, listening to records, discussing the techniques of different singers. And they would both be agreeing that Daniel was better than any of them. If only someone had once had the courage to tell him that he wasn't. He'd spent his entire career being told by everyone — herself included — that he was brilliant. How could he not believe it?

Instead of Daniel coming to the phone, it was Isaac. He told Anna that his son had just left, as she rang. Anna asked if Daniel was on the way home. Isaac replied that he believed so. Anna thanked him and put down the receiver, willing herself to be patient until Daniel returned.

Daniel got home twenty-five minutes later. When she showed him the food she had thrown into the garbage can, he looked sheepish and explained that his parents had been sitting down to dinner when he arrived. He'd suddenly felt hungry. Her anger at him was tinged with relief that he had not stopped off at a bar.

'I'm going back to being a *chazan*,' he said. 'I talked it over with my father. I'll still be welcome in Paterson on a full-time basis.'

'Is that really what you want?' she asked, knowing it was not. She guessed Daniel had mentioned the idea to his father, and Isaac, thinking Daniel really wanted it, had encouraged him.

'It'll have to be, won't it? Until Duguid decides that I've done my time. If he ever decides that.'

'Daniel, for Christ's sake!' Anna's voice rose high above the level she'd intended as her frayed nerves began to show. 'What do you expect Duguid to do? Come crawling to you? Begging you to go back? Let me tell you something. There's only one Grand Opera Company, but there are a thousand tenors who can sing Rodolfo. Now you figure out who should go crawling to whom!'

201

'What do you mean by that?' In Anna's outburst Daniel recognised the erosion of her support.

'I mean exactly what I say. You need Robin Duguid a darned sight more than he needs you.' Tears sprang hotly to Anna's eyes as she, too, realised that she was pulling away the prop she'd promised him. She was betraying his trust, but how long was she supposed to put up with his refusal to face reality? 'Daniel, you're driving me crazy, you're ruining us, splitting us apart with your selfishness.' She watched him wilt under the barrage of words and felt ashamed of the savage delight that pulsed through her. She should have acted like this ages ago, cut Daniel down instead of pampering his ego. It would have done him more good than all the encouragement she'd offered. It would have made him see the truth.

Anna found it impossible to hold back now. It felt like floodgates had been opened; a safety valve finally turned to let out dangerous pressure in the system. 'I also want to go back to the Grand, Daniel. It's my career, too. But I'm suffering because you've got me worried sick about you all the goddamned time!' She paused only for the shallowest of breaths. 'Each time you walk out of that front door, I'm not sure whether you're going to come back under your own steam or whether you'll have to be pulled out of a bar!'

'Wait a minute!' he finally managed to yell back. 'Do you think I'm a wino, is that it? It's the pressure that's doing it to me, that's what! And you'd think I'd get a little bit of help from my wife, wouldn't you?'

Anna put her hand on her hips, threw back her head and laughed. 'Pressure? Do you think no one else suffers from it? Believe me, any pressure you've got right now is of your own making.'

Unwelcome parallels began to form in Daniel's mind as he faced Anna, stunned by the ferocity of her assault. One moment it was Anna he saw, the next it was Lucy and her attack on him after he had been relieved of his job at the B'nai Yeshurun in Washington Heights. Lucy had told him almost the same, accused him of mooning around at home instead of getting out and making things happen for himself. Why had he married an opera singer for the second time around? Didn't he learn enough of a lesson from the first miserable encounter?

Anna finally lowered her voice after realising too late that the housekeeper upstairs in her room must be hearing every word of the argument. 'Daniel, if you want to go back to being a *chazan,* go ahead. If you want to be a bus driver, go ahead. Do whatever you want to do. But please, for my sake, for Benjamin's sake, do something before you drive us all into the madhouse!' With that, she turned around and ran up the stairs. Seconds later, Daniel heard the bedroom door slam.

For the better part of fifteen minutes, he walked aimlessly around the living room while he ran the argument through in his mind, trying to spot what had triggered it. His eating out and causing Anna to throw away the meal she had been making? No. That he wanted to be a cantor again? He shook his head in bewilderment. Women, he thought; there was never any way of knowing which way they'd turn. No rhyme or reason to their actions. She'd stuck by him all this time, and now, when he had reached a decision, she was turning on him. Who could understand that kind of logic?

He walked across to the old mahogany secretary that he'd brought over from the Greenwich Village apartment and pulled out the scrapbook. If Anna didn't want to stand by him anymore, the words of praise the critics had written would give him all the support he would ever need. They'd show him he was right in waiting for Duguid to come to him. How could anyone who had received the acclaim he had be shut out of any opera house? Sooner or later, Duguid would realise it. He'd want Daniel back, and he would return on his own terms.

Reviews passed before his eyes as he read and reread of his many triumphs. Had any other lyric tenor gone back to being something like a cantor while he waited for the right opportunity to arise? Or had they chased endlessly after a general manager like Duguid until they were patted affectionately on the head, well-trained dogs that had learned to obey their master's bidding. He wasn't a well-trained dog. Duguid could contact him, otherwise it would be the Grand's loss and Temple Isaiah's gain.

He fell asleep in an armchair. After a while, the scrapbook dropped to the floor, its noise muffled by the thick broadloom, and he slumbered on undisturbed.

At breakfast the following morning, Anna passed no comment about the previous night's argument. Daniel ate sullenly, then went upstairs to play with Benjamin before showering. Shortly after ten o'clock, he walked through the entrance of Harry Feldman's real estate office in Paterson.

'Pleasant surprise,' Feldman exclaimed when he saw Daniel. 'Business or pleasure?'

'Business.' Daniel pulled up a chair and sat down opposite the temple president. 'How would you like a former opera singer as your full-time *chazan*?' He made the offer grandly, as if he were giving Feldman his greatest opportunity ever.

Feldman sat still for a moment while he thought over the question. He knew all about Daniel's troubles with the Grand; everyone in the congregation did. 'What about the *chazan* we've already got?' he asked. 'What do I do with him? Give him a month's pay in lieu of notice and say it's been nice to know you?'

Daniel opened his mouth to answer, then closed it again. He'd expected Feldman to jump at the offer; he hadn't counted on a negative question in return. 'I'm a million times better than he is. You know it and so do I.'

'Sure you are,' Feldman acknowledged. 'You've got one of the most beautiful voices I've ever heard. And so you should because you're an opera singer. That's where you belong. In an opera house.'

'I've had enough of opera,' Daniel protested. 'It's full of frauds, people who clap you on the back and stick a knife in you the next moment. I want to get back to what I love most of all.' He was forced to struggle hard to find the right words. He'd figured out what he would say to Feldman, just as he'd figured out how the temple president would jump at it. Only

Feldman had not been shown the same script. He wasn't jumping. He wasn't even walking slowly towards Daniel's offer. 'How come I'm okay to sing for you on *Rosh Hashanah* and *Yom Kippur,* but you don't want me back on a regular basis?'

'Because you're a celebrity. A celebrity as *chazan* for the *yomtovim* is a big draw,' Feldman explained, although he did not know why he was bothering. Daniel knew why they hired him for the High Holy Days. 'The *chazan* we've got now is singing for a living. Sure his voice isn't as sweet as yours, but he's doing it to support his family. And we can rely on this guy. He won't leave us the moment something breaks in his major field, because being a *chazan* is his major field.'

'I told you, Harry, I'm finished with the opera. Too many sharp characters, too little sincerity. I want to be a full-time *chazan* again.'

Feldman chuckled deeply. It annoyed Daniel even more than Anna's laughter had. 'Who are you trying to kid?' Feldman asked. 'You'd jump straight back into your so-called world of frauds the moment the opportunity arose. We'd be without a *chazan* again, and no one would touch us with a ten-foot pole because of the way we threw out our regular guy to make room for one of your whims. Besides, I don't think the *shul* can afford any more of those contracts your crazy lawyer friend would throw at us. I hate to think what his special clauses would be now.'

Daniel stood up and loomed over Feldman's desk. 'Is that so? You just wait until the next *Rosh Hashanah* and see what kind of crowd your regular *chazan* draws. All by himself. Because I won't be there to give your services a touch of class.'

To his further annoyance, Feldman continued to laugh. 'Daniel, do me a favour and get out of here before you ruin the day for me. Go back to your opera company, to your wife, to your baby. Just leave me alone. I've got work to do.'

Daniel stormed out the door and walked blindly back to where he had parked the car. Now they were laughing at him as well. He was an object of ridicule.

They could all go screw themselves!

Robin Duguid was poring over the Grand Opera Company's books with the accountant when his secretary entered the office to announce that a gentlemen was waiting to see him.

'He doesn't have an appointment, Mr. Duguid. But he says that it's very urgent.'

A brief expression of annoyance flitted across Duguid's face. He believed in appointments, just as he believed in running his personal and business life to a determined routine. Without it, you were lost. Routine, to Duguid, was the lifeline to sanity in a particularly insane business. 'Who is it and what's it all about?' he asked testily.

The secretary held out a business card.

Duguid took the card and scrutinized it. The expression of annoyance returned when he saw the words attorney-at-law under the name of Maurice Waterman. Lawyers always meant trouble. 'Who is this Mr. Waterman?'

The secretary took a deep breath. 'He says that he represents Daniel Kerr.'

Duguid nodded in sudden enlightenment. He had met Moishe at the housewarming party when Hammersley had introduced him as the Grand's next general manager. 'Tell him I can spare five minutes,' he said. 'In about half an hour if he wants to wait that long.' He turned back to the balance sheet.

The secretary returned to the reception area and passed Duguid's message onto Moishe. Moishe accepted it without any fuss. He had spent hours summoning up the courage to call on Duguid; he might as well wait for the man to find the time to see him.

Moishe thanked the secretary and sat back while he wondered exactly what he was doing in the opera house. Guilt hadn't pushed him into making the visit. He had done nothing to feel guilty about. Daniel had accepted Joel Pomerantz's proposal for making *South Side Serenade* with his eyes wide open. Sure he might have been temporarily blinded

206

by seductive visions of a rapid escalation to Hollywood stardom, but he was still old enough to recognise his own best course.

Like hell he was.

Despite any rationalisation, Moishe knew he did harbour guilt feelings. Daniel could always bring them out in you, like your mother. He was a big kid, that was all. You could push him this way and that just as long as the direction appealed to his ego; he'd walk down any dark tunnel if there was the slightest chance of finding applause at the end of it. And somehow he always made you feel you were to blame if something went wrong, even through his own fault. The only time Daniel did not try to pass the buck was when something turned out to be successful, and then he had done it all on his own.

Moishe sighed as he identified himself in the role of martyr. Daniel had blamed him for enough things before now; he should be used to it. It was his own fault as much as it was Daniel's because he usually accepted the blame and tried to find ways of correcting the situation. If you wanted to remain friends with a guy like Daniel, you had to be willing to carry the can for him. Did he want to remain friends? he suddenly asked himself. What was the point of even thinking about it? He'd been friends with Daniel for so long, helping him out of one jam or another, that life without him seemed almost unthinkable.

'Mr. Duguid will see you now, Mr. Waterman.'

Moishe looked up at the secretary, then down at his watch, surprised to find that twenty-five minutes had slipped away while he had been thinking over his long relationship with Daniel. He must have covered everything in those twenty-five minutes, the first meeting on the way to Joey Bloom's hotel in the mountains, through Larry Kahn and the radio station to the present time. Smiling at the memory, Moishe followed the secretary into Duguid's office.

'Mr. Waterman, nice to meet you again.' Duguid walked around the desk to greet his visitor, then he tempered the welcome with an immediate, 'I can give you five minutes and no more, I'm afraid. You've caught me at a very busy time.'

'Thank you.' Moishe was uncertain whether he had the time to sit down or not. Duguid pointed to a chair and Moishe took it. 'I've come here on Daniel Kerr's behalf, Mr. Duguid.'

'Yes?'

'He wants to come back to the Grand. He wants to sing here again.'

'Has he told you this?' Duguid began to look vaguely interested in what Moishe had to say.

'No. But you can see it. It's driving him nuts being out of here. It's not doing his family life any good either.'

'The last time I saw Daniel was in Wheeler's after our opening night production of *Turandot*,' Duguid interrupted, 'and I didn't get the impression he wanted to return. If anything, I received the opposite impression. Daniel couldn't seem to care less about the Grand.'

'He keeps it bottled up inside of him,' Moishe said quickly. 'That's the reason I'm here. To ask on his behalf what he's got to do to come back.'

'I see. So you're the errand boy, is that it?'

'Hardly,' Moishe answered and called himself a liar immediately. Of course he was the errand boy, even if Daniel had not sent him. He'd been Daniel's errand boy from the moment he'd first met him. 'He doesn't even know I'm here.'

Duguid studied Moishe for a long moment. 'If I set out the conditions and you relayed them to Daniel, would it make any difference? Would he accept them?'

Behind the thick glasses, Moishe's eyes widened as he saw a ray of hope in Duguid's words. There were conditions. Which meant the Grand would have him back. 'I believe so, Mr. Duguid. I just think he's too embarrassed to come here and ask you himself.'

'Embarrassed? High and mighty is a more accurate description,' Duguid pointed out. 'Never mind,' he added quickly, as if he regretted allowing his personal opinion to

208

slip out. 'Mr. Waterman, Daniel Kerr has never shown the slightest remorse for the way he acted. He made a fool out of himself, which he's perfectly free to do. But at the same time, he dragged the name of this opera company through the mud.'

'No one knows that more than Daniel does.' When Moishe saw Duguid sneak a look at the clock on the wall, he realised he was wasting time. Half of his allotted five minutes had passed and still he had not made any inroads. To hell with diplomacy, he decided, and asked straight out: 'What does Daniel have to do to return to the Grand?'

'The hardest thing of all,' Duguid replied.

'What's that?'

'He has to apologise to me.'

'That's all?' Moishe asked, amazed at the simplicity of the reply.

'That is all.' Duguid stood up. 'Now if you'll excuse me, Mr. Waterman, I have an opera company to manage. Thank you for dropping by. I found our talk most enlightening.'

Moishe stood up, shook Duguid's hand and left the office in a happy daze, a man who had discovered gold. Daniel was on the way back, and Moishe had found out the magic words, the open sesame for him.

By the time he reached the street, Moishe's euphoria had all but disappeared. The words would be anything but magic. Duguid hadn't been kidding when he'd said Daniel had to do the hardest thing of all. Getting Daniel to apologise for anything was like trying to squeeze blood out of a rock.

CHAPTER TWELVE

Moishe glanced nervously at the hands of his watch as they neared twelve-thirty. Any minute now he'd hear Daniel's voice outside, informing the receptionist that he had an appointment with Mr. Waterman. And Moishe didn't know what to tell him when he came in.

Following the meeting with Robin Duguid, Moishe had called Daniel. Instead of coming right out and admitting he had been to see the Grand's general manager, Moishe had suggested lunch the following day to discuss a business deal in which Daniel might be interested. Daniel had pressed him for details but Moishe had declined. There was no point in telling Daniel over the phone. Daniel would probably resent his intrusion, tell him to look after his own affairs. Face to face, though, he might have a better chance of explaining why he had been to see Duguid.

'Hi, I've got a lunch date with Mr. Waterman.' Daniel's voice filtered through Moishe's closed office door. Moishe stood up, straightened the jacket of his dark grey suit, slipped on his topcoat and prepared to leave.

The door opened and the receptionist stuck her head inside. Moishe nodded and came out to find Daniel standing by the woman's desk, huddled up inside a navy blue cashmere coat. The heavy coat made him look like an overstuffed teddy bear, and Moishe knew it wasn't just the coat that made him appear so bulky. Daniel had been trying to eat away his troubles again. Either that, or he was picking up all the extra calories from booze. As Yetta Kirschbaum had once been alarmed to discover, Moishe could see physical similarities between Daniel and his Uncle Benny.

'What's doing, Moishe?' Daniel greeted him. He enjoyed using his friend's familiar name in front of the receptionist, certain that it shocked her prim and proper outlook on how a lawyer should conduct his business.

'Not too much. What do you say to a bite on West Forty-seventh Street?' Now that the diamond business had all but moved from Canal Street to West Forty-seventh Street between Fifth and Sixth Avenues, Moishe liked to frequent the area. The constant nonstop bustle of activity never failed to fascinate him.

Daniel fell into step as they headed down the stairs to the street. 'Why walk all the way over there?' he complained, although it would take no more than five minutes. 'There's a good place downstairs. Great corned beef.'

Moishe knew Daniel was referring to the Irish bar a few yards away. He shook his head firmly. 'I don't like drinking at lunchtime. Kills the afternoon for me.'

'Who said anything about drinking?'

'I thought it might come up.' Moishe shoved his bare hands deep into the pockets of his coat and started to walk eastward towards Sixth Avenue. Daniel followed sullenly, his bright mood at anticipating Moishe's latest piece of lunacy already dampened. Since Harry Feldman had turned him down for a full-time cantor's position with Temple Isaiah, Daniel had been in a state of numb depression. Wandering around the house, going out for long, aimless drives which more often than not finished up in local bars, or sitting idly with Little Benny. Hearing Anna practise only served to make Daniel more despondent. Everyone was following a rewarding career while he was being squeezed out on all sides. When Moishe had called and mentioned a business deal, Daniel had sensed another wild scheme which, if nothing else, might temporarily relieve the monotony. Now Moishe wouldn't even have a drink with him.

211

The delicatessen into which Moishe led the way was crowded with lunchtime traffic from the diamond district. Anonymous men filled the tables, talking and eating simultaneously as if unwilling to allow a single second of the day to pass without accounting for it. Two overworked waitresses scurried among the tables, carrying orders from the counter, dirty plates, cups and cutlery back to the kitchen. Daniel found little to appeal to him in the activity that captivated Moishe. He stared moodily around the delicatessen, wishing they had gone to the bar instead.

'Let's get out of here,' he pleaded. 'It's too crowded for me. I feel claustrophobic.'

Moishe ignored the request. He spotted two men leaving a table and immediately pushed his way through. He and Daniel reached it one step ahead of two other men and sat down quickly, claiming the territory. 'What do you want to eat?' Moishe asked.

Deciding to make the best of an unavoidable situation, Daniel scanned the menu and selected a pastrami sandwich on rye and potato *latkes*. Moishe settled for only a sandwich and sat back, waiting for the order to be delivered.

'Okay, what's all this secrecy about?' Daniel asked impatiently. 'What's so big that you wouldn't mention it on the phone?'

Moishe passed a hand across his shining head while he debated how to answer. He decided on a delaying tactic.

'How's Anna? Benjamin?'

'Fine. They're fine. Just like they were when you asked me last night.' Daniel sounded like he was grumbling. 'You didn't drag me all the way down here to ask me that. What do you want?'

'Why are you so edgy?'

'Edgy? You're crazy.'

The order came before Daniel could say any more. He watched helplessly as Moishe started on the sandwich, without making any attempt to explain the reason for the meeting.

Moishe's jaw worked automatically as he consumed the sandwich. Then he turned his attention to a bowl of pickled cucumbers in the centre of the table. Only when the coffee arrived did he decide to end Daniel's wait. 'You working at all?'

'You know damned well I'm not. What ideas have you got?'

'What about Feldman and Temple Isaiah?' When Daniel had mentioned returning to the temple, Moishe had not thought much of the idea. Those days were over for Daniel. Being a cantor would be a stopgap measure at best, something to keep him occupied until another opportunity opened up.

'I didn't bother in the end,' Daniel lied. Moishe didn't have to know that Feldman was not interested, that he'd seen right through Daniel's reason for asking.

'You want to go back to the Grand?' Moishe asked quietly.

If he had lit a firecracker under Daniel's chair, he could not have received a sharper, more startled response. 'Do I?' Daniel almost leaped to his feet, spilling coffee onto the table as his hand knocked against the cup. 'If you know how I can do that, let me in on it!'

Moishe took a deep breath and pushed his glasses to the top of his nose. 'I met Robin Duguid yesterday,' he began.

'Where?' Daniel wanted to know. 'How? Did he have anything to say about me?'

Moishe held up a hand for Daniel to stop. 'I didn't meet him by accident.'

Daniel looked confused. 'What do you mean you didn't meet him by accident? Did you go up there to see him? To his office at the Grand?' The questions were tinged with disbelief.

Moishe nodded. 'I went up to his office. He gave me five minutes. It was all I needed.'

'Needed for what?'

'To find out his conditions for allowing you back with the company.'

Daniel stared across the table, at first uncomprehending. Then his face reddened as his anger grew. 'You asked Duguid what he wants me to do before he'll allow me back? What goddamned business is it of yours?'

213

'Do you want to go back or not?' Moishe snapped.

'Of course I damned well want to go back! But I'll do it my way when I'm good and ready. I don't need other people sticking their noses in for me!'

'What is your way? Eating yourself sick until you're the size of a zeppelin?' Moishe injected his own anger into the questions as he tried to deflate Daniel's dangerous complacency. 'Drinking yourself into a sponge?'

'Is that what Duguid said about me? Or is that just your expert opinion?' Daniel demanded loudly. A waitress passing by the table looked nervously at the two men as their voices rose.

'All Duguid said is that he wants a personal apology from you. Nothing more. That's his sole condition for allowing you back. Seems reasonable to me.'

'An apology for what?'

'For making a fool of yourself and denigrating the company.'

Daniel pushed back the chair and stood up. In one furious motion, he pulled on the cashmere topcoat and started to stride away from the table. When he had gone five yards, he swung around, face almost crimson, finger shaking with rage as he pointed it at Moishe. 'You see him again!' he shouted across the delicatessen. 'You tell him he can kiss my ass! The same goes for you, too! You keep your face out of my goddamned business from now on! You've cost me too much already!'

Moishe shuddered and closed his eyes as if the simple action would make all the curious faces in the delicatessen disappear. When he could bear to open his eyes again, Daniel had disappeared. The delicatessen was back to normal, the momentary disturbance swallowed up and forgotten in the normal run of activity.

'Anything else for you, honey?' the waitress asked as she cleared the table.

'Just the check,' Moishe muttered. He leaned back in the chair while he tried to decide what to do next. The most attractive alternative was to drop the matter altogether. If Daniel was hell bent on hanging himself, no one had the right to stop him. He had picked up the pieces for Daniel too many times already; maybe they were better off being left where they fell.

Two minutes later, after he had paid the check and left the delicatessen, Moishe was exploring other possibilities, and by the time he had reached his office, his mind was made up. He'd give it one more try. If Daniel accused him of sticking his nose where it wasn't wanted because he had seen Robin Duguid, God alone knew what he'd accuse him of once he'd spoken to Anna.

The housekeeper answered the phone and asked Moishe to wait. Anna sounded surprised and worried when she came on the line. Daniel was meeting Moishe for lunch; was something wrong?

Using the barest minimum of words, Moishe explained what had happened during his meeting with Duguid and what had followed when he'd tried to tell Daniel that Duguid wanted nothing more than an apology to heal the wounds.

'Why do you stand by him?' Anna asked when Moishe had finished.

The unexpected question floored Moishe. He'd asked himself the same thing dozens of times and had never yet come up with a satisfactory answer. 'I need a regular dose of aggravation,' he replied flippantly. 'Daniel makes me realise how sane the rest of the world is.'

'Or maybe you're like all of us,' Anna suggested, 'and you care more about him than he does himself.'

Moishe smiled thinly at Anna's words. It was the story of Daniel's life for as long as he'd known him. There had always been someone around to help Daniel to his feet; he found himself wondering where Daniel would have wound up if he'd been on his own. 'Will you talk to him about it?' he asked.

'I guess I don't have much choice, do I? You've dropped the ball fair and square in my lap.'

'Thanks. You might have more luck than me.'

'Don't bet on it.' Anna started to put down the receiver, then she stopped. 'Are you still there, Moishe?'

'Yes.'

'Thanks for calling. I mean it. Thanks a lot for everything.'

Daniel did not return home until almost eight in the evening. Anna did not have to be told where he'd been; she could smell it on his breath. She asked if he had eaten, and he replied he'd had dinner in the city. Then she questioned him about the lunch date with Moishe.

'Some *meshuggeh* idea he's got,' Daniel shrugged off the question. 'You know what Moishe's like. I can do without his brainwaves.'

'Is an apology to Mr. Duguid so crazy?'

Daniel's eyes narrowed. 'Who said anything about an apology to Duguid? Oh, I get it. Bigmouth called here, did he?'

'Right after you screamed at him in the delicatessen. Is that all your beautiful voice is good for now, yelling abuse at people who try to help you?'

Daniel stamped away. Anna grabbed him by the arm and spun him round with a force she never knew she possessed. Her eyes were blazing when she looked into his face. 'If you're so desperate to kill yourself, why do it the hard way? Why don't you just take a loaded gun and blow your brains out? Put us all out of our misery!'

'Leave me alone, will you?' He tried to escape from her grip. She held on tenaciously, refusing to let him go. She didn't have to be a psychologist to know that Daniel was purposely punishing himself by holding out against Duguid. Punishing himself for some wrong — real or imagined; she didn't know — by refusing to take what he wanted most. Perhaps it was his own way of exacting retribution against himself for *South Side Serenade,* because he'd known all along he was doing the wrong thing. When he'd hurt himself enough, he'd look around and decide it was time to stop. Then and only then would he go to Duguid. Or would he just carry on because he was bent on destroying himself completely?

'Daniel, you might hate yourself right now, but do you care about me? Do you care anything about Benjamin? Do you?'

'Of course I do!' he snapped back.

'Then will you damned well start acting like you do?'

'I am not apologising to Robin Duguid or to anyone else!' he shouted. 'He can come to me!' With a savage tug, he tore himself loose of Anna's grasp and stormed out of the house, leaving the front door wide open to let in the wintry wind.

When he returned home after midnight, a strange car was sitting in the driveway. Daniel got out of the Cadillac and examined the blue Chevrolet, curious to know what it was doing there. He saw the New York plates and realised it belonged to Moishe..

What was he doing in the house? Hatching up more mischief with Anna?

The knowledge that Anna was still awake sobered Daniel. He had expected her to be sleeping when he returned, but the living room light was shining in the darkness of the street. Anna would be in there with Moishe; they were ganging up on him now. They'd both want to know where he'd been. He wasn't ashamed to tell them. He'd been sitting in a bar in Hoboken, down at the water's edge, drinking and talking with seamen. They had made more sense to him than his own family and friends.

'What the hell are you doing here?' he growled when he saw Moishe sitting alone in the living room. 'Where's Anna? Upstairs?'

'She's not here, Daniel.'

Daniel did not seem to notice it was one of the few times Moishe had ever called him by his full name. 'What do you mean she's not here?'

'Nobody's here but me.' Moishe stood up, ready for the onslaught he knew would greet his next words. 'Anna's taken Benjamin with her. I drove them and your housekeeper to a hotel in New York. They're not coming back.'

'What? You slimy, four-eyed sonofabitch!' Daniel closed the gap in two large strides. Moishe saw the punch coming and tried to duck. He never had a chance. Daniel's right fist grazed the side of his face and sent him staggering backwards, knocking his glasses into the air. As Moishe tried to regain his balance, Daniel brought over the left. It smacked solidly into Moishe's mouth, splitting his lips, smashing them back onto his teeth.

The sickly-sweet taste of his own blood was adrenalin to Moishe's system. He swung his arms furiously, aiming blindly in Daniel's direction, aching to feel his fists pound savagely into flesh. Years of frustration, years of playing straight man to Daniel's clown, lent energy to the wild punches. Daniel stepped back in amazement, dodging the punches with ease. If he had not been so mad at Moishe, he'd have laughed. Moishe wasn't a scrapper. He was a bookworm, a milquetoast. He'd fight you with words. With jokes. With cunning. Never with his fists.

'You self-centred bastard!' Moishe yelled at the indistinct figure in front of him. He whirled his arms like a windmill and landed a glancing blow on Daniel's shoulder. 'Don't you ever think of anyone but your fucking self?'

Another punch thudded into Daniel's arm as he stood perfectly still, at last providing a target that Moishe could identify without his glasses. Daniel moved only to dodge the roundhouse right that whistled dangerously towards his head, then he grabbed hold of Moishe's arms, pinioning them to his sides. 'Hold on, will you, for Christ's sake? You'll kill yourself!'

'Since when do you fucking care?' Moishe lashed out with his foot, surprising Daniel as the shoe thudded painfully against his shin. 'Since when are you concerned about anything but your own damned self? You couldn't give a shit about anyone! About Anna! About me! Even about Lucy!' The foot swung again and Daniel jumped back, releasing Moishe's arms in his haste to dodge the kick.

'You killed Lucy because you didn't give a shit about her!' Moishe screamed.

Black rage enveloped Daniel at the accusation. Feet planted firmly on the ground, he slammed his fist into Moishe's face. The punch landed just below Moishe's right eye and toppled him backwards. He sat down in the middle of the carpet, spitting blood from the earlier blow. He shook his head and tried to lever himself up.

Daniel looked down at him, suddenly horrified by what he had done, even more frightened that Moishe would struggle to his feet to continue the fight. 'Don't get up, Moishe. Please.'

'Fuck you! I'm not jumping out of any windows just to please you.' With an almighty shove, Moishe staggered to his feet. 'You didn't like hearing the truth about Lucy, did you?' It was torture to form the words. He didn't care because he knew hearing them would hurt Daniel even more. Whoever wrote that sticks and stones could hurt your bones but names would never harm you was full of crap. Moishe knew the taunts he was yelling were going through Daniel like red hot knives. 'You think Lucy jumped? You pushed her!'

'Shut up!' Daniel yelled. 'Do you hear me? Shut up before I kill you!'

'Now you're trying to do the same thing to Anna. I won't let you. That's why I took her away. One Lucy was enough!'

Daniel's fist exploded like a shell burst in the centre of Moishe's face. Arms flailing for balance, Moishe fell across an armchair, tipped it over and hit the floor with a sickening crash. A groan escaped from his mouth as the breath was driven out of him. His body wriggled sluggishly like a crushed worm.

'Moishe?' Daniel's head cleared. 'Moishe?' He ran across the room and knelt down beside the prostrate figure. 'Are you all right?' He turned Moishe's face upward and felt sick when he saw the smashed lips and nose, the large bruise that was already puffing up the right eye.

Moishe groaned again. No recognition showed in his eyes. His breath erupted in ragged, painful gasps. Daniel stood up slowly, unable to tear his terrified gaze away from the destruction he had wrought. He could not believe he'd done it. Couldn't understand why. Just as he was unable to comprehend why Moishe would throw up all those terrible lies about Lucy. Daniel felt like a man living through a nightmare which had somehow managed to make itself real, found the back door of his mind to invade his very existence.

He spotted Moishe's glasses lying on the carpet and picked them up. One lens was smashed. 'Here's your glasses,' he said quietly, kneeling down again. 'I'll pay to get them repaired.'

Moishe's eyes blinked and Daniel stepped away. He stopped by the living room door long enough to look back once more, willing himself to believe that Moishe was all right. Then he fled from the house, dived into the car and tore up the street in a protesting scream of skidding tyres.

Lying on the floor, still dazed by that final blow, Moishe was barely aware of the sound of the Cadillac accelerating along the street. He was confused, trying to piece everything together. The fight — if a fight it had been — and his own screaming rage at Daniel. For the first time since that night in the Deuces Wild in Harlem, when he had jumped on the back of the man attacking Daniel, Moishe had resorted to violence. He'd lost, but what had he expected to do against someone of Daniel's physique? Using fists was almost second nature to Daniel. Winning, though, had been a secondary concern to Moishe. Most importantly, he had shown Daniel that he wasn't scared of standing up to him.

He reached out for the glasses and slipped them on. The smashed lens covered his puffy eye. As he struggled to his feet, leaning heavily on the overturned armchair, a staccato hammering came from the front door. Unsteadily Moishe walked towards the noise. He opened the door a crack and saw a police officer standing outside, face illuminated by the porch light.

'Mr. Kerr?'

Moishe shook his head. 'He's not here,' he mumbled through swollen lips. He ran the tip of his tongue along his top teeth and felt jagged edges; two of them were broken.

The police officer peered closer, suspicious when he saw the smashed spectacles, bleeding nose and mouth. 'Who are you?'

'I thought I was a friend of Mr. Kerr. I guess I was mistaken.' He opened the door wider and allowed the policeman into the house.

The policeman looked around the living room, noticing the overturned chair, the total disarray. 'We had a report of a disturbance. A neighbour complained.'

Despite the pain, Moishe managed to smile. 'Your disturbance just left.'

220

'Everything all right?' the police officer asked. 'Nothing you want to tell me?' He hoped there wasn't. It was a cold night and he wanted to get to the all-night diner half a mile away for a cup of coffee and a cigarette.

'Nothing at all,' Moishe said, to the man's relief. He held the front door open and followed the policeman out.

Daniel pressed down the bell on the front door of the house in Van Cortlandt Park. All the lights were out, but his parents would hear him. He'd keep on ringing the damned bell until they woke up.

Ten seconds passed, and he added to the noise by banging on the door with his clenched fist. A light came on in the front bedroom. Drapes were pulled back. Daniel saw his mother's face peering out into the night. He stepped back and waved for her to open the door. The drape fell back into place and other lights began to glow. He rang the bell again and the door opened. Yetta stood facing him, dragging a heavy woollen dressing gown around herself.

'What's the matter, you wake everyone up this time of night?'

'I want to speak to Pa.' He pushed his way past Yetta and walked into the living room.

Yetta followed him, annoyance at being woken up yielding to curiosity. She thought she'd smelled liquor on his breath as he'd walked past her.

On the stairs, Daniel heard his father's slippered tread. He waited for Isaac to enter, then said, 'Anna's left me. Taken the baby and cleared off.'

'What?' The single word of disbelief came simultaneously from both Isaac and Yetta as they stared in horror at their son.

'She's gone to some hotel in New York. Moishe took them and the housekeeper.'

'How come Moishe?' Isaac asked.

'Because . . . oh, I don't know,' Daniel finished lamely. He'd caught himself just in time from heaping all the blame on Moishe's shoulders, just like he always did. 'I suppose Anna called him up while I was out.'

'Where were you?' Yetta asked. 'In some bar?'

'Yes, I was,' Daniel replied belligerently. 'Is there something wrong with that?'

Isaac rubbed the sleep from his eyes and tied up the belt of his dressing gown. 'Why did she leave you?'

'Because I've been making her life a goddamned misery, I suppose.' He turned angrily to his mother. 'That's what you're waiting to hear, isn't it? That I've been on the skids ever since I got slung out of the Grand?'

'From your own mouth you admit it,' Yetta said. 'Why should I say anything?'

'Which hotel?' Isaac asked quickly. He felt dizzy at being woken up. An argument between his wife and son would only make him feel worse.

'I don't know. Moishe was waiting for me at the house. He told me he'd taken them, but he wouldn't say where.'

'Why did you come here?' Yetta asked. 'If you're so concerned about Anna and Benjamin, why aren't you trying the hotels?'

Concerned! Moishe had used the same word, asked him why he was suddenly concerned about anyone else. Now his mother was using it. 'Do you think I don't give a damn about anyone either?' Daniel snapped at her. 'Yeah, that's it! You're just like Moishe. You all think I couldn't give a shit about anyone but myself.'

Yetta stood her ground silently at the outburst, but Isaac was shaken. 'Is that what Moishe told you?' he asked quietly. 'Or did Anna tell him to say that?'

Daniel turned on his father, ready to attack him as well. He couldn't. The strength seemed to drain right out of him, leaving his body weak and limp.

'You've been friends with Moishe since you were fourteen,' Isaac pointed out. 'It's part of a friend's duty to tell the truth, as painful as it is. If he tries to protect you from the truth, hide it from you, then he's not a real friend.'

Confronted by his father's reasoning, Daniel slumped into a chair. Before his eyes danced an image of Moishe staggering back from that final punch, the shattered face, the smashed glasses on the floor. How long had Moishe bottled up his feelings? Kept them inside as he had struggled to maintain the friendship? Tonight they had spilled over. Moishe had seen all along what Daniel had refused to acknowledge. That he was hurting everyone — not just himself — in his selfish quest for vindication at the Grand. He'd driven Anna to distraction, left her despairing just as surely as he had left Lucy in torment. After giving up trying to communicate with him, Anna had turned to Moishe, hoping that he would be able to make Daniel understand.

'Pa, will you come out with me? Try a few hotels? Persuade her to come back if we can find her?'

Despite his own weakness, Isaac nodded. 'I'll get dressed.'

He turned away to trudge upstairs to the bedroom when Yetta called him back. 'You'll do no such thing. It's freezing cold outside and you're not going to make yourself ill because of his foolishness. There's the phone.' She pointed to the instrument. 'Let him phone the hotels. You don't have to go out with him.'

Isaac opened his mouth to argue, but Daniel saw the sense in his mother's suggestion. 'Okay, Pa. You pick the hotels from the directory and I'll call them.'

'You sure?' Isaac asked, relieved that he would not have to go out.

'Sure.' Daniel already had the receiver in his hand.

Watching, Yetta nodded her approval. 'I'll make you some coffee,' she offered. 'You might be here a long time.'

From the window of her room in the Statler Hilton on Seventh Avenue, Anna looked out over Penn Station and thought about the phone call she'd just had from Moishe. His words had been almost inaudible, a sudden attack of toothache, he'd explained. He'd told her that he'd waited until Daniel arrived home and informed him that Anna had left with Benjamin and the housekeeper. Moishe made no mention of the fight, or of the police coming. He finished up by saying that Daniel had left in the car.

Anna turned her gaze to the crib the hotel had provided. Benjamin slept soundly, undisturbed by the night's panic; the housekeeper, too, in the suite's other bedroom. Anna supposed Daniel would come looking for her. She wished

223

him luck. She'd taken steps to prevent his discovery of where she was by registering in the name of Wasserman, a nice little touch suggested by Moishe.

Daniel. She repeated his name quietly while she wondered what to do. Leaving him permanently never crossed her mind. She knew she would go back to the house in Teaneck, to Daniel. But before she returned, she wanted him to suffer a dose of the medicine he'd been handing out. Eating humble pie might do him a world of good, give him a more honest perspective. Perhaps he would have had a better outlook already if he had struggled the way she had, started with smaller parts until she'd attained a reputation by hard work. It had all come too easily for Daniel. Now, faced with a real crisis, he did not know how to cope.

She remembered writing that first letter of apology for him. She'd be damned if she'd do it again.

Isaac Kirschbaum felt the first twinges of pain in his chest when he read out the eighteenth hotel for Daniel to try. He excused himself and went upstairs to the bedroom for his white pills. Yetta was sleeping, having divorced herself from the crisis. Isaac looked at her still form for an instant before slipping one of the pills under his tongue and quietly returning downstairs. He was just in time to hear Daniel ask one night clerk if the hotel had anyone registered under the name of Anna Markova, Markowitz or Kerr. Again the answer was no and Daniel slammed down the receiver in disgust.

'I bet that sonofabitch is putting her up at his apartment,' he cursed, totally oblivious of his father's discomfort.

'So call there and find out.' Isaac settled carefully into a chair, the Manhattan telephone directory balanced on his knees. He did not approve of his son's language, especially when it concerned Moishe. How long would it take Daniel to realise that in Moishe he had one friend he could trust?

'No. Give me another hotel.' He watched his father trace the names with his forefinger, seeming to take forever. 'Come on, Pa! We haven't even done twenty yet!'

'Daniel' — Isaac closed the book and let it drop heavily to the floor — 'all of a sudden I don't feel so good.'

'What?'

'I just took a pill. It hasn't helped.' Even as he spoke, Isaac's face grew paler.

'Do you want another one?'

Isaac pointed to the ceiling. 'I don't think I can manage the stairs. I left the pills in the bedroom.'

Daniel's senses sharpened. He forgot all about the phone calls to the hotels, all about Anna and Benjamin. He leaped from the chair and took the stairs three at a time, feet pounding with the urgency of his fear. Forgetting that his mother was asleep in the room, he turned on the light.

'What's going on?' Yetta asked, sitting up in bed.

Daniel didn't bother to answer. He searched feverishly through his father's clothes until he spotted the small brown bottle on the night table. He grabbed the bottle and raced from the room. Yetta climbed out of bed, put on her dressing gown and followed him downstairs in time to see him uncap the bottle and pass a pill to Isaac, who hastily slipped it underneath his tongue.

'What's the matter?' Yetta screamed. 'Are you killing him as well with your madness?'

Daniel spun around. 'I didn't do anything!'

'What do you mean you didn't do anything? You dragged us all out of bed in the middle of the night, got your father all excited, with his heart and all. And you did nothing?' She stepped closer. Isaac's eyes were closed as he fought against the constriction in his chest. Yetta wasted no time. She picked up the receiver and dialled the local doctor. Too bad if he was asleep; he got paid to heal, not to sleep.

The doctor arrived within fifteen minutes, jacket and topcoat thrown hastily over his pyjama top. He checked Isaac's pulse and heartbeat, then peered into his eyes.

'Nothing to worry about,' he assured Yetta and Daniel. 'Just to make sure, though, I'll get him into hospital.' He used the phone to call for an ambulance, then returned to the patient. Colour was returning to Isaac's face. His breathing had evened out, as if the pills had finally achieved their objective.

'Is it another attack?' Daniel asked.

225

'A spasm, that's all. But they can check him out far better in the hospital than I can here. Heartbeat and pulse seem normal.'

The ambulance from Montefiore drew up outside the house ten minutes later. The doctor followed the attendants outside while Daniel remained in the living room with his mother. 'I'll come by for you in the morning,' he said. 'We'll both go to see him.'

'Before you go near him again, you make sure you've sorted out this business with Anna,' Yetta warned.

It came as something of a revelation to Daniel that after all these years, his mother was really concerned about his father.

It was almost dawn when Daniel arrived home. He put the Cadillac away in the garage next to Anna's car and started for the house. Surprise struck him when he saw the open front door and deepened when he stepped inside the house. Chairs were overturned, furniture was in disarray. Then he remembered the fight with Moishe. This must have been how he had left the house, and Moishe had gone immediately afterwards, forgetting to close the door.

Then Daniel looked at the mantelpiece over the fireplace. Two heavy silver candlesticks given to him and Anna as wedding presents had disappeared. Suspicion darkened his mind and he began to explore further. Other ornaments were missing, the silver *bucha,* with which he made *Kiddush* every Friday night, silver dishes, an inscribed gold plate which had been presented to Anna and himself after their opening night in *La Bohème* the previous season. He ran upstairs to the master bedroom. Drawers had been pulled out, the mattress pulled off the bed. Anna's jewellery box had been rifled. His gold cuff links were gone. And worst of all, Fat Benny's gold watch was missing.

The house had been burglarised.

Without looking any further, Daniel returned downstairs, straightened one of the chairs and sat down. Then he leaned back and simply stared blankly ahead in the silent room, his mind replaying the day's events — and Moishe's accusations — until he was numbed by them.

226

CHAPTER THIRTEEN

At seven the following morning, Moishe was frying eggs in the small kitchen of his apartment when the phone rang. He turned down the gas and answered. When he recognised Daniel's voice, he made himself ready for a continuation of hostilities by pushing his spare pair of glasses up to the bridge of his nose.

'What do you want now?' He would have done better to stay watching the eggs. This sonofabitch was going to ruin his breakfast as well. He ran his tongue across the two broken teeth and tenderly touched his broken nose.

'I want to apologise for last night,' Daniel said meekly.

'You do, do you?' Moishe didn't know whether the feel of his own injuries, the obscured vision through his closed eye or Daniel's humility was giving him the courage to be aggressive. It didn't matter. On the phone he could say whatever he liked and not risk getting his lights punched out. 'What makes you think I give a shit whether you're sorry or not?'

'Because I need your help.'

'Huh?' Moishe couldn't help himself. This wasn't Daniel talking. It was Daniel's voice, sure, but the sentiments did not belong to him.

'I need your help,' Daniel repeated. 'I want to know where Anna and Benjamin are. My father's in the hospital again. And on top of all that, you didn't close the door when you left last night. The house got cleaned out.'

227

'Got what?' Moishe was glad Daniel was miles away because he could not stop himself from letting out a satisfied laugh.

'Cleaned out. Robbed. You left the door open and someone walked off with half the house.'

'Serves you goddamned right, asshole.'

'Never mind about that. Just tell me where Anna is.'

'I can't.'

'You can't or you won't?'

'Won't, then. Not till you straighten yourself out with your stupid opera company. I promised Anna I wouldn't.'

Daniel considered threats and discarded them. Moishe wasn't scared of him; he'd proved that the previous night. 'Screw you, too, Buddy.' There was a long pause, then Daniel said, 'Listen, I'm going to Montefiore to see my father this afternoon. He's in there because he got upset over Anna . . . over me. I don't want to see him before I've got everything straightened out.'

'Then you'd better start off by seeing your friend Duguid. Because that's the only place for you to start.' And Moishe hung up the receiver.

Daniel sat back in the chair and wondered what to do next. He supposed he should call the police about the burglary but the loss of material possessions was furthest from his mind. The loss of his family concerned him most. And the loss of Moishe as a friend. Not that he didn't deserve to lose them all. He'd gone out of his way to alienate everyone, that was for sure.

An apology, that's what Moishe said Duguid wanted. A simple apology. What was so terrible about that? Did it make him any less of a singer to apologise? Any less of a man?

Daniel recalled that Duguid liked to be first into the office every morning. He like the feeling of having the opera house almost to himself at least once a day, even if only for a few minutes. Probably a dreamer, Daniel had once decided. Stands up on the stage when there's no one present and pretends he's Rodolfo or Canio. Pretends he's me.

228

Dreamer or not, this would be one morning Duguid would be disappointed. Because Daniel would be there before him.

Robin Duguid walked along the corridor from the reception area to his own office and stopped dead when he saw Daniel standing by the door. He recovered quickly and produced the key to his office.

'Good morning, Daniel. Something I can do for you?'

'Yes, sir. I'd like to talk to you if you can spare me a few minutes.'

'Come in.' Duguid led the way into the office and pointed to a chair. 'Make yourself comfortable.' He hung up his coat and sat down behind the desk, facing his visitor. There was no need to ask what Daniel wanted. Duguid could tell. Following the visit Duguid had received from Moishe, Daniel could be in the office for only one reason. The rebel had finally realised his error and had come to ask forgiveness. In his moment of triumph, Duguid knew no sensation of righteousness. All he could feel was relief.

'I'd like to come back to the Grand, Mr. Duguid.'

'Yes?' The general manager made up his mind to offer no help. The apology had to come from Daniel, without any assistance from anyone else.

'I made a mistake with that movie. I wanted to get out of it, but I couldn't without getting entangled with a million lawsuits.' Daniel hesitated and looked hopefully across the desk. Duguid's expression was cool, an indication that Daniel had not gone far enough.

'I want to apologise for the way I let the company down, Mr. Duguid. And to ask you to consider lifting your ban on me.'

Duguid pursed his lips thoughtfully. 'Thank you, Daniel. I promise I'll consider it.'

Daniel debated whether to add anything else. As far as he was concerned, he'd said more than enough already. Nonetheless, he could see that Duguid remained unconvinced of his sincerity. He supposed he could throw himself on the general manager's mercy, tell him about his father's hospitalisation, about Anna taking the baby and leaving him. But his pride had suffered enough already; he had no intention of dragging himself lower.

'Yes,' Duguid repeated. 'I'll consider it.'

'I promise there'll be no repeat performances,' Daniel blurted out.

For the first time in the meeting, Duguid smiled. 'I'm certain there won't. From what I saw of your reviews for *South Side Serenade,* Carmel Studios wouldn't touch you again.'

'They weren't very good, were they?' Daniel admitted. He began to find it easier to talk. The bridge between himself and Duguid had been crossed, the apology made. Now they were talking as equals. 'They even killed the soundtrack.'

'So I heard. A pity, because I would rather have liked to hear the music, to learn whether it's possible to anglicise and modernise opera,' Duguid admitted. He stood up and Daniel followed suit, convinced that the meeting was already at an end. No doubt Duguid would inform his board that Daniel had made amends. Then there would be a message — probably a letter because Duguid believed in formality — asking him to come in for contract discussions regarding next season. Daniel didn't even know what productions were being planned for next season. Anna would, though; she'd be making her comeback then. Anna. He had to see her as well, tell her about the meeting with Duguid, persuade her that he had done enough.

As he started to walk towards the door, Duguid called him back. 'On the subject of reviews, you might have noticed that our *Turandots* haven't been faring very well either.'

Daniel stopped and turned around, stomach twisting, praying that his mind was not playing tricks by imagining what was not there. 'I didn't read them,' he lied.

'They were terrible, take my word for it.' Duguid smiled thinly as he saw through Daniel's denial. Of course Daniel would have read them; and he would have laughed over them. Duguid was glad to see the tact in Daniel's answer; it was another sign of his sincerity. 'You will sing Calaf for this Saturday's matinée performance.'

Daniel understood how much the offer meant to Duguid. *Turandot* was the general manager's first solo production at the Grand. Although the opening night performance had received reviews that were polite more than complimentary, the two performances since then had been panned. Critics had complained that the young tenor singing Calaf possessed a voice that was too thin. Furthermore, the Saturday afternoon performances were broadcast live on the radio. Duguid wanted the best at his disposal for the broadcast; with one outstanding performance, he would be able to salvage the production from the previous ravages of the critics. 'Thank you, Mr. Duguid. I can handle the role. I won't let you down.'

'I'm certain you won't.' Duguid held out his hand to seal the bargain. 'The last time we shook hands it was on a rather sombre note. This time we're both happier in our minds that an honourable settlement has been reached. Welcome back.'

Daniel grabbed the hand, scared that it might be withdrawn and the offer with it. His apology had been accepted, his return assured. All he had to do now was convince Anna.

He left the opera house and drove the few blocks north to Times Square. The receptionist in the law office recognised him and asked him to take a seat while she checked whether Mr. Waterman was busy. Daniel fidgeted awkwardly while he waited. Finally the woman reappeared and told him to go in.

Moishe was staring out of the window, his back to the door. Hearing Daniel enter he turned around. Two purple eyes gazed out mournfully from behind the spare pair of glasses; one eye was almost completely closed. 'See what you did, asshole!' he greeted Daniel. 'And this!' He stepped close to Daniel and touched his nose gently, to show where it had been broken. 'I'm going to need a goddamned nose job, thanks to you. And this as well!' He opened his mouth to display the two broken front teeth and the battered lips.

'Serves you right you got robbed. Pity they didn't take you as well.'

Daniel held up his hands in a gesture of peace. 'I'll pay to get your teeth capped,' he promised. 'I'll pay to get your nose straightened. Don't worry about it.'

'And the glasses you smashed. Don't forget the glasses. Those frames set me back a fortune.'

'I'll buy you a hundred pairs of glasses, a whole store! Just tell me where Anna is.'

'What about Duguid?'

'I just came from there. I'm in *Turandot* for this Saturday's matinee performance.'

Moishe studied Daniel's face, searching for the truth.

'If you don't believe me, call the Grand and ask!' Daniel grabbed the phone. Fingers fumbling in their haste, he spun the dial.

'Grand Opera Company box office,' a woman's voice answered.

'Who's in *Turandot* for Saturday's matinee?' He held the receiver between himself and Moishe so they could both hear.

'Just a moment, sir, I'll check.' The woman came back an instant later. 'There's been a cast change, sir. Daniel Kerr will be returning to sing Calaf.'

'Thank you.'

'Statler Hilton,' Moishe said. 'She's registered under the name of' — he began to smile — 'Anna Wasserman.'

No wonder he'd had no luck the previous night when he'd called the Statler Hilton. Anna Wasserman. What was it, a private joke on Moishe's part? Or wishful thinking? 'Thanks, I'll speak to you later.'

'What about your father?' Moishe called after him.

'I'm going up there right after I've seen Anna. I'll take her with me. That's the best medicine he could get.'

'Good luck!' Moishe called out. He meant it. The unpleasantness of the night was over. If it had taken getting the hell beaten out of him to set Daniel straight with his career and Anna, it was worth it. He called out to the receptionist to set up an appointment with the dentist. If Daniel was paying, Moishe wouldn't settle for having the broken teeth simply capped.

He'd have gold.

Anna was playing with the baby when she heard the urgent rapping on the door. She put down the child and listened carefully. The knock did not sound like someone from the hotel. Or Moishe; he would have telephoned. It could only be Daniel.

'Yes?' she called out.

'Anna, it's me. I want to speak to you.'

'Who told you I was here?'

'Moishe. I've been to see Duguid. Everything's straightened out.'

Wanting to believe him, she opened the door. He pushed in gently and put his arms around her. She was surprised to see tears glistening wetly in his eyes. Then he looked past her to his son. 'I've come to take you all home,' Daniel said. 'And to say sorry for the way I've been carrying on.'

''What about Mr. Duguid?'

'I saw him first thing this morning. We're friends now. I'm in *Turandot* this Saturday.'

'The radio broadcast? That's only three days away. You'd better get your voice in shape, make sure you know the role. There's no time for rehearsals. We'll start as soon as we get back to the house,' she said quickly, her enthusiasm mounting.

Daniel shook his head and told her they first had to go to the hospital. She looked shocked when he explained that his father had been taken ill again.

'Whenever I have a bust-up, he's the one who always suffers.'

Then he told Anna the house had been burglarised while he'd been out searching for her. She started to grin, then covered her face with her hands as laughter rippled through her.

'Thank God we're insured,' she finally managed to say.

233

'We're not. I forgot to renew the policy.'
She laughed even harder.

Once the housekeeper had been sent back to New Jersey with the baby in a taxi, Anna and Daniel drove up to the Bronx. They picked up Yetta and continued to Montefiore Hospital. Isaac was sitting up in bed, looking cheerful when they entered. He saw Anna and waved excitedly, beckoning for her to come closer.

'You malingering again?' she asked brightly. 'A young man like you spending all this time in bed! Shame on you!'

'Ah!' Isaac said in disgust. 'I'm protesting, that's all. When Daniel sings again, I'll get out of bed to hear him.'

'You'd better hurry up and find your clothes, then,' Anna told him. 'He's in the Grand's Saturday afternoon broadcast performance.'

'*Turandot*,' Daniel explained. 'I had a meeting with Robin Duguid first thing this morning and we're all squared away.'

'You sure you can step into the part after being away for so long?' Isaac wanted to know.

Daniel nodded instantly. Despite the confident way he'd assured Duguid he could handle the role, the same anxieties were plaguing him. He'd be damned if he'd let his father know, however.

'Good,' Isaac said. He turned to the man in the next bed. 'I won't be in this lousy place come Saturday, but you make sure you listen to my son, Daniel Kerr, on the Grand Opera broadcast. Okay?'

The man looked bemused but said he would.

CHAPTER FOURTEEN

Isaac had to be helped by Anna and Yetta to his seat in the circle on Saturday afternoon. The doctor had been loath to discharge him from Montefiore. Isaac had argued and had finally signed a waiver of responsibility. He still felt weak and could not walk without the aid of a cane. Nevertheless, he was determined not to miss his son's return performance.

He sat down and looked around the almost empty auditorium. Only a scattering of people had so far taken their seats. The performance was not due to begin for another forty-five minutes, and Isaac was struck by the awesome silence of the opera house when it was empty. It allowed his imagination to play tricks, to lift the heavy gold curtain and impose his own characters on the stage, in his own opera. He could see Daniel playing Eleazar in *La Juive,* with Anna as Rachel. Closing his eyes, Isaac offered up a prayer to God that he might live long enough to see that production. It was just a wish, though. One that he felt would not be fulfilled. Daniel had never made any serious mention of wanting to perform the role. It was a killer. Look what it had done to Caruso! And the Grand, to Isaac's knowledge, had never discussed the feasibility of resurrecting it.

If they did a production of *La Juive,* it would have to be soon, Isaac knew. He'd kidded Daniel about it. Told him he'd have to hurry with the part if he wanted his father to see it. Only it wasn't really a joke. Despite the way he'd walked out of Montefiore Hospital, telling the doctor he felt as sprightly as a two-year-old, Isaac knew his heart was failing. He'd worked too hard, seen too much sorrow for it to be any other way. The other night hadn't helped either, although he would never blame Daniel for the second attack. Daniel had come to the one person he trusted the most, his father. How could a father refuse to help his son? He'd have gone willingly into the cold to search for Anna if Daniel had thought it would help.

Anna's voice intruded on his thoughts. 'I'm going backstage to be with Daniel.'

Isaac smiled at her. He knew how hard Anna had worked with Daniel over the past three days to prepare him for this return. She had told Isaac when Daniel had stopped vocalising, ceased practising in the depths of his depression. The sessions with Anna had been long and painful, with Daniel constantly complaining that he had lost his voice. Anna had persisted, going over the score again and again until she was satisfied. Daniel was like an athlete deciding to come out of retirement to run against the best in a mile race, and giving himself only three days to tone his body to peak fitness. Maybe he wouldn't win the race, but Anna had made damned sure he'd finish in style.

'Tell him I'm praying for him,' Isaac said.

'I will.' She walked away, leaving Isaac and Yetta alone in the circle, two solitary figures in the vastness of the auditorium. When she reached the exit, she looked back and could barely make out their shapes. She hurried to the dressing rooms and found Daniel sitting disconsolately in front of the mirror, already in costume and make-up.

'What's the matter?'

'Worried,' was the one-word reply.

'What about?' She pulled up a chair and sat down next to him. 'This is your big chance to kill them stone-dead. You've got no cause to be worried.'

He turned to look at her, his face frightened behind the false beard and heavy make-up. 'I'm more scared than ever

236

of going out there. Scared I'll forget the words, miss a note, fall over a loose prop and break my neck. Everything.'

'Don't be ridiculous. You wanted to come back. Now you're back. Come on, it's time to do your exercises.'

Feeling like a man preparing for the scaffold, Daniel stood up and began to vocalise. Despite knowing his voice sounded almost as clear as it ever had, he could not shake off a feeling of impending catastrophe. Surely his vocal cords must have suffered from the abuse he'd subjected them to. Duguid should have given him more time, not just three days' notice. If something went wrong, it wouldn't be his fault but Duguid's. Only it would be Daniel whom the critics would lambast. Or was that what Duguid was hoping for? That he'd make a fool of himself?

'It sounds fine to me, Daniel,' Anna said, listening carefully. 'Don't even think about the opera. Just think about afterwards, when everyone will be on your side again and *South Side Serenade* will have been forgotten.'

Daniel grew more confident as he listened to her words.

'Think about Benjamin. He's waiting for you at home. He's expecting a hero to come back.'

'And what about you?'

'Think about me as well. And your parents. Moishe too.'

Instead, Daniel thought briefly about the two shots of whisky he'd always enjoyed before a performance. There was none today. Anna made sure of that.

He stood in front of the mirror, thinking about what she had said. He breathed in deeply and puffed out his chest. The nervous tension still ran through his body but now he knew how to cope.

At two o'clock, Moishe tuned in for the radio broadcast of *Turandot*. He didn't have the slightest idea what the words meant. He wasn't even sure about the story. All he wanted to do was listen to Daniel's voice, to learn if he could live through the holocaust he'd created for himself.

He held his breath as Daniel's voice first came from the radio speaker. The snatches of music, short duets, told him

237

nothing. He waited patiently for one aria, 'Non piangere, Liù,' when he would be able to decide if Daniel had retained the quality.

When the aria began, Moishe sat up tensely, eyes closed, fists clenched as he willed Daniel to succeed. The voice coming from the radio started off uncertainly and Moishe cursed. Then it seemed to gather strength and sweetness as the aria continued. At last, it coalesced into the silver clear and vibrantly warm tenor that Moishe had always associated with Daniel.

'Sonofabitch!' he yelled triumphantly into the apartment, eyes gleaming in the triumph he felt for his friend. 'That sonofabitch did it!'

He leaped off the chair and jumped into the air, yelling encouragement at the radio. He'd call Daniel that night and drive over to the house. They'd all have dinner together. It would be just like old times.

During the intermission preceding the third act, Isaac allowed his eyelids to droop. He sensed rather than saw other members of the audience moving about him as they went outside for refreshments or a smoke. He was too tired to move. He wanted to conserve his strength for the last act, the most enjoyable of the entire opera as far as Isaac was concerned. Daniel was beyond comparison with Caruso now. Caruso had died before Puccini wrote *Turandot*. For once, Isaac knew that his judgment would not be clouded with comparisons.

He heard applause as the conductor returned to his rostrum. The noise grew in volume as the conductor signalled the entire orchestra to stand. Isaac opened his eyes again, mind refreshed by the short rest. He glanced sideways at Yetta, whose eyes were riveted on the stage.

'Enjoying it?' he asked.

'He's lucky,' Yetta said. 'All that he did to himself and they've given him another chance. He should get down on his knees and thank everyone.'

Isaac smiled and turned to Anna. 'What do you think?'

'He's singing like an angel.' He was — he was singing as well, if not better than she had ever heard him. He'd started hesitantly and she'd caught him looking towards the prompter's box a few times. Then he'd picked up strength, gathering it from the rest of the cast, the audience, the opera house itself, until he'd broken free of his bonds during 'Non piangere, Liù.'

Anna's description satisfied Isaac. He knew there were no angels, but if there were, they would sound like Daniel did this afternoon.

The curtain lifted and the final act began. Isaac felt the warm wetness of a tear beginning to form in his right eye. He made no attempt to stop its flow. It rolled down his cheek and caught the corner of his mouth. He could taste the salt. Too late he pulled out a handkerchief and dabbed at his eyes. With the passage of the first tear, the flow had grown. He put away the handkerchief and let the tears fall unchecked.

So what if people saw him cry? They'd seen him cry during *Bohème*. It wouldn't do them any harm to see him cry again.

The orchestra's triumphant refrain thundered in on the final *'Vincero!'* of 'Nessun dorma' and Daniel did something he had never done before. Disregarding the discipline that had been drummed into him by Roger Hammersley, he faced the audience and took a solemn bow.

The audience responded to the unexpected action by increasing the volume of its ovation. Daniel glanced swiftly at the orchestra. The musicians had set aside their instruments and were joining in! Welcoming him home by sharing in the audience's applause! He caught the eye of the conductor. Daniel nodded and the man lifted his baton, ready to end the applause and continue the act.

Then, from somewhere in the circle, a woman screamed.

Anna clapped her hands enthusiastically when Daniel bowed. He'd broken the Grand's tradition and got away with it. Capped his successful return by doing what no one else dared to do. Accept applause by taking a bow. Her gaze

239

strayed to Duguid's private box. The light in the box was on and Anna could see Duguid and his party. All were clapping; two of the women in the box were even standing, calling praise down onto the stage. Anna had known Duguid would let Daniel get away with the bow. The prodigal son had returned home duly repentant. He'd turned in a performance that would never be forgotten. And at the same time he'd shown that he still wasn't above tweaking a few noses.

She turned her head a fraction to look at Daniel's parents. Yetta was applauding, a formal action that held none of the spontaneity others were injecting into the ovation. It was a major aria, and major arias were always applauded; so Yetta was applauding. It was as simple as that. Then Anna looked at her father-in-law. At first, she was curious why he was doing nothing. She had heard him sniff, seen the tears start at the beginning of the act. The show of emotion was understandable. She'd even felt like crying herself. Was Isaac so overcome now that he couldn't even clap his hands?

She looked closer. Isaac's cheeks were glistening from the tears, but his head was bowed as if he were praying. She reached out and took his hand. As she pulled it towards herself, Isaac's body toppled in the seat and fell against her.

It was then she screamed.

Robin Duguid stood uncomfortably in front of the closed gold curtain and looked out into the darkness of the auditorium. He was unused to such silence. Whenever he had walked out into this position before, his appearance in the spotlight had always been greeted with groans of displeasure because the audience knew he had to announce that a leading singer would not be playing the role advertised. The general manager only appeared with bad tidings.

'Ladies and gentlemen,' Duguid began quietly, wondering if they could hear him in the rear of the balcony. 'On April the twenty-fifth, 1926, when *Turandot* was first performed at La Scala, in Milan, the conductor was Arturo Toscanini. On that occasion, he laid down his baton in the third act after the death of Liù and said to the audience: "Here at this point, Giacomo Puccini broke off his work. Death on this occasion was stronger than art." Today, unfortunately, death is again stronger than art.

'As some of you may now be aware, Mr. Kerr's father has passed away during this performance. Although Mr. Kerr has professed willingness to continue with the final act, it is my feeling that it would be most respectful if we emulated Maestro Toscanini. Thank you all very much for listening to me. Good day.'

Duguid stayed in front of the curtain while he watched members of the audience rise and begin to leave the suddenly silent auditorium. Then he turned away and walked quickly up the stairs to the dressing room.

Daniel couldn't feel a thing. From the moment he had heard the scream of horror from the circle, his world had collapsed. Even without knowing who had screamed, some inner sense had warned him that he would be affected.

There had been immediate consternation in the audience. The lights had come on and he'd looked up to the circle where his parents and Anna were sitting. He'd spotted the green of Anna's long dress as she bent over his father. Attendants had come cascading down the aisle. He had followed the drama from the stage, now part of the audience to another production. A man's voice — Daniel supposed it was one of the attendants — had yelled down that it was his father. He had jumped off the stage, rushed through the orchestra pit and raced up the stairs to the circle. A doctor was already there, a woman who had been sitting in the row behind. When Daniel pushed his way through the throng of people, the woman had looked at him with despair in her eyes.

He remembered telling Duguid that he would carry on. God knows how he would have managed it, though. He barely had the strength to return to the dressing room and fall into the chair. They would have had to carry him back to the stage. Duguid had rejected the idea immediately, before going onstage to announce the abrupt termination of the performance. Daniel was grateful to the general manager; it hadn't even crossed Duguid's mind to let the understudy complete the final act. If Isaac knew that his passing had been elevated to the level of Puccini's, he'd be thrilled, Daniel reflected.

'The ambulance has come.'

Anna's soft voice made Daniel look up. Her face was tear-stained, a mirror of his own. He had made no attempt to check the tears that had started as soon as he'd arrived in the circle and seen the woman doctor's face. 'My mother?' he asked.

'She went with him.' Anna watched him warily, guessing the tumult in his mind . . . that Isaac's death had been caused by the way Daniel had behaved; or by the way she'd left him that night, taking the baby. Daniel always had to find a reason for everything bad that happened to him. Anna wondered which way he would swing.

He reached out suddenly, grasped her around the waist and buried his face in her breasts. She could feel him shake, feel the dampness of his tears as they penetrated the fabric of her dress. Before he could say a word, she knew he was taking the blame all on his own.

'That goddamned stupid movie!' he cursed. 'All because I took that goddamned stupid offer! If I hadn't gone, none of this would have happened.' His grip become tighter until it threatened to crush the breath out of her. She let him hold on, gazing up at the white-painted ceiling until at last she closed her eyes.

'Stop it, Daniel,' she whispered. 'Don't say that.'

He didn't seem to hear her. He kept repeating over and over 'That goddamned movie!' until at last the words became quiet, less distinct.

A knock sounded on the dressing room door. Gently Anna eased herself out of Daniel's arms and walked slowly to the door. 'Who is it?'

'Robin Duguid. May I come in?'

Anna turned around to look at Daniel. His head was on the dressing table top as he sobbed quietly into his arms. She opened the door a fraction and looked out. 'What do you want?'

'How is he?' Duguid tried to look past Anna. She blocked his view.

'Upset. Is it something important?'

Duguid shook his head. 'Tell him if he needs anything to contact me. I'm sorry.'

'Thank you.' She closed the door and returned to Daniel. 'I think we'd better go. Your mother also needs you.'

Daniel raised his head from the table and looked at Anna through red-rimmed eyes. He understood that she felt the shock as deeply as he did and looked for some way to ease her grief; his own as well. Finally he pointed to Calaf's costume that he still wore and to the make-up on his face. 'Do you think I should change before we go? Or should I go like this?'

A feeling of unity passed between them at his words. Anna held out both hands. He took them, brushing them against his lips. Thank God he had Anna. He couldn't even begin to think what this would be like without her.

The house in Teaneck was crowded. Daniel, his brother Jack who had flown in from Chicago for the funeral, and Yetta Kirschbaum sat on small wooden chairs, accepting condolences from visitors.

The *shivah* period was in its third day. Evening prayers had just finished and everyone was sitting down. Cups of coffee were appearing, passed around as the housekeeper took charge of the kitchen. Daniel tried to spot Anna, wanting to ask her how the baby was. He could not see her and guessed she was in the kitchen, helping the housekeeper.

Since the funeral, Yetta had hardly spoken a word to him. When he had followed her to the hospital on the day of Isaac's death, she'd hysterically accused him of causing it. Anna had stepped in quickly, leading Daniel away, knowing how troubled he was already by the possibility. During the funeral — at the same New Jersey cemetery where Fat Benny and Tessie were buried — Yetta had remained aloof to all that was taking place around her. Daniel had cried. So had Jack.

243

Tears were the only bond between them; otherwise they treated each other as strangers, polite exchanges of words about work and family.

Daniel looked up as a cup of coffee was passed to him. Moishe was acting as waiter, eyes still purple, nose swollen, teeth still broken. He gave a weak, encouraging smile as he passed across the cup and touched Daniel's hand lightly. Daniel nodded his thanks, knowing how grateful he should feel to Moishe. Old reliable. Always there when you need him; and sometimes when you reckoned you didn't. The thought brought a slight smile to Daniel's face. Moishe had been waiting inside the house when they had arrived home on Saturday night. He had heard the commotion over the radio and rushed to the opera house to find that everyone had already left. No one could tell him which hospital Daniel had gone to, so he had driven to Teaneck to wait there, the offer to help in any way he could springing from his lips the moment Daniel and Anna arrived there.

'I'll take your mother home tonight,' Moishe offered, as he had done every night. Yetta refused to stay in Teaneck. Both Daniel and Anna had insisted, but Yetta had firmly rejected the idea. She had her own home; she was perfectly capable of taking care of herself. The sentiment was new to Daniel's ears. This was a moment when his mother should be bringing into play every act she could, every frailty that would assure her of attention. Instead, she was backing away. He was certain he knew why. She did blame him for Isaac's death. It hadn't been just hysteria that had made her shriek at him in the hospital. She'd meant it.

Because of it, Daniel felt sorry for his brother. Not wanting his mother to be alone in the house, he had sent Jack with her each night. As a dutiful son, Jack had gone. Daniel knew he had not been happy about the chore. What would happen when Jack flew back to Chicago and his own family at the end of the *shivah* was anyone's guess, Daniel decided. He had a career to get on with again. Anna also had her career.

And they both had a child to share.

BOOK 2

LA JUIVE

CHAPTER ONE

Richard Milhous Nixon and John Fitzgerald Kennedy were dominating the news again. Daniel was getting sick of the sight of the two names. No matter which newspaper he read, which radio programme he listened to, which television station he watched, the names of the two presidential candidates plagued him. Even the New York Board of Rabbis was getting into the act now, according to the story on the front page of that Saturday's New York *Times*.

A man's religion had never been a factor in a presidential race before, Daniel thought, while he read about the rabbis deploring any attempts to inject religious conflict into the current campaign. To his memory, though, the country had never had a major Catholic candidate either. If Kennedy got the vote two months in the future, the country would have its first Catholic president. Good luck to him, Daniel decided, knowing he'd probably vote for the Massachusetts senator. Just give us all a break from the damned thing.

He flicked through the newspaper. Miami was getting slammed by Hurricane Donna. He wondered if his mother was all right and prayed that the weather did not get so bad that she would come back up north. He'd done the clever thing by shipping her off to Miami where she could sit and chatter all day long with other old women and stay out of his hair.

Kennedy and Nixon. There they were again, on page ten,

a story about the television and radio debates they would have. What were the political campaigns of the country becoming? A three-ring circus?

Eager to escape, he moved on to the sports page, past the results from the Rome Olympics. A smile lit his face. The Yankees were doing it again, beating the Tigers, 4-1, to get within a half game of the league-leading Orioles. He'd have to take Benjamin to a Yankee game one of these days. The kid was old enough now to understand what was going on, and he had been promising him. He'd wait till Maris or Mantle hit one a mile, then he'd casually tell Benjamin about Ruth and Gehrig. How they used to bunt that far.

Thinking of Benjamin, Daniel put down the newspaper and left the den, looking for his son. The kid should be almost ready by now, all dressed up for his regular Saturday morning visit to the temple. Daniel did not understand where Benjamin had inherited his religious zeal; certainly not from himself or Anna. Although he no longer conducted High Holy Day services at Temple Isaiah in Paterson, Daniel attended services in the local temple in Teaneck. But he had never shown the ardent love for religion that his young son did. Ever since Daniel had first taken him, the kid had been turned on by the history of the Jews and by the tradition of their religion. Hebrew classes, which Daniel had loathed when he was Benjamin's age, were like an outing to the shore for his son. At nine years old he could stand up in the *shul* and take the service all by himself.

Daniel called Benjamin's name. His son's high voice came back from upstairs; he was still getting dressed. Daniel grinned. The kid was like this every *Shabbos* morning, a bridegroom making certain that every last detail was perfect before he finally met his bride. Still grinning, he returned to the den to continue reading the newspaper until Benjamin was ready.

He glanced quickly, disinterestedly, at some more stories. Nikita Khrushchev was on his way to New York to head the Soviet Union's delegation to the United States. The *mamzer* should take a *misse meshinah,* Daniel wished;

drop dead before his boat ever docks in New York.

His attention was attracted by a British movie called *Carry on Nurse*. After perusing the report, Daniel decided not to bother seeing it.

A familiar face on page twenty-one startled his eyes. The three words 'Italian Operatic Roles' shrieked at him from the top left hand corner. Daniel stopped turning pages. A choking sensation enveloped him. A pounding started in his head and chest as he read the complete headline:

Jussi Bjoerling of Met is Dead;
Noted for Italian Operatic Roles

Bjoerling was dead at forty-nine, swept away in his summer home on the island of Siar Oe, in the Stockholm Archipelago, by the third of a swift succession of heart attacks.

Daniel felt dazed as he read and reread the lengthy story in the *Times*. The uncomfortable knowledge of his own mortality brushed against him for an instant and he shuddered. Bjoerling had been only four years older than himself. Now the voice that had thrilled a worldwide audience for thirty years was still.

He heard the door of the den open and looked around. His son stood in the doorway, sparkling clean, dressed in a short-trousered grey suit. 'I'm ready to go, Pa.'

Suddenly Daniel did not feel like taking Benjamin to the temple. He did not feel like moving out of the chair. He wanted to sit, to be alone with his memories, to think about the death of his contemporary, the man who had been one of his inspirations to become an opera singer himself. 'Ask your mother to walk you down to the *shul*, will you, Benny? I don't feel so good.'

Daniel felt guilty at disappointing the kid. At the same time, he knew he was robbing himself of one of the pleasures of being a father. He enjoyed the times he went to the temple with Benjamin, the short walk where they would talk about baseball, about school, about anything; it did not matter just as long as they talked. Then, in the temple, he'd get a huge kick out of witnessing his son's enjoyment, the total absorption in the service and everything around him. If he went this morning, though, Daniel knew he would be silent throughout the service, too caught up with the tragic news to communicate anything but grief.

'What's the matter with you?' Anna asked after Benjamin had relayed the message.

'This. Take a look at it.' He held up page twenty-one for Anna to see. She sucked in her breath in shock as she read of Bjoerling's death.

'So young,' she murmured. 'Such a terrible waste.'

Daniel understood what she meant. The *Times* report had not mentioned it, but the stories of Bjoerling's drinking problems were almost legendary. The insecurity that had plagued him, particularly towards the end of his career. The abrupt dives into the bottle as if he could find the answers there. Daniel had come close enough to know how it felt. He had been lucky, though. He had managed to make the return journey.

He heard the front door close as Anna left the house with Benjamin. From the kitchen came the noise of the housekeeper cleaning up after breakfast. Daniel paid no attention, his mind riveted on one subject. With Bjoerling gone, who was left? Tucker and Peerce, the brothers-in-law. Del Monaco. Bergonzi. Di Stefano. Himself. Three Italians and three New York Jews. And Gedda, a Russian-Swede. And soon how many of those tenors would be left? And who would take their places? More cantors? More Italians?

Roger Hammersley was also dead, another heart attack victim. So was Harry Feldman from Paterson; when he had died, Daniel had ceased to conduct the High Holy Days services at Temple Isaiah. Gigli was dead as well. Many of the father figures, the men Daniel had looked up to or tried to emulate had died during the fifties, just like his own father. Now Bjoerling had started off the sixties in the same manner. Daniel allowed himself the luxury of becoming maudlin while he wondered who would still be around when the seventies began. His mother? If she was, she'd be in her middle-eighties. Somehow the knowledge that Yetta Kirschbaum would probably die before the end of the decade did not bother Daniel. She was living in Miami with money he sent her each month in addition to her Social Security. If he saw her once a year, it was a lot. When she needed anything, she telephoned him. And when the Grand's tour encompassed Florida, she always expected free tickets to each performance so she could point Daniel out to her friends. Daniel felt that being on show like that was a small price to pay for not seeing his mother for the remainder of the year.

Daniel thought about Martinelli, retired from his practice in Milan. The last time they had met was two years earlier, when Anna and Benjamin had accompanied him to Milan where he had sung Radames in *Aïda* at La Scala. Martinelli had shared the honours of the performance after Daniel had insisted on introducing the doctor from the stage as the man who had been instrumental in making him select an operatic career. Martinelli had loved it; so had the audience and the Italian press. Now Daniel was forced to think about Martinelli in another, darker light. Would the last of the people who had been responsible for his career be alive when the sixties ended?

He thought about Moishe as well. Would that clown be around when the sixties passed into history? And finally, reluctantly, he focused on himself. Would Daniel Kerr be alive when the big ball dropped in Times Square to celebrate the birth of 1970? Of course he would; he laughed at his own fears. Life without himself wasn't possible. Then he realised that Bjoerling had probably thought the same thing only a year earlier, before the heart attacks had started to shake his faith.

Daniel's mood of weeping sentimentality changed slowly to regret. There was really so little time left and so many things to do. At forty-five, his life was well past the halfway mark and he had not done one tenth of the things he'd promised himself he would do. There were still countless roles he wanted to perform, places he wanted to visit, stages

251

upon which he wanted to sing. He had started late, that was the trouble; he had let too many years elapse. If only he could have known earlier what he wanted to do with his life. All that precious time wasted, playing the clubs with Moishe. Even the years spent on the *bima* praising God had been wasted; he could see that now. He should have met Martinelli earlier, listened to him earlier. Or listened to his father, who had loved the world of grand opera just as dearly as the Italian did. Why did his final decision have to wait until a German flying bomb had dumped an American soldier into a hospital in Britain so an Italian doctor could explain the beauty of opera and start him on a road he should have taken a lifetime earlier? Even Lucy! Why hadn't he listened to what Lucy had tried to tell him?

He read the story in the *Times* yet again and recalled the occasions he had seen Bjoerling at the Met. The Swede had not possessed outstanding stage presence. Daniel, with the advantage of height, knew he possessed more. But the wondrous instrument of Bjoerling's voice had more than compensated for what he lacked in stature and dramatic talent. Each season had added even more style and technique to his singing, and somehow the voice had never showed signs of darkening, never achieved the downward movement towards the baritone range that affected so many tenors. Daniel knew his own voice was beginning to darken, becoming richer yet deeper. It was a natural, physiological transformation that came with age, affecting some more than others. He had made up his mind to quit if it showed signs of becoming too deep, like Caruso's had done. Daniel wanted to be remembered as a true tenor, not as a baritone changeling.

As he stood up the newspaper fell to the floor, its pages scattering across the carpet. Stepping carefully to avoid the pages, he walked to the phonograph. The recording he selected was Bjoerling's 'E lucevan le stelle' from *Tosca*. This time Daniel did not seem to notice how much it resembled 'Avalon.' Nor did the music bring to mind Lucy's dramatic plunge from the window of the house in Paterson.

He just thought of Bjoerling and of the story in the *Times*. The Swede had been scheduled to sing in *Manon Lescaut* the following month at the Met; now a replacement would get his big chance.

When the track finished, Daniel selected another. From the *Turandot* Bjoerling had only recently recorded with Birgit Nilsson and the Rome Opera House Orchestra and Chorus, Daniel played 'Nessun dorma.' No tenor had ever sung it like Bjoerling; not even himself. No tenor ever would again.

Anna returned from taking Benjamin to the temple to find Daniel still sitting in the den. Tears cascaded down his face.

'Hey, you've got a recital tonight.' She tapped him gently on the shoulder. 'Carnegie Hall's expecting Daniel Kerr, not Johnny Ray.'

He felt her touch but could not tear himself away from the poignant memories aroused by the voice and the music. His father had died during 'Nessun dorma.' Now Bjoerling, too, was dead.

Anna tried again. 'Daniel, you've got a recital tonight. Don't get yourself all upset.' She had not seen him this despondent since the days of his fight with Robin Duguid and the Grand's management. He had lost a god, she realised that. A fellow artist whom he had looked up to, whom he had tried to emulate because he thought he was the best.

'So I have.' He wiped his eyes with a handkerchief and stood up to clasp his arms around Anna. 'But I'm still allowed a brief period of mourning for a departed comrade, aren't I?'

'Sure you are.' She stood on tiptoe to kiss him. The early morning sunlight shining in through the den window highlighted the grey that was spreading along the sides of his thick mane of hair. If she met him now for the first time, she knew she'd fall in love with him all over again. The only difference was that it would happen quicker this time. While other couples had drifted apart, she and Daniel had grown closer together, tied by more than just respect and love. They shared everything, their work, each other's experiences on stage. Anna knew that without Daniel she would be Laurel without Hardy, Crosby without Hope, me without my shadow; and she was strengthened by the knowledge that his devotion to her was just as fierce.

When she had first met him — the indignant novice who refused to make his operatic debut in anything but a lead role — she had been intrigued by his stubborn tenacity, the dogged determination to stick it out no matter what the cost. He had been a fighter, even if sometimes in his enthusiasm he picked the wrong causes to champion. Now he was approaching the level of a respected elder statesman, an established artist the new generation of singers could look up to, admire, use as their own inspiration, as Daniel had done with Bjoerling. Because of it, Anna loved him even more.

'What time will you be home from the city?' she asked.

'Around eleven, eleven-thirty.' He was disappointed that she would not be accompanying him, but the housekeeper had been promised this particular evening off for months and the babysitter had come down with a cold the previous night. Daniel would give Anna's ticket to Moishe instead, make him sit through the recital.

'Will you eat dinner before you leave, or shall I hold it till you get back?'

'When I get back.' He'd stop off at a delicatessen for a couple of sandwiches on the way in, or maybe he'd eat at the Russian Tea Room.

'No snacks,' she warned, reading his mind.

'No snacks.' It amused Daniel that after all these years, Anna was still fighting the battle of his bulge. For her own sake, he allowed her to believe she was winning, although his weight never seemed to drop below two-twenty these days. It was his metabolism, he claimed. Even if she starved him on a diet of dry crackers and water, he wouldn't get any thinner. She accepted his story and knew all along that he was cheating. But if she hadn't managed to change him yet, she reasoned, what chance did she have now?

The gnawing possibility of his own death preoccupied

254

Daniel throughout the entire journey to the city that evening. He knew the idea was preposterous. He should be laughing at the very thought. He was in the best of health. The last check-up, two months earlier, had assured him of that. Just watch your weight, the doctor had advised. He had nothing to worry about. Aware of the strain that being a lyric tenor put on the heart, Daniel watched his health carefully. Still, he could not bring himself to laugh. Reading in the *Times* of Bjoerling's sudden death — even if the Swede had suffered previous heart attacks — had guided Daniel's own mind down an unwelcome but inescapable avenue.

Death happened to everyone, sure; other than taxes it was the only certainty in life. He'd never worried about it before, though. The possibility itself was not so terrifying, he reflected; it was just the knowledge that he was thinking about it all.

He parked the car in a lot on West Fifty-sixth Street, stopped in at a delicatessen to pick up a pastrami sandwich and a cup of coffee and then hurried to Carnegie Hall, acutely conscious of the curious stares that followed his white tie and tails. Everyone probably thought he was a waiter at some restaurant. Maybe he'd have been smarter to wear a light topcoat or carry a change of clothes. After leaving the spare ticket for Moishe, Daniel made his way to the dressing room. He was very early, but he had decided on some last minute changes to the published programme and needed time to go over them with the conductor.

A few minutes before the scheduled commencement of the recital at eight o'clock, Daniel stood in the wings and watched the conductor take centre stage, his back to the orchestra.

'Ladies and gentlemen. By now you are all aware of the tragic passing of Jussi Bjoerling.'

A slight murmur from the audience greeted the conductor's words. He waited patiently for silence.

'To honour the memory of this magnificent artist, Mr. Kerr will now open his recital with ''Cuius animan'' from Rossini's *Stabat Mater*. Mr. Kerr askes that instead of applauding, you remain silent for one minute after the completion of the work.' The conductor took up his position on the rostrum, baton raised. Daniel walked out solemnly from the wings.

Never before had he experienced a silence that was so complete. It would be so easy to believe that the auditorium was empty, that it was not filled with people who were expectantly waiting to hear him sing. The silence emanated a power of its own, an eerie, intangible force that reached out to embrace and smother him just as strongly as any enthusiastic ovation could ever do. For several seconds he allowed the utter quiet to sweep over him, to lull him. This reverential silence alone was homage to Bjoerling. Every member of the audience, the orchestra, the Carnegie Hall employees, were sparing a few moments of their own lives to remember one man. Many, like Daniel, had seen Bjoerling at the Met. Others, less fortunate, had heard him only on record. Now they were all joined as one to show their respect for the man who only two days earlier had been the world's outstanding tenor, but who was now only a treasured memory.

Daniel moved his head a fraction in a signal to the conductor. The baton fell and the slow, dramatic sound of Rossini's music filled the hall. 'Cuius animam' was a work Daniel had never sung before, never thought he would sing although he was familiar with it. As a boy, he had sung 'Ave Maria' in the school choir, but since his first days in the B'Nai Yeshurun choir under Kawolsky, he had never performed Christian liturgical music. The Latin words sounded strange to his ears, felt strange to his lips. The unaccustomed repetition of words and line took up all of his concentration, did not allow him time to think how he sounded.

One member of the audience forgot about the conductor's request for no applause. A single handclap rang out, embarrassingly loud, as Daniel ended the hymn; it was just as abruptly terminated as the culprit remembered where he was. The pistol-shot of noise only served to make the following silence even blacker, more awesome. Daniel bowed solemnly, turned to his left and walked offstage. Behind, he left total quiet. From the wings he looked back onto the stage at the silent orchestra, at the mournful blackness of the auditorium. The king had died and his subjects were paying homage to his memory. In sixty seconds, the crown prince would appear triumphantly to take his rightful place on the vacant throne. The man who had sent Daniel a cable on his debut saying 'Now I know who you are' had stepped aside to leave the path clear for his successor.

At the end of the minute, the conductor's baton rose and dropped once more. The orchestra moved sweetly into the introduction for 'M'appari' from Flotow's *Martha*, the aria that was to have started the recital originally. Daniel walked out from the wings, head held high to meet the overwhelming applause that almost drowned out the music. He bowed formally to the conductor, to the audience. The new king's coronation had begun.

The recital continued as planned with arias from *La Bohème*, *Tosca*, *Turandot*, *Carmen*, *Un Ballo in Maschera*, *Pagliacci*, *Cavalleria Rusticana* and *Faust*, along with a selection of Neapolitan favourites, interspersed with orchestral arrangements. Shortly before ten-thirty, when the recital was due to finish, Daniel walked off into the wings again, leaving the stage to the conductor.

'Ladies and gentlemen. As Mr. Kerr opened this recital with "Cuius animam", he wishes to close it with another religious work. From the Jewish *Yom Kippur* service — the Day of Atonement — Mr. Kerr will sing . . .'

Even before the conductor could finish the sentence, the applause began to ring out. In the wings, Daniel chewed his top lip thoughtfully, wondering if he was doing the right thing. Seven years earlier he had made a recording of Jewish religious music that was still selling steadily, but he had never taken his cantorial background into the concert hall before. 'Kol nidre' was a classic, easily on the same level as 'Cuius animam' or the 'Ingemisco' from Verdi's *Requiem;*

257

still, he hesitated about doing it. Too late now, though. He had made the decision during the intermission and the conductor had just announced it. He walked slowly back to his position at the centre of the stage, head bowed, working himself up to the emotional level he needed for the hymn. There would be no orchestral backing here. He would be on his own, just like when he had conducted services in the temple, his voice against everything else while he beseeched the Almighty.

'*Kol nidre ve-esoray . . .* '

Never had a temple or a congregation been more receptive to his voice as was his Carnegie Hall audience at that moment. An entire mass of people hung on his every note. Gentiles and Jews together prayed with him that all sins committed by them would be forgiven, all forced vows overlooked. He would be singing 'Kol nidre' again soon enough, part of a congregation while he watched another cantor lead the service. *Yom Kippur* was only three weeks away. He would be praying to be inscribed in the Book of Life for the following year. The prayer seemed to take on more meaning. He had never thought about it before. It was automatic that he would be inscribed in the Book of Life. He was too young not to be. After Bjoerling, Daniel knew he had to pray. There was nothing automatic about it anymore.

The audience refused to let him go. Daniel, happily, refused to leave. After the two encores he had decided upon before the start of the performance — 'O paradiso!' from *L'Africaine,* and 'Ah! lève-toi, soleil!' from *Roméo et Juliette* — Daniel conferred hurriedly with the conductor. Then he stood at the edge of the stage and looked down at the front row.

Requests were called up to him. He smiled and nodded at each suggestion, undecided which one he would sing. Then he decided against all of them. He would do an encore just for himself, a selection of his own choice. He returned to the conductor for another discussion. The conductor nodded approval and passed the message on to the orchestra. A shuffling of paper followed as the musicians found the score.

Daniel stood in the centre of the stage while he listened to the long, slow introduction to the aria he had chosen. More than anything, he wished his father were out front. Isaac would have appreciated this particular aria more than anyone. Perhaps he was not appearing in a full production of *La Juive*, but singing 'Rachel! quand du Seigneur' was as close as he would ever likely come.

As he began to sing, he wondered how many of his audience had heard the aria before. It was a first for him; probably a first for most of his listeners as well. To his knowledge, other than Caruso, only Gigli had recorded it. It was almost an unknown.

'What the hell was that last thing you sang?' Moishe wanted to know when he met Daniel in the dressing room after the performance.

'From *La Juive*. Any the wiser?'

Moishe shook his head. 'That was a nice gesture you started off with, that business with Bjoerling. I think the audience appreciated it.'

'Did you?' Daniel asked. Whenever he spoke to Moishe, he had difficulty tearing his eyes away from the flashing gold teeth in his friend's mouth, the constant reminder of the havoc he had created that night. Moishe had never mentioned the incident. He'd locked it away in whatever part of his mind he kept unwelcome memories; or maybe he'd forced himself to forget all about it. Whenever he opened his mouth, though, Daniel was reminded.

The gold teeth shone as Moishe grinned. 'Kind of struck me as the president elect finding something nice to say about the guy whose job he's just taken, if you want to know.'

'Struck me the same way.' Daniel stood up and gave himself a final inspection in the mirror. 'Doing anything now?'

'What have you got in mind?'

'Come home with me for a bite to eat. Anna's preparing a late dinner. Stay over the night.'

Moishe weighed up the offer. 'Sure, why not?'

'Here's the keys. Pick up the car from the lot and meet me

outside. I don't want to walk around looking like a penguin anymore.'

Moishe took the keys and told Daniel he'd see him in ten minutes. When he drove up to the main entrance of the hall, he saw Daniel gladly signing autographs for a large group of fans. He honked and Daniel waved at him to wait. He signed another dozen pieces of paper that were pushed at him before climbing into the car.

'Will Benny still be awake?' Moishe asked.

Daniel checked the dashboard clock. 'I hope not. If he is, there's something wrong.' He looked sideways at Moishe, just in time to catch the flicker of disappointment. 'You'll see him in the morning before he goes to Hebrew classes.' Prompted by Moishe's interest in the child, Daniel decided to satisfy his own curiosity. 'How come you never got married?'

'Never found anyone who could stand me I guess.' Moishe kept his eyes fixed on the road while he answered quietly.

'You never thought about it?' Daniel pressed. Moishe would have made some kid a good father. He always made a big fuss over Benjamin whenever he saw him, spent a lot of time with the kid, brought him presents by the armful.

'I thought about it once or twice,' Moishe admitted. 'Long time ago.'

'So what happened?

'The girl wasn't thinking the same thing. Who wants to take a skinny, four-eyed, bald-headed bastard like me home to meet the family?'

Moishe laughed as he spoke, as if he found the whole idea a huge joke. To Daniel's ear the sound was forced. He remembered once thinking the same thing about Moishe and felt guilty. 'It's still not too late.'

'I'm too settled in my ways now.' Moishe guided the car off the George Washington Bridge onto Route 4 and picked up speed. Motels and gas stations flashed past as they left Fort Lee.

'Don't you ever get lonely?'

Moishe took his attention off the highway for the instant it needed to turn around and glare at Daniel. 'Hey! What's with the sudden third degree?'

'I'm interested, that's all. You've stuck your face in my affairs often enough. I'm repaying the favour.'

'You needed help from time to time.'

'Are you saying you don't?'

Moishe made no reply and Daniel decided to let the subject drop. Somehow he had exposed a nerve. Perhaps Moishe had been turned down a couple of times and it continued to rankle him. Or was he jealous of Daniel for his family life? At first, the idea seemed absurd. The more Daniel thought about it, however, the more plausible it became. After all, under what name had Moishe registered Anna and the kid when they'd left the house that time?

'Are you interested in meeting someone?' Daniel asked out of the blue.

The front of the car veered slightly as Moishe's hands involuntarily jerked the steering wheel. 'What the hell are you trying to do? Play *shidduch*-maker?'

Daniel ignored the frightened questions. 'Anna's got some single girlfriends. Do you want to meet one of them?'

'I don't know.' Moishe hesitated, uncertain whether he wanted this conversation to continue.

'What harm can it do, for crying out loud? The worst that happens is that you spend a couple of hours with one of them. You don't have to see her again if you don't want to.'

Moishe lapsed into silence. Daniel did not know whether he was thinking about the prospect of a blind date, or whether he was scared dumb by it.

An hour after he had gone to bed, Daniel continued to lie awake, thinking about Moishe who was asleep in the guest room. How many times had Moishe gone to bat for him? Plenty. Now he had the opportunity to return some of that friendship, whether Moishe thought he wanted it or not. How come he'd never realised it before, that Moishe was frightened of women, frightened of meeting them,

261

frightened of being alone with them? If it were not for Daniel's company, the guy would be a hermit, a scared, lonely man who had built up a defence of bluster.

'You sleeping?' Daniel whispered to Anna.

'I was trying to.' She rolled over to face him in the darkness. 'It's damned near impossible with you tossing and turning all night long. What's the problem?'

'Moishe. Have you got any single friends who are looking for someone?'

'Why do you want to fix him up?'

'Why not? I'm as miserable as sin. Why shouldn't he be?' Anna dug him playfully in the ribs with her elbow. 'Are you sure he wants to get fixed up?'

'He doesn't know what the hell he wants. If we show him a nice girl, he'll want to get fixed up.'

Anna closed her eyes in thought. 'There's Lena,' she finally said.

Daniel considered the suggestion, a middle-aged secretary who had never been married. 'Too aggressive,' he decided. 'She'd scare the living daylights out of him. Anyone else?'

'Helen Silver?'

'Helen?' The idea appealed to him, a young attractive widow in her late thirties with a daughter who attended Benjamin's school. Her husband had died three years earlier, and Anna had done as much as anyone to help her through. She came to the house at least once a week for dinner and often kept Anna company while Daniel was away. Moishe would like Helen, a soft, gentle soul who would not frighten him away. He just hoped that Helen would like Moishe. 'Think she'll be interested?'

'I'll ask her around for lunch tomorrow. It's supposed to be fine so we can eat outside. Does Moishe have any clean clothes with him?'

'I'll run him back to the city first thing in the morning.' Daniel began to smile as he thought over the idea. What would Moishe say when he learned he'd been fixed up?

The smile turned to a throaty chuckle and Anna asked

what the joke was. He did not try to explain. All he could think of was that the day had started on a bad note but it was finishing brightly.

CHAPTER TWO

The bat swung freely in Moishe's grip, lifting the white plastic ball high into the air. In slow motion it reached the peak of its climb and began to drop, twisting lazily in the light breeze. Glove raised in optimism rather than confidence, Benjamin circled under the spinning orb, lips stretched tightly in concentration, brown eyes alert.

From a chair on the patio, Daniel observed the scene with amusement. His kid was never going to play in the Yankee outfield, that was for damned sure. Moishe had been shagging flies for all of ten minutes and Benjamin had only caught two. Three, if you counted the attempt that had skipped twice out of the clutching glove and had been snatched finally as it made contact with the lawn; charitably, Moishe had called it a fair catch. Even as Daniel thought about it, Benjamin made a despairing grab at the ball. It hit the end of the glove and bounced away into a flower bed. Benjamin charged enthusiastically after it, and Daniel winced as he watched a rhododendron shrub being hammered almost flat beneath his son's pounding feet.

'That's enough!' Daniel called before more damage could ensue. Anna took enough pride in her garden to go wild when she saw her flowers flattened, and he would take as much of the blame as Benjamin. 'You've got to get ready for *cheder*!'

The boy climbed out of the flower bed, dropped the bat in

the middle of the lawn and ran into the house to clean up. Moishe followed, face covered in sweat but smiling happily.

'Great kid you've got there.' He picked up his jacket from a chair and slipped it on.

'You want to try getting one of your own,' Daniel said. He did not begrudge Moishe the time he spent with Benjamin. The kid enjoyed it every bit as much as Moishe did. But now was as good a time as any to get Moishe in the proper frame of mind for meeting Anna's friend at lunchtime.

'Where do you buy them?'

'You don't. Or didn't anyone bother explaining that to you?'

Moishe laughed. 'What's the big deal about my going back to the apartment to change? Why can't I stay like this?'

'Because by lunchtime you'll be smelling worse than the Hackensack River.' Would he be better off by letting Moishe continue to wear old clothes? That day he had proposed to Anna he'd needed a bath and a change. Helen might take pity on Moishe if she saw him like this, figure here was a man who needed someone to look after him. Or maybe she'd stick a clothes pin over her nose and run a mile. 'We'll drop Benny off at *cheder*, then I'll run you home.'

They entered the house to find Anna sitting at the kitchen table while she read the Sunday *Times*. Both she and Daniel had been disappointed to learn there was no review of the previous night's Carnegie Hall recital until they realised they had the early edition which had gone to press before the performance ended. Above all, Anna had wanted to read what the critics had thought of Daniel's rendition of 'Rachel! quand du Seigneur.' She had been delighted that Daniel had decided spontaneously to include the aria from *La Juive* and wondered if there was any point in using a good review to persuade the Grand's management to stage a revival of Halévy's opera. There had been talk about the Grand giving Daniel an entirely new production for the following season to celebrate his fifteen years with the company. *La Juive*, she believed, would be perfect for him. Daniel, however, was not keen on using the opportunity of a new production to revive *la Juive*. Although he had experimented with the aria, he thought the opera was too heavy for him, too taxing, both physically and mentally. To keep Anna happy, he had promised to talk to Robin Duguid about the possibility when he met with the general manager the following week.

'See you in a couple of hours,' Daniel told Anna. 'I'll drop Moishe off home and then come back. Give you a hand getting the lunch ready.' He winked at Anna as he spoke, keeping his face turned away from Moishe.

'What's the big occasion anyway?' Moishe demanded. 'Why do I have to go home and get changed?'

'Because none of my clothes will fit you!' Daniel laughed.

'Don't take any notice of him,' Anna advised. 'We've got some friends coming over this afternoon, that's all. We thought you might like to meet them.' She had called Helen Silver while Moishe had been playing in the garden with Benjamin. At first, Helen had been wary of the unexpected invitation. Only when Anna had stressed the intensity of Daniel's friendship had Helen agreed to meet him.

'You're not trying fix me up with some broad, are you?' Moishe asked suspiciously.

'What?' Daniel choked back another burst of laughter. 'There's no one we dislike that much.'

'I find a measure of consolation in your abuse.' Moishe kissed Anna on the cheek, said he'd see her later and went looking for Benjamin.

'You think he'll be mad when he finds out?' Anna asked.

'No. Helen's probably one of the first women he's been introduced to in years. Inside his puny chest, his little heart will flutter wildly and he'll fall hopelessly in love.'

'I know,' Anna replied. 'That's what worries me.'

Moishe returned just after one in the afternoon, his arms loaded down with a football uniform, helmet and ball for Benjamin. 'Baseball season's almost finished,' he called out cheerfully. 'Time for a new game.'

'What did you do?' Daniel asked in amazement as he surveyed the pile of equipment. 'Raid a locker room?'

'Stopped off on Canal Street. Where's Benny?'

'Upstairs. Getting changed. Come out back, there's someone we'd like you to meet.'

Still clutching the football gear, Moishe allowed himself to be led through the house into the back garden. Chairs were set out on the patio; drinks and appetisers crowded a small table. Moishe saw Anna talking to a petite blonde woman whom he had never seen before. On the lawn behind them, a young girl played with the white plastic ball Benjamin had been using that morning.

'Where are the rest of your guests?' Moishe asked. He looked around anxiously, hoping to find more people.

'You're looking at them,' Daniel answered. He stepped in behind Moishe to cut off any avenue of escape. A sheen of perspiration started to appear on top of Moishe's head. Daniel knew it had nothing to do with the heat. 'Helen Silver, meet Maurice Waterman.'

Moishe dropped the football equipment onto the ground, jammed his glasses to the top of his nose and stuck out his right hand. 'Pleased to meet you,' he mumbled.

Helen pushed herself up from the chair, an action that combined grace with an economy of movement. Watching and comparing, Daniel wondered whether he and Anna had been too smart. On appearances, Moishe and Helen were a total mismatch. Moishe was ungainly, awkward, obviously disconcerted by the sudden appearance of the woman. Helen was neat and confident, elegant in a bright cotton print dress while Moishe looked slovenly, his trousers rumpled, shoes scuffed.

'Anna's been telling me a lot about you, Maurice. Or is it Moishe?' Helen asked as an afterthought.

'His friends can call him . . . ' Daniel began before he saw Anna's warning glance and fell silent.

'Moishe's okay,' Moishe said. He grasped the woman's hand uncertainly. The greeting over, he dropped to his knees to gather up the football equipment. A sharp movement startled him. He looked up to find Helen kneeling beside him on the concrete, helping. 'I can do it,' he protested. 'I don't need any help, thanks.'

'All this stuff's for Benny?' Helen asked, taking no notice of Moishe's protests.

'Yes.' He collected the last piece of padding and stood up. To his dismay, Daniel and Anna had moved back into the house, leaving him alone on the patio with this strange woman. On the lawn the little girl continued to play, unaware of the trauma that Moishe was experiencing. Desperately he tried to think of something to say. He felt embarrassed at being left alone with Helen Silver. At the same time he was angry with Daniel and Anna for putting him in this position. He'd been taken; he knew that now. Offered the chance to meet a few friends of Daniel and Anna and then set up.

'You must think a lot of Benny,' Helen said, recognising Moishe's awkwardness and finding it appealing. 'Daniel was telling me how you were playing with him this morning.'

'He's my godson.' Moishe glanced around, spotted the little girl on the lawn and recognised his salvation. 'Is that your daughter?'

Helen nodded. 'Susie!' she called out. 'Come over here and say hello to Mr. Waterman.'

The little girl dropped the ball and ran obediently towards her mother. Very formally, she offered Moishe her right hand. 'How do you do, sir?'

Despite his own discomfort, Moishe could not resist a smile at the little girl's primness. 'I do pretty good. How about yourself?'

The girl looked at him oddly before releasing his hand and running back to the ball.

'Looks like I scared the hell out of her,' Moishe said regretfully.

'Oh, I doubt that.' Helen sat down in the chair again, delicately crossing her legs. 'Daniel tells me you're a lawyer. Where's your practice?'

'Manhattan.'

'Do you specialise in any particular field?'

'Just in paying the rent and keeping some food in the fridge.' Moishe was surprised to realise he had made a joke and the woman was smiling. 'Not really. I handle everything. But I do a lot of immigration work, visas, green cards. I suppose you could say I specialise in that.'

'I've heard about your immigration work from Daniel. He says he owes you quite a few favours.'

'What do you do?'

'Schoolteacher. I went back to it a couple of years ago, after my husband died.'

'Your husband?' Moishe appeared lost.

'He died from a heart attack. He was only thirty-nine.'

'I'm sorry.'

The little girl wandered back from her game for a second and looked at Moishe. She stood perfectly still on the edge of the patio, finger to her lips while she studied him. Moishe waved at her. She turned around as if to run again, then stole another furtive glance at him. This time Moishe made a face and she laughed happily.

'So much for scaring the hell out of her,' Helen said.

Just then Daniel reappeared, carrying plates from the kitchen. He bgan to set the table on the patio, every so often looking at Moishe and Helen while he tried to gauge the situation. When he returned to the kitchen, Anna asked him what was happening outside.

'He hasn't run away yet.'

'Has Helen?' Anna asked, and they both laughed.

Daniel realised he should feel guilty about the way he had dropped Moishe into what was obviously an uncomfortable situation for him. Instead, he felt amused. Moishe had stuck him in enough awkward messes by trying to help him. It was only fair that he retaliate. Anyway, he was doing it for Moishe's own good. As long as he kept telling himself that, there was no way he was going to feel guilty.

By late afternoon, Moishe was in his shirtsleeves, playing on the lawn with the two children and obviously enjoying it. Daniel sat in a lounge chair on the patio, watching, convinced finally that he had done the right thing.

'Has he asked her out yet?' Anna wanted to know.

Daniel twisted his head around to see where Helen was. Satisfied she was out of earshot, he replied, 'One thing at a time. She might not want to go out with him.'

'She does.'

'How do you know?'

'She told me she thinks he's sweet. He likes kids and they like him. That's very important to her.'

Sweet? Moishe Wasserman sweet? 'Where's the wedding going to be?' Daniel asked, giggling like a kid himself. It was a new sensation, introducing two total strangers to each other and watching them hit it off. It made him feel good.

'Give them a chance, Daniel. And don't go opening your big mouth about it either. Let them do whatever they want.'

'Okay, I promise.' He clapped a heavy hand over his mouth, like one of the three wise monkeys.

Later on, when Daniel suggested the six of them go out to dinner, he was surprised to hear Moishe reject the idea. 'Helen's already agreed to come out for dinner with me tonight,' he whispered after pulling Daniel off to the side. 'Would you mind very much if we took a raincheck on you and Anna?'

'Not at all. You like her, eh? You're not so mad anymore about being fixed up.'

'She's not bad.'

Daniel could not resist turning the screw. 'She's got a lovely house, Moishe. Play your cards right and you could move out of that solitary confinement cell in the Village.'

'How far are you and Anna planning on taking this thing?' Moishe asked, frightened as possibilities opened up in his imagination.

Daniel just laughed.

'Can you do us one favour for tonight?' Moishe asked.

'Sure. Anything.'

The laughter died when Moishe asked Daniel to babysit Helen's daughter while they went out for dinner.

Daniel's poignant tribute to Jussi Bjoerling dominated

the reviews of his recital that appeared in later editions of the Sunday newspapers. Needlessly, he carried copies when he went to his meeting the following week with Robin Duguid, certain that the general manager would have seen the notices already.

'A wonderful gesture of respect,' Duguid acknowledged when Daniel entered his office at the Grand. 'You had the opportunity to do the proper thing and you did it.'

Everyone seemed to be telling him that. It was fate again, that same force of destiny that Roger Hammersley had once said intended Daniel to make his operatic debut as des Grieux and not the lamplighter. Fate had decreed that Daniel would have a Carnegie Hall recital scheduled for the day he read of Bjoerling's death. It would be his respect, his sorrow, that would make the headlines; his name would be prominent.

'And the world's a magnificent tenor poorer,' Daniel said in reply. 'To tell you the truth, Mr. Duguid, reading that obituary scared the living daylights out of me.' Even after nine years with Duguid, Daniel could not bring himself to call the general manager by his first name. Only four years separated them in age, and since Daniel's return to Duguid's good graces in *Turandot*, a professional friendship had flourished between the two men, nurtured by a common desire to see the Grand succeed and a respect for each other's abilities. Intentionally, Duguid kept himself socially aloof from the members of the company, but during the tours he would often pass the travelling time by playing chess or talking with Daniel. Nevertheless, Daniel felt more comfortable keeping the relationship on a formal level. Duguid was in charge of the company and should be treated accordingly; familiarity would only erode his authority.

'I doubt if you were alone in your fear,' Duguid said. 'His death frightened a lot of people. When a man of forty-nine dies at the very peak of his career, it makes a lot of his contemporaries take a long, hard look at themselves. What did you learn?'

Daniel's pride was tickled to hear Duguid refer to him as a

271

contemporary of a singer like Bjoerling; the Swede had won enough triumphs to fill an entire career before Daniel had even decided to become an opera singer. 'I learned that there are still plenty of roles I'd like to do.'

'I see. Was that why you included "Rachel! quand du Seigneur" in your Carnegie Hall recital?' Duguid asked. 'To see how it was received? Whether it would be worth using a good review to push for a full production?'

'Have you been talking to Anna?'

'Why do you ask that?'

'Well' — Daniel felt uncomfortable, as if he had overstepped the mark — 'there's talk about offering me a new production to celebrate my fifteen years with the company. Anna seems to think that *La Juive* would be a fine choice.'

Duguid mulled over the suggestion. 'What about you? What do you think?'

'I don't know,' Daniel admitted. '*La Juive* —has got a lot of sentimental pull for me. It was my father's favourite of all Caruso's works. I grew up listening to Caruso sing that aria. But' — he let the word hang suggestively — 'it's far heavier than anything I've taken into my repertoire so far.'

'It's a very powerful opera, Daniel, but it's not a very popular one. We were thinking, instead, of *La Gioconda.*'

Daniel seemed relieved. He had not been enthusiastic about tackling *La Juive*. As Duguid had said, it was not a popular work. Off hand, Daniel could not even remember when he had last heard of it being performed. Maybe Caruso had been the last one to sing it. He had only mentioned it for Anna — and for his father's memory. Now Duguid had removed the responsibility of taking the matter further. The role of Enzo Grimaldo was much easier. He had sung it before. Even a new production would not need the vast amount of work that would be required to learn *La Juive*.

'We're also hoping Anna will appear with you in this production,' Duguid continued. 'She's due for a new production even more than you.'

Daniel smiled at the general manager's comments. Although Anna kept her appearance to a minimum and never went on tour anymore — preferring to be a full-time mother instead of a full-time soprano — Anna had been with the company longer than anyone else.

'See if you can have a word with her, Daniel. Persuade her. Get her in the right frame of mind for when I contact her next week. There aren't so many top-level sopranos that we can afford to let Anna's talents go to waste in the wilds of New Jersey.'

'I don't think she'd be very thrilled to hear you say she was wasting away. Being a mother's a very serious business for Anna.' Daniel knew he would have no trouble in getting Anna to appear with him in the production. She would support him to the hilt. It would be an honour for her as well; she'd share the glory of the new production with him.

'I'm sure it is,' Duguid agreed. 'How's Benjamin? Is he showing signs of following in his father's footsteps?'

'Hardly.' Daniel had to laugh as he remembered the kid playing with Moishe on the lawn. 'The only thing he does worse than sing is catch a ball.'

'Not to worry,' Duguid concluded philosophically. 'There are many other ways to earn a living.'

Sure there are, Daniel thought. But not one of them is anywhere near as rewarding and exciting as this one.

After finishing the meeting with Duguid, Daniel headed up to Moishe's office, eager to learn how his friend was progressing with Helen Silver. Anna had spoken on the phone for almost half an hour with Helen the previous evening, two teenaged girls eagerly exchanging gossip about their newest dates. Daniel had ribbed Anna about it. He'd told her she was too old to be spending hours on the phone talking about men; nevertheless, he wanted to find out how his machinations were working out.

He entered Moishe's office, unannounced by the receptionist. Moishe looked up in surprise and tried to sweep the two framed photographs off the top of his desk and bundle them into the drawer. Daniel was quicker. He grabbed Moishe's hand and, to his friend's embarrassment, picked up the photographs. One was of Helen, the other was of Helen and her daughter.

'Leave them on the desk,' Daniel said. 'What do you want to hide them for?'

'Helen wanted me to have them,' Moishe said defiantly, determined to prove to Daniel that it was not his idea. He came out from behind the desk and Daniel noticed that his shoes were shined to a high gloss, his trousers were pressed and his shirt was crisp, well-laundered.

'Like hell she wanted you to have them. You asked her for them.' Daniel knew that much from Anna.

'All right, so I asked her for them! Is there a law against it?'

'Of course not. When are you seeing her again?'

'Tonight,' Moishe answered proudly. 'I'm going there for dinner.'

'Are you taking her more red roses?'

'Who told you about that? Is my life going to be a gossip column item from now on?' Moishe demanded.

Daniel sat down heavily on the chair, his body shaking with helpless laughter. There was no fool like an old fool! Thank God he'd got it all out of his system early on and could concentrate on more important matters, be able to see the world without having his vision clouded over by dreams of wild love. Although what Helen could see in Moishe was beyond him. Getting on well with kids must be more important than he'd ever realised.

He dreamed that night, shadowy images that drifted in and out of his subconscious, fleeting, tantalising, as he tried to reach out and grasp them. He dreamed of death and of life; of those who had gone and those who remained.

His father appeared, the lined face solemn, an admonishing finger raised. The lips moved. No sound came to invade the silence of the dream, but Daniel knew the words his father was speaking. 'You had the chance to sing *La Juive* and you let it go. It might never come again.' Daniel heard his own voice screaming in reply, 'I don't want

274

anything to do with an opera where a father watches his daughter boiled alive! I've already lost one daughter. Can't you understand that?'

Isaac's face disappeared. Another took shape in its place. Fat Benny, whom Daniel could have helped and had not. Slumped beside a hot dog stand in Yankee Stadium while the crowd which had just witnessed one bloodletting stopped to gawk in fascination at another. If only he had been more concerned with his uncle's welfare instead of his own indignation, he could have helped Fat Benny, helped him to live long enough to see his nephew succeed on stage.

Who else had been disappointed by him? At one time or another, he'd let down everyone; his irresponsible actions had caused grief to those he loved and respected.

He dreamed of Moishe. If one person had stood by him, it was Moishe. His support had been as strong as Anna's. The dream brightened momentarily as he recalled their hapless journey back from the hotel in the mountains when they had first met. Then it darkened again as memory made an unwelcome visit to the final act of that meeting in an apartment on Park Avenue, figures in uniform, the crashing sounds of explosions in a confined space and a woman's vengeful, hysterical screams. But he was paying Moishe back, wasn't he? Helping his friend to share in a relationship that would bring him contentment if he'd let it. He began to laugh as the final, fragmented sequence of the dream found Moishe standing under a *chuppah* with Helen. The idiot was wearing mismatched socks!

Bright light penetrated his eyelids. Through them he sensed a shadowy figure looming over him.

'Daniel? Daniel?'

He recognised Anna's voice, calling quietly as she tried to wake him. Slowly he opened his eyes and looked around. The light on Anna's night table was shining. Anna was kneeling on the bed, staring at him anxiously.

'Were you having a dream?'

'I think so.' He sat up, dazed by the abrupt return to consciousness. 'Why do you ask?'

275

'You were shouting. And all of a sudden you began to laugh.'

'What was I shouting?' For the life of him he could not remember a thing. The dream had vanished like a mist when the morning sun burns through it.

'Something about a daughter, that was all I could understand. And then you started laughing. Daniel, you frightened me.'

'I'm sorry.' As he moved to kiss Anna, he felt his pyjamas sticking uncomfortably to his body; he was soaked through with sweat. 'Shouldn't have had that grilled cheese sandwich before I went to bed,' he joked feebly. 'Cheese always gives me nightmares.'

'You didn't have any. Unless you sneaked down in the middle of the night to raid the refrigerator.'

'Would I do a thing like that?'

'Damned right you would. Where are you going now?' she asked as he clambered out of bed.

'To take a shower and put on fresh pyjamas. I'm sticking to myself.' He padded softly across the carpet to the *en suite* bathroom and ran the water almost cold.

Anna was asleep, a comfortable bundle under the covers, when Daniel left the bathroom. Without turning on a light, he crossed the bedroom and tiptoed downstairs to the kitchen. As he opened the refrigerator door, a flash of vivid blue light blinded him. He blinked furiously, rubbing his eyes with his hands. By the time he had regained his sight, the kitchen light was on and Anna was sitting in a chair, a camera and flash on the table next to her.

'Sleepwalking?' she teased.

'I thought you were in bed.'

Anna began to laugh delightedly. 'Stage prop, Daniel. Nothing more than a bolster shoved under the blankets. Do you really think I'm that shapeless?'

Four weeks later, after a whirlwind courtship that Daniel witnessed with a mixture of amusement and amazement, Moishe turned up at the house late one night with a request.

'Will you be my best man, Danny boy?' he asked before he even passed over the doorstep.

Daniel pulled the dressing gown tighter around himself, the initial annoyance at being pulled out of bed to answer the door after eleven o'clock yielding to pleasure. 'When did you pop the question?'

'Just now. I left her at the house and came right over here to reserve your services.'

'I assume she said yes.'

'Damned right she did. So did Susie.'

'You asked them both?' Daniel put the kettle on the gas and hunted for cups; at this time of night, instant coffee would have to do.

'I had to.'

'So when's the big day?'

'January.' Moishe paced from one end of the kitchen to the other, hands clasped behind his back while he recounted how he had gone to Helen's house that night for dinner and had ended up by asking her to marry him. 'I never thought I'd get married, Danny boy. You can't even begin to know how I feel.' He turned around and walked in the other direction. 'I owe you, kiddo. I owe you.'

'Be happy and quit wearing out the kitchen floor and you'll have paid the debt,' Daniel told him. 'You thought about what you're going to do yet? What *shul* you're getting married in?. Reception? Junk like that?'

'Helen wants to get married in the local *shul*. And ...' Moishe seemed to lose some of his enthusiasm. ' ... we're going to have the reception in the house.'

'Nice.' Daniel made a big show of making two cups of coffee. As an afterthought, he added another cup, then went upstairs to wake Anna. She'd want to be in on this as well; in fact, she'd be miffed that he'd found out before her.

'What is it?' she wanted to know.

'Moishe's downstairs. The nervous bridegroom.'

'Bridegroom?' She sat up in bed, suddenly alert.

'He just asked Helen the big question and got the right answer. They're getting married in January.'

277

'I'm coming down.'

'I thought you would. Coffee's all poured. By the way, I'm the best man.'

'I always thought you were.'

As he walked out of the room, he saw Anna pick up the bedside phone and spin the dial to call Helen. He knew he shouldn't have poured the third cup; it would be stone cold by the time she got downstairs.

Moishe had not touched the coffee when Daniel returned to the kitchen. He was still walking nervously across the floor. At the sound of Daniel's footsteps, he spun around.

'Danny, I need a favour.'

'Ask.'

'Can you lend me a thousand bucks. It's for —'

Daniel held up a hand. 'I'm not interested in what it's for.'

He left Moishe alone in the kitchen, went to the mahogany secretary and pulled out his cheque book. When he returned, he was holding a cheque for one thousand dollars. 'Is that enough?'

'Fine. Thanks. I'll pay you back as soon as I can.'

'Don't worry about it.' He stuffed the cheque into Moishe's top pocket. 'Now drink your coffee and relax, will you?'

While he watched Moishe pick up the cup, Daniel wondered why he needed the money. Despite saying he didn't want to know, he was curious. Honeymoon? It did not seem to make any sense. Moishe's law practice must be making money. Or was it? Hadn't Moishe said that he and Helen planned to hold the reception in the house and not in a hall?

Anna entered the kitchen, rushed up to Moishe and kissed him on the cheek. Coffee splashed all over the floor. No one paid any attention to the accident. 'Helen says you're going to be our neighbour,' Anna exclaimed.

'Maybe the real estate taxes will come down,' Daniel muttered. 'Bad elements moving into the district.' It still didn't seem to make any sense to him. Helen had the house; it was paid for, surely, by the insurance her late husband

278

must have taken out. He decided to talk to Anna about it once Moishe left.

Through Anna asking Helen, Daniel learned a lot of things he had never known about Moishe. With the exception of Daniel, Anna and his receptionist, Moishe had no one to invite to the wedding. He was lonelier than he had ever admitted. And he was broke. The law business on West Forty-fifth Street barely made enough money for him to pay his way. Helen told Anna of clients that never paid, of cases Moishe took without ever having a hope of collecting his fee; he accepted cases because he felt sorry for people. Moishe did not have the money to pay for a reception. Neither did Helen. That was the other thing Daniel learned. Claims under the mortgage insurance policy and life policy her husband had carried had been denied. Her husband had failed to inform the insurance companies that he had suffered from rheumatic fever when he was a child. He had died from a heart attack, and the companies, on finding out about the rheumatic fever, had said the risk would have been greater had they known. So Helen was struggling to pay the mortgage while bringing up her daughter on a schoolteacher's salary.

Daniel listened to Anna's information with a feeling of helpless disbelief. Helen's problems did not shock him as much as Moishe's straits. He had known Moishe for thirty years; why hadn't the idiot said something?

'He's crazy. I would have helped him.'

'Maybe he's too proud to ask for help,' Anna suggested.

'That's not pride. That's stupidity. I'm going to call him right now. Tell him he can have whatever he needs.'

'Don't you dare,' Anna warned. 'You'll make him feel small. If he needs anything he'll ask, just like he did with the thousand dollars.'

'Then why the hell did he never ask before? I know what to do. I'll call that thousand bucks his wedding present. That'll help him out.'

'That won't help at all. It'll just embarrass him even

279

more. He'll pay you back and you make sure you take every penny. Don't shove your wealth and success down his throat. You'll choke him.'

Daniel recognised the wisdom in Anna's words. Nonetheless, he continued to feel terrible. He had to do something for Moishe. Hadn't Moishe done enough for him? If it had not been for Moishe, who knew what would have happened to his marriage, to his career? He was the one friend Moishe had; a friend couldn't stand idly by and do nothing. 'What about if we arrange the reception for them?' he suggested. 'Instead of letting Helen arrange it at the house, why don't we organise a big do for them? Hire the hall, the caterers. Spring it on them as a big surprise.'

Anna shook her head. 'They don't have that many people to invite.' Lines appeared on her forehead while she concentrated. Then she raised a hand in the air, fingers trembling with excitement, eyes sparkling. 'I've got the perfect idea, Daniel. You'll have to do it, but for God's sake be tactful. If you're not, you'll lose Helen and Moishe as friends.'

Daniel listened to Anna's idea and his face creased up into a huge grin. Hell, next to this, the thousand dollars he had been willing to give Moishe as a present paled into insignificance.

There weren't many people in the temple the Sunday afternoon that Moishe and Helen got married.

Daniel arrived early to ensure the flowers he had ordered were in place. A nice little touch, he decided; nothing that could make Moishe offended. Wasn't it part of the best man's duty to see that everything went smoothly?

Anna arrived with Benjamin and Susie, Helen's daughter. Benjamin was dressed in blue silk and a pristine white shirt with ruffled collar and cuffs while Susie wore a pale blue frilly dress; as pageboy and bridesmaid they made a fine pair, standing in the still empty temple, holding hands to encourage each other. Daniel reckoned Benjamin would enjoy himself over the next couple of weeks when Susie stayed with them. The kid would have company his own age. They'd be with each other at school and in the house; a couple of childhood sweethearts.

Moishe had bought a new suit for the occasion, a dark blue pinstripe from Brooks Brothers. Daniel had never seen him looking so smart. While he waited under the wedding canopy for Helen to be escorted in by an uncle who was giving her away, he glanced around nervously. 'Who arranged for all the flowers?'

Daniel admitted that he had. 'Got to have something attractive in here to make up for you.' He reached an arm fondly around Moishe's shoulders and hugged him tightly. 'Got a fast car with the engine running waiting outside. Say the word and I'll smuggle you out of the state.'

'You think I want that?'

'No. You'd be a fool if you did. You're doing the best thing you've ever done. Except you should have done it a long time ago.'

'I didn't meet anyone a long time ago.'

'That was your own damned fault.'

Moishe took off his glasses and wiped the lenses. His eyes were moist, and a vein in his temple throbbed to a regular beat.

'Nervous?' Daniel asked unnecessarily.

'Bet your ass I am. Look what I'm giving up.'

'What?' Daniel reached out to straighten Moishe's tie, which was threatening to slide around to the side of his neck. He changed his mind and left it alone; maybe Moishe would be better off retaining some of his slovenliness. 'A shoebox of an apartment? Talking yourself to sleep every night? Being as lonely as a leper?'

'You'll take good care of Susie, won't you?'

'Like she was our own daughter. What are you worrying about?'

More guests entered the temple and took their seats. Moishe glanced around, uncertain of himself as he hesitantly acknowledged their smiles. 'I never told you this before, Danny, but I was jealous as all hell of you.'

'Of me?' What was Moishe trying to do to him. Alleviate his own anxiety by throwing it on someone else's shoulders? 'In God's name why? Because I sang?'

'No. Nothing to do with that. I still don't understand half that crap you wail from the stage. I was jealous of your family. Of the fact that you had someone. You always had someone. You made friends easy. I never did.'

'Okay, so you've changed. Now we're equal. You've got a family just like me.' He tried to switch the subject by asking Moishe who were the people in the temple; anything to make him relax. If he carried on like this, he'd be in tears by the time the ceremony began. So would everyone else.

Moishe refused to be sidetracked. 'You know, if there's anything I can ever do for you . . .'

'You've done more than enough for me already. Now will you just shut up so we can get on with this thing?' To his relief, he saw the rabbi take up his position. He pushed Moishe around to face the rabbi, then glanced behind as the temple door opened and Helen arrived on her uncle's arm. Daniel felt in his pocket to make certain he had the ring. His fingers came in contact with a bulky envelope, the present he would give to Helen and Moishe during the reception. Moishe might be a lot easier in his mind if he knew the envelope's contents. The idea of such a gift had been a stroke of genius on Anna's part. Daniel knew he would never have thought of it. He'd have gone ahead and told Moishe to forget about the thousand bucks, probably made him feel about an inch tall. Anna's suggestion had been more subtle. It would raise a few tears, protests that they shouldn't have done it. But it would be appreciated. And it would remove a lot of the headaches from the new marriage.

Daniel's eyes shifted downward as Moishe fidgeted nervously. Typical, he thought. The guy buys his first new suit in years and the trousers don't talk to the shoes; the cuffs of the pants finished a full half inch above his shoe tops. Daniel felt himself beginning to laugh and choked it back. The dream had been right. The stupid *klutz* was wearing one dark blue and one light blue sock!

Forty people attended the reception held in Helen's home. Moishe walked around in a semi-daze as if he could not believe he was married. Helen took the duties of hostess on her own shoulders, compensating for her new, bemused husband.

'Got lots of little white envelopes?' Daniel kidded. 'Just like a *bar mitzvah*.'

'A couple,' Moishe answered. 'And tea services, things like that.'

'Stick this with your collection.' Daniel pulled the heavy envelope out of his pocket, glad to be rid of it at last. Moishe regarded it questioningly. 'Helen will probably understand it more than you will, although it's written in the kind of gobbledygook only a lawyer would appreciate.'

Moishe balanced the package in his hand, gauging the weight. 'May I open it?'

'Sure. You're going to have to open it eventually, so do it now.' Daniel gazed into Moishe's face, wanting to treasure the expression that would come when his friend recognised the contents. Moishe peeled back the flap and pulled out the contents.

'You son of a bitch!' Tears sprang to his eyes, just as Daniel had known they would. 'What the hell did you go and do a thing like this for?'

'Because Anna and I wanted to. And do you know what kind of a performance it was to track down the little old lady who held the mortgage on this place?' Gently he pried Moishe's fingers off the title to the house and the documents that settled the outstanding mortgage. A little over eleven thousand dollars had been outstanding. With one signature on a cheque, Daniel had wiped off the entire amount and given Moishe and Helen a clean start to their marriage.

Moishe looked around the room, past the buffet table from which guests were helping themselves, past Helen talking to some friends. Finally his eyes settled on Benjamin and Susie, two children lost in a world of adults, standing solemnly while they witnessed what went on around them.

'Looks like a perfect match,' he said. 'Maybe you and me will be in-laws yet.'

'God forbid,' Daniel muttered. 'Not that I've got anything against Helen and Susie, but you I ain't too sure about. I'm not even certain whether I'm happy living in the same town now. Come on!' He slapped Moishe on the back so heartily that his glasses almost flew off. 'Be the good host and look after your guests.'

CHAPTER THREE

Even before he had asked Benjamin what he wanted for a *bar mitzvah* present, Daniel knew what the answer would be. The kid was so hyped up about being a Jew that he could ask for only one thing. So sure was Daniel, he even had a bet with Anna on the answer. And he won a dollar.

Benjamin wanted a trip to Israel. Following his *bar mitzvah,* he wanted to spend the entire school summer vacation in the country. He wanted to visit every site mentioned in the Old Testament that was encompassed by the modern boundaries. He wanted to walk where Abraham, Isaac and Jacob had walked, to live on a *kibbutz,* to worship where Moses had worshipped. In the end, he settled for two weeks split between West Jerusalem, Tel Aviv and Natanya, the longest that Daniel could afford to be away.

The trip was a first, also, for his parents, one of the many things Daniel had always meant to do but had somehow never accomplished. They didn't even need a guide book. Ever since Daniel had told Benjamin they would be making the trip, his son had been avidly consuming every tourist pamphlet, every book, every scrap of information he could about the country, adding to his already vast store of knowledge. The child became the guide, and Daniel swore he could see his son growing up in those two weeks.

An alert *Daily News* photographer recognised Daniel as he

passed through the airport on the return journey. Smiling at the camera, an arm each around Anna and Benjamin, Daniel explained the reason for the trip. The photographer jotted down the information before turning away in search of other celebrities. Daniel dimmed Benjamin's joy at the recognition by telling him not to bother looking for the photograph the following day; the newspaper had more important pictures to print.

He was wrong. The *Daily News* carried the photograph the following day on its show business page. Daniel would not have known about it had not Moishe read the paper. He brought the copy around to the house that evening. Daniel, in turn, gave the clipping to Benjamin to begin his own scrapbook.

The woman started appearing outside Benjamin's school the week he began the fall term. When he first mentioned her to his parents, neither Daniel nor Anna paid much attention, thinking she was probably the mother of one of the other children. Only after the woman had appeared three more times in the space of two weeks, and sought Benjamin out to speak to him, did Daniel take notice.

'She said she knows you, Pa. She saw your picture in the *News*.' Benjamin said. 'She knows you.'

'She didn't give a name, nothing like that?' Why was he getting worked up over this, some woman who'd spoken to Benjamin outside school three times? Lots of people knew him; lots of people must have seen the family photograph in the *News*. What was so strange about that? 'None of the other kids know who she is? Like she doesn't belong to one of them?'

'Did she speak to anyone else?' Anna wanted to know. 'Who were you with today when you left school?'

'Just Susie. She ignored Susie completely. She came up to me and said I should say hello to you for her.' He looked hopefully at his father to explain the mystery.

'What did she look like?'

Benjamin made a face 'She was old.'

286

That did not mean much. Anyone over twenty was old to Benjamin. 'What colour hair did she have?'

'Blonde. Very stiff, like she sprayed loads of gook all over it. And her face was all lined.'

Listening to her son, Anna decided to call Helen. Maybe Susie would be able to offer a better description. 'Do you think we should tell the police?' she asked Daniel after Benjamin had gone to his room.

'What the hell for? It's just some harmless, crackpot old woman. Doesn't mean a thing.' Nonetheless, he decided to walk Benjamin to school and pick him up each day. He would see for himself who this strange blonde woman was. And what, if anything, she wanted from him.

A week of fruitless journeys passed. Each morning Daniel took Benjamin to the school gate and waited until the children had been called into class. At lunchtime, while Daniel was in the city rehearsing for the coming season, Anna or the housekeeper would act as escort. Daniel made certain he was back from the city to collect Benjamin at the end of the afternoon session. He even had to cut one rehearsal of the opening-week production of *Il Trovatore* to be there. After explaining the reason to Robin Duguid, the general manager overlooked the unusual behaviour and filled in the role of Manrico with an understudy for the rehearsal.

On the eighth day, as Benjamin rushed out of the school towards his father, he abruptly stopped in mid-stride, eyes suddenly wide, finger pointed. 'There she is, Pa!' he yelled. 'That's the woman!'

Daniel swung around, determined to get to the bottom of the mystery. He caught just a glimpse of the woman from the back — wearing brown slacks and sweater with blonde hair piled high — before she dived into the passenger seat of a blue Mercury which sped away from the kerb immediately. The car was too far away for him to read the number; all Daniel could make out was that it was a New York plate. If he had been right and it was some crackpot old woman, why had she taken off like that? He'd been wrong all along. He did have something to worry about.

287

'We're going inside.' He grabbed Benjamin by the arm and pulled him into the school building. He passed Susie and didn't even recognise her. 'Where's the principal's office?'

Benjamin led the way. Daniel confronted a startled secretary and demanded to speak to the principal. The woman looked from Daniel to Benjamin, whom she knew by sight, then asked what the problem was. 'Mr. Palmer is in a meeting right now.'

'I'm not interested in what he's doing,' Daniel growled. 'My kid's being molested outside this school by some woman and I want to get to the bottom of it.'

'I see, Mr. . . . ?'

'Kerr. Daniel Kerr.'

'Just a moment, Mr. Kerr. I'll check if Mr. Palmer can see you.'

'Don't bother. I'll check myself.' Dragging Benjamin behind him, Daniel pushed past the woman and barged through to the door to the principal's office. Four startled faces turned around at the noisy intrusion. The principal pushed himself to his feet, face reddening with indignation.

'What is the meaning of this?'

'Mr. Palmer?'

'Yes. Who are you?'

'I'm this boy's father. Three times in the past couple of weeks he's been accosted outside this school by some woman. I want it stopped.'

'Perhaps you'll come outside with me, Mr. Kerr.' He excused himself to the three people present and led Daniel and Benjamin into the secretary's office. The woman picked up her purse and left. 'Now what's all this about, Mr. Kerr?'

Briefly Daniel told the principal what Benjamin had told him, finishing off with the incident of the blonde woman leaping into the Mercury. The principal asked why Benjamin had never notified any of the school staff before. Daniel replied that they had never thought it worthwhile. Until today, when the woman had caught sight of him and fled.

'Did you get the number of the car?'

Daniel felt foolish when he had to say no. 'Just a blue Mercury with New York plates. Maybe a sixty-two. Two people in the car, the blonde and a driver.'

Palmer picked up the phone and dialled the local police. 'If they're heading back to the city, perhaps we can get them stopped at the bridge. We can settle this here and now.' He got through and passed on the information. 'The Port Authority police will be on the watch for the car. If it hasn't gone through yet, we might get lucky.'

'Can I wait here?'

'Surely. I'll just break up that meeting and we can have the office to ourselves.' He went back into his office. Moments later, the three people who had been sharing the meeting came out. Palmer asked Daniel and Benjamin to wait in his office.

The telephone rang fifteen minutes later. Palmer picked it up. 'Teaneck police have checked Route 4 from here through to the bridge. They've seen nothing of a blue Mercury with two people in it that answers your description. Port Authority police have also come up with nothing. Are you certain the car had New York plates?'

'Of course I'm certain,' Daniel said irritably. 'I'm not that blind that I can't tell the difference between an orange-and-blue plate and a black-and-beige one.'

'Pity you didn't get the number.'

'Isn't it? So what are the police going to do?'

'I don't think there is very much they can do, Mr. Kerr. If the matter had been brought to our attention before we might have been able to do something. But now I'm afraid we're helpless.'

'Well, you'd better stop being helpless damned quick!' Daniel roared. 'Because my kid's not coming back to this school until you've got some kind of security system around here.' He lowered his voice. 'Come on, Benny, we're going home.'

Palmer rushed to reach the door before Daniel. 'Mr. Kerr, please try to understand that I'm the last person who would want anything to happen to one of our pupils.' His tone was placatory, the words carefully chosen. 'Ultimately, I'm responsible for everything that happens here. But you must realise that what we do now will be from scratch.'

Slowly Daniel simmered down as he realised that his own rage was even more dangerous than the blonde woman in the blue Mercury. If she was dangerous at all. Of course she was! Otherwise why had she taken off like that when he had turned to look at her?

'I'd suggest that you take Benjamin down to the police station. In the meantime, I'll try to find out if there are any other children who saw this woman. Between them, they might come up with a reasonable description for the police artist. Then, at least, the police will know whom they're seeking.'

'I will. Thanks.' Daniel offered his hand apologetically. 'Sorry if I was rude. I'm just worried.'

Palmer took the hand which Daniel held out. 'Of course, Mr. Kerr. Let's hope we can solve this riddle quickly.'

The local police were as helpful as they could be. Benjamin, Susie and three other schoolchildren who claimed they had seen the blonde woman at one time or another offered their descriptions. The artist came up with three different sketches and the children argued among themselves about which one was correct. They turned it into a game until finally the seargeant who had organised the meeting told Daniel he thought that nothing could be gained by continuing it. Regretfully, Daniel was forced to agree with him.

'Who do you think it is?'

The question came from Moishe, brow lined in thought, head shining dully as it reflected the light in the centre of the living room. He shared the couch with Helen, while Daniel sat in a straight-backed chair. Anna was in the kitchen making coffee; upstairs, Susie and Benjamin played.

'If I knew that, we wouldn't have this problem, would we?' Daniel shook his head in exasperation as he struggled to think of a reason why any woman would be interested in either him or Benjamin. He had called Helen when he got home from the police station to arrange a meeting for that evening. Between all of them, they might be able to force a reason to surface. It was all well and good for the local police department to make sure a man was posted at the school when the kids came and went, but what about the rest of the time? Was Benjamin going to have an escort for everything he did? Every time he played in the park, went to the public library, or went to the temple on Friday night and Saturday morning, would a police officer be tagging alongside?

'Is there an old girlfriend you've been keeping quiet about?' Helen joked, desperate to lighten the oppressive atmosphere.

'No.' Daniel dismissed the idea with uncharacteristic curtness, failing to see any humour in it. There was nothing to laugh about when his son was being threatened.

'And the police still think it's just some crank,' Moishe murmured. 'Some nut with nothing better to do.'

'Why would some crank come all the way over from New York just to pester me?' Daniel demanded of Moishe.

'Beats the hell out of me.' As much as he was concerned for Benjamin, Moishe was also worried how it would affect Susie. She wasn't his own flesh and blood, but he cared for her just as strongly as if she were. He'd watched the girl grow up for four years now and bitterly regretted that he had not been there for the first nine, and even before. All the favours he had ever done for Daniel, all the times he'd stood by him, had been paid back with any interest due by the introduction to Helen. Before he had met her, Moishe could not even conceive what it would be like to share his life with another. After he'd met her, he couldn't bear to think what it would be like any other way.

The door opened and Anna came in carrying a tray with four cups, coffee pot, cream and sugar, and homemade cheesecake. Very pointedly she indicated the smallest portion of cake. 'That's for you,' she told Daniel.

'No. I don't want any. Just the coffee'll do.'

Anna regarded him oddly. He was more worried about the mysterious blonde than he was showing. Any other time he would have battled for a bigger slice; this time he was passing it up altogether. 'I'll confess to you all now,' she said. 'I invented this mysterious blonde just to put Daniel off his food. How else could I make him lose weight?'

The sound of Moishe's and Helen's laughter passed right over Daniel's head. He hadn't even heard what Anna had said to start them laughing. All he could think of was the woman. If he had to go over to New York himself and check out every blue Mercury registered in the state to find out what was going on, he'd damn well do it.

The tension was increased another notch the following morning. The mailman brought two letters addressed to Daniel. One was a telephone bill. The other, with his name and address printed on the envelope in clumsy block capitals, contained the page from the *Daily News* with the photograph taken at the airport circled in red and an accompanying sheet of white paper. On the paper, letters cut from different publications spelled out, 'What a happy family. You don't deserve it.'

Furiously Daniel crumpled the envelope and its contents into a small, tight ball before he remembered that the police would need to see them. Not that they would be able to learn much; he was certain of that. Anyone who took the trouble to write in block capitals and then use letters cut from magazines for the message would surely avoid leaving fingerprints on the paper. That's if fingerprints could be left on paper to begin with. Hell, he was out of his depth here. He was struggling against something he didn't understand. For a reason he didn't understand.

He debated whether or not to show the letter to Anna. He could take it straight to the police and not give Anna additional worries. There seemed little point in making her as upset as himself. Then he realised she would be even more upset if she knew he was keeping anything from her.

'You've got no idea what any of this means?' Anna looked

at the New York postmark on the envelope. She was more perplexed than worried, confused as to why anyone should go to these lengths to harm them. Was this the price of fame — that any nut who could read enough to look up a celebrity in the telephone directory could start pestering them? She had argued years earlier with Daniel about having their phone number and address unlisted, but he had insisted on its inclusion in the Bergen County directory. He was a public figure, he had reasoned, and if people wanted to contact him, they should be able to. The idea to make himself accessible had been good. Daniel had enjoyed talking both to fans and aspiring singers who wanted advice. But now nuts were getting through. Accessibility was suddenly a peril.

'Do you think if I knew what it meant, I'd be standing here?' Daniel asked in return. 'I'd be out there with someone's neck between my hands.' He clenched his fists, subconsciously relishing the sensation of having the blonde woman's throat in his grip.

Anna watched him carefully while she tried to gauge the turmoil she knew was raging inside him. Whatever it was, whatever grudge, real or imagined, that this woman held against her family, she wished it would come to a head before it wrought havoc with Daniel.

Easing the heavy sword from its scabbard, Daniel stared pensively at the shining blade. From dressing rooms on either side he could hear fellow artists loosening up their voices for the performance of Verdi's *Il Trovatore*. He fingered the dull edge of the blade; no sense in having it sharp in case he got carried away during a performance and took someone's head off by mistake. He knew whose head he'd like it to be. Visions of a bloody head with blonde hair bouncing across the stage into the orchestra pit briefly lightened his mood.

Three more letters had followed the first. They had contained originals of old reviews, even one from his debut as des Grieux in *Manon Lescaut* from the New York *Times*. The police had jumped on that one. They had checked with the *Times* morgue and with libraries in New York to see if they had records of anyone checking out that particular issue. The replies had come back, all identical. No library in the city had a record of anyone asking for that particular copy of the *Times*. Also, all their copies were intact; nothing had been ripped out. Whoever was plaguing Daniel had been holding the grudge for a long time. Long enough to have collected the reviews from almost twenty years before.

At least the pestering of Benjamin at school had ceased. Daniel was grateful for that. Obviously, the perpetrator had decided to alter the method of attack and use the mails to unnerve him. That had one advantage. Using the mails made it a federal matter, although Daniel seriously doubted if the FBI had enough spare time to go chasing after some lunatic woman who was making a nuisance of herself.

Not much point in dwelling on it, Daniel decided. Whatever will be will be. Whoever's behind it will get an even bigger kick if I go out there and blow a note to hell and back. He stood up, attached the scabbard to his belt and left the dressing room. He met Robin Duguid in the corridor outside, as the general manager was making his rounds of the dressing rooms to wish his artists good luck. When he spotted Daniel, his face became serious.

'Anything new on your phantom letter writer?'

'I wish you hadn't mentioned it, Mr. Duguid. I'm doing my best to try not to think about it.'

'I'm sorry. I didn't realise.'

'Not your fault. Nothing new. Every so often I get another old review in the mail. The cops think whoever's behind it has had it in for me since day one in this business. Now they're digging through their scrapbooks to send me a few reminders. I just wish they'd send something that could give the cops a clue.'

'Anything I can do to help?' Duguid asked gently as he accompanied Daniel downstairs to stage level.

'Come up with a motive.'

'I wish I could.' Duguid clapped Daniel on the shoulder in a rare gesture of closeness. 'Good luck.'

The blonde woman was winning her war of nerves. During the second act, Daniel forgot a line. He looked around blindly, mouth gaping, face blank while he prayed silently for assistance. The panic was contagious. Instead of calling out softly, the prompter shouted with enough force to be heard halfway around the auditorium.

When Daniel came off for the intermission between the second and third acts, he spoke to no one. If he still kept a bottle in the dressing room, he would have emptied it without a second thought. Duguid was sympathetic. He knocked gently on the dressing room door and stood just inside. 'Do you want me to go onstage and say you've been taken ill?'

Daniel glared moodily into the mirror while he shook his head: *Il Trovatore* was an opera, like so many others, where the tenor could rescue a mediocre performance with a powerful third-act aria. In this instance it was 'Di quella pira.' Daniel, as the insurgent leader, Manrico, would stand at the front of the stage, sword raised valiantly aloft, and rouse his followers to storm his enemy's castle. 'I'll make them forget that blunder,' he promised Duguid.

The general manager smiled at his tenor's confidence. 'That's what I was expecting you to say. Go blow their eardrums out.' He patted Daniel on the shoulder and left the room.

Daniel continued to stare in the mirror until he heard the call go out that only five minutes remained to the beginning of the third act. As he prepared to leave, the telephone rang. It was Anna. The tactics had been changed yet again. First it had been Benjamin, then the newspaper clippings and the old reviews had started to arrive. Now, whoever was plaguing them had turned to the telephone. When it had rung three minutes earlier, Anna had answered it to hear the first-act duet from the *La Bohème* she and Daniel had recorded fourteen years earlier. As she listened, the speed was changed, first fast then slow. When Anna screamed, the receiver at the other end was put down.

Daniel felt sweat begin to bead on his brow. Someone was

turning the screws, and there wasn't a damned thing he could do about it. 'Call the cops,' he said. 'And call the phone company. Better still, get the cops to do it. Maybe they can get some kind of permanent trace on the line, listen in if this nut calls again.'

'Daniel, I'm frightened.' It was the first time Anna had ever admitted fear. Daniel knew how deeply frightened she was.

'Don't worry. I'll finish off this third act and come straight home. Call Moishe. Get him to come and sit with you.'

'All right.' She blew a kiss into the mouthpiece and hung up.

Daniel walked slowly down to stage level, his face wet and ashen. People asked if he was feeling all right. He nodded brusquely. He would feel better once the third act began and he immersed himself again in the character of Manrico, ready to redeem his poor performance so far.

A popular tenor's performance can recover from many ills. He can compensate for a frigid start with later sweetness and warmth and his audience will welcome him back into their hearts. A forgotten word or line can be forgiven in the time it takes to draw the next carefully controlled breath and come back with a cluster of high notes that will shake the chandeliers. But no tenor ever recovers from a cracked high-C.

Daniel knew he was going to fall short of his high-C in 'Di quella pira' even before he tried to reach for it. He wasn't into the part at all. He wasn't Manrico trying to save his mother from being burned at the stake. He was Daniel Kerr, trying to sing while he was worried stiff about some nut who had singled out his family for an experiment in psychological terror. Some nut who was doing a damned good job . . .

The high-C cracked. Daniel felt his throat closing up as he went for it. Where before his voice had soared effortlessly, now it faltered. He sounded like a man choking, drowning, a final scream for help that turned into a weak gasp as the waters closed over him. His eyes bulged. His mouth froze in a wide, helpless circle. His lungs burst and his heart stopped. The sword, held so proudly aloft moments earlier, clattered from his hand onto the stage. Daniel stared down at the conductor's concerned face, at the blackness of the auditorium where the audience sat, all witness to a catastrophe instead of the expected triumph.

Was the blonde woman out there even now? Watching and listening to the havoc she had created? Was this her triumph? The objective of her terror campaign? To be on hand when he tried to hit the top and collapsed? Was she the friend of someone who wanted him out of the way? Doing a more frightening version of what Moishe had once done for him with an Italian tenor named Cesare Scarlatti?

A shocked gasp exploded from the audience as realisation finally hit home. Their hero of countless productions had been vanquished. It was time for another hero. The heavy gold curtain dropped down in the middle of the scene. Daniel spun around and walked quickly into the wings. He passed his double, the understudy dressed up as a second Manrico, all ready to go on. Duguid had sensed problems and had been prepared for it. While he watched the understudy take up his recently vacated position in the centre of the stage, Daniel heard Duguid's voice in front of the curtain, telling the audience that Mr. Kerr had been taken ill and would be replaced by tenor Paul Lankau. Daniel did not wait to hear any more. When the curtain rose and the orchestra began again with the introduction to 'Di quella pira,' Daniel was racing up the stairs to the dressing room. He did not even spare a sympathetic thought for Paul Lankau, his understudy, who had been flung into the lion's den without the least protection, forced to sing a 'Di quella pira' without the slightest recitative to ease himself into the part.

When Duguid reached the dressing room, Manrico's costume was already on the floor in an untidy heap and Daniel was clambering into his trousers.

'Are you all right?'

'Yeah. I'm going home.' He realised that Duguid did not know about the phone call Anna had taken, the distorted playing of the duet from *La Bohème*. While he continued dressing, he related the story. Duguid nodded understandingly.

'Daniel, if you want a leave of absence from the company, for God's sake say so. You went on just before when you know damned well you shouldn't have.' Daniel opened his mouth to speak in his own defence. Duguid held up a hand. 'I know what you're going to say. That the audience paid to hear you sing Manrico. That's the risk they take when they book, whether you'll be in the part or not. Instead, they heard you give what was probably the worst performance of your entire career. You cheated everyone, yourself included.'

Daniel saw no sense in arguing with Duguid. The general manager was right in everything he said. Daniel had cheated everyone. He'd cheated himself by turning in a performance so bad he'd never be able to forget it; and he had cheated his audience by offering them second rate when they had come to expect only the finest.

'Do you want a leave of absence from the company?'

'I think I'd better.' He slipped into his jacket, paused long enough to make sure he had his car keys and wallet, then grabbed his topcoat. 'I'll give you a call tomorrow. Let you know what's happening.'

As he clattered down the stairs towards the stage door, he heard the sound of voices. The performance was continuing without him. It would have to remain that way until the police got to the bottom of this mess. Daniel prayed that it did not take so long that the audience would forget him.

The house was full when he arrived; the entire world seemed to have congregated in his living room. Benjamin and Moishe sat talking quietly. Anna, eyes red but dry, sat alone on the couch, hands clasped on her lap as she talked to two men Daniel had never seen before. They introduced themselves as FBI agents. A Teaneck police officer was also present, representing the local municipality.

'Mr. Kerr.' The senior of the two agents addressed him, a

298

man with greying hair and blue eyes that somehow managed to remain warm. 'I'm Jack Regan. I'll be handling the case from now on. From talking to your wife' — he indicated Anna, still sitting on the couch — 'I'd suggest that we monitor all your phone calls in future.'

'What about changing the number?'

'That would just avoid the issue, sir. We'd like to trace where the calls are being made from; that way we can get a lead on whoever is behind this campaign against your family. We've already notified the phone company. And for your personal safety, we'll be leaving an agent in the house.' He motioned to the second man.

'Guess you'd better watch your personal calls from now on, Danny boy,' Moishe called out. The words brought an involuntary grin to Daniel's face; even Anna laughed.

'I doubt if we'll be listening in on those, sir,' Regan remarked drily.

'If you want juicy calls, try eavesdropping on some of the deals he tries to pull over the phone,' Daniel shot back. 'Your ears would drop off.' He was pleased to see Moishe's face redden.

'What was the name of your friend who was with the FBI?' Anna asked suddenly. 'You know, the one we met in the Village that night before we got married? The one you promised to send tickets to.'

'Tommy?' Daniel asked, surprised that Anna should remember. 'Tommy Mulvaney. Either of you guys know him?'

Regan nodded. 'He's with the New York office, a senior investigator.'

'Where do you work out of?'

'Hackensack. You know Mulvaney well?'

'Used to,' Daniel admitted, shamefaced. 'We were friends as kids. Then kind of drifted apart.'

'When I run into him next time, I'll let him know you're still alive.' The agent turned to the local cop. 'Anything you want to ask?'

The police officer shook his head.

299

'Okay, then, Mr. Kerr. I'll be taking off. Your housekeeper's kindly made up a room for my man. He'll be living with you for a while. Just treat him like one of the family.'

'Does that mean you can claim him as a tax exemption?' Moishe wanted to know. Laughter rocked the room, dissipating the tension and anxiety that had greeted Daniel only a short while earlier.

Moishe was the last to leave, standing by the front door while Daniel thanked him for coming round. Not only had he supported Anna until Daniel had arrived home, he had also acted as a release valve for the presure with his insane jokes. After watching Moishe drive away, Daniel returned inside. He checked that the FBI agent was comfortable before looking in on Benjamin who was already in bed.

'You're going to have an escort when you go to school tomorrow,' Daniel promised. 'You'll be the talk of the school.'

'Do you think I'm the one who's in danger?' his son asked. 'Or is it Ma and you?'

Touched by the intelligence and consideration of such a question, Daniel was uncertain how to answer. 'I hope that none of us in in danger,' he replied at last. 'The cops seem to believe we're just facing some crank who picked on us. With the forces we've got on our side now they should pick them up soon.'

'I wish I'd taken more notice of that woman those times she spoke to me,' Benjamin said wistfully. 'Then she might be out of our hair already.'

Daniel chuckled at the sentiment. 'That's a problem Moishe will never have,' he joked. 'Good night.' He turned off the light and left the room. In the hall, he passed the FBI agent on the way to the bathroom.

'Anything you need?'

The agent shook his head. 'Nothing at all, thanks, Mr. Kerr. I'm being looked after here better than in my own home. Sleep well.'

Daniel entered his own bedroom. Anna was waiting for

him, sitting in the chair by the dressing table. They were alone at last, and she could ask him what had happened at the Grand. He had arrived home much too early to have completed the performance.

'I blew the ''Di quella pira.'' Cracked the high-C.'

'What did Mr. Duguid say?' Anna knew she did not have to ask the question; the answer was already obvious.

'He dropped the curtain, and then went onstage to say I'd been taken ill. They picked up the third act again from ''Di quella pira'' with my understudy.'

'Did you see Mr. Duguid afterwards?'

Daniel nodded. 'He insisted that I take a leave of absence until this thing blows over. He says I'm harming myself more than anyone else by persisting.'

'He's right. How do you feel?'

'Rough. And mad. I'd like to get hold of the sonofabitch behind all this. What the hell did we ever do to deserve all this crap?'

'Daniel, have you really combed your memory? Are you sure there isn't someone with good reason to hold a grudge against you? You know, you did some pretty wild things in the old days.'

'You mean Pomerantz? Still mad at me because of what I cost Carmel Studios?'

'Pomerantz. Anyone. What else did you get up to?'

'What's the point in going back before then? No one holds a grudge for twenty or thirty years.'

'Then why have we been singled out? Daniel, it's terrifying to know that someone out there' — she waved vaguely at the bedroom windows — 'is jerking us around like a puppet on a string.'

'Ah, there are more nuts out than in,' Daniel said as he tried to assure Anna. 'The cops'll nail this one as well. Quit worrying about it.'

'And what about you? You're not worried? You're so calm that you blew a high-C for the first time in your life.'

'That wasn't fear. That was age. I'll be fifty soon.' He pulled off his shirt and stood in front of the full-length

301

mirror, sucking in his stomach. 'There. That's not bad for half a century, is it?'

'Now let it out,' Anna told him. 'You won't be able to see your feet.'

A knock on the door made Daniel hastily throw on a dressing gown. The FBI agent stood outside, bedsheets and pillow bundled up in his arms.

'Mr. Kerr, I think it would be better if I slept downstairs on the couch. Good night.'

'Good night.' Daniel closed the door and continued preparing for bed. He decided to shower. The make-up from the aborted performance was still on his face and he could smell the sweat on himself. Fifteen minutes later, when he emerged from the bathroom, Anna was sitting up in bed.

'I was wondering whether you'd notice,' she greeted him.

'That I smelled?'

'No. That you were still wearing Manrico's face. God knows what that man from the FBI must have thought when you came marching in looking like that.'

'Or just now,' Daniel added. 'Seeing me all ready for bed with a pound of heavily applied make-up on my face. Thanks for telling me.'

'There's probably a standard police officer mentality that thinks all artists are freaks and should be accepted as such,' Anna said. 'You didn't disappoint them.'

Daniel slid into bed, reached across Anna and turned out her light. As he pulled back his hand, Anna grasped it. 'Daniel, I don't want to go to sleep. I'm frightened.'

'You and me both,' Daniel admitted. 'The only one who's not scared out of his wits is Benny. He's more worried about us than anything else.'

'Talk to me.'

He put his arms around her, closing his eyes for an instant while he tried to remember Anna as he had first known her. She'd had a body that was kept as fit and lithe as any athlete's. Years of being a singer, of being a wife, of being a mother had taken their toll. Anna was heavier, with comfortable folds of flesh that he could grasp where before there had been only skin. Her hair, like his own, had streaks of grey, and she had taken to wearing glasses for reading. She had considered having her hair tinted to remove the visible signs of age, only to decide against it after making the appointment. An old man like you would look peculiar with a young girl on his arm, she'd told Daniel. People will think you're out with your daughter, not your wife. Daniel found it comforting that Anna was content to age gracefully with him. The grey hair did not have to be there; nor did the lines that were showing in her face. She could have them camouflaged, removed. Daniel was grateful that she had chosen not to.

'What shall we talk about?'

'Anything. Anything at all. Just as long as it's not this hell we're being put through.'

He kissed her tenderly on the forehead, feeling her snuggle closer to him. Slowly he moved downward, caressing her eyelids, the tip of her nose, her lips. Anna moaned softly and pressed against him. There was no need to talk.

CHAPTER FOUR

The reason for Daniel's leave of absence somehow reached the press. Newspapers were sympathetic, atoning to some degree for the doubts critics had expressed about the continuation of his career when he had been replaced in *Il Trovatore* by the understudy. Questioned by reporters, Daniel had admitted that threats were being made against his family, adding that the FBI and local police were adopting protective measures to combat the menace. Jack Regan, the agent heading the investigation, came down hard on Daniel for his tactlessness. Then, when nothing happened for a month — no phone calls, no letters, no visitations — Regan told Daniel that his error might have been advantageous. Publicising what the police were doing had probably forced the crank to seek new victims to harass.

The police and federal agents decided to end their vigilance. Daniel and Anna agreed, relieved, wanting to believe that the campaign of terror was over. No reason had existed for it to commence; similarly, for no reason, it had finished. Daniel met with Duguid and made arrangements to return to the Grand. Duguid decided to make him wait a further two weeks, until the next scheduled production of *Il Trovatore* in which he was to have starred. He had left the company with Verdi's opera. It was only fitting that he should return in the same role. He would dispel any doubts about his voice and simultaneously set to rest any rumours that the threats plaguing his family had been nothing more than a cover-up for his failure to sing.

Publicised beforehand in the press, Daniel's return to the Grand was an unqualified success. A ten-minute, foot-banging, hand-thrashing ovation greeted his 'Di quella pira.' At the end of the final act, the audience — his audience — refused to let him go. They called him back again and again until at last he raised his hands in the air, as he'd seen Joe Louis do those many years earlier at Yankee Stadium.

In Wheeler's, the post-performance atmosphere was festive — July the Fourth, Thanksgiving and Christmas all rolled into one. Daniel played the gracious host to Anna, Moishe and Helen. He had wanted Benjamin and Susie to attend the performance also, but they had school the following day and could not afford to go to bed at three in the morning. Susie was staying over at the house with Benjamin, watched over by the housekeeper, and would go straight to school in the morning.

Fans who stopped by the table to compliment Daniel on his performance were greeted with open arms. Autographs were scribbled on linen napkins. Robin Duguid stopped by to offer his congratulations yet again, staying long enough to chat with Anna about putting in more time with the company. Gently she rejected his persuasion. One production each season was all she would allow herself.

The party broke up just before two-thirty, when Moishe complained that he had to go to work in a few hours. Daniel's offer to drop him at the office on the way home met with muttered obscenities.

'Don't forget to set your alarm,' Daniel told Moishe when he dropped off his passengers. 'You don't want to take a chance on oversleeping.'

'I'll wake you up just as I leave,' Moishe said sourly.

'You just try and your head'll get to the office half an hour before the rest of your body does.' Still full of pleasure from the performance and the following celebration, Daniel laughed loudly. 'Glad you're not handling any cases for me in the morning. See you.'

When they reached their own house, Anna waited under the front porch while Daniel put the car away in the garage. He took the key from her and opened the door softly. The lower hall light was on and as he closed and bolted the door, he heard Anna gasp.

'What . . . ?' He spun around just in time to see Anna raise her hands to her mouth as she tried unsuccessfully to stifle a scream of terror.

By the light spilling from the hall into the living room, Daniel could see two figures tied to chairs, hands bound behind them, mouths covered with white adhesive tape. Susie and the housekeeper. The television was still on, a late-night movie sending light and dark shadows flickering across the room. Benjamin was nowhere in sight.

Daniel lunged into the room and tore the strip of tape from the housekeeper's mouth, unaware of the pain the violent action must have caused. 'What happened?'

The woman gulped, straining against the bonds that held her to the chair. As Daniel struggled to free her, she blurted out that two men had come to the house shortly before ten o'clock. When she had answered the door, they had pushed their way inside, tied her and Susie to chairs and . . .

'And what? Where the hell is my son?' Daniel snapped off the last of the ropes. The woman staggered to her feet, stumbling as her circulation-deprived legs refused to take the weight. He dragged her upright and pushed her into an armchair.

'They took him with them,' the housekeeper mumbled.

Daniel's expression was grim as he watched a technician dust the chairs that had held Susie and the housekeeper for fingerprints. Come on, you sonofabitch, find something! Anything! Even a smudge, he prayed for, a minute clue that could be quickly identified and would lead to the apprehension of the men who had stolen Benjamin. Two men only, Susie and the housekeeper had told the police and FBI agents who had flocked to the house. No sign at all of a blonde woman.

Daniel spared a moment to think of Anna, lying upstairs under a strong sedative, blissfully asleep. She'd screamed like a madwoman when she realised what had taken place. When the screaming had stopped, the crying had started, continuing until Anna had no more tears left, only dry, choking sobs as she blamed herself for not being in the house that night. Daniel had called a doctor who lived three houses away. The man had come right over and administered a shot. When Anna woke up, she'd remember and cry again, but that wouldn't be for a few hours yet. Daniel wondered how the experience would affect Susie and the housekeeper. Susie had been sent home as soon as the investigators had finished with her, picked up by a flabbergasted Moishe who had been woken up to be told about the abduction.

'I'm afraid all we can do is sit and wait now, sir,' said Regan, the FBI agent with greying hair and blue eyes who had led the investigation into the nuisance letters and phone calls.

'What?' Daniel had not heard a word; he was too busy thinking about Benjamin, whether the kid was all right, where he was.

Regan repeated his statement. 'It's a very unusual case, Mr. Kerr. With kidnapping, the victim is normally abducted and a ransom demand follows. Here, you and your family have been harassed for some time, like you were being warned something was going to happen. I'll be frank with you. I'm wondering if we're going to get a ransom demand at all.'

Daniel pondered the agent's words. Someone had yanked the kid, not for money, but for some other reason, all tied in with those letters and phone calls.

'Are you a rich man, Mr. Kerr?'

'I suppose so.' Personal wealth was the furthest thing from his mind. He would give away the whole bundle and start again from scratch if it would get his son back. 'What happens should a ransom demand come through?' He preferred to stick with that possibility; money, at least, was a motive he could comprehend.

'Well, the choice is up to you.' Regan stopped talking as the telephone rang. He motioned for Daniel to pick it up. Simultaneously he lifted an extension that had been installed early that morning.

'Yes?' Daniel could barely force himself to utter the single word.

'Danny? It's Moishe. What's happening?'

Daniel breathed out heavily, relieved that it was only Moishe. And at the same time disappointed. 'Nothing. Where are you?'

'Just got in the office. Anything I can do?'

'Pray.'

'I already did.'

Daniel believed him. 'Thanks.' He saw Regan waving at him to get off the line. 'Moishe, I'll speak to you later.'

'Okay. Good luck.'

'Stay off the phone,' the agent warned. 'Just in case a call should come through.'

'What were you saying before about the choice being mine?'

'Either to pay whatever ransom they want and hope to get your son back that way, or let us handle the drop and try to nail whoever's behind it.'

'Which way ensures my son won't be harmed?'

Regan shook his head sympathetically. 'There's no guarantee about anything. We prefer that we're allowed to handle it. But it's your son who's involved so the choice is yours.'

Daniel didn't need to think it over. 'If I can raise the cash, I'll pay to get my son back. You can worry about catching the bastards responsible afterwards.'

Regan glanced through the living room window as a grey Chevrolet pulled up outside the house to join the cluster of automobiles already there. A man wearing a heavy camel coat and a snap-brim hat pulled low over his eyes walked quickly from the Chevrolet up the path to the front door. Before the bell could ring, Regan left Daniel and went to open the door.

'Hi, Cherrybum.'

'Hi, copper.' There wasn't the faintest trace of pleasure in Daniel's voice as he greeted Tommy Mulvaney. It might just as well have been a total stranger standing in front of him. Benjamin's abduction drained him of all emotion but fear. 'What are you doing here?'

'Helping out if I can. I saw the report and came right over.' He let his eyes drift over Daniel, then he smiled. 'You haven't changed a bit, Cherrybum. You're still fat enough to make damned good plate blocker.' He clapped Daniel on the shoulder and wandered away to watch the man dusting for fingerprints.

'You've got the big hitters going to bat for you,' Regan said. 'If anyone can direct this case, Mulvaney can.'

Daniel nodded absently while his eyes followed Tommy. The guy had turned out just like his old man, a solid, uncompromising face, hardly an ounce of fat on the body. Only the hair had changed, the bright red, angry ginger fading to a salt-and-pepper mixture of red and grey.

Tommy came back and pulled Daniel aside. 'Where's Anna?'

'Upstairs. Sleeping.'

'You've got no idea who's out to get you?'

'None.'

'Has Regan explained the procedure to you?'

'That I can pay up or leave it in your hands. If there's a ransom demand.'

Tommy nodded. 'What do you want to do?'

'What will get my kid back for me?'

'If I knew that . . .' He left the sentence unfinished.

'What about the blonde woman who started all this?' Daniel assumed that Tommy knew the history of the case, right back to Benjamin being pestered outside school.

'Do you know how many blue Mercurys there are? Sure we've got people looking for a blonde driving one with New York plates, but don't get your hopes up over that. The only line we'll get is when the kidnappers contact us.'

'How long does that normally take?'

'Depends. Some do it immediately because they want to get it over with as quickly as you do. Others? Well, they take their time to build up the suspense.'

Daniel forced himself to ask the question from which he had been hiding. 'Even if I pay, is there a guarantee . . . '

'That you'll get your kid back in one piece? I wish I could tell you yes, but I can't.'

'Thanks for being honest.'

Tommy gave him a sardonic smile. 'That's what we're supposed to be. If we're not, who is?'

Anna awoke shortly before midday. When she ventured downstairs, her mind was still numbed by the sedative, but she remembered Tommy from the meeting more than fifteen years earlier in Greenwich Village. 'How's your wife?' she asked, a question that Daniel had neglected.

Tommy grimaced. 'She gave me an ultimatum about six years ago. Her or the job. I guess I took too long making up my mind.'

'Any children?'

'Three. A boy and two girls. They're with her.'

'Are you divorced?' Daniel asked, surprised.

'No. Just separated. She won't even mention the word — a good Catholic — and I don't see any point in getting one. We see each other weekends.'

The telephone rang, a single sharp jangle that cut through everyone in the room like a winter wind. Daniel's hand jerked spasmodically as he reached out for the receiver. Tommy slammed his hand down on top. 'Let it ring a couple of times, Cherrybum. Don't show them you're sitting on it.' He strode to the extension, his eyes on Daniel, waiting for him to answer.

Daniel picked it up on the third ring. 'Yes?'

'Mr. Kerr.' A woman's voice. 'Your son is well.'

Daniel flicked a glance at Tommy, who nodded encouragingly. 'Where is he?'

'Never mind where he is. You will only see him again if you do exactly as we say.'

310

'Who are you?' Daniel asked stupidly in response to Tommy's mimed command to keep talking.

The question was ignored. 'We'll speak to you again at five o'clock this evening.' The call ended abruptly.

Tommy got through to the telephone company. There was nothing, no way of getting a bearing on such a short call. 'Looks like we've got to wait.'

'Do you think it was the blonde woman?' Anna asked.

'Who knows?' Daniel had never felt so helpless in his life. The joy and triumph of the previous night had turned sour, leaving him desperate and impotent, unable to do anything. He realised what course he had to follow. Tommy and Regan, the other FBI agent, had laid out the cards clearly. Either he could deliver whatever ransom the kidnappers demanded in the hope that Benjamin would be released, or he could let the FBI use the drop as a lead to cracking the case — which would probably endanger his son. Only one course appealed to him — give them whatever the hell they wanted just to get Benjamin back. He'd worry about the money afterwards.

Five o'clock came and went without another phone call. Tommy tried to ease Daniel's fears by saying he had expected it. The kidnappers were playing with Daniel, teasing him, psyching him up to such a degree of anxiety that he would do anything when they finally decided to reveal their terms.

Moishe arrived just before six, battling his way through the reporters camped outside the house, to offer any help he could. He knew of Tommy's presence from radio reports on the kidnapping. They shook hands formally, two men at a business meeting; old friendships could be continued at a later date.

The telephone rang many times with friends and colleagues anxious to learn what was happening. Daniel kept the calls short, explaining that the line had to be free. At seven-thirty, the call he was waiting for came through.

'Mr. Kerr.'

He recognised the woman's voice immediately. 'Where

were you at five?' he demanded angrily. 'You told me you'd call back at five!'

On the extension, Tommy raised a hand to caution him to remain calm. Then he dropped it. If Daniel got involved in an argument with the kidnappers, he might keep them on the telephone long enough to get a trace; anything was worth a try.

The woman took no notice of Daniel's furious questions. 'We want two hundred thousand dollars for the return of your son. In cash. By midday tomorrow.'

'Where the hell am I supposed to come up with that?'

'You're worth it.'

'Not in accessible cash I'm not!' He looked around the room wildly, searching for ideas to prolong the call. 'I'll need more time. I can't raise that much by midday.'

'You'll have to. We'll call back at midnight with directions for the delivery.'

'Ask to speak to your kid,' Moishe mouthed.

'How do I know my son's all right?' Daniel asked the woman. 'I want to speak to him.'

'You can't.'

'Lady, I'm not putting together ten bucks until I know my son's all right.'

The woman hung up.

Tommy cursed quietly and fluently. 'Let's see if we had any luck this time.' He called the exchange and shook his head. 'Too quick again. Can you get that kind of bread?'

'From the bank. They'll loan me.'

'How much do they want?' Anna and Moishe asked simultaneously.

'Two hundred grand. By midday tomorrow.'

'I'm going outside to talk to the reporters,' Tommy said. 'Keep them off your back by giving them something to chew on.'

Daniel watched through the bay window of the living room as Tommy answered reporters' questions. He had no idea what Tommy was saying; he just wished he had the answers himself.

By five minutes after midnight, Daniel knew he had to make the hardest decision of his life. Do it Tommy's way, or the way he wanted to. The woman had called at precisely midnight to ask Daniel if he had arranged for the money. Daniel said he had, in used fifties and twenties. The bank manager would have it ready for him at ten-thirty the following morning. The woman had then specified that the money was to be delivered to a drive-in movie in Little Ferry, four miles away from where Daniel lived. The movie lot was abandoned for the winter, and the surrounding area was deserted enough for any police tails to be spotted. If the pick-up man was satisfied that whoever made the delivery had not been followed, the woman had said, he would accept the ransom. If not, the pick-up would be aborted and the woman promised Daniel he would never see Benjamin again.

'I'm a father, too, Cherrybum,' Tommy said softly. 'I know exactly what you're thinking right now. Do you want us to handle it, or do you want to make the drop yourself and hope for the best?'

Daniel did not know how to answer. He had dreaded this moment, when the life of his son would hang on his words.

'Do it Tommy's way,' Anna said quietly. 'We have no guarantee of Benjamin's safety even if we do it their way.'

Tommy didn't wait for Daniel's opinion. As far as he was concerned, Anna had spoken for them all. 'We'll set the place up. The only thing remaining now is whether you want to make the drop yourself, with us keeping watch, or you'd rather one of my men did it.'

'I'll do it.' The offer came from Moishe. 'Give me the directions and the money and I'll make the drop. They take one look at me, and they'll know I'm not a cop.'

The comment brought a smile to the faces of the people in the room. Tommy asked Daniel for a large suitcase he could use. 'We can fix it up, plant a homing device that'll give us an idea where they go. We don't want to follow too closely in case they tumble onto us.'

Daniel went upstairs for the suitcase. When he came back down, Tommy was briefing Moishe on what he had to do.

Moishe set out from the house at eleven thirty-five the following morning. The suitcase containing two hundred thousand dollars was locked in the trunk of his car. The instructions were clear. He was to enter the empty drive-in, drop the suitcase in the garbage container close to the entrance and leave immediately. Six FBI agents in three vehicles had already staked out the drive-in, and local police had been warned to give the vicinity a wide berth.

Daniel remained in the house with Anna, Tommy and another agent. The two FBI men showed no signs of the anxiety that was eating away Daniel's stomach like acid. He guessed they were used to the tension, hardened professionals, men who had been through it a thousand times in a thousand similar situations.

A radio transmitter on the table next to Tommy crackled into life. One FBI team disguised as a telephone repair crew had seen Moishe entering the drive-in. 'There's something wrong. Another car's just pulling in behind him.'

'What kind of car?'

'A dark blue Mercury with New York plates. Just the driver, a male Caucasian.'

Daniel sat bolt upright in the chair, his hand clasping Anna's at the mention of the blue Mercury. The agent read off the licence plate and Tommy told the other man in the living room to run it.

'Stay with it,' Tommy advised the stake-out man. For the first time a tremor showed in his voice.

'Why have they changed their plans?' Daniel asked. 'Moishe was supposed to drop off the money in the garbage container. He wasn't supposed to be met.'

'I don't know. Maybe they had the house staked out, just like we're doing to the drop-off point. They saw a man leave with a suitcase so they followed to make sure Moishe wasn't being tailed by us.'

Suddenly a babble of voices erupted from the transmitter, shouted words about suspects and deliveryman and shooting. Tommy grabbed the transmitter. 'Move in!' he snapped. 'Pick him up!'

'What happened?' Daniel asked.

'They forgot the rules, Cherrybum. The guy in the Mercury just shot your buddy and tried to run with the suitcase.'

'Where are you going?' Daniel screamed as Tommy ran towards the front door.

'Where do you think? Down there.'

Daniel forgot all about Anna as he leaped after Tommy. 'Not without me you're not!'

Tommy and Daniel arrived at the drive-in moments after an ambulance had whisked Moishe off to the hospital. Regan was waiting and Tommy demanded to know what had happened. Twenty yards away, past a line of audio hook-ups for the movie, Daniel could see a man in handcuffs.

Regan related the events in a dull monotone; he might just as well have been reading off a shopping list. 'The suspect was waiting by the entrance. As Mr. Waterman drove in, he followed. Mr. Waterman got out of his car with the case, intent on depositing it in the garbage container. When the suspect tried to take the case from him, Mr. Waterman put up a struggle. The suspect then pulled out a gun and fired one shot.'

'How is he?' Daniel burst out. 'Moishe. What happened to him?'

Regan seemed to notice Daniel's presence for the first time. 'It was a flesh wound. The bullet just nicked his left shoulder. If you ask me, Mr. Kerr, your friend fainted the moment he saw the gun. He was already on his way down when the suspect fired. We came out before he could fire again.'

Daniel's head dropped onto his chest and a sigh of relief shook his frame. Until he remembered Benjamin. He grabbed Tommy by the arm and pulled him around. 'What happens to my son now?'

'I don't know. All we can do is grill this guy. If we get nothing out of him, we have to go back and wait for another phone call.' He turned to Regan. 'What have you got on the suspect?'

Regan didn't have to consult any notes. 'Name's Paul Fulford. Address 73-12 Thirty-seventh Avenue, Jackson Heights. An apartment. We're checking his sheet now.'

Daniel followed Regan and Tommy across to the handcuffed suspect, who was being guarded by two more agents. On the ground next to the man was the suitcase containing the money.

'Has he been told his rights?' Tommy asked. One of the agents nodded. Tommy directed his attention to the suspect. 'You want to help yourself? Or do you want to protect your friends?'

The man said nothing.

'Kidnapping is a capital crime. Do you know what that means? You can burn for it. Is that what you want, while your friends get off scot free?'

'I don't know anything about any kidnapping. I was trying to grab that guy's suitcase, that's all.'

'With a gun?' Tommy asked sarcastically. 'You needed a gun for that?'

Watching, Daniel felt the fury of his own temper building up inside him. He shoved his way between Regan and Tommy and lunged at the handcuffed man. 'Where's my son?' he bellowed. 'What have you done with my son?' Before any of the federal agents could make a move to stop him, he pounded a huge fist into the man's face and sent him staggering backwards. Unable to break his fall with his hands, the man crashed awkwardly to the ground, skinning his face on the hard, frozen earth.

Hands grabbed Daniel's shoulders, lifting him as he tried to dive onto the prostrate figure. He shook himself free and pounced again, fists still flying. One punch hammered into the concrete ground. Daniel never felt the spasm of pain that flashed up his arm. All he knew was the blind, hopeless rage that consumed him. The man on the ground knew where his son was being held. That man could stop his son from being harmed. 'Tell me where he is, you bastard! Before I kill you!'

Hands grabbed him again, this time like steel claws which yanked him upright. 'Knock it off, for Christ's sake!'

Tommy yelled. 'We want a suspect for questioning, not a goddamned corpse!'

'He knows where my kid is!' Daniel screamed back.

'He's not going to tell you anything if you split his head open and spill his brains on the earth. Will you listen to reason?'

One of the agents interrupted the argument with news about the suspect. 'He owns a bar on the Northern Boulevard in Queens. No record at all. The Mercury's registered to him.'

'No record?' Tommy asked. 'Are you sure?'

'Not under his own name. Clean as they come.'

Tommy turned to face the suspect. The man was slowly getting to his feet. Blood was trickling from his nose and one side of his face was badly scraped. 'Fulford, you help us and I promise you the judge'll let you down lightly. You've got no record and my word'll help.'

What did letting down lightly mean? Daniel wanted to know. Five years? Ten? No matter how much the guy helped, Daniel did not want to see him let off. He'd put Anna and Benjamin through misery and torment; why the hell should he be treated leniently?

A crowd had gathered, attracted first by the sound of the shot, then by the flurry of action in the deserted drive-in theatre. Local police had to be called in to keep onlookers at a distance. Tommy decided that the area was becoming too public. He gripped Fulford by the arm and steered him towards the fake telephone repair truck. Police officers cleared a path through the crowd. Tommy shoved the handcuffed suspect into the back of the truck and slammed the door on him.

'You ever hear of the nice-guy-bad-guy routine?' he asked Daniel.

Daniel stared at him blankly, unable to understand.

Tommy explained briefly. 'A subject is interrogated by two men. One's reasonable while the other wants to break every bone in the suspect's body. It's a psychological deal. I reckon you're the most believable bad guy around here right

317

now. We're going for a ride.' He told Regan to get in and drive. Then Tommy climbed in the back of the truck with Daniel.

As the truck began to move, Tommy opened up. 'We're taking a trip, Fulford. By the time we're finished, you're either going to tell us where the Kerr kid is, or you're going to be carried out of here in a bag. Take your choice.' He sat back against the wall of the truck while he let the words sink in. Daniel watched carefully, looking for his cue. Not that he needed one. He didn't need any kind of cue to launch himself across the confined space and slam the bastard's head to pulp against the wall.

'Where do you want me to go?' Regan called from the driver's seat.

'Go on 46 back towards the Bridge. Keep it slow.' Satisfied that Regan was going in the right direction, Tommy turned back to Fulford. 'Tell me where the kid is. Otherwise I'm going to let his father loose on you.'

'I don't know anything about any kid.'

'He's all yours, Cherrybum.'

Daniel crouched in the low space. His hands shot out and caught Fulford around the neck. Four times in quick succession Daniel smashed the man's head into the side of the truck. Each blow was accompanied by a scream of pain. In the front, Regan glanced in the mirror to see what was happening, then he looked back at the road.

'That's enough!' Tommy called out. Daniel moved back and Tommy confronted Fulford again. 'That's just a taste of what you're going to get. When we were kids, this guy beat the hell out of me with a baseball bat. That's nothing to what he'll do to you. And we'll swear on a stack of bibles that you were trying to escape. That you jumped out of the back of the truck and bounced on the road a few times.' Tommy heard the radio but paid no attention.

Regan's voice came from the front. 'There's been another phone call to the house. The woman. Says the bagman's late and if he doesn't get back in half an hour, they're going to dump the kid.'

318

Daniel pushed Tommy out of the way. 'Where's my kid?' His clenched fist crashed into Fulford's face. The suspect's head bounced sickeningly off the side of the truck. Tommy made no attempt to intervene, as if he had realised that Daniel's way was now the only way. Time was the most important factor now.

'Where's my kid?' Daniel's fist slammed into the man again. His knuckles were bruised and bloody, throbbing with pain from where he had hit the frozen ground before, but all he knew was the release of the fury that had been boiling up inside him like a volcano since the blonde woman had first appeared. 'Where is he? Where are they holding him?'

Tommy pulled back Daniel's arm as he was about to strike again. Fulford's head was hanging loosely. A froth of blood covered his nose and mouth. As he breathed, red bubbles formed and burst obscenely. 'He's going to beat you to death and I'm not going to raise a finger to stop him,' he warned quietly. 'Unless you tell us what we want to know.'

The man tried to say something. A gurgling came from his battered mouth and he spat out blood. 'Empty apartment in the Bronx. University and One Fifty-ninth.'

'Move it!' Tommy shouted to Regan. 'University and One fifty-ninth! Call in more units!' Regan sent out the call and put his foot down on the gas pedal; as an afterthought, he called the house to keep the agent posted there informed.

'Will we get there in time?' Daniel asked.

'Easy,' Tommy replied. 'Other units will be there before us.' He turned to Fulford. 'Who else is in the apartment?. How many?'

'Two,' the man mumbled painfully. 'Man and a woman.'

'Names?'

Daniel felt the truck pick up speed as Regan headed towards the George Washington Bridge.

'Jack Harris.'

'The woman?'

'I don't know her name.'

'You don't know her name?' Tommy asked incredulously.

'She came into my bar a few times. Felt us out, Jack and me, to see if we were interested in this job.' The man's voice became clearer. 'Said we could keep all the money. She didn't want any part of it.'

'What did she want?'

'She wanted him.' The man nodded at Daniel.

'Why did you shoot the guy who made the drop? Why didn't you keep to your part of the bargain and let him drop off the money in the garbage container?'

'The broad was planning on stringing it out. I was going to take the money, and she'd call you to say the money wasn't where it was supposed to be. She'd threaten to have the kid killed. Then she'd call again to say we'd got the money but now it wasn't enough. She told us maybe we would end up with half a million between us this way.'

'Were you going to let the kid loose?'

'I don't know what she'd planned. I never meant the kid any harm, honest. You've got to believe me. I didn't mean to hurt the guy who made the drop either. I never thought a skinny runt like that would put up a fight.'

Tommy turned around to look at Daniel. 'Someone's sure got it in for you, Cherrybum. Got it in for you so much that they're not even interested in the money. Any ideas?'

Daniel shook his head. He must have made enemies along the way. Everyone did. But no one, surely, would strike back this fiercely. He thought about Moishe and asked Tommy to check how he was. Regan called the agent stationed at the hospital.

'Your pal's all right. A graze, nothing more. He'll be home by tonight.'

'Thank God for that.' Now all he had to worry about was Benjamin.

CHAPTER FIVE

Anna sat quietly in the living room, willing herself to remain calm. From time to time she looked at the federal agent who had been left behind. He had answered the telephone when the woman last called, and had relayed the information to Tommy Mulvaney. Anna had been unable to help but overhear the urgent message. When he realised what he had done, the agent tried to cover up. But Anna knew the truth. The dreadful knowledge from which she had tried to hide had made itself felt. Her son's very life was in danger.

She felt cold, encased in a block of ice, unable to think or act. The role of operatic heroine had invaded reality. All the tragedies in which she had ever starred had combined into one greater tragedy. Only now there was no comforting knowledge that when it was all over, she would stand in front of the gold curtain and accept ovations, flowers. The ending to this particular production had not been written yet. The composer was penning in the notes while he went along, changing in mid stroke to give another twist, another dimension to the performance. Or — the most chilling possibility of all — had the final act already been written? Was Benjamin even now dead?

'Are you all right, Mrs. Kerr?' the agent asked, concerned at her silence. 'Is there anything I can do for you?'

'Just get my son back to me.'

The agent laid a reassuring hand on Anna's arm. 'Try not

to worry, Mrs. Kerr. They know where he's being held. They're on the way there now. They'll get him out.'

Anna searched the man's eyes as she tried to find the truth. She saw nothing; the certainty in his voice had not reached his eyes.

'Can't this thing go any faster?' Daniel snapped at Tommy. 'We're crawling along, for Christ's sake. We'll be too late!'

'We're doing seventy-five,' Tommy replied as the truck streaked across the bottom level of the George Washington Bridge. From somewhere a flashing red light had appeared on the truck, accompanied by a strident siren to clear its path; inside the truck, the clamour was amplified tenfold. Daniel looked around and saw the bloody face of the man who had shot Moishe. Tommy had handcuffed him to the pipe leading from the gas filler to the tank. With each bump and jolt he swung around drunkenly, his unprotected head banging violently against the side of the truck. Daniel could not care less.

Four hundred yards from the apartment where Benjamin was being held, Regan turned off the siren and the light. The sudden silence was eerie. Daniel felt as if he were in an aircraft and his ears had just popped under pressure. He dug his fingers into them as he tried to clear the blockage, wanting to hear more than just the truck's straining engine note and the noise of other traffic. Without the piercing sound of the siren, the urgency had disappeared; and with it the chance to save his son.

'Up there.' Tommy pointed past Regan's shoulder at a corner apartment block. 'There are four cars there already.'

Daniel saw a lot of cars. He could not tell which ones belonged to the FBI. A man dressed in Con Edison overalls stepped from the sidewalk into the road and waved the truck to a halt.

'We're evacuating the building,' he called in through the open window to Regan.

'Won't that tip them off?' Daniel asked.

322

'Give us some credit, Cherrybum,' Tommy replied. 'They won't even know what's happening until we go in there.' He switched his attention to the man in Con Ed overalls. 'Can you see into the apartment at all?'

'We've got a lookout across the street.' The man pointed to another apartment block; a man was on the roof with a pair of binoculars. 'He hasn't been able to see inside though. They've got sheets or something over the windows.'

'Okay.' Tommy reached inside his jacket and withdrew a revolver. 'Let's get this thing over with.'

Daniel started to follow him into the building, but Regan blocked the way. 'Hey! I'm going with you!' Daniel protested.

'Nothing doing, pal,' Tommy said. 'You stay right here.'

'But —'

'I told you, nothing doing. This is our job, not yours.' He dismissed Daniel and led the way into the evacuated apartment building. Powerless, Daniel watched him go, followed by six other men. Regan stayed behind, alternately watching Daniel and the people who had gathered around the entrance to the building as they sensed something happening.

'Go on, beat it all of you!' Regan hissed. 'You're putting a kid's life in jeopardy.'

The crowd did not move. Regan edged towards the nearest people, waving his hands. In the instant it took the federal agent to make the move, Daniel darted into the building's doorway, looked around to orient himself and pounded heavily up the stairs. Behind, he could hear Regan's desperate shout for him to stop. Screw you! Daniel muttered. No one's keeping me out of something like this. That's my kid they're holding in there, and I want to see what happens.

As he reached the third floor, heart pounding, breath ragged, he recognised one of Tommy's men, pressed flat against the wall while he waited for a signal. The man turned at the sound of Daniel's heavy steps. Anger flashed across his face and he waved furiously with his hand for Daniel to keep back. Daniel stopped for an instant, then ran to where the agent stood.

'Get the fuck out of here!' the man spat out. Further down the hallway, Daniel could see Tommy and three of the other men; two were still out of sight and he guessed they were hiding somewhere, ready for action.

'I'm not going anywhere,' Daniel growled

The man made no further attempt to argue. His attention was on Tommy, who raised a hand in the air, then made a sharp cutting motion. One of the agents with him lifted a foot and slammed the door at the lock. Wood splintered. The door flew black and slammed against the wall with a noise like a bomb exploding. Tommy dived through with two other men hard on his heels. Shouts echoed along the narrow hallway. Daniel waited fearfully for the sound of shots. There were none. He rushed forward, charging into the apartment after the last of the agents. Confusion greeted him. Two agents held a man over a table; one had a gun jammed into his ear while the other searched him. Another two agents, their backs to Daniel, were grappling with a blonde woman. The bitch who had made the calls, molested Benjamin outside the school, threatened to kill him. Tommy stood in the centre of the room, the revolver back in its holster, supervising.

'What the hell are you doing up here!' he yelled as he recognised Daniel standing in the doorway.

'Where's Benny?'

'In the bedroom.' Tommy turned back to the two men who were struggling with the blonde. She was kicking and clawing like a fury. One man already had a deep red furrow down his cheek. Daniel ignored it all as he raced into the bedroom. A figure was crouched in the corner, mouth gagged, hands and feet tied. Daniel stared before he recognised the trussed-up parcel as his son. He leaped across the intervening space and scrabbled furiously with the ropes that bound Benjamin, fingers fumbling in their haste to release him. A noise from behind made him turn,

'Try using this.' Tommy held out a pocket knife. Daniel

324

slashed through the gag, then attacked the ropes that bound Benjamin's hands and feet.

'You all right?'

The boy tried to speak. A dry croaking sound came from his mouth. Tears welled up in his eyes and dribbled down his cheeks.

Why? Daniel wanted to scream. Why did these animals pick on someone who'd never harmed a soul? Gradually he forced himself to be calm, to ease Benjamin's anxiety by displaying none of his own.

'She said I was going to be killed, Pa,' Benjamin finally managed to say. 'Even if you paid what they wanted, she was going to kill me.' He started to cough and more tears sprang to his eyes. Daniel waited. 'She said they were going to leave me here after they left. I'd starve to death before anyone found me.'

'No one's going to hurt you, Benny.' Daniel could feel tears beginning to burn his own eyes. 'We're taking you home right now. Your mother wants to see you. When we get downstairs, we'll call her. You can talk to her. Tell her you're all right.' He helped Benjamin to stand up, watching in pain as his son hopped from one foot to the other as he fought against the agony of returning circulation. Tommy stepped forward to help, taking one arm while Daniel held the other.

They reentered the living room. All six agents who had entered the building with Tommy were present. The situation was under control. The man was sitting on the floor, hands cuffed behind his back. The woman, blonde hair awry, make-up smeared grotesquely, was being held by two men. Daniel stood in front of her and looked hard into her face. She was in her fifties, lines on her forehead and around her mouth. He could swear he had never seen her before in his life.

'What did I ever do to you?' he asked. 'What?'

She laughed harshly. The sound sent shivers down Daniel's spine. Then she spat at him, striking him under the right eye. He made no attempt to retaliate. The saliva dripped down his cheek like another tear. 'I hope you crawled,' she whispered. 'Writhed like I did when you killed my father, you bastard!'

The woman's words had more effect on Tommy than on Daniel. He grabbed hold of her chin and jerked her face around. 'Joey Bloom's daughter!' he exclaimed, voice full of wonder. 'Joey Bloom's daughter, Linda!'

'Linda?' The single word came out as a whisper, and Daniel stared at her in disbelief.

'Linda,' the woman said, a malicious edge in her voice. 'I waited years for this. It was worth waiting for. Just as it'll be worth rotting in prison for you, you sonofabitch!' She spat at him again, hitting his coat. 'I hope you burn in hell!'

'Get her out of here,' Tommy said. He'd seen enough. Any second now Daniel would lose control of himself, and this time Tommy was not sure he could handle him. The two men holding Linda began to move. Daniel motioned for them to stay, but let Regan take Benjamin outside.

'Why did you wait all this time?' he asked. 'And why my kid? Why not me?'

She regarded him coldly, debating whether to administer the ultimate injury by refusing to answer his questions. 'I watched you climb, Daniel, and I wanted you to fall off the ladder so badly that it burned a hole in my gut. Then I decided you'd fall harder once you got right to the top. So I waited. And I collected the ammunition I'd need to make your life a misery.'

Daniel listened, unable to find a reply to the hate in Linda's voice. The first girl he'd ever been with, ever made love to. He knew he should be yearning to strangle her right now. He had been until he found out who she was. Instead, he could feel nothing toward hers, no animosity, no anger. That had died. If he felt anything, it was pity.

'When I saw that picture of you, your wife and kid coming back from Israel, I knew how to hit you.'

'But why Benny?'

'Because I wanted you to live with it afterwards. Just like I

326

had to live with the memory of being there when you got my father killed.'

'Take her away,' Tommy said. This time Daniel did not try to stop the two agents who guided Linda out of the apartment, down to one of the waiting cars. He was exhausted. His own anger he could have coped with, understood. But how could be comprehend a woman who had nurtured a hatred for twenty-seven years?

'Come on.' Tommy put a hand on his shoulder and led him towards the hallway. By the door, he stopped. 'Hey, Cherrybum, I've got something for you.'

Daniel looked up expectantly. He saw Tommy's fist swing through a short arc before it impacted just below his left eye. He stumbled backwards, his own hands raised to defend himself.

'What the hell was that for?'

'For not staying downstairs when I told you to. You could have screwed up the whole deal by rushing up here the way you did.' He began to laugh when he saw the anger looming on Daniel's face. 'Besides, how in the name of heaven do you hope to claim self-defence for what you did to that guy downstairs when you haven't got a mark on you? Him with his head smashed in and you without a scratch!'

As Daniel comprehended, he dropped his hands. Self-defence. He had to have some mark on him, otherwise no one would believe it. Tommy didn't have to hit him so hard, though. The sonofabitch had put enough into the punch to knock out an ox.

Tommy's fist flashed through the air again and slammed into the same spot. Daniel spun around and collided with the wall. 'That's for what you did to me with a baseball bat when we were kids,' Tommy called out over his shoulder as he left the apartment. 'Now we're quits. Come on down and look after your kid.'

Daniel clawed at the wall for balance. He felt his eye, relived to find it was still in the socket. That Irish bastard could still hit, even if he was past fifty. Slowly he followed Tommy down to the street. There was no sign of Linda or the

327

man who had been with her in the apartment. Only Tommy and Benjamin remained outside the building. Regan was off to one side, pushing back a crowd of onlookers who wanted to see what the commotion was about. He was telling them they could read all about it in the newspapers that evening.

'Some shiner that guy gave you,' Tommy said. 'No wonder you hauled off like you did.'

Benjamin's eyes opened wide in fright as he saw the rapidly swelling bruise under his father's left eye. He could not make up his mind whether it had been there before. 'What happened, Pa?' He ran towards Daniel and threw his arms around him.

'Some other guy did it. Earlier. When we went to drop off the money they wanted.'

'What did you do to him?'

'Your father almost killed the guy,' Tommy answered. 'We had to drag him off, kicking and screaming.' He accompanied the words with a smile and Daniel could not help joining in. 'Isn't that right, Cherrybum?'

'That's right. No one hits your old man and gets away with it, Benny. And no one takes off with you and gets away with it either.'

'About time you made that call,' Tommy reminded him. 'Otherwise Anna's going to be going out of her head with worry.'

While the seconds ticked past, the vestiges of hope passed from Anna's breast. Either they had not found where Benjamin was being held, or — and the thought was even more frightening — they had found him and did not want her to know.

What did a mother do when she lost her only child? And when she was too old to ever hope for another? Daniel already knew how it felt for a father to lose his child. He'd been through it once already. He'd know how to cope. No; she changed her mind. He might cave in completely, be powerless to shrug off another tragedy. What would she do to numb the loss? Throw herself wholeheartedly back into her work? Lose herself in the embrace of the stage, of opera? Robin Duguid would like that. He was always trying to persuade her to become more involved with the Grand. For someone, at least, her own tragedy would present a silver lining.

The telephone rang. The FBI agent's hand reached out to lift the receiver before the first ring could end. He listened for a few seconds. 'For you,' he said, passing the receiver to Anna.

She searched his eyes for the truth. Did he know already what the call was about? And couldn't bear to tell her himself? 'Yes,' she said hesitantly into the mouthpiece.

'Ma? It's Benny.'

'Where are you?' How could she speak so calmly? Was she acting, using lessons she'd learned from the stage?

'I'm with Pa. I'm all right.'

The receiver dropped from Anna's hand, bounced on her lap and thudded dully onto the carpet. The agent started from his chair. He stopped when he saw Anna's closed eyes, the rhythmic movement of her chest as she sobbed quietly in relief. He got up from his chair and walked quietly from the room.

Daniel visited Moishe at home that evening to find his friend sitting up in bed, apparently well. As Regan had said, it was a graze, nothing more serious. Moishe insisted on displaying the bandages that swathed his left shoulder, all the while telling Daniel how it felt to face a man with a gun, to see the orange flame spurt out, to feel hot metal burn through flesh. While he listened, Daniel glanced at Helen. Every few words, she would pretend to dab tears from her eyes. Suddenly cast in the role of hero, with his picture in the newspapers and on television, Moishe was embroidering the story more with each telling.

'Who told you to go for the guy?' Daniel asked. 'Have you been reading Dick Tracy again?'

'What would you have done if it had been my kid?' Moishe retorted. 'If it had been Susie? You wouldn't have done the same thing for me?'

Daniel was too tired to argue. Today had seen the most strenuous performance of his life and he was mentally and physically shattered. He had spent almost an hour talking with reporters. Tommy had claimed another two hours of his time. Now he knew he had to go home to Anna and explain why a middle-aged blonde woman would organise a kidnapping against his son. That would be the most difficult part of all. He had kept Linda from Anna all this time; now that she had surfaced, Anna was entitled to know the connection. 'I guess I'd have done the same thing,' he finally admitted.

'I hear you did some job on that guy who shot me,' Moishe said, wanting to keep the excitement alive. 'Beat him black and blue.'

'Look what he did to me first.' Daniel pointed to his discoloured eye, already convinced that Tommy had not been responsible. 'Besides, if someone tried to shoot me, wouldn't you have done the same thing?'

'Only if he was chained up,' Moishe replied honestly.

'He was.'

While Moishe stayed in bed, Helen walked Daniel downstairs to the door. 'You know he thinks the world of you, don't you?' she said quietly. 'He wouldn't have volunteered to deliver the money for anyone else. Even for me, I don't think.'

Daniel thought about her words and smiled. 'Moishe and I have known each other for too long, I guess. He's had so much practice in going to bat for me that it's got to be a habit.'

'Moishe wouldn't have it any other way.'

On the doorstep, Daniel kissed Helen on the cheek. 'Neither would I. But don't tell him that.'

During the short journey home, Daniel reached his decision. He would be completely open with Anna about Linda. They had been married for too long, shared too much for it to be handled any other way. He would tell her about Linda and Joey Bloom. He'd leave nothing out. How he had

330

first met Linda in her father's hotel. The relationship between them. Then Fat Benny's murder, and how he had used Linda to trap her father. The whole episode had been closed more than seven years before he had met Anna, so what did it matter anyway?

Anna listened carefully to Daniel's account of his experience with Linda. It had little effect on her. She was just grateful that it was all over and that Benjamin was safe. If anything, she could not help sharing Daniel's sentiments, feeling sorry for Linda, sorry for a woman who had stored and nourished her hatred for twenty-seven years.

'What a terrible waste of a life,' she said when Daniel finished speaking. 'To spend it like that, plotting to wreck someone else's life.'

'I'm glad you can feel sorry for her.'

'Don't you? Or is it going to help if she goes to jail for the remainder of her life?'

'You know something? Pity's all I did feel when I recognised her in the apartment. First confusion. Then, when I realised who she was and why she'd done it, pity. I wonder if Tommy can do anything to her if we don't press charges.' The idea appealed to him. 'They can get the guy who shot Moishe for attempted murder. Probably nail that other clown for something. But I wonder if there's any sense in sending Linda to prison for the rest of her life.'

Anna was amused by Daniel's change in attitude. 'Before you were ready to kill. Now you're thinking about forgiving and forgetting.'

'Not forgetting.' He shook his head vehemently. 'Just forgiving. I'm getting too old to be vindictive anymore. I'm grateful that Benny's safe and sound. I don't want revenge because I can see what it did for Linda.'

'Why don't you ask Benny?' Anna suggested. 'See what he thinks.'

'Good idea,' Daniel agreed, pleased with it. Benjamin had been in the eye of the storm. He should be the one to decide what course of action to follow. Daniel got out of the chair and went upstairs, followed by Anna. He knocked

331

tentatively on the door of Benjamin's room, scared of waking his son if he was asleep. When a voice called out to enter, Daniel and Anna went inside. Benjamin was sitting up in bed, reading.

'Hi, how do you feel?'

'All right I guess.' Benjamin set the book on the night table. Daniel glanced at the cover and saw it was Leon Uris's *Exodus*. The kid must have read it half a dozen times by now; he kept on going back to it as if it were the Bible.

'We want to talk to you, Benny. We want to ask your advice.'

'What about?' The boy seemed disturbed at the prospect of adults coming to him for advice.

'That blonde woman. What do you think should be done to her?'

'She'll go to prison won't she?'

'Is that what you want to happen to her?' The question came from Anna.

Benjamin looked confused as he pondered the question. He didn't have the answer and his face showed it. 'I don't know. When I was in that room, all tied up, I wanted to kill them all. For what they were doing to me. And to you.'

Daniel nodded, understanding his son's emotions. They had been his own. 'And now?'

'Now I don't really care. It's over and I want to forget about it. I just don't ever want to see that woman again.'

'Okay, Benny, you won't.' Daniel leaned over the bed and kissed his son on the forehead. 'Good night. Get some sleep.'

Downstairs, he faced Anna. 'I'm going to call Tommy and tell him to forget about Linda. Let the poor bitch go free for all I care.'

'What if she tries something again?'

'Do you really think she would?'

It took Anna only a moment to decide. 'No.' She threw her arms around Daniel and hugged him tightly. 'You're just a big softie, you know that? A big soft teddy bear. And I love you for it.'

'Get off,' he protested, embarrassed that the housekeeper might come down and see Anna plastering his face with kisses. 'We're middle-aged. We're not supposed to be acting like this.'

'There's a little scrap of paper somewhere that says we can act any way we damned well like. Unless you want to let me go free as well.'

'You've got some hopes.'

'That's what I thought.' She became serious again. 'Don't forget when you speak to Tommy to mention those two tickets you offered him a million years ago. He might want them now.'

If Daniel were in front of him now, Tommy knew he would have no hesitation in closing his other eye to knock some sense into him. The whole idea was preposterous, wanting to let the woman go.

'You listen to me and you listen good!' Tommy yelled into the phone. 'That woman is going for trial with the other two. And she's going to be convicted with them. Nothing's going to interfere with this case.'

'But, Tommy ...' Daniel knew it was hopeless to continue. The whole idea was crazy, asking Tommy if he could let Linda go free. He and Anna were so overcome with relief at getting Benjamin back that their minds were clouded by a charity that didn't belong in the situation. 'Hasn't the poor bitch suffered enough? What's the point of sending her to prison?'

'Who the hell said anything about prison?' Tommy demanded. 'Kidnapping's an offence punishable by the death penalty.'

'What?' Daniel was horrified.

'Don't worry too much about it. We don't execute many people these days.'

'But can't you just let her go and forget about it?'

'Cherrybum, get this through your thick skull, will you? If you pull out on us, Uncle Sam's going to take a good, hard look at you. He'll want to know why you don't want to press kidnapping charges, why you're backing out. With a person in your position, there can be only one reason. There was no kidnapping. You needed publicity, that's the reason. Maybe your career's in trouble, who knows? But you needed some good, sympathetic publicity so you arranged to have your son kidnapped.'

'What? That's crazy! You know it's not true.'

'Sure I know it's not true. But you can't afford to be charitable because there are a whole gang of people who'll think you fixed the whole thing. And I wouldn't blame them.'

'What will happen to her then?'

'Life. Don't feel sorry for her, Cherrybum. She was a loser. Came from a family of losers. Just be thankful you got out of it okay. You hear me?'

'I hear you.' The euphoria of finding his own solution had been disintegrated by Tommy's cold realism. If it were not so serious, it would have been funny, setting himself up for an investigation by trying to show mercy to Linda. She would have had the last laugh after all.

'So forget all about this crazy idea. We'll let you know when we need you.'

'Hey, don't hang up!' Daniel remembered what Anna had told him. 'Do you want a couple of tickets for a performance? I'm doing *Il Trovatore* again before the end of the season.'

'You're doing what?'

'Never mind. It was just an idea. Be speaking to you, copper.' He replaced the receiver and went upstairs to Anna.

CHAPTER SIX

'Pa! Wake up! Wake up!'

Like a tornado in full, destructive flight, Benjamin burst through the door of his parents' bedroom to send it slamming back against the stop.

'What time is it?' Daniel asked groggily as he struggled to shake off slumber and sit up. Next to him, Anna poked fists into her eyes, trying to force them open. 'Is the house on fire? It had better be.' He saw his son standing over the bed. The kid was already dressed in jeans and a T-shirt. Perhaps it was late, and he and Anna had slept through the alarm.

'Six o'clock.'

'What?'

'Six o'clock' Benjamin repeated. 'Turn on your radio, quick! There's a war on!'

A war? Everyone knew there was a war on. Vietnam. Why was the kid getting so excited about it all of a sudden? Because he figured he might get drafted in a few years? Daniel reached out to flick on the bedside radio which was tuned to an all-news station. He didn't have to wait long. While Benjamin perched excitedly on the edge of the king-sized bed, Daniel and Anna listened to the announcer read out the latest information from the Middle East. Claims and counterclaims from Israeli and Arab spokesmen — all to Daniel's ears exaggerated. On the one hand, the Arab air forces claimed to have shot down hundreds of Israeli planes

335

during major air battles; on the other, the entire forces of Egypt, Syria and Jordan had supposedly been destroyed by the Israelis on the ground in the opening minutes of the war. Daniel felt giddy as he listened. Egypt was claiming its army was cutting across the thin waist of Israel in a drive to join up with the Jordanians, while the Israelis said they were pushing into the Gaza Strip and the Sinai.

'What do you think is happening?' Benjamin asked. 'Who's telling the truth?'

'Who do you think?' Daniel asked back. He wasn't sure himself, but he'd be damned if he'd let his son know that.

Benjamin looked from his father to his mother and back. 'I don't know. The Israelis, I hope.'

'So do I.' Daniel swung his feet clear of the bed and stood up, pulling the cord of his pyjama trousers tight as he felt them slipping. Like everyone else, he had followed the events of the past weeks with close, anxious attention. The threats by Nasser, the blockading of the Straits of Tiran, the ever more ardent flirtation with war. He had relaxed when the Israeli government had said it would try to seek a peaceful solution. If the Israeli claims of wholesale destruction of Arab air power were to be believed, the Arabs had also relaxed.

'Where are you going?' Anna asked.

'Downstairs. Make some coffee. Come on.' He put his arm around Benjamin's shoulders. 'We can listen downstairs. Give your mother some peace and quiet.'

By six o'clock that evening, Benjamin was arranging fund-raising activities through the local Zionist group to which he belonged, and Daniel had agreed to perform three concerts during the coming two weeks to raise money for Israel. He felt as if he had been in the middle of an explosion, like that time in London when the buzz bomb had landed a hundred yards away. Jewish organisations had called him up to ask if he'd perform in benefit concerts. Carnegie Hall had already been booked for one; so had the Grand. In the end, he stopped answering the telephone. There were only

336

so many hours in his day; he could not do anymore.

Benjamin arrived home after ten-thirty, eyes blazing with excitement. In his hand was a Manischewitz *gefilte* fish jar, full of money, coins and bills. While Daniel watched, fascinated, Benjamin counted the money out on the kitchen table. It amounted to one hundred and thirty-five dollars and twenty cents, all made from knocking on doors in the neighbourhood. Seven other boys of Benjamin's age had gone out that night; they expected to have more than one thousand dollars to send to Israel.

'When can we go there again, Pa?'

'How about we pack our bags and go right now?' Daniel asked, trying to keep his face straight.

'Can we?'

'Get out of here,' Daniel laughed. 'One, there's a war on right now. Two, you're in the middle of school. Maybe in the summer, if this thing has quietened down.' He had meant to answer if Israel won but could not bring himself to say the words. No such doubt existed in Benjamin's mind. The kid was convinced that Israel would emerge victorious. To dampen that ardour would be nothing short of sinful. Daniel, also, was beginning to feel confident. That evening, the most comprehensive news report had emerged from the war zone, and it appeared that Israeli claims to have destroyed the Arab air forces on the ground were true. Perhaps they'd reach the Suez again. Perhaps . . .

'Do you think they'll take the old city of Jerusalem?' Benjamin asked, reading his father's thoughts.

'Be something, wouldn't it?' Daniel answered with a huge grin.

'Pa, make me a promise. If they take the old city, we'll go there this summer. I want to see the temple.'

'I promise.' He pointed to the money on the table. 'Let's check that and I'll sign for it. We can talk about going to Israel in the morning.'

With a brightly coloured *yarmulke* perched dangerously on top of his thick brown hair and a *tallis* draped around his

337

shoulders, Benjamin merged into the Saturday-morning crowd of shirt-sleeved worshippers thronging the Western Wall of the temple and disappeared from view. The effect was not lost on Daniel and Anna, who stood at the back of the crowd, unwilling to be separated into the men's and women's sections of the makeshift synagogue that had been organised at the wall.

'He's one of them,' Anna marvelled. 'We brought up a middle-class American kid, and he fits into a bunch of Israelis like he was born here.'

'I know.' Daniel did not find it amusing. He saw a time in the future when his son would not ask to be taken to Israel for a vacation; he'd just up and leave. The United States and luxury weren't for Benjamin. He wanted to work for his pleasure, his fulfilment, wanted to work for it in the land he'd dreamed about ever since the first time he set foot inside a temple. When that day came, Daniel knew he would not fight his son. If Israel was what he wanted, Daniel would be proud, not regretful. He wondered if Anna realised it yet. He thought about discussing it with her now but refrained. She was the kid's mother after all. Mention something like Benjamin wanting to live in Israel — far away from the warmth and safety of home — and Anna would have a fit. She'd need time to adjust to it; now was not the moment to spring it on her.

As he listened to the congregation chanting prayers, Daniel was overcome by a sudden thought. He had not conducted a temple service since Harry Feldman at Paterson had died. Because of Benjamin's involvement in the local Jewish community, he went as regularly as he could to temple, but leading the service had become a memory. He preferred to be one of the congregation. Here in front of the Western Wall, all that remained of the biblical temple, Daniel wanted to take a service again. Here was where it had all started a hundred lifetimes earlier.

Taking a prayer shawl from the stack, he slipped it on and eased his way through the crowd of men to where Benjamin stood. His son looked up, surprised to see him.

'Thought you were just going to watch.'

'What's the matter? You think you're a better Jew than I am?' Daniel challenged. 'I tell you one thing, I'm a better *chazan* than the guy they've got.'

'Go ahead,' Benjamin invited. 'Show them what it's all about.'

Daniel did not need further prompting. He pushed his way gently towards the front of the congregation. The man who was leading the service, a white-bearded chaplain in the defence forces, regarded Daniel with curiosity as he squeezed himself out of the front row. As he waited for a pause in the service, Daniel hoped the old man spoke English.

'I'm a *chazan* in the States,' he whispered. He was certain enough people in Israel knew him, that the name of Daniel Kerr would be recognisable. He didn't use it. All he wanted right now was to be a cantor again. 'Can I take a part of the service?'

'Surely.' The chaplain accepted the request as a *mitzvah,* a good deed.

'I'll wait until the end of the service. The "Adon olom," if I may.' On his way through the congregation, Daniel had decided which hymn he wanted to sing, the closing piece from the Sabbath and High Holy Day morning services. He'd use the tune he had always reserved for the High Holy Days, a slow, intricate melody that only a cantor with the utmost faith in his voice would dare to use.

'Very good.'

Daniel made his way back to Benjamin. He looked towards the barrier separating men from women and spotted Anna. He waved and grinned triumphantly.

Benjamin seemed disappointed when he saw his father returning. 'What's the matter, aren't you good enough for this house?'

'Bite your tongue. You'll hear me.'

Towards the end of the service, Daniel moved again to the front. The bearded chaplain stepped aside and Daniel took his place on the raised dais. He faced the wall where an ark

339

had been erected to hold the sacred scrolls of the Torah. He changed his mind. He would sing to his audience, his congregation, give them a finale they had not anticipated.

Heads in the congregation lifted at the sound of the new voice, a world removed from that of the chaplain who had been conducting the service. The voice was recognisable, known by Americans in the congregation who had heard it on religious recordings. Smiles of pride and pleasure appeared to lift the solemnity of the service as the Americans recognised one of their own.

It was the first time Daniel had ever sung in the open air. He had no acoustics to worry about, no sounds bouncing back at him. There would be no applause either. It didn't matter. He was enjoying himself, even experiencing some of the feeling of coming home that his son felt. The fine temples of the United States, the grandeur of the opera houses he had graced held little at this particular moment against this sensation.

Daniel did not sing with the congregation. He sang above it, far above, letting his voice ring full as he aimed for the optimum combination of sweetness and sheer power. He improvised, interjected higher notes than normal, wished that the hymn could last forever.

Worshippers had come that morning to the Western Wall to witness a miracle. They were not disappointed. The miracle was the voice they heard. At the end of the hymn, the chaplain grasped Daniel's hand and shook it enthusiastically. He was besieged by well-wishers. Worshippers told him they had seen him at the Grand, had heard him on records; some even embarrassed him by pulling out pens on the Sabbath and asking for his autograph. He declined. When he saw Benjamin, he grinned happily. 'See? Your old man had them stomping in the aisles!'

'Mr. Kerr?' A middle-aged man pushed his way to the front of the crowd of admirers surrounding Daniel. 'I'm Mordecai Katz, of the Hebrew National Opera.'

'How do you do?'

Katz struggled to pull Daniel away from the crowd.

Benjamin followed and they walked towards where Anna was waiting. 'How long will you be staying in Israel, Mr. Kerr?' Katz asked.

'Another ten days.' Daniel introduced Katz to Anna.

'That's a pity. As I listened to you before, I thought that perhaps you might be interested in appearing in Israel.'

'That's something my agent would have to handle.'

'Would you at least do us the honour of stopping by the company if you are in Tel Aviv?' Katz asked. 'We have some interesting productions at the present time.'

'Lohengrin?' Daniel did not understand why he attempted such a feeble joke.

Katz smiled thinly. 'I doubt if you will ever hear Wagner played in this country, Mr. Kerr. Liszt, perhaps. He only wanted to give us our own country so we would leave his. Wagner wanted much worse done.'

'I know. I'm sorry. Look, we'll be in Tel Aviv in a couple of days. I'll drop by and say hello.' He shook hands with Katz and led Anna and Benjamin away.

'That was in bad taste, Pa,' Benjamin chided him.

'Don't know why I said it. I got turned off Wagner a long time ago.' He thought of Martinelli. Should he send the Italian a postcard showing the temple's Western Wall, inscribe it that his latest performance had been there? Maybe they could arrange their return flight with a stopover in Milan. He had not seen Martinelli since that night at La Scala nine years earlier, when he had dragged him onto the stage after *Aïda* to share in the acclaim. Martinelli had told him once that a cantor could never thrill his audience as a lyric tenor could. Well, he was wrong. And today Daniel had proven it.

'Want to stop off in Milan on the way home?' Daniel asked Anna.

'To see your friend Enzo?'

'I was just thinking about him.'

'I'd love to.' Anna linked arms with her husband and son, feeling secure and happy as she walked between the two men in her life.

Daniel only intended to spend a few minutes with Mordecai Katz at the Hebrew National Opera in Tel Aviv. He allowed himself to be shown around the opera house, nodding politely to everything Katz said, barely listening.

'. . . In 1947, when the British were still here, we began with Opera Israel,' Katz said. 'The first performance was *Thaïs* by Massenet, with Edis de Philippe who, with her husband Eben Zohar, formed the current Hebrew National Opera nine years ago.'

'That's right,' Daniel said automatically. 'Who's singing now with the company?'

'We had Placido Domingo with us for three years, until 1965 when he moved to the New York City Opera.'

Daniel nodded. He wanted to get outside, back to Anna and Benjamin who were waiting in a restaurant. 'If I can find the time, Mr. Katz, perhaps I'll drop in on one of your productions while I'm in Tel Aviv.'

Katz was so thrilled that he did not even notice the boredom enveloping his guest. 'I think you would like what we are doing,' he enthused. 'Especially our production of Halévy's *La Juive,* such a fitting work for this company.'

'*La Juive?*'

'Yes.' Katz didn't understand the questioning tone Daniel put into the name. 'Is there something wrong with that?'

'No. When is it?'

'Tomorrow night.'

'Let me have three tickets, will you? I'll be here.'

'Of course, Mr. Kerr. Of course. We will be delighted to have you and your party as our guests.'

Daniel sat through the performance of *La Juive,* totally absorbed by the story. He did not understand French, the language of the opera. The libretto, written in Hebrew, was not much use to him either. All he understood was the one aria, 'Rachel! quand du Seigneur,' which he had chosen as his final encore at Carnegie Hall. Nonetheless, he found himself wrapped up in the role of Eleazar, the proud Jewish

342

goldsmith in the Swiss town of Constance who sacrifices himself and his daughter in preference to bending to the will of the Church. Never before had he realised what a powerful role it was, far more dramatic than anything he had ever attempted.

'You want to do it, don't you?' Anna whispered as the audience called back the cast for curtain calls.

'Should I?' he asked uncertainly. He moved in the seat and found that his clothes were sticking to him. He had sweated as much during the opera as he did during his own performances. He felt as if he had sung every note with the tenor playing Eleazar. 'Depends on whether a certain soprano would come out of semi-retirement to sing Rachel.'

'It depends on a lot more than that, Daniel.'

He knew exactly what she meant. The choice of productions was not his decision. It was Robin Duguid's, based on a very simple yet effective formula. Check what had done well over the previous couple of seasons and use them as staples — *Bohème, Tosca, Rigoletto*. Then start to fill out the production roster. Add a few daring ones, modern operas that would have limited appeal but needed to be aired to round out the repertory. Where would something like *La Juive* fit into that?

'I could do it better than that guy.' he pointed towards the stage, where the young tenor was taking another curtain call. 'He doesn't have the depth Eleazar needs.'

'Of course you could do it better.' Anna wasn't trying to flatter him; that was an approach she had never used. She was telling the truth. Daniel was an established singer, a man who had held the spotlight for more than twenty years. He had the depth and experience needed for such a role.

'I'm going to talk with Duguid when I get back,' he decided. 'See if I can persuade him to revive it at the Grand.' He leaned across Anna and directed his next words to Benjamin. 'Whatever the Israelis can do, the Grand can always do better.'

Before leaving Israel, Daniel sent Martinelli a cable with

343

the flight number and time of arrival; he would be able to spend a few hours between planes in the city. When they landed in Milan, Daniel was surprised to find the Italian doctor was not there. Instead, he saw a smartly dressed young man holding up a piece of card with the name 'Kerr' printed on it.

'Did Enzo send you?' Daniel asked.

'I am his grandson, Benito. My grandfather regrets that he was unable to meet you personally but he said he is looking forward to seeing you again.'

'Benito, huh? Meet Benny.' Daniel introduced Martinelli's grandson to Benjamin and Anna. They checked the baggage onto the onward flight, then followed the young man out to the parking lot. A rusty, beige Fiat 600 awaited them. Somehow they managed to cram themselves into the minute car. Daniel was almost crouched double on the front passenger seat. Benjamin and Anna shared the tiny back seat, squashed against each other, the sides of the car and the seats in front.

'How is your grandfather?' Daniel asked as the youth swung the car out of the airport and joined the stream of traffic. He closed his eyes as the tiny car abruptly changed lanes and cut in front of a heavy truck. The truck driver's irate blast on the horn was rewarded with a derisive wave of Benito's hand through the open sunroof and a stream of Italian invectives.

'Not very well, I am afraid,' Benito replied, grinning as he glanced in the mirror to see the truck he had cut off. 'His arthritis has become very bad.'

'I didn't know he had arthritis.'

'My grandfather is not a man to burden others with his problems. You will see how he is when you meet him.'

Daniel had wondered if Martinelli had got arthritis by sitting in a car like this for long periods of time. He knew if the journey did not end soon, he would never be able to stand up straight again. He'd be able to play Rigoletto without a costume that was tailored to make him crouch. Only Benjamin seemed to be enjoying the ride, laughing loudly as he described to Anna how he would tell his friends about his trip in a mobile sardine can.

They stopped outside an apartment block. Daniel helped Anna and Benjamin out of the confines of the back seat. 'Come, Mr. Kerr,' Benito invited. 'We will meet my grandfather.'

'What happened to the house he used to live in?' Martinelli had sent Daniel his address change, but he had never mentioned moving into an apartment.

'The house was too big for him alone. He moved into an apartment complex for older people. Here he is looked after.'

Daniel was beginning to worry. The doctor had never mentioned any of this in his infrequent letters. Daniel knew Martinelli's wife had died, but never had the Italian admitted he was ill.

Benito rapped loudly at a door on the ground floor. A middle-aged woman answered, smiling pleasantly as she recognised the youth. He rattled off long sentences in Italian which Daniel did not understand. 'My grandfather is awaiting you,' Benito finally said. He led his three guests into the small apartment. Daniel glanced around as he walked through. The place resembled a hospital ward, everything neatly placed, everything plastic. The difference from the house Daniel had seen nine years earlier was staggering. The doctor had loved antique furniture. Here there was nothing old. There wasn't even the piano that Martinelli had loved to play.

'What is this place?' he whispered to Benito.

'It is a nursing home for elderly people. An old age home for people who have enough money to pay for their own apartment. My parents wanted my grandfather to be with us, but he refuses to be an imposition. He came here instead.' He stopped talking as the woman opened the bedroom door. Martinelli was sitting in a chair by the window, looking out. When he heard the door open, he turned around. Daniel was shocked. The once black hair was a dirty grey. The face was heavily lined, a piece of dark,

345

wrinkled leather. As Martinelli stood up with the aid of two metal sticks, Daniel could see how badly bent his back was.

'Daniel! Have you come to sing for an old man?' He crossed the room slowly, his movements restricted. Daniel started to go towards him but stopped when he felt Anna's restraining hand on his arm. He let Martinelli come to him.

'How are you, Enzo? What's with the sticks?'.

Martinelli looked disparagingly at the two sticks which supported him. 'She makes me use them,' he said, glaring at the woman who had opened the door. 'She runs my life for me. Do you let Anna run your life for you as well?'

The woman took Martinelli's words as a signal. She left the room; moments later, Benito followed.

'I'd be in a whole mess of trouble if I didn't,' Daniel replied to Martinelli's question. 'You remember Benny, don't you?' He pulled his son forward. 'From nine years ago?'

'He was a child. Now he is a giant.' Martinelli looked up and down the boy. 'He is truly your son, Daniel. Is he going to be a singer like you?' He looked to Benjamin for the answer.

'I don't think so, Mr. Martinelli.'

'He's going to be a farmer instead,' Daniel cut in. 'Working on a *kibbutz* in Israel. We've just come from there. We had to drag him away from the place, he didn't want to leave that much.'

Martinelli laughed delightedly. 'Your father worked with his hands, Daniel. You did not, but your son wants to. What can you do, eh?' He sat down on the edge of the bed and invited his three guests to make themselves comfortable. When Daniel told him they had only a few hours between flights, Martinelli could not hide his disappointment.

'I hoped to hear you sing at least once.'

'What's wrong with those?' Daniel pointed to the stack of opera records that were piled neatly next to a turntable. Each of his recordings he had inscribed and sent to Martinelli.

'A plastic disc with something that sounds like your voice. Come, Daniel. Perform a favour for an old man. A favour for your longest-standing admirer.'

346

Daniel blushed. He didn't know how to refuse Martinelli's request. 'Without a piano?'

'You do not need a piano. Your voice needs nothing.'

'I'll sing for you what I sang at the Western Wall of the temple in Jerusalem,' Daniel offered. 'You won't understand a word of it, but it's beautiful.'

Martinelli nodded happily. Glancing at Anna and Benjamin, who sat in rapt attention, Daniel began to sing 'Adon olom.' He kept his voice low; he was in a small room now, not in the open spaces surrounding the wall.

'Beautiful,' Martinelli murmured when Daniel had finished. 'What does it mean?'

'It praises God. Sabbath and High Holy Day morning services are terminated with it.'

'And people go home with glorious music ringing in their ears.' Martinelli closed his eyes as he envisaged it.

'Daniel's going home with *La Juive* ringing in his,' Anna said.

'Oh?' Martinelli became alert again. 'Your father's favourite. Did you see a production of it?'

'The Hebrew National Opera put it on. I was interested.'

'Interested enough to try for it?'

'I don't know whether I'm equipped for such a heavy role,' Daniel admitted. 'I know I can do better than the tenor who sang Eleazar in Tel Aviv. Whether I can do it well enough to satisfy myself is another matter.'

The years suddenly seemed to roll off Martinelli's face and body. His eyes became sharp and his hands moved quickly in time with his words as he said, 'For a role like that, you have to understand the true meaning of tragedy. The meaning of irony. And the meaning of revenge. All that before you even sing a note. You are a Jew clinging stubbornly to your faith in the middle of Christian pressure to change.' He assumed the role of teacher easily. Daniel sat down to listen, entranced as he had once been in a house with a thatched roof in the English countryside. 'And your daughter, the light of your life, the sole reason

347

for your existence, is the weapon of your terrible vengeance against those who despise you for your faith.'

'The Israeli tenor didn't have that,' Anna said. 'He had a pleasant voice, but the drama was missing.'

'What did you expect?' Daniel turned to face her. 'He was a kid. I'm not. I can handle a role like that.'

'Then go to see Robin Duguid when you get back. Tell him you want to choose your own production. It'll be your twenty-fifth anniversary with the company in three years' time. The 1970-1971 season will mark your quarter century.'

Faced with the direct challenge from Anna, Daniel's enthusiasm waned. He looked to Benjamin, who shrugged his shoulders; decisions like this were not his mete.

'Maybe Duguid will be against it as he was the last time.' Daniel seemed to forget Martinelli's presence as he argued with Anna.

'You'll never know if you don't ask him. Besides, you'll have something big to celebrate in three years' time. You'll have leverage.'

'I'll mention it to him.' He glanced down at the watch on his wrist and was amazed to see that more than two hours had passed so quickly. 'Guess it's almost time to say goodbye, Enzo. Sorry it was so short.'

'Next time it will be longer. I am grateful that you remembered me.' Martinelli struggled to his feet again. Daniel resisted an impulse to offer help; he did not want to injure the older man's pride.

'My grandson will drive you back to the airport. It was good to see you again, Daniel.' He shook hands formally with Anna and Benjamin, then grasped Daniel around the shoulders and kissed him on both cheeks. Daniel could not help noticing the tears that misted the Italian's eyes.

Robin Duguid rejected the idea again when Daniel met him for lunch the week following his return from Israel. Duguid's argument against the production was the same one he had used seven years earlier. *La Juive* was too removed

348

from the popular arena to be worth the new production the Grand would give Daniel to commemorate his silver anniversary with the company.

The last time Duguid had turned it down, Daniel had not been unhappy. He had been relieved. This time, though, the refusal did not sit well with him. He was determined to push for it; if not for his twenty-fifth anniversay, then he would aim for some later date. On the way home he stopped off at the library in Teaneck, where he began to peruse the section on opera, searching through the shelves of scores until he found what he wanted — the score for Halévy's *La Juive*. When he checked it out, the woman at the counter smiled knowingly.

'Will this be one of your next roles, Mr. Kerr?'

'Perhaps.' He smiled back. If he put it around that he was studying the score, people might begin to talk. Rumours would spread. A push would start to get *La Juive* back into production.

By the time he reached his car, the idea had vanished. Robin Duguid would no more listen to gossip started by a librarian then he would to an astrologer's chart when it came to setting the Grand's production schedule.

A telegram was waiting for him at home. Anna had already opened the envelope and read the message. Wordlessly, she handed it to him. It was from Benito, Martinelli's grandson, in Milan.

'Regret to inform you that my grandfather passed away in his sleep last night.' Daniel read aloud; the lump in his throat grew larger, more uncomfortable. 'Your kind visit made his last days joyous ones. Thank you.'

CHAPTER SEVEN

Shortly after the family had returned from Israel, Benjamin's personality underwent a transformation. Daniel was certain it had something to do with the trip, the visits to ancient biblical sites that had been impossible before the Six-Day War, the sensation of peace and homecoming they had all experienced while walking the gentle slopes of the West Bank. Benjamin became even more religious, aggressively so. Every morning he zealously put on *teffilin,* the phylacteries wound around his left arm and head. He started to talk incessantly about the Jews' right to the occupied territories, how they were not negotiable, how Israel would again be the master of the entire Middle East with the boundaries it had enjoyed in Old Testament days.

Daniel chuckled to himself while he listened to his son's theories. He recognised the young man finally coming to the surface, politically and socially aware, knowing what he must do to change the world to the way he wanted it. Anna found nothing to laugh at, though. Her son was beginning to mix with a new crowd, not the friends he had made in Teaneck and neighbouring towns, but radicals in New York, where he would spend the evenings and Sundays.

'He's a kid,' Daniel had argued when Anna first brought up her objections. 'He's just finding out that he wants to change the system. Let him be.'

'He's our son,' she had replied. 'Do you like the way he

dresses now? The long hair, the denim jackets and jeans, like he belongs to some secret army? He's mixing with this bunch of bums in the city and I'm frightened he'll turn out like them. Is that what you want for a son?'

'I'll talk to him.'

Talking to Benjamin did not help. Since his second trip to Israel, he'd found out what it really meant to be a Jew, he told his father. It meant you had to fight to stay alive, and there was only one country where you could continue that fight. Israel. If they gave in on Israel and negotiated with its enemies, they would all be lost. When asked about the group he mixed with in New York, he said he preferred it to the Zionist organisations he had belonged to in New Jersey. 'They do more things over there. They act! They don't sit around talking.'

'Act?' Daniel was mystified. 'How do you mean act?'

'You'll see,' Benjamin promised. 'When the time comes, you'll see how they act.'

Political literature began to adorn the walls of his room, posters from Betar, the right-wing Zionist group that included Menachem Begin among its alumni. One poster even Anna had to laugh at — a bearded *Hasid* complete with long *payis* emerging from a telephone booth in a Superman costume.

Anna was not alone in her concern. The same group that Benjamin had joined had attracted Susie. She would accompany Benjamin into the city for meetings whose purpose they refused to share with their parents. Their schoolwork suffered as they spent more time with their new friends in New York. From being childhood sweethearts the two had become co-conspirators. Both sets of parents got together one night to discuss their children's fascination with this new Zionist group — they assumed it was Zionist — but no decisions were made. Daniel was firmly set against restricting his son. The kid was flexing his muscles, that was all. He'd get over it. His schoolwork would pick up again.

Instead, Daniel tried a different tack. On Friday night, during the *Shabbos* meal, he gently steered the conversation

351

around to the difficulties the Israelis were facing in controlling the occupied territories. Benjamin jumped in immediately, as Daniel knew he would, defending any actions Israel took to maintain its authority.

'Is that what your new friends teach you?' he asked quietly.

'When are we going to meet these friends of yours?' Anna asked. 'You keep telling us about them. All about what they teach you. But we never get to meet them. Are you ashamed of them? Ashamed of us?'

Daniel could see Benjamin was becoming flustered under the assault. He pushed on. 'Invite them over here for one of the meetings. You can use the house. Or don't they know enough to get out of New York?'

Benjamin turned red and raised his voice to his parents. 'Do you want to see them? You come to the Soviet Mission on Sunday and you'll see them!'

'Why the Soviet Mission?' Anna asked.

'Because that's where the action's going to be. We're going to let the Russians know they've got a fight on their hands when they start with the Jews.'

'What kind of fight?' Anna was scared of the belligerence that had suddenly asserted itself in her son.

'Since the Six-Day War, there's millions of Jews in Russia who have remembered they're Jews,' Benjamin answered. His voice was lower but his tone was no less enthusiastic. 'They've all renounced their Soviet citizenship and declared themselves to be Israelis. They are Israelis under the Law of Return and they want to be allowed to go there. The Russians won't let them out. Starting this Sunday, we're going to make sure that what happened to six million Jews under Hitler doesn't happen to three million more under the Soviets.'

'Wait a minute.' Daniel held up his hand, deciding it was time to bring this nonsense to a halt. 'What kind of favour would you be doing Israel if you got three million Russian Jews dumped on them? Where the hell would they put them?'

'Where?' Benjamin repeated the word incredulously. 'They'll build settlements. On the West Bank. In the Sinai.'

'They're not going to keep those territories forever.

352

They'll negotiate for peace and security with them.'

'Of course they're going to keep them forever. They belong to Israel!'

Daniel fell silent, choosing to concentrate on his meal. He did not wish to carry the conversation any further. He was certain now that he knew what group his son and Susie had joined, and he was as anxious as Anna.

Benjamin came downstairs just before midday on Sunday, wearing faded army fatigues with all insignia removed. The *yarmulke* he had taken to wearing permanently was pinned to his bushy hair. Around his neck, dangling outside the fatigue jacket, was an oversized Star of David. Pinned to the jacket was a round badge that depicted the clenched fist thrust through a Star of David. Written underneath were two words. 'Never Again.'

'Jewish Defence League?' Daniel asked.

'You'd better believe it, Pa. We're going to let the world know that we care enough to fight. Before they do it to us all over again.'

'Susie's going with you? Dressed up like that?'

Benjamin nodded. 'I'm picking her up. We're getting the bus across the bridge to the "A" train.'

Daniel debated whether to offer his son a lift, then decided against it; he refused to be an accomplice. If Benjamin was that set on going to demonstrate, he could get there under his own steam. 'What time does this shindig of yours start?'

'Three o'clock. Are you coming?'

'Maybe.' He watched as Benjamin kissed Anna goodbye and left the house. Walking up the street, his back was ramrod straight and he swung his arms stiffly, like a marching soldier. That's what he is, Daniel reflected. Another one of King David's soldiers marching off to war. And to think I was worried about him being drafted to fight in Vietnam when he's old enough; he's going to find his own war long before then.

'Do you think there'll be any trouble this afternoon?'

Anna asked as she watched through the window with Daniel.

'No.' He forced himself to sound confident. 'These kids don't mean any real harm. They're just letting off steam.'

'You've got to do something to stop him, Daniel. Before it's too late.'

'What can I do?' he asked helplessly. 'He's found a cause he believes in. I should tell him to quit it?'

'What about when he wants to go over there to live?'

'We'll worry about that when it happens,' Daniel replied curtly. And it's going to happen damned soon, he realised. He doesn't give a hoot about school anymore. All he cares about is Israel. Being a Zionist, supporting the country wasn't enough for him; he has to belong to this bunch of lunatics as well.

Daniel, Anna, Moishe and Helen stood in a small group on East Sixty-ninth Street, across from the Soviet Mission to the United Nations. Outside the mission, under the watchful yet amused eyes of police officers, some fifty youngsters paraded in a large circle. Many carried placards that read 'Let my people go.' Most of the youngsters were students but the hardcore phalanx of the group was composed of boys and girls dressed like Benjamin and Susie. They all wore the JDL badge and shouted the loudest.

'I think we were worrying for nothing,' Moishe said optimistically after they had watched the protest for fifteen minutes. 'They're just a bunch of kids fooling around.' There had been no sign of trouble. The demonstrators had maintained an orderly formation. And there had been no evidence of any reaction from the Soviet Mission. Press photographers had stopped by to snap a few pictures and a camera crew from one of the New York television stations had shot some film.

'If this is all they were planning to do, you're right,' Daniel agreed. 'It depends on how set they are on getting some reaction out of the Soviets.'

'No, this is it. They've had their say and they'll pack it in.' As Moishe spoke the words, the lieutenant in charge of the police detail moved in and told the demonstrators their time was up. Obediently they dispersed. A scattering of applause broke out from the people watching. Daniel did not join in as he watched Benjamin and Susie cross the road towards them.

'Feel better now you've got it out of your system?' He looked at some of the other JDL members as they marched past him. Their ages were anywhere between sixteen and eighteen, he guessed; some looked as if they weren't tough enough to push their way past a paper bag, let alone sway Kremlin policy.

Helen reached out a hand to Susie. The girl recoiled as if contact with her mother was repugnant. Daniel noticed the shocked, hurt expression on Helen's face. She felt as Anna did, unable to understand the change that was overtaking her child.

'Are you coming with us?' Moishe asked quickly, wanting to gloss over the awkward moment. 'Grab a bite to eat?'

Susie shook her head. 'We've got a meeting first.'

'Where?'

'At headquarters. To discuss what we achieved today. And make plans for the future.'

'Just what did you achieve?' Daniel asked.

Benjamin answered. 'We showed everyone we cared. That we're not afraid to stand up for our own people.'

'Nobody even looked out of a goddamned window!' Daniel heard his voice rising, but he couldn't control it any more than he could control his son, stop him from associating with these religious fanatics who wanted to wield swords and spears again in the name of God. 'That's how much you showed them!'

Benjamin refused to be cowed by his father's anger. 'Wait till next time,' he vowed. 'Wait until you see blood. Theirs, not ours!' He backed away, turned around and began to run down the street after his comrades. Susie followed him.

'The young revolutionaries,' Moishe commented. 'Maybe we were like that at their age, only we've forgotten.'

'The hell we were,' Daniel muttered.

Anna went to bed early but Daniel waited up. He wanted

to have this out with his son once and for all. Find out why he was getting mixed up with a gang of zealots, what he had to do to get Benjamin away from them.

A little after eleven, Benjamin arrived home. The JDL badge was still pinned proudly to his shirt as he swaggered into the house.

'How was the meeting?' Daniel asked. 'Where do you meet anyway?'

'A loft in a building on Forty-second Street. And it was fine, just fine.' He walked through to the kitchen. When he returned, he was holding a glass of milk and a peanut butter and jelly sandwich. The sight of his revolutionary son on such a diet brought home the ridiculousness of the situation.

'So what did you and your friends decide to do for an encore?'

'We're going to wait.'

'Wait for what?'

'To see what the Soviets do. If they let our people go to Israel, we'd have won.'

'And if they don't?' Fat chance of the Soviet Union taking any notice of today's puny parade, Daniel thought.

'Then nowhere in New York, nowhere in the whole United States and Canada is going to be safe for the Soviets. We've got people in Canada, too. Do you know what we are, Pa? We're the children of the holocaust. We learned. And what we learned we're going to put to good use. No one pushes the Jews around anymore while we're in business.'

'Who drummed all this nonsense into your head? Meir Kahane?'

At once, Benjamin's expression changed from righteous anger to one of awe. 'Pa, you should hear him speak. He rips into you. All he has to say are those two words, ''Never again,'' and you realise what your existence is all about.'

'I don't want to hear him speak. I don't like extremists, no matter which side of the field they come from.'

Listening to his father denigrate his idol, Benjamin became belligerent. 'What did you do to save the Jews during the war? Eh? If Kahane had been there, plenty would have been done. For every Jew that died in a gas chamber, ten Nazis would have been killed!'

Under his son's tirade, Daniel began to feel guilty. He knew damned well he had no reason to; you didn't feel guilty when you were compared with a fanatic, even if he was your son's messiah. But what had he done? Got blown up while learning to play cricket with a young boy in someone's back garden on a sunny Sunday morning? 'Your enemies aren't here, Benny. If Kahane wants to fight so badly, let him go to Israel and take his crazy organisation with him.'

'Where do you think we're going?' Benjamin shot back. 'As soon as I've finished high school, I'm off. So is Susie. We're all going.'

'Susie can do whatever she likes. So can the rest of that mob. But you're not going anywhere, young man.'

'Who's going to stop me?'

'I will, that's who?'

'What for? So I can stick around to become cannon fodder in Vietnam? If I'm going to fight anywhere, it'll be for my own people, my own kind.'

'You're going to stay here so you can go to college and learn something.' Daniel heard footsteps and turned around. Anna had come downstairs, woken by the loud argument in the living room.

'Are you two going to come to blows or are you planning on settling this peacefully?'

'Ask your son,' Daniel said sarcastically. 'He's all ready to pack his bags and take off for Israel. Can't wait to pick up a gun and kill someone. It used to be kill a Commie for Christ; now it's kill an Arab for Kahane, the new messiah. The man who's going to lead the Jews back to what they owned in bible times. And lead them back four thousand years while he's doing it.' He turned to Benjamin. 'What damned good do you think you're going to be to Israel? They need professionals, skilled craftsmen, builders of a country. The way you're heading right now, you won't even finish high school!'

'Then I'll be a farmer. I'll shovel chickenshit on a *kibbutz*. And I'll carry a gun for the country.'

'What's the matter with you?' Daniel yelled. 'You think farmers don't need a decent education? Israel's not the promised land you seem to think it is. It's not a place where you throw a few seeds into the ground and wait for a bountiful harvest to come up. Who the hell do you think figured out the irrigation systems that make crops grow in the deserts? High school dropouts like you and your crazy friends?'

Benjamin's aggressiveness, his dream of becoming a pioneer, wilted in the face of his father's angry logic. He stood in the centre of the living room, looking around himself foolishly. His fingers toyed with the large Star of David dangling around his neck. Daniel watched him carefully, feeling the tension seep out of his own body; he had finally managed to make his son understand the realities of life.

'Do you want to go to bed and think it over?' he asked Benjamin quietly. 'Make up your mind what you want to do?'

Benjamin nodded.

Daniel waited until his son began to climb the stairs, then called him back. 'You finish high school and go to college. Study something you'll be able to use over there, for your own good and for Israel's good. Then I'll help you get over there. But if you drop out of school, I promise I won't lift a finger to help you.'

Benjamin nodded again before continuing on his way upstairs.

A period of quiet descended on the house. Benjamin continued to attend the meetings in New York, but he no longer brought his enthusiasm home with him. Daniel was grateful to see his son's grades improve, glad to see the kid was taking notice of him. Hell, Benjamin wasn't a kid anymore. Kids didn't talk about killing their enemies and making the world safe for their own kind. That was adult language; fanatic adults at that. Daniel supposed he should be grateful that Benjamin was only protesting against Soviet treatment of Jewish dissidents; everyone else seemed to be taken up with the anti-Vietnam War crusade.

The truce ended when Benjamin learned that a Soviet ballet troupe would be putting on a performance of *Swan Lake* at the Grand, and that his parents intended going. For weeks he urged them not to attend, arguing that it was hypocritical to support Israel and then watch Russian dancers who were representative of a government that was oppressing the Jews. Daniel did not even bother to argue with him; he simply made it clear that he and Anna were going and nothing would change their minds.

On the night of the performance, Benjamin cornered his parents in their bedroom as they were dressing.

'Do you have to go tonight?' he asked yet again.

'What's it to you?' Daniel asked, continuing to tie his bow tie in front of the full length mirror. The topic had worn thin and he didn't want to argue anymore.

'You're paying money to see Russian dancers. Money that will be used to suppress Jews in the Soviet Union.'

'We're not paying anything,' Anna said, weary of the subject. 'Robin Duguid gave us complimentary tickets.'

'That doesn't matter,' Benjamin shot back. 'Just by your presence you're giving them support. Think what would happen if no one showed up. Maybe the Russians would get the message.'

'Just like they got the message when you and your friends paraded outside the Soviet mission that time, eh?' Daniel asked. 'You're flogging a dead horse, Benny. Give it up.'

Benjamin changed tactics. He dropped his aggressiveness. In its place was an abject plea. 'For my sake, will you stay at home tonight?' he asked quietly. 'Just miss this one performance, that's all I want. Is that too much to ask? Too much to do for your son?'

Daniel breathed out loudly. 'I'm sorry, Benny. We told Robin Duguid we'll be there. We've got to go.'

Anna tried to humour her son. 'We won't go to the next one,' she promised.

Benjamin stared silently at his parents, willing them to

change their minds, When he saw they were still bent on going, he left the room and ran downstairs. Seconds later the front door slammed after him. Daniel glanced at Anna and shrugged his shoulders. The kid was *meshuggeh*.

'Does it feel different to enter as a spectator?' Anna asked when Daniel held open the door to the Grand's lobby.

He grinned. 'Feels easier. Maybe I'll even manage to fall asleep during the performance.'

'Don't you dare,' she warned. She knew that Daniel disliked sitting through a ballet and had come only because she wanted to see the performance. He would have given in willingly to Benjamin's demands that they miss out on the performance if it had not been for Anna. 'Why do you think Benny got so upset?' she asked Daniel as they walked down the centre aisle towards their seats.

'How would I know?' he answered. 'I don't understand how that kid's mind works.' They sat down and Daniel looked around. 'So this is how it looks from the other side of the fence,' he said in mock wonder. 'Gee, I never would have guessed the curtain was that colour.' He grinned hugely when his words made nearby members of the audience turn in his direction and recognise him.

'Now you daren't go to sleep,' Anna whispered. 'You'll be talked about if you do.'

'Let them talk.' Daniel made himself comfortable and purposely closed his eyes. Seconds later, he grunted quietly when Anna jabbed him in the ribs with her elbow.

Daniel never got the opportunity to fall asleep. As the gold curtain rose on the first act, half a dozen figures in jeans and denim jackets erupted along the centre aisle and began to converge on the stage. Daniel's first amazed thought concerned their style of dress. Who came to the Grand dressed this casually? And motorcycle crash helmets? What were they doing in motorcycle crash helmets? What the hell was going on?

A girl's voice next to him screamed 'Never again!' He turned around in time to see an arm raised, a missile launched towards the stage. The dancers scurried to the safety of the wings as a plastic bag full of blood arced over the orchestra pit and splattered against the set.

All hell broke loose. Uniformed attendants and men in tuxedoes raced along the centre aisle. Fights erupted. Woman among the audience screamed in terror. Daniel jumped out of his seat and threw his arms around the girl who had thrown the bag of blood. She kicked and punched at him, surprising him with the ferocity of her attack. He let go and she raced away, back up the aisle, straight into the arms of one of the attendants. Savagely, the man tore the motorcycle helmet off her head. Daniel gasped in shock. The sight of Susie struggling vainly in the attendant's arms brought home to Daniel why Benjamin had been so hostile about his parents attending the ballet.

The performance was cancelled. While other members of the audience went to restaurants or drove home to talk excitedly about the incident, Daniel and Anna went to the police station where the demonstrators had been taken. They were both certain that Benjamin would be there.

They found him in the police station, sitting with Susie and four other members of the JDL, young boys like himself. Benjamin showed no surprise when he saw his parents. Daniel forced down his fury when he confronted his son.

'Are you happy now? I was a member of that audience. You embarrassed the hell out of me.'

'Good!' the boy spat back. 'You had no business being there, supporting the enemies of the Jews!'

'Wrong! I had every business being there. I work there. I'm an artist. I was watching other artists work. Your kind of stupidity comes to a screeching halt when it affects my work.'

'Is music sacred?' Benjamin demanded. Other members of the group who had been sitting sullenly began to take more interest in the argument. Susie cut in with, 'Don't you know they played classical music at Auschwitz? That's how sacred it is. They played it while Jews burned.'

'Does your mother know where you are tonight?' Anna asked Susie. She took in the rest of the group with a

361

concerned gaze. 'Do any of your parents know where you are?'

No one answered.

Daniel turned away and sought out the seargeant who seemed to be in charge of the situation. 'What's going to happen to them?'

'Who are you?'

'I'm Daniel Kerr. I'm the father of Benjamin Kerr. I was in the audience at the Grand.'

'They'll spend the night in the cells. We're notifying the parents. Tomorrow morning they'll go before the judge and set bail.'

'What charges will there be? They're all still juveniles.'

'So what? Assault. Creating a disturbance.'

'Thanks.' He went back to Benjamin. 'You're going to spend the night in a cell. Maybe that'll knock some sense into you.'

The prospect didn't bother the boy. If anything, it appealed to him. An even stronger bond would be forged between himself and the others, jailed for a cause they'd die for.

'Stick around here,' Daniel told Anna. 'I'm going to call Moishe and Helen; better I do it than the police. Then I'm going back to the Grand to try and see Duguid. He'd better hear it from me first that my son was involved in that disgraceful mêlée.'

He asked the seargeant if he could use the telephone. When he got through to Moishe, he told him what had happened. Moishe stayed calm, but Helen went hysterical, screaming into the phone about the injustice of her daughter being kept overnight in jail. Daniel told Moishe there was no point in coming into the city. They'd all be released on bail the following morning. Finally he promised to stop off at their house on the way home.

Leaving Anna in the police station, he returned to the Grand. He found Duguid —still white-faced and shaken by the episode — in his office, talking with a heavy-set man whom Daniel did not know.

'I've come to apologise,' Daniel said simply.

362

'For what?' Duguid asked, surprised by Daniel's unexpected appearance and the offer of an apology. He turned to the heavy-set man. 'Daniel, this is Igor Redenko, the manager of the Soviet dance troupe. I'm sure you've heard of Daniel Kerr, one of this country's outstanding singers.'

'Of course.' The man stood up. 'I'm delighted to meet an artist of your reputation, Mr. Kerr.'

Daniel acknowledged him briefly before returning his attention to Duguid. 'My son, Benjamin, was one of the demonstrators.'

'What?' Duguid stood up, mouth open in amazement.

'He was one of them. He's a member of the Jewish Defence League. He's at the police station now with the others.'

Duguid sank back in the chair while the Russian's expression of greeting turned to one of hostility. 'What do you want me to do, Daniel?' Duguid asked.

'What were you going to do?'

'Press charges, of course. I will not tolerate that kind of behaviour in my house.'

'Then go right ahead. It might teach him a lesson.' Daniel moved towards the door, eager to get back to the police station and Anna.

'Daniel.' Duguid called him back. 'Thank you for coming by to tell me. I appreciate it.'

'Good night.' Daniel left the opera house and hurried back to the police station. The six JDL members were no longer in sight. Anna told him they had been taken away. Daniel checked with the seargeant on the time of the court appearance the following day. Then he drove back to New Jersey. Moishe and Helen were waiting nervously. Daniel could see Helen had been crying and he couldn't blame her. Anna seemed the calmest of them all, as if she had convinced herself that the entire episode was only a dream. Her son spending a night in jail, like a common criminal? It couldn't happen. But it had, and now they had to face up to it, decide what to do in the future to make sure it never happened again.

'Short of banning them from seeing these lunatics, what can we do?' Moishe asked.

'That wouldn't work.' Daniel knew the quickest way to make Benjamin do something was to forbid him. Maybe he should encourage his son with this JDL madness, egg him on. Then he'd rebel against his father's wishes and revert to being conventional. Reverse psychology. Some hopes! With a normal kid it might work. Not with someone indoctrinated by these madmen.

'Do you think a night in jail will help?' Helen asked. 'Bring them to their senses?'

'No way,' Daniel replied. 'They're revelling in it as if being flung in jail confirmed that they were right all along. They'll get a fine. And a record,' he added sourly. 'Why is it that I'm almost fifty-three years old and I haven't got a record? Yet my son — and your daughter — are going to have records by the time they're seventeen.'

'You were lucky,' Anna said. 'No one ever caught you.'

Despite his aggravation, Daniel laughed. Anna had hit the right spot. For what he had done in Los Angeles while tied up with Carmel Studios, he should have gone to jail for life.

Moishe followed Anna's lead, seeing they would get nowhere by beating their breasts. 'If we need a good lawyer tomorrow morning, I know just the guy.'

'I want those kids out of there,' Daniel shot back. 'I don't want to see them sent up for life!'

Daniel lay awake in bed, eyes fixed on the ceiling while he reviewed the events of the evening. One night in jail and they'll both be martyrs, he reflected. Brother and sister in idealism. Or is terrorism the word I'm looking for? Is this how terrorists start out, how urban guerrillas get their training?

What do they do next? Hijack a plane when they're not even old enough to get driving licences yet?

CHAPTER EIGHT

Benjamin graduated from high school and started college, his mind made up to become an engineer. He wanted to work with his hands, to accomplish miracles with them. Others in his class talked of the dams they would build, the hydroelectric plants; the student who attended college with a *yarmulke* on his head dreamed of the bridges he would erect across the Suez Canal, the tanks and fighter aircraft he would design.

In his second year at college, news began to reach the American press of show trials in the Soviet Union for Jewish dissidents. Benjamin's group called an urgent meeting. The decision was taken to launch an anti-Soviet terrorist campaign. The first Daniel and Anna knew of it was when Benjamin and Susie were arrested in a sit-in outside the Soviet Mission.

'This has got to stop! Right this instant!' Daniel yelled at Benjamin after he'd bailed him out the following morning.

'It hasn't started yet! Can't you understand that?' Benjamin shouted back just as loudly.

'Sit-ins are going to change the world? Is that your answer? Harassing the hell out of Soviet diplomats by putting their phone numbers in ads for hookers?'

'You wait,' Benjamin promised. 'You'll see what we can do.'

Daniel did not have to wait long. Two days later a bomb

wrecked a car with DPL plates that belonged to the Soviet Mission. The Jewish Defence League proudly claimed responsibility. The following weekend Benjamin was arrested yet again, with Susie, for charging police barricades outside the Soviet Mission as they tried to force their way into the building. More fines followed, which Daniel paid. Benjamin's name began to appear in newspapers. The first couple of times he was identified as the only son of Grand Opera tenor Daniel Kerr; after that, he achieved a fame of his own. He was one of the leaders, one of the vanguard of Jewish belligerents who would do anything, risk anything to help their fellow Jews in the Soviet Union.

Colleagues offered Daniel sympathy. He refused to accept it. He didn't want sympathy from anyone for the way his son behaved. In some strange, inexplicable way he was coming to terms with Benjamin's ideals. He was becoming used to them, the furtive meetings of an organisation in which the Federal Bureau of Investigation was interested, the sudden embarrassing, destructive strikes at the Soviets, the promise to protect Jewish lives and property. Once even a sensation of pride touched him, the time that Benjamin showed him a press clipping that said the Soviet Union was allowing a handful of Jews to leave the country for Israel.

'We're winning, Pa! Can't you see that now?' Benjamin said exultantly. 'They're giving in.'

'Do you really think it's you and your pals who are doing it?'

Benjamin came back immediately with, 'Who the hell else bombs their offices?' And Daniel realised, to a degree, that he was right.

The telephone rang late one night. Daniel answered it and listened carefully. When he replaced the receiver, his face was serious, the features tightly set.

'What is it?' Anna asked.

'I have to go out.'

'This late? Why?'

'I'll explain later. It's about Benny.'

For an instant Anna thought that he had been arrested again, until she remembered that he was in his bedroom, reading for an exam the following day, 'He's here in the house.'

'I'll tell you when I get back.' He called Moishe and told him to be in front of the house in ten minutes; he'd be by with the car to pick him up.

Daniel and Moishe drove in silence for thirty-five minutes until they reached an almost deserted street in an industrial section of Newark. Empty factories stared down at them; the shadowy figures of night watchmen making their rounds flitted into sight like ghosts. One other car was in the street, a late model Dodge, engine and lights off, a figure behind the steering wheel. As Daniel pulled in behind the Dodge, the driver's door opened and the man got out. Bent low, he hurried towards Daniel's car, opened the back door and climbed in.

'Hi, Cherrybum. Moishe.'

'What's the big emergency, copper?'

'I'm doing you both a favour and I don't know why.'

'Spit it out, Tommy,' Moishe said.

'You've got a couple of crazy kids there. And they're running around with an even nuttier group.'

'They're fighting for what they believe in.' Daniel was surprised to hear himself defending Benjamin and Susie.

'Maybe. I just wish they'd do it somewhere else where it doesn't give my people headaches.' Tommy lit a cigarette and rolled down the window to toss out the spent match. 'Their big chief, Kahane, has split and moved to Israel. I'd suggest your two kids do the same. And damned quick.'

'Why?'

Tommy ignored the question. 'Have they got passports of their own. Valid ones?'

Daniel and Moishe nodded.

'Then get them on a plane out of here first thing in the morning. Before it's too late. Get them on a flight to Israel and let them stay there.'

'For God's sake, why?' Moishe asked.

'Any day now there's going to be a whole bunch of Grand Jury subpoenas handed down. About an attempted bombing a few months back. Two of them have got your kids' names on them. It won't be fines this time. It'll be jail.'

'Hey, come on!' Moishe protested. 'Okay, they're a couple of hotheads. They might have got involved with the sit-ins, crap like that. But not bombings!'

'I'm just telling you what I know. Take my advice, be safe and get them the hell out of the country.' Tommy opened the car door and slid out. He didn't look back as he jogged to the Dodge, jumped in and drove away. Only when he reached the intersection a hundred yards away did he turn on the lights.

'What do you think?' Moishe asked nervously.

'I think the man's giving us a break and we'd better do as he says.' Daniel gunned the engine and sent the car streaking towards the intersection. Benjamin was probably in bed by now. Anna, too. He guessed that his son wouldn't mind being woken up to be told he was flying to Israel the following day. For an extended stay.

They all travelled to Kennedy in one car. The few pieces of baggage that Benjamin and Susie needed did not fill up half the trunk. Who needs suits and fancy dresses in Israel? they had asked. Jeans. Work clothes. We're going there to help build the country, not to dance. And to escape a Grand Jury subpoena, Daniel added quietly.

'Do you think the immigration people will stop them from going?' Moishe asked, worried by the possibility.

'I doubt it. The subpoenas haven't been issued yet. Might be a different story in a few days' time.' He was more concerned with what Benjamin and Susie would do when they arrived in the country. They would be accepted as legal immigrants; that was no problem. And they had enough money for their immediate needs. But what about after that? Benjamin swore he knew people over there, members of the JDL who had already left the United States and were now working on *kibbutzim*.

Only Benjamin and Susie showed no signs of sadness when the flight was called. They were like two small children going off on vacation, eager to be on their way, enthusiastic about the sandcastles they would build once they reached the shore.

As the flight was called, Daniel grasped Benjamin and hugged him tightly. 'Take care of yourself. Don't be in too much of a hurry to pick up a gun.' Benjamin started to pull away but Daniel held on tightly. 'What about that bombing?'

'It was a Soviet trade office, Pa,' Benjamin whispered. 'It never went off.'

'But you did it?'

Benjamin nodded. 'I made it and I planted it. I didn't make it too well.'

'Were there others?'

Again, Benjamin nodded. 'Some others went off, but we never killed anyone. Only property.'

Daniel gulped back a sob. His kid was talking so casually about making bombs. What had happened? To him? To the world? 'Go get your plane,' he finally said, releasing his grip on Benjamin.

The four adults waited until the El Al flight took off, then they trudged slowly back to the car. No one spoke a word during the entire journey back to New Jersey. Once Daniel glanced in the rearview mirror and saw Moishe taking off his glasses to wipe his eyes.

Bombs, he thought. He's studying to be an engineer so he can build bigger and better bombs. And I'm the one who forced him to go to college.

The subpoenas calling Benjamin and Susie to appear before a Grand Jury arrived two weeks later, the same day as letters which told their parents they had settled into a *kibbutz* in northern Israel, a few miles from the Lebanese border. Benjamin was working on a building crew while he continued his interrupted engineering studies. Susie was working on a chicken farm.

Daniel passed Benjamin's subpoena over to Moishe. He was the lawyer; he could handle them. It was time, after all the excitement and anxiety, to get back to worrying about his own career.

Why should he have to worry? He had already reached the peak of his career. One of the finest lyric tenors in the United States, if not the world. Hadn't Robin Duguid introduced him as such to the manager of the Soviet dance troupe, that night Benjamin and his friends had run down the centre aisle of the Grand and thrown bags of chicken blood at the Russian dancers, screaming 'Never again!'

There was no longer any need to feel concerned, he decided. He could retire whenever he liked, although he would prefer to see it through until the 1975-1976 season, his thirtieth with the company. If he paced himself carefully, he could last out with plenty to spare. His voice had not darkened any more. In his thirtieth year he would still be fresh; and sound a damned sight better than some of the younger singers who were coming through.

Suddenly he knew why he was worried. It was easier to be anxious about himself than about Benjamin. With his own life, at least, he had some control. He could afford to worry because he could always find the means to solve the problems.

'Want to sell the house?' Daniel asked.

Anna looked across the living room in surprise. 'What made you ask that?'

'We've been here a long time. Maybe we should make a move. Who needs a house this big when there's just the two of us?'

'What about when Benny comes back?'

Daniel laughed at the question. 'He's not going to come back, is he? And even if he did, even if the impossible happened and he returned to this country, do you think he'd want to live with his old-fashioned establishment parents?'

The knowledge pained Anna. 'Where would you want to move?'

'Maybe back into the city.' Daniel had been thinking it

over for some time. Without Benjamin, the house seemed like a mausoleum, empty, just like that night after his debut when he had sat alone for a few seconds in the vastness of the Grand's auditorium. It was full of shadows and echoes, a scrapbook he could look into whenever he felt the urge. He needed somewhere smaller, a place that took less work to run. He didn't even appreciate the garden anymore; the swimming pool hadn't been used since Benjamin had gone away. 'We'll buy a coop,' he decided. 'Somewhere nice on the East Side.'

'Next you'll be wanting to move into a retirement village somewhere,' Anna chided him. 'Is a coop in the city what you really want?'

Daniel did not answer the question directly. 'Maybe after we come back from Israel next summer we'll look around. Who knows,' he added, as if he had misgivings about his earlier words, 'maybe Benny'll tell us he wants to come back.' There wasn't much chance of it, he thought as Anna dwelt on the possibility. When they had been to Israel the previous summer, Benjamin had given them no hint that he would ever return to live. His Hebrew was as fluent as that of any native. He'd put on weight, hard-packed muscle, and looked fitter and happier than Daniel had ever seen him before. He'd grown up, matured, accepted the responsibilities of being an adult. The talk was no longer of building a modern-day Jewish empire. It was of making peace with the Arabs and turning the entire area into a productive part of the world instead of a constant battlefield.

Daniel was used to the idea that his son would never return, just as Moishe and Helen had become accustomed to Susie staying out there. Anna was the holdout, the only one of the four to keep alive a hope that her child would come home. Daniel could never bring himself to argue with her; it was kinder not to quench that hope.

CHAPTER NINE

The two-week vacation to Israel Daniel and Anna had originally planned for the following year was rapidly changed to a two-month trip after Benjamin wired that he and Susie were getting married towards the end of the summer. Both sets of parents knew they had been living together in a two-room apartment in Beersheba after leaving the *kibbutz*. It was a subject left unmentioned. Even when Susie wrote to Moishe and Helen that she was expecting Benjamin's child, little was said. Without Anna's knowledge, however, Daniel wrote to Benjamin to ask if he planned to marry Susie; he was proud that he was still old-fashioned enough to expect such a progression of events. It was one of the few letters Daniel had written in the past few years. He preferred to use a telephone. If he thought a call would have helped this time, he would have done so, but he reasoned that the printed word would carry more impact. It did. The reply was the telegram announcing plans for the wedding.

Benjamin followed up the wire with a lengthy letter. Towards the end, like a postscript, he casually informed his parents that all his friends knew of Daniel Kerr — and he was certain his father would not mind staying over a few weeks after the wedding to conduct the *Rosh Hashanah* and *Yom Kippur* services at the local synagogue. Benjamin had already offered his services; and the offer had been immediately accepted.

'*Chutzpah!*' Daniel declared when he read the letter aloud to Anna. 'Goddamned cheek to think I'm going to stay out there for six weeks after his wedding to sing for free at some little *shul!*'

'You know you'll love it,' Anna told him. 'You're a born showman. You'll sing anywhere, anytime someone gives you an invitation. And sometimes when they don't.'

The first glance Daniel had of the synagogue where he would conduct the services was during Benjamin's wedding. His initial reaction was one of scepticism. The place wasn't a B'nai Yeshurun or a Temple Isaiah, that was for sure. He doubted if it held two hundred people; even then they'd have to be crammed in like sardines. The temple was on one level, with the women's section separated from the men by nothing more imaginative than a rope. If he sang in this place as he used to sing in Paterson or Washington Heights, he'd blow every window clean out of its frame. He'd bring the walls down like Joshua with his trumpets at Jericho.

Susie made no attempt to conceal that she was five months pregnant when she entered the synagogue on Moishe's arm. Daniel stole a look at Helen and wondered what was going through her mind. Any other mother would have been screaming blue murder, hammering down our front door, he decided, telling us what a little bastard we had for a son, getting her daughter knocked up. Helen hadn't said a word and neither had Moishe. We're still the best of friends. What would have happened, though, if he had not written that letter to Benjamin? Helen and Moishe would have been grandparents without a son-in-law.

The *chuppah* was held up by four men, friends of Benjamin. The service was quicker than any Daniel had heard before. There was no English at all. Here, Hebrew was not only the language of religion. It was the language of the people.

An outdoor reception was held after the ceremony. Food and drink were abundant. Lively music encouraged even the most staid guests to dance. Daniel joined a circle, one arm around Moishe's shoulders, the other around Anna, and kicked up his legs to a *hora* tune. In the centre of the circle, two teenaged boys did a *kezatske* with more flourish than any pair of Cossacks. A Jewish wedding's a Jewish wedding, Daniel thought; whether you're wearing a tuxedo in New York or an open-necked shirt like here.

'Never thought we'd be in-laws, did you?' Moishe yelled above the din. Sweat poured off his brow and glistened on his head as he worked at the dance, obviously enjoying himself.

'You don't know how many times I prayed it would never happen!' Daniel shouted back. The music ended and he came to a grateful halt. His shirt was soaked and he wanted a cold drink. He smiled broadly as he remembered the skinny kid who'd walked towards him along Grand Concourse and waved, forgetting he was holding a folder full of sheet music. *Golem,* Fat Benny had called him. Now the *golem* was his in-law. 'You sure you and Helen can't stay any longer than a couple of weeks?'

'We have to get back. I'm not a big-time singer like you. I can't afford the time. We won't even be here when Susie has the kid,' he added sadly.

'Neither will we.' The Grand's season started two weeks after *Yom Kippur*. Daniel would have just enough time to get back for the final rehearsal of *Pagliacci*, his first performance of the new season. If he was lucky, he would be able to swing a few days to make another trip with Anna; otherwise, she would have to come out by herself to be with Benjamin and Susie when the baby was due.

All the jokes Daniel had ever heard about small towns that rolled up the sidewalks paled beside Beersheba on *Yom Kippur;* especially when the fast fell on a Saturday as well. The only sounds on the streets were the footsteps of worshippers on the way to the temple. A cloudless blue sky added to the purity of the day.

Daniel didn't miss the constant hum of the air conditioners he knew would be working in the temples back in the States, drying out the soaking humidity so that worshippers could pray for forgiveness in comfort. Here, the weather was dry. A perfect day that did not sap the strength from you.

He sensed that something was wrong around midday, when two men in uniform entered the temple. Not that there was anything unusual about that; soldiers prayed as well. These men, however, carried no prayer books, wore no prayer shawls. They held sheets of paper in their hands and walked quietly along the rows of seats, seeking out other men. Worshippers rose, folded their prayer shawls, set down their books and just as quietly left. Within five minutes, the congregation was halved. Puzzled, Daniel looked to where Benjamin sat; he wanted an explanation. He was just in time to see his son, tight-lipped, join the exodus.

A man came up to the *bima* and whispered to Daniel that Egyptian forces had crossed the Suez Canal in depth and attacked Israeli positions in the Sinai; simultaneously, Syrian armour in unprecedented strength had broken through the weak Israeli defence line strung precariously along the Golan Heights. The country had been caught unawares. Its much vaunted intelligence system had failed.

By two-thirty, Daniel was performing to a congregation of elderly men, women and children. Everyone of military age had been called away to their units. Sirens had sounded, followed by an all-clear. While he prayed, Daniel wondered where Benjmain was. He knew his son was a reserve officer with a tank unit, but he had no idea where he would be sent. Probably to the Sinai to face the Egyptians. The air force would take care of the Syrian thrust in the Golan. Would it be another six-day wonder? With everyone safely home by the end of the week? The prospect did not seem quite so probable this time. The Arabs had chosen their time of attack with care. When the entire country was in *shul,* the defences at their weakest. The Israelis had not received the slightest warning. Their intelligence had let them down. This war would last longer. How many would die this time to protect the integrity of the tiny Jewish state?

How many, Daniel asked himself, of those who had just prayed to be inscribed in the Book of Life were already dead?

Late that evening, after *Yom Kippur* had finished, Daniel and Anna sat up with the elderly owners of the guest house in which they were staying. The man translated the latest radio bulletins for his visitors. There seemed to be fighting everywhere, and the guest house owner enthusiastically declared that soon, very soon, the Arabs would be pushed back even beyond the earlier boundaries. This time, he declared, the Jews would occupy Damascus, Cairo and Amman; they would wrest such a victory from their foes that the Arabs would not bother anyone again for twenty years.

Daniel tried to decide what to do. He was too old to fight, not that he would have been able to. He was an American, a visitor in the country. He could sing, though. He could entertain. He could be a Jewish Bob Hope in a time when entertainment would be appreciated tenfold. Anna could join him. They could form a team. He broached the idea to her and she agreed immediately.

His enthusiasm waned only when he realised he did not have the slightest idea how to put his scheme into operation. He asked the guest house owner, who recommended Daniel approach the local military command.

Two days later, after signing a release form that relieved the Israeli government of any responsibility for their safety, Daniel and Anna were performing in camps and military hospitals. Back in New York, Robin Duguid was studying a telegram which told him that Daniel would be unable to sing Canio in the season's first *Pagliacci*.

They had just finished a series of duets at the hospital in Jerusalem, finishing with 'Un dì felice' from the opening act of *La Traviata,* when a man in uniform approached them.

'Mr. Kerr? Mrs. Kerr? I have some news for you.'

Daniel looked into the man's dark brown eyes and knew even before a word was spoken that the information he had was bad. 'Benny?' he asked.

'Your son. I am afraid he has been wounded in a battle in the Sinai.'

'How bad?' Daniel took a deep breath and braced himself for the worst.

'His leg was crushed when his tank exploded. The doctors had to amputate.'

Daniel heard Anna's terrified gasp. He reached out and gripped her wrist, trying to instil his own strength into her. 'Where is he? Does his wife know?'

'He's in a military hospital in Tel Aviv. I will take you there. His wife is already with him.'

Still holding onto Anna, Daniel followed the man out of the small hall, unaware of the puzzled stares from wounded soldiers that followed his abrupt departure. He was no longer interested in their wounds, in helping them over their injuries. His own son had been hurt; that was all he could think of.

The helicopter journey passed in a daze. A jeep with blue-painted lights met them at the landing pad and whisked them to the hospital. A doctor was waiting. Benjamin, he said, was sleeping under sedation. He had lost his right leg below the knee. Daniel felt himself go cold. Immediately he thought that his son was a cripple, a helpless shell who would have to depend on someone else for the remainder of his life. The doctor tried to explain that with the artificial limb with which he would be fitted once the wound had healed, he would be able to lead a normal life.

'Will he be able to run, play baseball?' Daniel wanted to know. How the hell could anyone lead a normal life without two real legs? Was this where Benjamin's zest for religion, his Zionism had landed him? In a hospital bed while his lower leg was somewhere else? What did they do with amputated limbs anyway? Did they bury them? Burn them? Pickle them in formaldehyde so they could be interred at some later date with their original owner when he eventually died? Like the American Indians who believed they wouldn't go to their happy hunting grounds if their bodies were not intact?

'When can we see him?' Anna asked quietly. She had calmed down during the journey and now seemed more in control of the situation than Daniel. The doctor addressed his reply to her.

'Perhaps tomorrow. In the meantime, I am certain we can find you some accommodation.'

'What about Susie? His wife?'

'She is also here.'

'How is she?'

'Bearing up strongly. Accepting the news.'

She would, Anna thought. Anyone who graduated from Meir Kahane's Jewish Defence League would not be turned off by an injury like this. They had all been prepared to die for what they believed in, and to accept the deaths of those close to them in the same cause.

They found Susie waiting calmly in a small anteroom. Her face was dry; no tear streaks marred the perfection of her skin. 'He's going to be all right,' she greeted her parents-in-law. 'It's a below-the-knee amputation so he'll retain full use of the joint. They're much more serious above the knee.'

A pregnant child speaks so unemotionally, Daniel marvelled. Like ice. Devoid of all feeling. Was this the child who used to play ball on his lawn in New Jersey with Benjamin? 'Have you seen him yet?'

Susie nodded. 'After they took him to the ward. He was barely conscious but I know he recognised me.'

Gradually their fears were eased by the girl's serenity. What right did they have to be frightened when their son's wife was so unafraid?

Accompanied by Anna and Susie, Daniel was allowed to see Benjamin the following afternoon. His son was in a large ward with twenty other men; burn victims caught up in the inferno of the Sinai front who groaned in pain even under the strongest sedation; limbless soldiers who, like the rest of the country, had been taken by surprise when the Arabs had attacked; boys who weren't even old enough to shave, with tubes sticking out of their bodies.

Benjamin was awake and alert. He managed to coax a weak smile onto his face when he recognised his visitors. Susie leaned over the bed and kissed him. Anna stood nervously by the side of the bed. Daniel could not tear his eyes away from the flat spot underneath the sheet where a healthy man's right leg would be.

'What happened to you?' Daniel asked, forcing himself to speak.

'I didn't get out of the way. It was a New York-style mugging. We got jumped by four of the bastards.'

'Where?' His eyes flicked from his son's face to the flat spot under the sheet again.

'Somewhere in Israel,' Benjamin answered, giving the government's standard line for designating areas of military activity. 'You know better than to ask that.' He turned his eyes from Daniel to Anna. 'Why so glum, old lady? It's not the end of the world.'

'Not so much of the old lady,' she warned, smiling in spite of herself.

'I hear you two were giving concerts,' Benjamin continued. He propped himself up on his elbows, knowing he had to keep talking, anything so that his parents would not have time to dwell on his injury. 'Someone told me the only reason we got reinforcements to the front so quickly was because of the pair of you. You both sang so badly you cleared all the camps and hospitals. Our reinforcements were really trying to emigrate.'

'Benny, don't try so hard. We're not worried about you,' Daniel lied. 'So you can quit acting.'

Benjamin lowered himself slowly and stared up at the ceiling. 'You're both worried as hell. If not about me, then about this country. We got caught with our pants down and we got clobbered. We're not invincible, are we?'

'Who is?'

'We were. Until we got soft.'

'You think you can stay on guard the whole time? Always combat-ready? Is that any way to live?'

'It is when you've got neighbours like we do. How much longer are you both staying for?'

'Till this things blows over. A couple of weeks, I guess.'

'It'll be sooner than that. As soon as we reverse the

379

position, the United Nations will step in and blow the whistle. In the meantime, you keep on entertaining the troops. That was how you started out, wasn't it?'

'I was one of the troops.' He looked sideways at Anna and guessed the question that was on her lips.

'Are you coming back home when this is over?' she asked.

Benjamin smiled at his mother. 'I am home, Ma. You still can't understand that, can you?'

'I can,' Daniel answered. 'But I don't think your mother ever will.'

The Egyptian Third Army was saved from obliteration by the United Nations after the Israelis crossed the Suez Canal to surround it. Benjamin left the hospital to return home pending being fitted for his artificial leg. Anna stayed on, wanting to be with her injured son and pregnant daughter-in-law. Daniel returned alone to the United States, after promising Anna he would be back when the baby was due.

The morning after he arrived home, still exhausted by jet lag on top of the exertions of the past three weeks, he telephoned Robin Duguid and asked to meet him for lunch. Duguid cancelled the appointment he already had and agreed.

They met in a quiet restaurant close to Central Park. Daniel told Duguid about Benjamin and the general manager sympathised. When Daniel told him he had wanted to stay on, to be with the soldiers, Duguid merely nodded, understanding that as well, the desire to be with the family rather than with the audience. From being youthful antagonists, they had progressed through the years to professional comrades, able to understand and appreciate each other's needs.

After lunch they walked in the park, enjoying the fall scenery. The leaves were turning and Daniel stopped to admire the colours, regarding nature with a new appreciation. He thought of Anna back in Israel; how was she faring? Duguid watched him thoughtfully for several seconds, then said, 'Was there something else you wanted to talk to me about, Daniel?'

Daniel let Duguid wait for the answer until he had walked down to the lake and sat on one of the benches. When Duguid joined him, he said, 'I think I'm nearing the end of the road. I want a little time for myself, for my family. I've given enough.'

The admission caused no expression or word of shock from Duguid. It was as if he had been expecting such a decision. 'Not this season, though, I hope.'

'No, not this season. I wouldn't let you down like that.' Daniel became quiet as he tried to imagine life without his work, the stage at the Grand that would no longer echo to his applause. 'I was thinking about giving it another couple of years, making the '75-'76 season my last. That'll make a round thirty years with the Grand.'

The sound of Duguid's gentle laughter made Daniel swing around in the seat. 'What's so funny?'

'Coincidences, Daniel. Coincidences are funny. That was the season I set for my retirement as well. I'll be sixty-five then, a good age to slip gracefully away from the limelight. You know, we'll have been together for twenty-five years then. It'll be our silver wedding.'

Daniel smiled at the comparison. 'Our marriage had a stormy start, didn't it?'

'It did indeed. But we worked out our differences far better than some couples. What do you plan to do with your spare time?'

'Live, I suppose. Try to get in a few ball games. I used to be a great Yankee fan when I was a kid, and that doesn't seem so long ago.' He looked down at his hands resting on his lap. 'I suppose I'll split my time between here and Israel. Anna and I are moving back into the city, and Benny's going to be staying out there.'

'Sounds good, Daniel.' Duguid paused for a moment to watch two children under the care of their mothers try to launch a small sailboat from the edge of the lake. 'Do you still want to sing *La Juive*? Have it as your finale at the Grand?'

381

'There's only one thing I want more, Robin.' It took both men several seconds to realise it was the first time Daniel had ever called Duguid by his first name. They laughed together, almost embarrassed, at the destruction of the final barrier. 'Above anything else I want to see my kid with both legs. That's not going to happen. I'll settle instead for singing *La Juive* in my final season.'

Duguid clapped him on the thigh. 'I'm going back to the Grand right now to begin making the arrangements. Two years should be enough time to make sure nothing goes wrong.'

Daniel watched him walk away. When the general manager was lost to sight, he turned his attention to the lake, sharing the success with the two children as the sailboat floated triumphantly away from the bank.

CHAPTER TEN

Moishe pushed his plate away and sat back in the chair, hands massaging his swollen stomach. 'I've eaten too much,' he complained to Anna, 'but it was too good to leave alone.'

Anna laughed as she cleared away the plates from in front of Helen and Daniel. On the way into the kitchen, she looked through the living room window of the co-op apartment she and Daniel had bought when they'd returned to the city. It was still raining. Pedestrians scurried across the intersection of Park Avenue and East Sixty-eighth Street, dodging both cars and rain. She placed the dirty plates in the dishwasher and returned to the living room.

'Guess we should be going now,' Daniel said.

Moishe looked up questioningly. 'Going where?'

'Kennedy Airport.'

'Kennedy? Why?' Helen asked.

'We're meeting an El Al flight. Some people we know are on it.' Daniel smiled broadly as he witnessed the stunned expressions on Moishe's and Helen's faces. He wished he had a camera in his hand to capture them.

'Benny and Susie are coming in?' Helen managed to ask.

'And David,' Anna added.

'What? When did . . .' Moishe spluttered.

'We wanted to surprise you,' Anna said. 'Daniel arranged it a couple of months ago. They're coming in for his final performance.'

'They never said anything in their letters,' Moishe said.

'Of course they didn't. We swore them to secrecy.' Anna went to the closet and started bringing out coats. Moishe forgot all about his full stomach as he grabbed his coat, thrust his arms into it and looked impatiently at the others.

'Come on! What are we waiting for? We don't want to be late for the flight. What time's it due in anyway?'

'Seven twenty-eight,' Daniel answered. 'Don't worry. We've got plenty of time.'

'There might be traffic jams in this rain,' Moishe called over his shoulder. He was already out of the door and halfway down the hall to the bank of elevators.

The El Al flight touched down at Kennedy two minutes ahead of its scheduled arrival time. Daniel felt his stomach give the faintest tremor as he watched the word 'arrived' click jerkily into place beside the flight number on the information board.

His kids were home! With a kid of their own. A son called David who was almost two years old. He had a grandson who was almost two! It didn't seem possible. The years didn't pass that quickly. But he knew they did. They'd flown by, clouds scudding across the sky, one moment on the far horizon, the next moment overhead, and then, in the time it took to blink, they were gone, racing, chasing each other out of sight.

'How long will they be in customs?' Anna asked.

'Maybe half an hour before they're through.' Daniel looked past Anna to Helen and Moishe. Were they as thrilled as he was? So excited they could not stand still in one spot for more than ten seconds? He knew they were. They had surprise to contend with as well. Until an hour ago they had not even known Benjmain and Susie were making the long trip to New York for Daniel's finale. At least he and Anna had seen their grandson only a few months earlier when they had made their regular summer trip to Israel. Moishe and Helen had not been over there for more than a year. Daniel knew the child would have grown by leaps and

384

bounds in just the few months since he had seen him. How would the other grandparents reconcile themselves to seeing a grandchild who had doubled in size and now walked and talked incessantly?

'Nervous?' Anna asked quietly.

'What do you think?' He kept his eyes fixed on the doors leading to the customs and immigration area, willing the El Al passengers to come through. On the edge of his vision he saw Moishe walk away and ask a question of one of the porters. He came back and told the group that the porter reckoned anywhere from ten to twenty-five minutes before the passengers came through. Daniel was grateful that someone else was struggling on the same tenterhooks on which he was impaled.

'This had better be your best performance ever,' Anna warned. 'Their first trip back in five years and they're doing it just for you.'

Daniel did not have to be told. He knew. The new season opened in just a few days with Halévy's *La Juive*. The Grand had invested a small fortune on the sets. They were all new, designed from scratch. They had to be, because the company had none in its inventory. *La Juive* had never been performed at the Grand. It was a first. And, for Daniel, a last, a triumphant exit which would mark his thirtieth season with the Grand and the end of a long, distinguished career. Both he and Duguid had spent hours trying to coax Anna out of retirement for the production. They had pressed her with the sentimentality of the occasion, how much her presence would add. She had declined. The role of Rachel, Eleazar's daughter, called for a younger woman. Besides, the work that was involved, not only in learning the score and rehearsing, but in trying to bring her voice back to something resembling its former beauty, would be awesome. She had not sung at the Grand for ten years. A comeback was not in her plans. *La Juive* would be Daniel's production, Daniel's triumph. The entire season would belong to Daniel. She would do nothing that might detract from his hour of supreme glory.

La Juive would be Daniel's only work of his final season. He would star in the opening night production, then in two more performances over the following six weeks. The third production, shortly before Christmas, would be his last. After that, *La Juive* would belong to someone else, and Daniel would become a spectator. All three of the performances had been sold out the moment tickets were released, and the final performance would be broadcast live on public television to allow millions more across the country to share in the historic occasion. Gala festivities were planned following the last performance. Wheeler's would be taken over for the night, and the Grand was paying the bill for anyone whom Daniel wanted to invite. Invitations had already been sent by the Grand to local dignitaries. Duguid was determined to make the evening a fitting climax to an outstanding career.

To make Daniel's final weeks even fuller, Benjamin and Susie had arranged to be in the States for the entire time, from before the opening night production until after Christmas, sharing their time between Daniel and Anna in the co-op apartment in Manhattan and Moishe and Helen in Teaneck.

A scattering of passengers began to drift through the doors from the customs area. Moishe darted forward to look at their baggage tags and came back smiling. He'd spotted the El Al stickers on the bags. The long wait was almost over.

Anna was the first to spot them. As the door opened to allow a large group of passengers through, she caught a glimpse of Susie pushing the baby in a stroller while Benjamin struggled with a baggage cart towards the customs inspector.

'There they are!' she shrieked. 'I saw them!' Other people waiting for passengers turned around and smiled in amusement at her enthusiasm.

Before Benjamin and Susie could see the welcoming committee, the doors swung closed again, cutting off the view of the customs area.

'Relax, will you?' Daniel said. 'Hysterics won't make them come out any quicker.'

Helen answered. 'You relax. We'll shriek.'

The doors opened and closed four more times before Benjamin and Susie came through. Anna and Helen tried to press forward but their progress was impeded by the security railing. 'Look how David's grown!' Helen cried. 'He's not a baby anymore. He's a big boy!'

Daniel threw a swift glance at Moishe. He had never satisfactorily figured out how Moishe fitted into this scene. Did he feel like an outsider because Susie wasn't really his own flesh and blood? The huge, almost childish grin that spread across Moishe's face dismissed any doubts that Daniel had; no real grandfather could be getting more *naches* out of the moment than Moishe was.

Susie bent down and untied the harness holding the child in the stroller. She pointed to the four people leaning over the railing, but it was unnecessary. The child remembered Daniel and Anna from their visit a few months earlier, and anyone standing with them had to be all right. He waddled towards the group, arms outstretched, his diaper-distorted bottom sticking out like a soccer ball. Daniel reached over the barrier and lifted David high into the air. Then he handed him to Moishe, who held the child for an instant before passing him over to Helen and Anna.

Daniel turned back to the barrier. Benjamin came through and clasped his father around the shoulders. 'No tears,' Daniel warned sternly. 'I promised your mother no tears.' There were tears all the same. 'How's the leg feeling?'

'Did you see me limp?'

'No,' Daniel lied. The limp was there, slight but noticeable all the same. The artificial leg could never take the place of a real one. 'What happened when you went through the security scanner in Israel?'

'It sounded like World War Three had broken out,' Benjamin retorted. 'I carry a doctor's slip, but they insisted on making me roll up my trouser leg anyway.'

Susie kissed Moishe and Helen, then turned to Benjamin's parents. 'You'd better be in good voice to drag me away from home for so long,' she told Daniel. 'The last time I heard you sing, you started a war all by yourself.' She threw her arms around her in-laws and kissed them ecstatically. 'Come on, let's get out of here and you can show me what's happened to good old New York while I've been away.'

Daniel signalled for a porter to take the baggage to the car. Moishe carried the child, tickling him under the chin, while Daniel pushed the empty stroller. Benjamin, Susie, Helen and Anna followed, all chattering excitedly.

'Benjamin Kerr? Susan Silver?'

Three men in raincoats blocked the exit. Benjamin glanced at them uncertainly. 'What is it?'

'We're federal agents,' the leader of the three men said. 'We have warrants for the arrest of you and your wife, the former Susan Silver.'

Moishe slammed down the telephone receiver in a rarely exhibited display of fury. Behind the thick glasses his eyes blazed wildly as he turned to face the others. 'They're bringing up that old shit from the JDL days! Can you believe that?'

'What specifically are the charges?' Anna asked. Purposely she slowed her speech. If she spoke slowly and clearly, thought carefully about each word, she would remain calm.

'Possession of a dangerous substance. Dynamite. They were conspiring to bomb some Soviet trade office.'

'I know all about that.' Daniel's admission brought shocked stares from Anna and Helen. 'It never went off. What the hell are they trying to prove after all these years?'

Anna hissed at Daniel to lower his voice before the noise disturbed the child sleeping in the apartment's second bedroom.

'A hundred lunatics planted bombs in those days,' Daniel said, dropping his voice. 'Why pick on Benny and Susie?'

'Because they came back,' Moishe replied. 'The warrants have been outstanding all this time. Extradition attempts failed. The Israeli government wasn't interested. So the feds waited.'

'How'd they find out?'

'I suppose their names were on the list when they came through immigration.'

'The big book the inspector checks?' Daniel asked, remembering the procedure from when he travelled.

'That's the one. He must have tipped off the feds. Damn!' Moishe suddenly swore. 'If you hadn't swung this whole thing as a big surprise this would never have happened!'

'What do you mean?'

'Because I should have known the warrants would still be outstanding, that's why! I'm a goddamned lawyer, remember? I got so worked up when you pulled the big surprise that I didn't even think!'

'So what do we do now?' The question came from Helen as she tried to settle her husband.

'There's a hearing tomorrow morning. I'll represent them. See if we can straighten this mess out. In the meantime, you call your pal Mulvaney and find out what the score is.'

Daniel picked up the receiver, surprised to find it was still in one piece after the battering it had received from Moishe. He caught Tommy at home and told him what had happened at the airport. Tommy cursed.

'Didn't you realise any warrants we had against them were still valid, could still be served?' Tommy demanded. 'What do you think we do with them, chuck them out with the garbage if we can't find anyone to serve them with?' There was a long silence while Tommy thought it over. From the second bedroom, Daniel could hear the baby's cries. They had woken David. He turned to see Anna walking quickly from the living room to comfort the child. 'I'll see you at the hearing tomorrow,' Tommy promised. 'Maybe we can come up with something there.'

Daniel let the phone buzz in his ear for ten seconds while

389

he tried to think of a plan of action. It would be like taking on Goliath. Just his luck the kids would miss the opening night *La Juive* as well. Hell, the way things were going they'd miss all three performances. They'd be able to read about the old man's grand finale in jail.

Anna returned to the living room, holding little David by the hand as he toddled behind her. Watching the child, Daniel's bleak mood lifted momentarily. The little tyke didn't even miss his parents; he was happy just as long as there was someone to play with him and feed him.

He put down the receiver and clapped his hands, laughing as David looked towards the noise and started to run in his direction. He lifted up his grandson and placed him gently on his lap, bouncing him up and down.

The joyful welcoming committee had been transformed into an apprehensive babysitting squad.

Daniel and Moishe met outside the courthouse the following morning. Each dreaded the approaching time for the hearing. Together they went inside where Tommy was waiting for them. He called them over to a corner and began a whispered conversation.

'Get hold of your lawyer.'

'I *am* the lawyer,' Moishe interrupted.

'You? Okay. It's an old case, we admit it. And it doesn't hold much water.'

'Thanks,' Daniel responded sarcastically. 'So why the hell are your people bothering with it?'

'Sheer bloody-mindedness, what else? It's on the books so we've got to go with it. Your kids skipped the country to get out of an investigation. We tried to extradite them from Israel and got nowhere fast. Not that we expected to. So we nailed them when they stuck their faces back here again. It makes us look like we're on our toes.'

'Three cheers for your public relations,' Daniel muttered.

'Cut it out, Cherrybum. I'm trying to help.'

'Sorry.'

Moishe cut in quickly, sensing the fire that was

smouldering inside Daniel, wanting to cut it off before it burst into open flame. 'So what do you want?'

Tommy looked around nervously, as if frightened someone might be spying on him. His voice dropped even lower. 'We don't like wasting taxpayers' money ...'

'More public relations.' Daniel couldn't help himself.

'Yeah, more PR. Besides, the feeling among a lot of people right now is your kids should have been given a medal, not arrested. Maybe we could come up with a deal.'

'What kind of deal are we talking about?' Moishe felt more comfortable. The bargaining had begun and he was on firmer ground.

'Benjamin and Susie weren't the only outstanding cases stemming from the old JDL days,' Tommy said. 'There were a bunch of them.'

'You want names?'

'Damned right we want names. You get those kids to cough up names that can tie up some of the other cases and we'll drop this one. I promise you.'

Moishe thought over the proposition. He pulled Daniel away and shook his head doubtfully. 'Can you imagine Susie or Benny finking on their pals to get out of this jam?'

'What if they don't?'

'The judge might throw it out of court anyway. Even Tommy said the FBI's case doesn't hold much water. We could plead for sympathy as well, Benny's artificial leg, your own fame.'

'Supposing the judge doesn't throw it out of court, though? They'll wind up in jail.'

'Then you and me had better get hold of them and make them spit out some names,' Moishe decided. 'Quick.'

Daniel and Moishe faced Benjamin and Susie across a narrow table in one of the courthouse's detention rooms. In the corner stood Tommy Mulvaney, arms folded across his chest while he witnessed the heated argument.

'All they want is names?' Benjamin shouted. 'Names? So

they can throw other people in jail? What do you think I am, crazy?'

'Who says they're going to throw anyone in jail?' Daniel demanded. 'They're just trying to tie up some other cases.'

Benjamin slammed his open hand against his forehead. 'Tie up some other cases, my ass! You're asking me to betray friends. Would you?'

Tommy coughed discreetly, a warning to keep down the noise.

'What will happen if we don't cooperate?' Susie asked.

'You'll get bail,' Moishe answered. 'Your passports will be confiscated and a trial date will be set. You won't be going home till David's almost *bar mitzvahed*.'

Susie paled at the information but Benjamin remained righteously irate. 'I'm not doing it,' he stated vehemently. 'I'd rather spend time in jail than turn traitor.'

'What about me, then?' Daniel asked. 'If you couldn't give a damn about yourself, think about me. This is the final moment in my career, my grand exit, and you're going to louse it up?'

The sound of laughter rocked the small room. The four people at the table turned around to see Tommy convulsed, hands clasping his stomach.

'What the hell's so funny?' Daniel wanted to know.

Tommy pointed a finger in Daniel's direction while his mouth tried to form words. Finally he spluttered, 'Jesus Christ, but you sounded like your mother used to.'

'What?'

'Guilt!' Tommy laughed. 'Fill your kids with guilt!' He burst out laughing again and turned to face the wall. His shoulders shook as more spasms tore through him.

Daniel lowered his head and grinned. Tommy was right. When he looked up again, he saw that the other three people at the table were also smiling.

'Did you lose any friends over there?' Tommy suddenly asked Benjamin.

'What do you mean?'

'During the last war. Did any of your JDL boys buy it?'

Daniel and Moishe stared uncomprehendingly at Tommy, but Benjamin seemed to catch on. 'A few.'

'Who had something to do with Soviet property over here being damaged?'

'There was Dov, Yehuda and Joel,' Susie cut in, also seeing where Tommy was leading.

'What are their full names?'

'Joel Lerner, Yehuda Kahn and Dov Stein,' Benjamin answered.

'You give me the details of what they did to Soviet property here and I'll call it a fair trade,' Tommy offered. 'I won't even put down that they're dead. The bureau can find that out when they try to extradite.'

Finally Daniel understood. He got up from the chair, walked across to where Tommy stood and embraced him.

Two anxious, middle-aged men had arrived at the courthouse that morning. At midday, when they walked down the courthouse steps, accompanied by Benjamin and Susie, the anxiety had disappeared.

'Tommy got a postponement,' Moishe explained. 'Sometime during the next couple of weeks the charges will be quietly dropped.'

Daniel clapped Moishe across the back, then he put his arms around the shoulders of Benjamin and Susie. The clouds had gone. His kids were back with him again and nothing would be allowed to mar those three performances of La Juive.

The atmosphere had built up slowly over the six weeks separating the opening night La Juive from Daniel's final performance at the Grand. A cauldron brought carefully to the boil by an expert chef, until at last the aroma of the dish was unbearably delicious and tantalising.

The opening night performance had been a critical triumph for Daniel. The reviews had centred upon the revival of La Juive, commending Daniel for his fine portrayal of Eleazar, the proud, vengeful Jewish goldsmith who uses his daughter to gain a chilling revenge upon the Christians he despises. The second performance had, perhaps, been Daniel's most satisfying. It was one where he could relax the most, project himself into the role without thinking about opening night or his own closing. He had brought the house down.

As the third and final performance neared, he found himself falling prey to the nagging fears that had plagued him in the early moments of his career. It was ridiculous. He had no career to concern himself about anymore. One more performance, that was all. After that, he could gracefully retire.

Three hours before he was due at the Grand, he left Anna, Benjamin, Susie and his grandson in the apartment and went out for a walk. He needed to be alone. He wanted time to review the thirty-year career that would end that very night amid a wild, sentimental celebration. After tonight, his voice would be nothing more than a recording.

What do you do with a voice when you retire it? he asked himself as he walked south along Park Avenue. Ahead he could see the Pan Am Building all lit up in preparation for Christmas. Do I get a Christmas wish? Can I start all over again? With one difference. Let me know, dear God, everything that I know now so I won't make the same mistakes again. I'd be even greater the second time around.

Wishing for the chance to start all over again brought a smile to his face. He should be grateful that he had been given the opportunity to make it to the top just once. God had given him a gift, that's what everyone had always told him. He'd laughed at them. A gift! What else was it then if it wasn't a gift? A voice like this could be nothing else. It was a gift direct from heaven. God had looked down and fixed his gaze on a fat kid in the Bronx called Daniel Kirschbaum. You, my boy, are going to have a wonderful voice.

Before he realised it, he was at the Pan Am Building. He stopped to look around, watching people as they scurried from offices on their way home. This is what the gift had saved him from. A humdrum life in some office, bent over a desk until he retired at sixty-five with a gold watch. He'd sooner die.

A middle-aged man approached him hesitantly, peering into Daniel's face as he tried to decide whether or not it was the Grand Opera tenor Daniel Kerr. 'Excuse me,' he said timidly, 'but are you Daniel Kerr?'

The simple fact of being recognised on busy Park Avenue brought home to Daniel all that he would be missing after tonight's performance. It wouldn't happen immediately. He'd slip gradually from the public eye. His recordings would still afford him recognition, but how long would it take before his pictures on the record sleeves bore little resemblance to himself? 'Yes,' he said to the stranger. 'I'm Daniel Kerr.'

The man offered his hand, more sure of himself. 'I'm delighted to meet you, Mr. Kerr. My wife and I saw you in *Rigoletto* three seasons ago. We're big admirers of yours.'

'Thank you.' Daniel was lost for words. How do you reply to compliments you once took for granted, but which you might never receive again after tonight? 'Thank you very much.'

'We'll be watching you tonight, Mr. Kerr. On the television.'

'Not in person?' Daniel didn't know why he asked the question. It sounded pompous and he regretted it.

The man shrugged his shoulders apologetically in case Daniel took offence that he would be watching *La Juive* on television. 'You don't know how hard I tried to get tickets for one of the *La Juive* performances, Mr. Kerr. They were like gold. My father, rest his soul, always told me about Caruso singing *La Juive*. I'll be watching tonight to compare.'

Daniel looked down and saw that he still held the stranger's hand. He could not remember taking it in the first place. 'Your father probably knew my father. All I ever heard as a kid was Caruso in *La Juive* as well.' He looked up from the clasped hands into the man's eyes. 'Do you want a couple of tickets for tonight?'

'I can't afford the expensive ones.'

'What's your name?'

'Benetti.'

'Mr. Benetti,' Daniel said grandly, 'you don't have to worry about affording anything. Stop by the ticket office and there will be two tickets waiting for you.' Before the surprised man could offer his thanks, Daniel added. 'And wear a tuxedo. You're invited to my farewell party afterwards. Give your wife my regards and tell her I'm looking forward to meeting her.' He turned around and walked away quickly, leaving the amazed man to stare after him, like a child watching Santa Claus soar off into the sky after leaving the present he always wanted.

Daniel arrived back at the apartment as gleeful as any child, eager to tell Anna what he had done. She questioned his charity, whether there were any tickets left; he had already given away more than his special allocation for the evening. Duguid will always find a couple more, he told her. Even if they have to stand at the back of the auditorium, it'll be all right. He hugged and kissed her on the lips, wanting her to share his own joy.

They left David with a babysitter and took a cab to the Grand, arriving ninety minutes before the performance was due to begin. Another last, Daniel thought, looking through the cab's dirty window; no more will I take a cab to the Grand as an opera singer, only as a member of the audience. When they arrived, he went immediately to the dressing room. The room had been gaudily decorated for the occasion. Streamers hung down from the ceiling. Gold and silver stars were plastered all over the walls. Piled in front of the mirror were letters and telegrams of congratulation. He leafed through them quickly, felt tears start to burn in the corners of his eyes as he recognised names, surrendered to sentiment. Even one from the White House.

The first president he had sung for was Harry Truman, that night Claudia Rivera had held onto her note in the final act of *Tosca* and sent him rushing shame-faced from the stage at the end of the opera. Memory made him smile; what had seemed so important then was now nothing more than an amusing moment. Since then he had sung before every president, including a recital at the White House for John F. Kennedy. There was a wire from Gracie Mansion, signed by the mayor who would be present at the dinner later on in Wheeler's. Remembering the dinner, Daniel left the dressing room and rushed to the ticket office. Two seats in the fifth row of the orchestra had just been returned. Before they could be snapped up by the hopefuls on top of the cancellation list, Daniel commandeered them, telling the woman in the office to reserve them in the name of Benetti; they'd be picked up later on.

On his way back to the dressing room, he ran into Robin Duguid. Daniel stood and stared. The general manager looked like a reincarnation of Roger Hammersley, dressed impeccably in white tie and tails. When he saw Daniel gaping, Duguid smiled.

'Some more telegrams have arrived, Daniel.' He handed over a thick bundle of Western Union envelopes. 'I hope I get one tenth of this adoration when I call it quits at the end of the season.'

'I'll send you one,' Daniel promised. He wanted to sit and chat with Duguid, to share a few precious moments of this final night with the man he had hated and then learned to admire. The make-up artist cut short any time for reminiscing. Daniel sat back in the chair and watched. On went a long white beard and wig. Then the artist went to work on his face. Not much to do anymore, Daniel thought. Once I played a Cavaradossi or a Turiddu with hardly any make-up; now I can play Eleazar the same way. He waited until the make-up man had finished, then turned to Duguid, who had remained in the room.

'What about tonight's programme? I haven't seen a copy of it yet.'

'I'll get you one.' Duguid left the dressing room and returned less than a minute later. In his hand was the commemorative programme for that night's performance. The cover was gold with black ink. Inside was the complete libretto of the opera, the cast, messages of good will from record companies and operatic organisations with which Daniel had been associated. He was interested in none of them. Quickly he turned to the first right-hand page and stared at the few words written there:

'This performance is dedicated to the memory of Isaac Kirschbaum.'

'Thanks, Robin. That makes everything just perfect.'

As much as he wanted to remember every note, every movement, every experience of his final performance, the first three acts slipped past Daniel as if he were sleepwalking. He was only vaguely aware of the subtle change in lighting that allowed the television crews from PBS to send the production live into homes across the country. A comfortable sensation of sadness enveloped him as the opera continued, as if he was finally realising that the major portion of his life was coming to an end. After tonight, his time would be his own. To be with Anna. To be with his family.

The fourth act opened with Daniel watching from the wings, waiting for his cue. If he had so far failed to cling to one moment of his final performance, he would make no mistake with this act.

As Eleazar, he walked proudly onto the stage to be told by his enemy, the Cardinal de Brogni, that only by renouncing his faith could he save his daughter Rachel from death. Scornfully he rejected the offer, and swore that even though he and his daughter might die, he would be avenged on one Christian — the cardinal himself. The cardinal's daughter had disappeared as a young child, rescued from a fire in which the cardinal had believed she'd perished. Eleazar knew where she was but he would not tell. After pleading with him for the information, the cardinal abandoned the fanatic to his fate. For a sweet moment, Eleazar gloated over the doubt he had instilled in the cardinal's mind. Then his heart softened as he thought about Rachel, his own daughter, whom he was sacrificing.

The last encore Daniel had sung at Carnegie Hall on the

night he paid homage to Bjoerling cast its spell for the final time over the Grand's audience.

'Rachel! quand du Seigneur la grâce tutélaire . . .'

Wheeler's had been rearranged for the gala celebration following Daniel's final *La Juive*. It looked as if a wedding was planned, a *bar mitzvah*, a family affair. Four tables had been joined together to form one long top table, with other tables clustered in front of it. At the centre of the top table sat Daniel and Anna, flanked by Benjamin and Susie, Helen and Moishe, Robin Duguid and a perplexed-looking Tommy Mulvaney, who was still trying to make some sense out of what he had seen and heard. Talking to him after the performance, Daniel knew he had been right in never getting back to Tommy with the tickets thirty years ago.

He looked out over the tables and spotted Benetti, the man he had met by the Pan Am Building earlier that day. Benetti and his wife were at the same table as the Mayor of New York and a host of other dignitaries. Daniel caught Benetti's eye and raised his glass in a salute.

The maître d' placed a bottle of Dom Pérignon on the table in front of Daniel. Attached to it was a small white card covered in dainty handwriting. Daniel read the note and laughed out loud. See how hard I prayed . . . Anna. He turned in the seat and kissed her, not caring who saw. Tonight was his night; he could do whatever he liked.

Speech followed speech. Fellow artists showered compliments on Daniel's head. The telegrams that had been waiting in his dressing room were read out. Each one was followed by a loud burst of applause; each round of applause seemed more sustained than the one preceding it.

Finally, Duguid stood up to the microphone, resting his hands on Daniel's shoulders. 'Friends.' The single word took in everyone. 'We have witnessed tonight the farewell performance of a truly magnificent artist.' Another round of applause greeted the statement. 'I am proud that for twenty-five years I worked with Daniel Kerr. It wasn't all roses —

anyone unlucky enough to have seen a movie called *South Side Serenade* will tell you that.'

Daniel joined in the laughter which swept through the restaurant.

'Those of us who have been fortunate enough to share this night will treasure the memory. I treasure far more than that. I treasure the relationship I shared with Daniel. He is a dedicated artist and a dedicated family man; in this particular business, those two are sometimes hard to find in the same man.' Duguid removed a hand from Daniel's shoulder and raised it to his mouth to cover a nervous cough.

'It's my privilege tonight to pass on to Daniel a memento of his thirty years with the Grand.' He reached into his pocket and pulled out a small package. 'Daniel, from the Grand Opera Company of New York; just so you won't forget us.'

Daniel took the package and opened it. Inside was a minute but perfect replica of the front of the opera house on West Thirty-fourth, cast in solid gold. Inscribed on the base was the date, his own name and the title of the opera he'd chosen for his finale. He stood up, knowing he had to respond, but he could not think of a word. His eyes lingered over the familiar faces and his mind captured a million memories. From now on, when he came to Wheeler's he would be a guest, another member of the audience stopping in for a meal after the performance. It was time. Other tenors were entitled to get their bite at the cherry, to carve their reputations.

'Has anyone,' he asked softly into the microphone, 'seen the *Times* review for tonight's performance yet?'

THE END